DEAD *or* ALIVE

THE ROMAN EMPIRE'S HUNT *for the* RESURRECTED REBEL JESUS

A Novel

MICHAEL KELLEY

ILLUMIFY
MEDIA.COM

Published by

Illumify Media Global

www.IllumifyMedia.com

"Let's bring your book to life!"

Library of Congress Control Number: 2025904104

Paperback ISBN: 978-1-964251-56-1

Hardcover ISBN: 978-1-964251-57-8

Cover design by Debbie Lewis

Printed in the United States of America

Dedicated to my mother.

Prologue

I KNEW I was dreaming, but I couldn't wake myself. Because I wasn't myself.

I wasn't pacing in my familiar Columbia classroom or preaching from my pulpit. Instead, I was an abbot in a Gothic medieval cathedral surrounded by flames and dodging debris as it rained down. My body was drenched in sweat, and my lungs burned as I gasped for oxygen in the caustic, smoke-filled air. It was my solemn duty, in extremis, to decide which works of art and holy relics to save and which to let perish. Impervious to fear and fatigue, I remained undaunted in my mission.

One last time, I rushed into the inferno to rescue the statue of the Holy Mother from a remote chapel—or to die in the flames. Suddenly, trumpets started blaring.

Shaken, I felt the tormented abbot rising out of me like a cloud—or maybe he was being buried deep inside me like a shadow. Cloud or shadow, he was gone, though the trumpets were still resounding in my ears as I opened my eyes. I was in my room and in my bed, my cell phone ringing on the bedside table. Only two people—my archbishop and Miles—could bypass the sleep setting to reach me at any hour. The trumpet-heralding ringtone could only mean one of two things: my archbishop, on a mission in Ethiopia, was drafting me back into service, or Miles had discovered a find of great historical significance in Kashmir.

"Ye-es?" I answered in a scratchy voice.

"Thomas, get packing!" It was Miles, my best friend and a renowned professor of archaeology. He was far too loud for—I checked the time—four o'clock in the morning.

I supported Miles at Columbia, particularly regarding his archaeological excavations in Kashmir, a volatile region. Since becoming an autonomous region and a police state in 2027, Kashmir remained wild and lawless, its promise for a constitutional democracy being perpetually deferred. One site within the wild eastern autonomous region, in the foothills of the Himalayas, was particularly promising for further reconnaissance. The previous summer Miles had found some Roman coins and two ancient spatha swords, used by Roman cavalry. They were bound together perpendicularly and hidden under the frozen earth in front of a Himalayan cave. I joked it was an X marking the spot. Miles corrected me, saying it looked more like a cross. He must be calling with an urgent update regarding his exploration of the site.

It was Easter morning, April 1, 2029. My body was still shaking from the aftermath of my lucid dream. My faith was silent on prior lives, or in denial, but I was convinced that *I* had been that heroic and humble abbot who had actually lived and perhaps died in that tragic cathedral inferno sometime back in the Middle Ages.

"I found the manuscript of the century," Miles said as I sat up in bed. "No, beyond that. Of the millennia! You were right: the swords were an X marking the spot, the burial site of a Roman text—amazingly well-preserved papyrus scrolls sealed in a bronze strongbox buried inside an icy cave. It was amazing. I wished you could have been there. Seeing those scrolls laid out like sticks of dynamite in near perfect condition I felt like I was opening the ark of God."

More likely Pandora's box, I thought. Still, his enthusiasm was palpable, shaking me from my vivid nightmare in the medieval cathedral.

"Not as many as the charred Herculaneum scrolls, but they are preserved in a readable condition. And not just random readable passages but a complete manuscript from the Roman Empire at the time of Christ."

Before I could say anything, he drew in a quick breath and added, "Thomas, the thing is, it reads like a historical epic or . . . fiction from Roman times. Could that possibly be right?"

The Herculaneum scrolls were the Holy Grail of ancient texts, an entire Roman library all but destroyed by the same volcanic eruption that blanketed Pompeii in AD 79. Like the mummified bodies, pages of the texts were also preserved by the ash. Each year, AI advances allowed a few more passages of the library to be read for the first time in two thousand years. But these charred snippets of letters and dramas were not full manuscripts and certainly not epics. Miles wasn't an expert in Roman-era Latin or Greek, so who knew what he'd actually found.

"Miles, people write historical fiction *about* that period; nobody was writing it back then. Maybe it's mythology or biographical propaganda. But it can't be—"

"That's why you need to be here now to determine what it is. Once you hear more, you'll be booking the next flight."

"I'm not Indiana Jones," I said as I got up and headed to the bathroom. I am Father Thomas Mann—not the German novelist of the 1920s, but a sixty-four-year-old adjunct professor of Christian history at Columbia University and an ordained priest and newly retired bishop. I had lost my fire for ministering to a dwindling flock. In my early retirement, I preferred to be called father rather than bishop emeritus. Living an academically accented spiritual life, I was researching and writing a book about the Blessed Virgin Mother, exploring her saintly life within the gospels and pivotal role in the life of Jesus. I also planned to examine her subsequent Church-recognized appearances to the faithful, concluding with the meaning of those Marian apparitions to Church doctrine, Christian contemplation, and prayer. This magnum opus will be my crowning achievement.

"And I'm on an Easter Sunday panel at St. Paul's Chapel after early mass in just a few hours," I said.

"Right. More of the same talk about the historical Jesus and the pillars of Christian theology. This manuscript may turn all that on its head, shaking those pillars like Hercules—"

"It was Samson," I said.

He was on a roll, so I let him talk, did my business, and headed to the kitchen for coffee.

"Although my Latin and Greek are limited, the little I can decipher from the long text—Thomas, the scrolls laid end to end would span a kilometer—is astounding. And if it's authentic. . . . You'll have to determine its veracity and decide whether it should see the light of day. I know you; you won't publish your findings if what you uncover goes against your articles of faith. You are so *by the book* and Church doctrine." He paused to get my reaction to his jibe, but I just shook my sleepy head. "When you get here," he continued when I didn't take the bait, "you won't have time to translate the scrolls verbatim. And you know me, I'll press for further access and the scrolls' full release when I return to the States, regardless of their content. You must promise not to burn them."

"I'm no book burner," I said, "but you're right. If the text is blasphemous, I won't publish it. And wait, why do I need to come to Kashmir? Can't we take pictures of the scroll pages and study them here first?" What was the point of technology if you weren't going to use it? "Were you able to at least authenticate the date of the scrolls?"

"They were written around the time of Christ. No pictures allowed, though. They erased the ones I took. You know Kashmir—*click, click.*"

We often joked about Kashmir being stuck in the ancient past, and his clicks were a signal that our conversation was probably being monitored. Although they lived in the past, the government did use advanced technology for eavesdropping and surveilling its still-peasant population. I was superimposing my dream over modern-day, anachronistic Kashmir, but the comparison wasn't that farfetched.

"The authorities here have me and the scrolls under house arrest in a monastery. I've negotiated for you to have three months to study the text before they seize and probably destroy the ancient manuscript. I'm being sent home as soon as you arrive."

"What? Your visa must be good for at least another six months."

"Revoked. They don't give a damn about Roman or Christian history. Hell, they might burn the pages as blasphemy or as treason against the fledgling state and its predominantly Muslim population. You know, guys like me." Miles was always eager to remind me of his Muslim heritage. I think he found it ironic that we could be such good friends. "They took the body and are denying it exists and are pissed that I keep insisting it did. I promised the rest of our grant, in gold, to guarantee you access for three months. Bring pens and lots of paper. No electronics are allowed here in the Buddhist monastery."

For a moment neither of us said a word. The only noise was my single-cup coffee maker percolating. I think he expected me to speak, but I had too many questions to pick from. Finally, I asked, "What body?"

"Oh, I forgot to explain that bit of mystery," he said. "It's like I've been brainwashed. This discovery is so astounding. Anyway, a frozen, mummified corpse lay undisturbed on top of the strongbox when I entered the cave. Maybe it was the author or a ritual guardian locked in the cave to protect the scrolls."

That at least made sense, as Romans had adopted from Egypt the process of mummifying their dead. "Where's the body now?"

"I don't know. They must have removed it. A monk here said they went to pray over the body, but it was gone. The Kashmir officials deny it was ever there. They're already messing with the site. That's the problem with using local diggers—they talk. It's their country, but . . . they don't . . . Anyway, the body's gone, like it never existed. And maybe I imagined it. Let's just let that go."

He made a clucking sound, his tongue snapping against the roof of his mouth. Not exactly a *click, click,* but I got the message. He wouldn't just let it go, but he wanted whoever was listening to believe he would.

So, we had a remarkable discovery; Miles was being kicked out of Kashmir; a mummified body had disappeared, and the scrolls might be next. Miles was right. I needed to be in Kashmir before the unearthed history was buried once more. Regardless of the content of the text, the discovery of the scrolls was a major find, and Miles deserved my support and skills; without my reactions being driven by personal fears that it might be the devil's work or desire for personal glory should the work shed light on the life and teachings of our Lord.

"Miles, slow down and tell me what the text covers." I didn't know how much he'd say while under surveillance, but I needed at least a few details.

"An official Roman hunt for the body of Jesus after the resurrection."

My cup rattled and coffee scalded my hand, as I instinctively made the sign of the cross. The historical importance and the sensational nature of the find were undeniable, but perhaps we were both allowing emotion and excitement to drive us. *We could be running ahead of the find and its implications. We could—*

Suddenly, I had a realization. Jesus was calling me to defend his honor from a Roman blasphemy. I shivered. I hadn't felt the Lord's touch so clearly in years. Or perhaps it was the Lord simply calling my attention to the magnitude of my mission, and I shouldn't rush to judgment.

"Now, that does sound like fiction," I said, using humor to collect myself and buy time to rinse my red hand with cold water before breathing in the aromatic dark roast remaining in my coffee cup and taking my first sip. I had to be sure I was acting on reason and heeding a true calling of my Lord rather than chasing the thrilling little cherry bombs of the epiphanies detonating within me.

"If so, then it's the first novel," Miles said with a mix of humor and aggravation.

I laughed. "The first novel was *The Tale of Genji*, written eleven centuries after the Roman era. More than likely, your text is simply a drama. And there was no record of an official Roman hunt for the body of Jesus. But the absence of a thing—"

I stopped because my soul shuddered as I thought about the abbot in the burning cathedral. I was being charged with a sacred duty. That had been no ordinary nightmare, but a prophetic dream. If the Lord wasn't sending a divine message for me to wake up and pay attention, then I was experiencing a stroke. But these illuminating tremors were no stroke. I prayed, *Dear Lord, I—*

"Perhaps I ought to reach out to our friend in the English department," Miles interrupted, his voice increasingly agitated. "He might show the appropriate level of enthusiasm. A lot of people say the Bible is fiction too."

He knew that people still disputing the historical Jesus and the gospel accounts of his life were a source of great irritation for me. I let his taunt go, realizing that Miles too, in his peculiar way, was trying to get me to focus and not jump to conclusions.

"So the Bible now has a sequel or Roman rebuttal?" I asked to taunt him in return, but he didn't laugh or even grunt. "You know, I was an English major in college. And I *am* excited, Miles. It's just . . . it's well before dawn here, and half of me is still lost in a vivid dream I was having ten minutes ago, leaving only half of me to deal with your shocking revelations." That was not entirely true. I was as awake as a saint being blinded by the light. "And I am trying to figure out where this is heading."

"To Kashmir," he said. "Start packing. They're watching me. They confiscated my equipment and electronics and have shown me the door.

They're not playing around." The man was relentless when there was work to be done, and his voice exhibited the strain of the recent events. "From what I could read, which you know is limited, the Romans suspected he survived the crucifixion. I *think* the author claims to be writing a historical account of the search for Jesus's body by a disgraced Roman tribune and his men—"

"Wait!" I glared at the silly date on my phone. It was April 1. It wasn't like Miles to play me for a fool, waking me for a prank, but a disgraced tribune sent on a search for Jesus's body, and someone just happened to capture the details of the search in writing and that work of art survived intact two thousand years? Crestfallen, I said, "Miles, is this some kind of April Fool's joke?"

"What!? No. You know me better than that—just serendipity. Get packing, my doubting Thomas."

Miles wasn't joking. Thank God. Relief rushed through me, followed by a jolting wave of urgency and reticence.

"But . . ."

"But what?" he demanded.

"Church protocol. Though I'm retired, I should still have the blessing of my archbishop for such a mission, and he may be difficult to reach."

"The scrolls are not Church property. This is Columbia University presenting you with this incredible opportunity. Reach out too him if you must but get on a plane."

He was right but still I worried.

The first item I packed into my carry-on knapsack was my bedside Bible. Then I grabbed my suitcase and opened it on the bed, putting Miles on speaker so he could tell me all he knew about the scrolls as I juggled taking notes and packing the gear I'd need for three months.

After arranging a Jesuit priest from Fordham to take my place on the panel at St. Paul's Chapel and writing the archbishop and his secretary, I headed to the airport to catch a ten a.m. flight east to Mumbai—where I'd catch a connection to Kashmir.

⌖ ⌖ ⌖

Moving backward into antiquity faster than the speed of sound, the flight into the past afforded me time to research the region and the monastery where I'd be sequestered for three months. And to gather my thoughts on my sudden and sacred expedition. Miles was trained in paleography and had authenticated the approximate date of the papyrus and ink. However, that authentication of the scrolls didn't mean the story they disclosed was true; it may have been written as propaganda. The story may have been a philosophical treatise or myth-making epic. But I wondered if Miles was right that a post-resurrection Roman search, if it took place and came to light, would rewrite Christian history.

My mission was to determine whether the "history" in the scrolls was fact or fiction and decide whether the story should be published or suppressed—the latter serving to deactivate a buried time-bomb capable of blowing up Christianity. Anti-Catholic conspiracy theorists latched onto every newly discovered Gnostic text as gospel. Roman histories were often mere propaganda for the empire, the emperors, or powerful senators. A history of a tribune's search for the risen Christ sounded fascinating but fanciful.

Even if the scrolls contained an accurate account of an actual search, what would an official Roman search for Christ's body, which remained undiscovered, reveal?

I had always hoped we might learn more about Jesus from age thirteen to thirty, a period the gospels are silent on. But I never imagined we'd discover an account of his last days on Earth after his death and resurrection. My mind began unspooling a catechism concerning the time between the Lord's resurrection and ascension.

According to the book of Acts, forty days after Jesus's resurrection—days that included multiple sightings—he ascended bodily into heaven. The gospels, except the Gospel of Luke, were mostly silent on the ascension and didn't report the Acts account. And it was Luke who wrote the book of Acts. Christian scholars over the years pointed out the significance of this omission—failing to report the final sighting of the resurrected Jesus on Earth and the miracle of his ascension into heaven to sit beside God.

Having studied Thomas Aquinas's writings, I reconciled this potential discrepancy by noting that during the entire resurrection period, Jesus's glorified body could appear and vanish—or ascend—*at the speed of thought*. And a still-living Christ could appear again today and ascend again if it were God's will, as he did to Saint Paul years afterward.

I closed my eyes to ponder the possibilities. A record of a Roman search for Jesus. No matter its result or veracity, the historical significance alone would be remarkable. I wasn't sure whether to pray for the story to be real or a newly unearthed Roman mythology.

— — —

Miles was permitted to meet me at Srinagar Airport before the authorities saw him to his departure gate. I showed him my unsatisfying response from the Archbishop's secretary:

The Archbishop is extremely busy. He didn't have time to fully consider your proposal but says whatever the manuscript is, it sounds like a fanciful fraud. If you need more guidance before proceeding, you should contact the dean of cardinals at the Vatican.

I didn't know what to think. The archbishop would surely realize that getting a response from the second most powerful man in the Vatican could take weeks.

"He didn't say no, bishop emeritus," Miles taunted. Still, I didn't know what to say.

"Should I have brought in a layman Latin expert from Columbia? You can't drop the ball here. There's no time to think. Time to act old man." He was twenty years my junior.

I agreed to move forward and would correct any misstep later.

We hugged goodbye.

He had done his job, finding and authenticating the mysterious Latin manuscript. It was now my turn.

My Kashmir driver was a black-bearded, plainclothes military police officer, who was built like the Michelin Man of firm, stocky rubber. After presenting his badge, he confiscated and bagged my phone and laptop. He then gave me a gruff pat-down that included the inseam up to and thoroughly around the crotch. After that moment of unwelcome intimacy, he looked me in the eye and stretched out his hand, waiting for me to give him a concealed camera for taking pictures of the manuscript. I shook my head. He put his hand down, but I was convinced that if I had blinked, a cavity search would have followed.

After I unsuccessfully tried to engage the black beard in conversation about the scrolls, our scenic ride in a mildew-scented 1990s Buick passed in silence for the almost two-hour drive. At the monastery, I was passed from bad cop to good monk. Dressed in a maroon robe and sand-colored sandals, my monk guide had a bowling-ball-smooth scalp, twinkling eyes, and an endearing smile. Without saying a word, he pressed the palms of his hands together, held them up to his face, and gently bowed. I returned the humble gesture. Though I had many questions for this monk, I respected his silence. He had a peaceful, spiritual way about him that allowed him to communicate without words. I followed him from the chilly stone entrance hall into the warm heart of the monastery.

There was a part of me that relished the idea of being holed up in an ancient monastery nestled in the foothills of the Himalayas and like a late-middle-aged monk, translating and scribbling into a big book the historically and culturally faith-building—or blasphemous and faith-shaking—story. Disconnected from all gadgets and my life in the city, separated from classroom and pulpit, I'd make the work a spiritual practice. I wondered if I'd have anyone to talk to, or if I'd pass three months in silent solitude without a friend and confidant.

The monastery was a marvelous relic dating back to AD 500. It wasn't an austere home for Christian monks but more a Gaudí and Dalí collaborative hallucination; the pungent incense may have been laced with poppy extract. As monks chanted like distant wolves from a mountain top, I followed my joyful guide and his flowing burgundy robe. We meandered through crooked corridors and various rooms from brilliantly lit large halls painted in playful colors that displayed angry deities with many heads and four to eight arms to ominously dark inner sanctums.

My tour ended with a gallant wave of the monk's arm, much like a bellhop ushering me to the threshold of a regal suite.

"Here, here," he said. "Cozy, cozy room for you to do your writing."

At least he spoke some English. That was helpful since I didn't speak Kashmiri, Hindi, or Urdu. He lit a candle and ushered me into a dank study where the manuscript scrolls were piled high on a long desk spanning the rear wall of the room. The monk lit three more candles. I inhaled sharply. The treasure trove of ancient text was being treated like a decade of daily newspapers in the room of a hoarder. The literary discovery of the millennium was only a toppled candle away from going up in smoke.

"May I have light brought into the room?" I asked my host. Still studying the haphazard pile, I prayed Miles's chronology of the scrolls had been maintained.

"Yes, but no, our electricity is not good most of the time, and we have no power in this room," he replied. "Candles are more reliable. Praise Lord Buddha, we have lots of snow and ice to keep our food fresh." He pressed his hands together and held them to his "Father Thomas, correct?" I nodded and smiled. "And I, Lama Chin-chin-a-na-ga, will be your guide." He beamed at the sound of the playful syllables of his name. "Please let me know when you have more questions."

In Buddhism, a lama was a high-ranking monk. I bowed low, and he giggled while returning my gesture of respect. I wondered if he knew I was also a bishop . . . emeritus. My ego wanted to tell him, so I dismissed the thought.

"I'd like to see where I will sleep. I need some rest, then I will get started."

He pointed to a mat on the floor. Apparently, I would sleep and work in the same small room for three months.

"How about food?"

"At dawn, after morning prayers, midday, and the eighteenth hour. In the temple dining hall. Yum-yum." He patted his stout belly and gave me another endearing smile. "I could also have tea brought with yak milk as you work, if you like?"

"Tea. No milk, please. Thank you." I'd ask later if coffee with cow's milk was on the menu.

"I'll leave you to start now. Please enjoy your retreat," he said. "And I hope we will have a chance to know each other better during your stay. I am interested in your faith, your work, and what you will find here. I cannot read the Latin." An obvious lover of antiquity, he looked longingly at the scrolls.

I liked my lama guide with his enchanting eyes. If tasked with spying on me for the police state, he was off to a good start, already putting me completely at ease with his aura of spiritual grace. Of course, that might be the candlelight reflecting off his shiny bald head.

He left me in the barely lit room that was no bigger than a sacristy or hotel room. One open ten-foot scroll might fit horizontally across the room but not vertically. I knelt to pray and to settle my spinning head from the thin mountain air. I knelt for a long time until an image of Jesus revived me. Mine wasn't a grand mystical vision of Saint Paul but the recurring image of Jesus's beatific face from long periods of reflection upon it. I would let nothing denigrate or mar that image.

Since it was already past three p.m. local time, I decided to put in a couple hours of work, get my bearings, eat, and then get some much-needed sleep on my two-inch-thick floor mat. If I could stay awake long enough, the delay would help me adjust to the time and elevation change.

A mouse squeaking across the cold stone floor before disappearing into a nook in the wall took with him my romantic notion of a monk's hermitage. I suddenly longed for the comforts of a Holiday Inn.

I opened my knapsack to remove my Bible, a pen, and one of my many oversized notebooks. I placed the Bible on a foot-high table by my mat. There was no place to hang or store my clothes—I would literally be living out of my suitcase, which I would keep closed to prevent my rodent roommate from making a bed of it.

From my suitcase, I unpacked the sterile wipes and cloths. After thoroughly cleaning and drying my hands, I began my inspection of the scrolls—108 according to Miles. The floral smell of the papyrus struck me as being as ancient as the text. The scent indicated that the scrolls were treated with some preservative, maybe camphor oil, before the lofty mountain permafrost entombed and preserved them. The fragrance was delightful and intoxicating, but sadly the scrolls' scent indicated a sweet and slow decay had started after centuries of preservation. The scrolls would soon decay from moisture if not moved to a museum for proper care.

To my relief, the scrolls seemed to be in chronological order, with the first scroll beginning with a Homeric-like invocation that called forth a godlike omnipotent narrator. I paced the room for a few minutes, once again contemplating how to approach my translation. I'd played with a few ideas on the plane, but now that I saw the true scope of the task, I refined my tactics.

My resources were limited. I had no access to the internet or colleagues. My time was even more limited; I would have to work through over a scroll per day. So rather than painstakingly try to translate word for word, a method that would get me less than halfway through the scrolls by my deadline, I would summarize and translate the text using understandable modern parlance, omitting lengthy political diatribes, complex genealogies, and all the mentions of crude toiletry and bathing habits that were commonly included in Roman histories.

I prayed that I or another translator—a team of translators—would later have an opportunity to perform a more complete and literal translation. Though I would be co-creating the text alongside the unidentified narrator from circa AD 33, I planned to limit my intrusions to adding observations where I could bring a Christian understanding of the story and, where necessary, to clarify or dispute challenges to the Christian faith that existed within the text.

I began reading the Latin words with the eye of an English major and noting that the author, following his invocation, introduced his characters and setting with omniscient narration, a common feature of Greek and Roman epic literature. However, the text soon shifted to a close third-person point of view, dropping into individual characters' heads—generally one character per chapter. The narrator created an intriguing bridge between ancient and modern literature with this viewpoint switching. The style allowed readers to know each character both from an observer's viewpoint and from the mind of the character.

This technique was odd for the era. I wondered whether the text might be a modern counterfeit. AI was already replicating the old masters' paintings and writing novels in the style of Dickens and Dostoyevsky, so maybe. . . . But I had to trust Miles and his dating of the ancient scrolls.

I switched hats and started reading as a religious scholar, recalling an essay in which I analogized the Greek narrator to God and the Greek muses to the Holy Spirit. The comparison served as a clever way to remind my readers that God knows their thoughts and that we should let him move through us to author the story of our lives.

As for the tale itself, after a brief introduction of place and characters, the story began in the thick of the action, with the Romans and the Jews desperate to find Christ's body to prove he hadn't risen as the Messiah.

What struck me as I headed down to join the monks for dinner—besides the potent fragrance of incense—was a sense of overwhelming responsibility to complete my task without bias or fear of the truth. I told myself that if the history seemed a truthful account but contained world-shattering revelations on Christianity, I'd let the pope decide what to do with the story and whether to press Kashmir for the manuscript's release; and if successful, whether to re-bury the scrolls in the Vatican's secret "private" archives.

All roads, then and now, lead to Rome.

Sing through me, muses and daughters of Jupiter. Hear me, incorporeal genius that hovers above men's minds. Descend and possess me so that I may give voice to our hero's Olympian battles and long journey home. Make him brave and undaunted as he endeavors to defend the innocent from evil and discern truth from lies.

Janus, you two-faced god, beholder of bold beginnings and heroic endings, bless this beginning and let the end be never ending.

—Invocation, author unknown, circa AD 33

CHAPTER 1

East and West

THERE CAN BE no doubt where and when the quest of the small military family under the leadership of disgraced tribune Marcus Antonius Decia began. It was late April when a carrier pigeon arrived from the emperor demanding that the new prefect of Egypt secure immediate passage for Marcus, his two men, and their horses on a vessel sailing from Alexandria to the port of Caesarea. The men completed their crossing without incident and began the last leg of their journey the next morning, riding to Jerusalem with haste to meet Governor Pontius Pilate for an undisclosed purpose.

The three men were very different in temperament and behavior but functioned as a solidary and formidable unit. Marcus followed orders and Poet and Boy followed Marcus, all three knowing exactly what was expected of them.

They were only two men left under Marcus's command—dedicated, loyal, and brave. Far from the thousands who'd formerly served under Marcus.

Boy, a sixteen-year-old slave whose given name was unknown to his companions, tended the horses. He was like a centaur himself, so attached was he to Sahara, his light brown Andalusian mare. Boy was tall, strong, and fast—a whirlwind of burgeoning manhood. His coloring was a rich bronze, and he would make a magnificent statue if he ever managed to stand still. Boy was the only slave in the empire to carry a spatha sword and ride a thoroughbred alongside Roman officers.

Thirty-three-year-old Marcus was a couple of shades lighter, with more muscle. But Boy looked enough like the tribune to pass for his son, the resemblance proving useful when slaves were not permitted into an establishment where all three of them wanted to enter. Marcus's stoic face was one women remembered and loved, and men remembered and feared.

Poet, slightly older than Marcus, had long ago shed his name for the literary title and looked like a stunted pine between tall oaks. He had a sharp, noble Roman nose on a handsome face and was the Hellenistic-inspired artist of the small company. Poet had been a commander of a five-hundred-man cohort of Marcus's legion. He had been Marcus's most loyal comrade through all his battles, with campaigns and postings ranging from Germania to Mauretania as they enforced Roman will and law on the untamed frontiers of the empire.

Those glory days were now behind them. After the tragic events in Rome—a bloody coup attempt supposedly led by Marcus's father, Senator Decia, which resulted in the emperor's Praetorian Guard massacring the entire House of Decia in Rome—Marcus was stripped of his legion and assigned to the position of rebel hunter. But Marcus was still called tribune; removing that title required a vote in the senate, and Caesar didn't have the votes he needed. Not yet.

Tribune Marcus Decia had been born for greatness but was laid low by treachery, yet still he and his two companions triumphed, successfully detecting rebellion and identifying and removing rebel leaders in Egypt and elsewhere in the empire. Making the best of his new ignoble station, Marcus was still of great value to Rome where he was likened to a hunting dog tracking the scent of sedition to the seat of rebellion.

Poet stayed with Marcus after his fall from commander of legions to rebel hunter, choosing loyalty and love over status and comfort. Neither man believed the official Roman story of the coup, and Poet still believed that Marcus's courage and righteous acts would be rewarded and that he would be crowned by glory.

Unfortunately, cruel fate had left Marcus, the fallen tribune, with little prospect of a valiant life story.

⌐ ⌐ ⌐

At the same time that Marcus and his men journeyed east, a pair of humble travelers moved slowly west. Ma and Swami Bhakti had departed India, following the Silk Road, on a pilgrimage to Jerusalem in search of Jesus of Nazareth.

Bhagawati Ma was a blissful spiritual woman whose small group of followers addressed as Ma, though she referred to herself as a *little girl* even as she approached her thirtieth year. The white sari covering her olive skin seemed too white for the dusty road on a donkey's back. She was quick with an authentic smile and a flash of her dazzling brown eyes. Her face emanated light and joy, casting peace like a tranquil sun. And like the sun, she cast no shadow. Stories circulated of this simple, graceful woman taking on the form of the fearsome goddess Kali to defeat manifestations of evil. Her devotees in need of physical or spiritual healing saw her simply as Ma. No one who met her with an open heart would deny she was blessed with divine grace.

Swami Bhakti, her attendant, cook, and student, rivaled Ma in his understanding of the ancient texts of Eastern mysticism. If Ma was the radiant sun, Bhakti was the full moon. As a sober and celibate religious scholar, he found his light in following her. A bright, orange robe dusted by the dirty road covered his leathered skin. And his long, drawn face was pockmarked by a childhood pox. His aged and weathered appearance served to illuminate Ma's physical brilliance.

Ma was being guided along the rough, poorly charted trails to the Silk Road by an inner compass, the assistance of her guru, Mahavatar Babaji, and the gods. Two moons ago, Ma and Bhakti had departed western India. Jerusalem and Jesus were still many more moons away.

And even as Bhakti pondered parables and paradoxes Ma posed to him to guide him to divine union with Bhagavan (God), Poet pondered Pythia, the great Oracle of Delphi, who posed the one question she said would answer all questions: *Where and when does east meet west?*

CHAPTER 2
Boy

BOY LIT THE campfire, pleased to be on an important and mysterious journey to Jerusalem with his master and with Poet. He was proud of his work as their horse and fire tender. He watched as Poet prepared their simple dinner, a stew of salted mutton with herbs and root vegetables. Poet was a fair cook with what he had to work with, but Boy missed the savory Moroccan flavors of the dishes his mother used to make. Marcus whittled a piece of wood, lost in thought and probably still contemplating the urgent imperial command delivered by a carrier pigeon, demanding that they immediately join the governor of Judaea in Jerusalem.

Marcus was not alone in his pondering. Boy knew pigeons carried concisely worded messages of only great political or military weight, but the reason they were summoned remained a mystery. The message-bearing bird also caused him to consider the cold calculus of the Roman saying that "*a good homing bird was worth more than a hundred slaves.*"

They had ridden hard from Caesarea to arrive at the outskirts of Jerusalem before nightfall. After a quick supper, Boy cleaned up while keeping the fire crackling. He was restless after finishing his camp work. "What are you writing, Uncle?" he asked Poet, who sat on a stone, scratching words onto papyrus. *Uncle* was the affectionate name Boy used for Marcus's brother-in-arms.

"Notes about our quashing the rebellion in Alexandria."

Boy nodded. He loved spying with Marcus and Poet. Boy had mastered playing whatever role was needed to elicit information otherwise not forthcoming from witnesses and sympathizers to insurrection. He embraced the most perilous role of all: infiltrating a clandestine rebel group as one of their own. Marcus and Poet would rather assign themselves to such risky work, but Boy's youth and non-Roman features often made him the best choice to serve as spy.

"That chapter of our lives may have closed," Poet explained, "and I want to chronicle our successes before I forget or before it is too late."

"Too late?" Boy asked, though he knew what Poet meant. They both glanced at Marcus, who ignored their banter.

Poet said, "Let us change the subject."

"Of course," Boy said. "Tell me again the story of the day you and Marcus found me."

He'd heard his origin story many times before, but each time Poet told the tale, he recalled or invented some fresh detail that Marcus would correct or clarify, and Boy would ponder the new detail for days. Boy was proud of his roots and liked to be reminded of his father's courage and nobility. Boy also worshipped his regal mother, and he prayed daily to be reunited with the woman who'd been taken from him when he was a child. Keeping her image alive in his mind had become a testament to his undying devotion.

The dramatic battle that had brought the three men together was his favorite of Poet's campfire stories. Boy hadn't yet lost his childlike imagination, nor his empathetic ability to live the story being told. And Poet used his words well to cast spells. A vivid storyteller, Poet allowed Boy to see the scenes flickering in the campfire as if he were taking part of the events.

"Again with that old story?" Poet said, setting aside the papyrus filled with neat writing, reminding Boy of the debt of gratitude he owed the man who had taught him to read. The ability to read made him one in a hundred men and was a gift he could never repay. "I should write it as verse. Then you could sing it to yourself," Poet said. He sighed and looked up to the night sky, and then he lifted the wineskin that was propped against his hip. He fondled the skin containing the last of their good Greek wine to gauge how much remained before pouring out three cups and putting the nozzle to his lips to suck out the last drop. Marcus liked to whittle while he thought. Poet liked to drink while he talked.

As Poet began the story, Boy was transported back four years, seeing the events unfold through Poet's eyes as Poet surveyed the battle scene at Marcus's side:

Stretched out before us was a flat, grassy Moroccan savanna dotted with thorny bushes that looked like little green fires lit by the blistering sun overhead. The scene was also dotted with very straight and very tall Moroccan men armed with long swords and small shields.

"We've been here half a day, yet they still stand firm, reddish-brown sandstone obelisks unprepared to yield," I said, looking out over the green vista that reached the horizon. "We are twenty-two horsemen to their thirty-three foot soldiers, so we will have a slight advantage on their field of battle." I wished we had brought a few more men from the legion on the excursion into the untamed region and was hoping Marcus would confirm our advantage.

Many times, I've marveled over the stoic composure Marcus exhibited in the face of battle and death. He had a masterful control over himself and his reactions, one that led to an ease of command that no man would question, and which imparted confidence to his men. That Marcus would die for any one of them made each ready to die for him.

We, and our twenty elite cavalrymen had stumbled upon a well-disciplined regiment of Mauri warriors and their chief while chasing a thieving Bedouin band. The Mauretania region was yet to be formally subdued by the empire, and warrior chiefs still controlled large parts of the wild western North African landscape.

"Let's see if we can talk them out of a fight today," Marcus said, motioning for me to follow. I lifted my arm and called the troops to attention as we strode out to meet our adversarial counterparts.

"We will leave the horses, but bring your shield in case they start pitching those spears," Marcus said.

As we marched across the ankle-high grassland—perfect terrain for a cavalry charge—I said, "They know how to use those spears. And even without armor, their bare, glistening torsos are intimidating."

"They look like the best of athletes built for fighting on the grand stage of the colosseum," Marcus said. "We have armor and horses, but they'll have the advantage of speed, numbers, and those long spears if they can topple us from our mounts."

The enemy got bigger, taller, and stronger the closer we came to their line. Their chief was tall and adorned with a gold, gem-encrusted breastplate. He had assumed a center position in their ranks and moved out alone to meet us.

"They will throw half their spears as we charge and probably bring down five of our men," Marcus coolly announced. "And then kill or maim another five more in battle before we can cut them down from our mounted position. But the battle will be ours. Let us hope the man will see reason and take my mercy instead."

"You don't suppose they might just leave the field?" I asked.

"They likely can get supplies from their village. Our garrison is over a hundred miles away; provisions and time are on their side." Marcus finished speaking before the chief came into earshot.

The warrior's face was the color of dark clay and fierce, as imposing as Marcus's battle mask.

"I knew the Romans would return after taking my queen," he said, speaking Greek. His breastplate was in the form of a cat; it had two emerald eyes that sparkled in the sun, poised to pounce.

"When was this?" Marcus answered. "We are the first Roman military excursion to these parts that I know of."

"Six moons ago, while my men and I were out hunting. Cowards took my regal wife. She was a goddess to me, my *drree*, and my people. Return her or die." His heart had been ripped from his chest and replaced by a burning desire for revenge. He looked like Mars's brother Vulcan about to erupt.

"I'm sorry," Marcus replied. "It may have been thieves wearing Roman military tunics, but I assure you that no sanctioned Roman unit passed through here six moons ago; I would know of any such activity. It sounds like rogue mercenaries who blunder without sanction or restraint."

Marcus despised such men and was displeased that Rome rewarded their actions by allowing them to keep the silver and gold of their spoils.

"Then leave your little officer here as a hostage until you can find those that took my wife and return her to me along with their heads."

Marcus told the chief, "That would be a *small* price to pay to avoid the unnecessary loss of life, including yours, that will ensue today. But I can't leave my commander here. Too many snakes," he added for my benefit.

Boy laughed despite himself. Poet gave him a sharp look. He didn't like to be interrupted when telling a story. Poet said, "Maybe I'll just enjoy the last of the wine." Boy's dark eyes pleaded with Poet, begging forgiveness. "Well, I am a half foot shorter than Marcus and your father. And my fear of snakes is real, Boy. Now, no more cackling and I will continue:

"You have my word as a tribune of Rome," Marcus told him, "that I will investigate and have your wife returned if she is to be found."

The chief didn't look impressed or convinced by Marcus's words.

"If I may?" I asked, looking to Marcus, who nodded. "Chief, this is Tribune Marcus Decia, a hero of many military campaigns, but more to the point, a man of great honor and integrity. If he gives his word, that bond is all you need. And if he agrees, I myself will lead your wife back here or come to report our failure to find her, but only after exhausting all possible means of searching."

I knew that finding the princess would be unlikely. The region and the entire Roman legion were under Marcus's command; Marcus's soldiers would not have done this. I knew the mercenaries who had seized the chief's queen were probably in Rome by then, selling the Nubian princess for a large bounty.

"Thank you, friend," Marcus said. "I don't expect that we'll find her, as I would have heard of the raid and of her by now. But

I will make every effort, and you will know whether we find her or not." I often wished Marcus was less honest or at least less direct. He continued with his blunt assessment, "If we find her, which is unlikely, I will hold those responsible to account by Roman law and justice. I won't lie: They may have broken no law, though I agree they should be put to death, and I'd bring you their heads if I could."

I could only imagine the pain this noble man suffered thinking of the cruel treatment and enslavement of his queen by Roman barbarians. The chief's expression was a mix of ferocity and grief. "Yes, she is not coming back, and there will be no justice. But for my *drree*, I had to try. And now I will have my revenge in battle with you, my worthy Roman foe."

The fates had brought the two warriors to clash, and their eyes locked in equal parts admiration and ferocity.

"Mars proclaims vengeance is a virtue that serves his bloodlust," Marcus said. "But vengeance will serve little purpose here today other than bloodshed, and with you gone, the enslavement of your village."

"Only if you win the day," the chief said, bouncing the dull end of his spear against the ground to make his point. "We shall see."

"It is your death," Marcus told him.

"My duty!" he sang out, his sword bouncing between his words. "Your duty!" Bounce. "My death." Bounce. "Your death!" Bounce. "Death means little." Bounce. "To those that live like lions." Bounce. "With honor!" Bounce.

The chief's voice resounded with determination as he steeled himself for battle. I wished we didn't have to fight the courageous man and his well-trained soldiers.

"You would have made a great tribune had you been born in Rome," Marcus told him. "You have my respect and soon will have my sword."

I would have worded it differently. Marcus tipped his head and turned to walk back to his battalion. I joined him in the long walk in silence.

As our soldiers rallied the horses to make ready the charge, I remember saying in jest, "We could just ride around them."

"And be chased like rabbits from the field?" Marcus responded. "I cannot deny that man his revenge or an honorable death."

"So we fight," I said.

"As the gods will," Marcus said. "He is smart. See, he has them forming a wedge to deflect our horses to either side." We had seen a lot of death and didn't like to see good men die on either side of the battlefield, but we always did what had to be done, and performed our duty. "I'll try one last attempt to avert the deadly tide, bloody though it will be," Marcus said. "Bring me a dodecahedron."

I brought him one of our three dodecahedra. The twelve-sided bronze projectile fit within the palm of Marcus's big hand. In flight, the dodecahedron emitted a loud, haunting wheeze and rattle sound that heralded death. Following my signal, one of the men brought a large slingshot to Marcus. The soldier soaked a rotten nub of wood in oil and placed it in the center of the projectile. I watched the drill with admiration—the flaming dodecahedron was Marcus's invention and art.

The attending soldier lit the oiled wood and crouched when Marcus twirled and then hurled the large bronze ball the length of an arena. It looked fearsome traveling through the air with its fiery tail, not unlike that of a comet—a touch of artistic military genius.

The dodecahedron hit the man standing next to the chief, separating his head from his body. I counted thirty-two soldiers left standing as Marcus glared at the scene. It seemed that he and the chief were maintaining eye contact over the great distance.

We had hoped the sight and damage of one dodecahedron would cause the Mauri to retreat, but they held ranks. I knew Marcus didn't like men to die in this unsporting way rather than in a fair fight, so I prodded him by saying, "It will save their lives and ours, if, with two more shots, you can make them yield."

Marcus shook his head sadly and called for another dodecahedron and then another, downing a man beside the chief both times. After each shot, the opposing leaders glared at each other. Though he was the best shot I had ever seen, it was still hard to believe Marcus would spare the chief's life on purpose, but so it was.

"Mount your horses, Romans," Marcus said to his men. "They came to fight and are not afraid to die. Mars wills us into battle. Men, make this charge as if it is the last of your life and raise your swords high to reflect the sun in their eyes as we grow near their wedge. We will introduce them to Roman fortitude and steel. May the gods be with us."

Of all Romans, the military was the most religious and never more devout than when heading into battle, but we all pray to different gods, like the Egyptian gods the Mauri people had adopted. I gave thanks to Apollo—the Horus-like god of poetry—that our men were already winning the battle, three to zero.

With the Roman cavalry mounted, Marcus pounded his chest and shouted, "Know no fear!"

I blew the big bone horn that was strapped to my saddle to commence the charge. The horses raced headlong into death. The Mauri released a primal battle cry, a fear-inducing blast of fury. Thorny bushes scraped at our rider's legs but were no obstacle to the attack. Halfway from their target, a barrage of spears flew at us, knocking six Romans from their horses—one more than Marcus had anticipated.

When the cavalry, swords raised, was about to ram the wedge of Mauri men, the soldiers collapsed into a single line with their chief out front. With his men lined up behind him, the chief crouched low and planted a metal spear into the ground so the blade was angled up neck high.

I couldn't prevent my horse from being impaled. I hit the ground hard and lay dazed, watching as the rest of the horses either passed by the single-file line, unable to stop or rearing up, throwing their riders to the ground. Events crawled along, as if time itself had slowed to watch the carnage. Yet once the fighting paused, the mayhem seemed to have passed in no time at all. Blood was dripping from my sword.

The next thing I remembered with clarity was scanning the field littered with men for Marcus. He was the lone man still on horseback. And he had locked eyes with the chief, the lone Mauri left alive and unwounded. The leaders were maybe thirty paces apart. The brave chief started sprinting, like a cheetah after prey. At less than ten paces from Marcus, he leaped in the air and aimed his spear at Marcus's heart. Marcus twisted aside to avoid a skewering but took a pounding from the chief's body, which knocked him from his horse. The chief rolled and bounced up from the hard earth, spear in hand. Marcus, weighed down by armor, rose to meet him. With his sword in one hand, he held up his other hand, which normally held his shield, to signal to us to stay out of the fight.

The chief continued to attack Marcus, jabbing his long spear in rapid succession, putting Marcus on the defensive, blocking the thrusts with his much shorter sword. I recalled Marcus saying the Mauri had the advantage of speed and length of weapons and imagined that those advantages might be the death of my master. Marcus removed his helmet between thrusts. On the next lunge, he flung the helmet at the chief, striking him in the hip and causing him to stumble. This gave Marcus an opening to grab the warrior's spear and pull him into his own blade, cleaving the right flank of his honorable foe.

The chief fell to his knees, at which point Marcus caught him, keeping him from dropping face first into the dirt. Marcus dropped to his knees too, holding the chief upright by the shoulders. Their faces were close; the men looked more like brothers praying than deadly adversaries. The brave Mauri said something to Marcus as he pulled his breastplate up and from around his neck and handed it to Marcus. Connected to Marcus by the breastplate and their unbroken gaze, the chief exhaled his last breath.

That final breath was slow and gentle; he left us in peace. And Marcus . . .

Boy looked up from the fire where he'd watched his father's death once more to steal a glance at Marcus who sat beside him, hoping Marcus might finally say what tribute or promise he'd made to his father as he passed away.

Marcus silently continued whittling the horse, with a faraway look in his eyes, but Boy knew Poet would keep prodding, inciting Marcus to engage.

Boy, once tormented by anger and resentment, now remarkably felt only gratitude for the man who had slain his father and who became his master and teacher of the great virtues of steadfast love and fidelity to one's duty. Marcus had taken Boy into his service and into his family, and Boy had come to love Marcus as a father.

Boy turned back to the fire, and Poet cleared his throat and continued, "After that good fight and noble death, Marcus laid your father on the matted grass. I felt an overwhelming sense of loss for a man I'd met only an hour before, and Marcus said a few words. Words we will never know, that Marcus will never speak—"

"He knows the story and how brave his father was that day," Marcus said finally. "What I've never owned up to is that but for my armor I'd be dead instead of him. Poet left out that your father's spear glanced off the metal on my breastplate when I twisted aside before he knocked me off my horse." He held up the wooden horse, narrowed his eyes, and continued to work the wood. "We found you, all of twelve years old, bound by rope in a nearby camp with the women and other children, but there was no mistaking you. You were his child, a true warrior's son. I saw him in your eyes. I freed you and made you my slave." He stretched his powerful arm over Boy's shoulder.

"I wanted to fight in the name of my mother," Boy said. He watched to see how those words affected Marcus, but the tribune's face remained unmoved. "My father knew only chains would stop me from joining the fight to revenge her being . . ." Boy stood, ready again for a battle that was over four years earlier as he continued, "Poet, you also didn't mention the final score was thirty to fifteen and that a cavalry should vanquish foot soldiers at least three to one. I don't count the three men killed by the dodecahedra." Boy liked to imagine how his people fought heroically, treating it like a personal mythology. One day, he would pick up his father's valiant attempt to find his mother and take vengeance as his own quest.

"I wish we had a dodecahedron to fire into Pilate's palace to rattle his cage," Poet said, again looking for Marcus to react.

When Marcus didn't reply, Boy filled the void, saying, "I'm glad you spared my father a death by dodecahedra before the battle began, so he could die a hero's death." Boy sat by Marcus and shuddered as a wave of remorse for his fallen father washed over him.

Marcus pulled Boy into his body for a comforting side hug. "There were no good men or bad men that day. And yes, your father died a brave and honorable death. His collapsing of the wedge of foot soldiers into a straight line to avoid the frontal assault of our charging horses is now part of the military training back in Rome. His regiment performed like a cohesive unit of humming, swarming bees. That brilliant tactic almost won him the day, as we were cut down to just five men," Marcus said as he resumed whittling. "All men come to death. In the meantime, the charioteer of the logos either rolls over us or passes us by. Some believe that if you're in a state of deep contemplation, you can hear the iron wheels of his chariot spinning faster and faster until they become a hum of the gods, and we become lost to this world."

"Master Marcus, the stoic with his logos," Poet said.

Boy appreciated that Poet, though not a slave, still called Marcus his master. Poet was as bound to Marcus as he himself was. And Marcus *was* a master, a master of war, of intelligence, of justice, of truth, and of men.

"You should read Zeno of Citium someday, Boy, if we live long enough," Poet said. "But you have a living teacher in Marcus, a stoic who doesn't let circumstance define him and who is a master of his reactions." Poet stood, looking sadly into his empty wine cup.

Boy shook his head and poured half his wine into Poet's cup.

"You're a good man," Poet said. "In Jerusalem, we'll be saddled with piss-poor wine from some local village, wine so foul that it has to be embalmed to keep it from turning to vinegar."

Boy patted his chest and the metal under his tunic, calling for Poet to finish the tale. It was sacrosanct that each retelling includes the ending—the full ending and not the shortened version that Poet had just recounted. Marcus pointed to Poet, indicating he should deliver the bittersweet ending, though it really was Marcus's story to tell.

"Marcus knelt next to your fallen father to see him off on his flight into Elysium and to hear his last words. Your father, struggling for breath, pointed to his heart and said, '*Drree.*' He pointed to Marcus's chest and repeated, '*Drree,*' as if he was giving this *drree* to Marcus. Your father then removed his breastplate, truly a rare work of art, and gifted it to Marcus, seeking some promise in exchange. Marcus agreed, not knowing what he was agreeing to. Your father closed his eyes and died a good death." Poet and Boy looked down to the earth, neither at liberty to ask what prayer and oath Marcus had offered in that moment of death. Marcus had once said it was a private matter between the two men and the gods and that they were not to speak of it again.

Poet broke the silence saying, "Upon entering the chief's village, Marcus held up the golden breastplate bearing its black cat with precious green gems for eyes. The women bowed to him as if he were now their leader. Marcus called out, 'drree,' and he was led to you. He learned that *drree* meant *boy* in your native tongue."

Boy removed the precious artifact from his tunic, kissing each emerald cat eye, as was his ritual. "My mother's mystical work of art," he whispered.

"Marcus gave it to you that day, and it has been with you, and you with us, ever since," Poet said.

Boy stood to add fuel to the fire. "I just wish . . ." His voice trailed off. There was no point in expressing again the deep-seated sentiment. They knew what he most desired, and it wasn't his freedom but to find his mother. He would run away, desert his duty and master, if he thought he could find her.

"And here we are," Poet said, "as a reward for our exemplary service in Egypt, we're summoned to Jerusalem to meet the sniveling *Pernicious* Pilate." Shifting topics was the sign the story had run its well-rutted course.

Poet turned to face Boy and said, "The first time we met Pilate, he sat atop his horse, giving orders while watching from the rear—" Poet twisted his long sharp nose and snarled his lips as if he'd just bitten into a green lemon "—as our cavalry charged."

Boy wished he had been there for the cavalry charge. Boy wished he'd been at his master's side for all of his battles—except one.

"You met him once again in Jerusalem, didn't you?" Boy asked.

"Yes, under the banners of Marcus's legion in a show of force and pride when he arrived as the new governor in Judaea. Now the emperor orders us to meet Pilate in his palace, giving us no idea why we're called from the comfort of Alexandria. But we must assume it isn't to sing our praises," Poet said, turning to face Marcus, "or to give you back your legion."

"No good deed," Marcus said. "His call must relate to our cunning ability and excellent reputation for ferreting out rebels in Alexandria." Marcus, branded a rebel's son, was charged with hunting rebel leaders. The irony was not lost on Boy. "Pilate is always looking for spies to do his indelicate work," Marcus continued. "I do not fear this governor and won't accept his mission if it's shameful or unlawful."

"Am I the only one concerned we might die tomorrow?" Poet asked. "Suppose he has summoned us only to have us killed like they did to your family?"

The question reminded Boy of the third saddest day of his life, the day Marcus was flogged in Alexandria for refusing to admit to colluding with the family in the coup attempt and for not denouncing his father's name to the emperor's emissaries. Despite being a tribune, he had submitted to corporal punishment as a sign of his conviction of his family's innocence.

Standing abruptly, Marcus flung the near-completed horse into the fire. Boy scuttled to rescue it, singeing his hand. The fire had scorched the horse around the mane. Boy placed the smokey sandalwood mare under his nose to capture its pleasant scent and packed it away for Marcus to finish later.

"Why must you harp on this? My father, mother, and wife were honorable." Marcus unclenched his fists with a deep sigh. "And now they are dead." Poet had finally riled up the otherwise unprovokable bear, inciting him to pace while speaking in his family's defense. "Father was a lone voice in the Senate, advocating for freeing the slaves. It was as pragmatic as it was moral—a rhetorical plea to recognize the dignity of all men. My wife had changed his mind with the wisdom of her Venus heart."

Marcus's wife, Beatrice, had been with child the day his family was slaughtered in Rome. Boy thought of Beatrice as a sister to his mother, both women sacrificed at the whims of evil men.

Marcus stopped pacing, clutched the wine cup to his chest, and raised his right hand and pointed the carving knife to the heavens. "My father knew his clarion call would not be heeded, but he used it to prod his fellow senators, many of which are brutish men, to recognize the goodness within all men."

Boy felt a quiver racing through him as he imagined he was listening to the renowned orator Senator Decia himself in the Forum.

"Offering slaves their freedom would hurt only cruel masters whose slaves craved freedom from the lash." Marcus continued waving his knife to make his points. "Even if the slaves of kind owners chose to leave, their departure wouldn't cause harm for every slave my father and other decent men lost, there would be ten able-bodied men dying for the same work in exchange for food and a place to sleep. And slaves in areas of conflict would remain in slavery until their leaders made peace with Rome."

Boy pondered Marcus's words. He had made an uneasy peace with his slavery. As a child, he hadn't given his enslavement much thought, but as he approached manhood, he wondered about being free. Boy wasn't like other slaves—he was a slave in name only. He knew this fall from royalty to slave was maintained for his protection. At first, Marcus had kept him as a slave to stop him from running off in search of his mother and getting himself killed by Roman authority. If he acknowledged his mother was a slave, that would mean by Roman law he was a runaway slave. Later, Poet explained that as a tribune's slave, he was afforded greater protections than a free man who was not a Roman citizen. No one dared steal, beat, or cross a tribune's slave other than maybe an emperor or governor. Finally, as long as Marcus lived and was unable to clear his family name, giving Boy the Decia name was a deadly liability. The emperor might still decide to finish the eradication of the entire Decia lineage, annihilating the House of Decia once and for all.

Still, he dreamed of taking what he'd learned from Marcus to search for his mother. Marcus, before his family's fall from grace, had used his good standing, family prestige, and connections to find Boy's mother, but found no trace of her. The empire was as vast as the ocean, and they would have given her a new name. She was one of the ten million slaves—if she was still alive. Boy had heard the tragic tale of Cleopatra and feared that his regal mother might have chosen death over life as a slave. Yet each night he prayed, somehow, some way, they would be reunited.

"Boy, are you listening?" Marcus asked, as Boy was caught lost in thought about his mother. "The military, regardless of rank, has long been enslaved by strict codes of conduct and punishments. Sure, the non-constricted-soldier-citizen is free to leave the service and wander the earth, competing with slave labor, but absent family connections, will die destitute. Are we not all of us slaves to Mother Roma? She spends more silver and gold enforcing slavery than it would cost to abolish it. The empire will fall by the same hands that built her." Marcus stomped off, but pivoted immediately to face Poet and added, "My father's speeches put him at odds with the emperor, but he would never have supported a treasonous coup. And I will never disown my family or believe they committed murder and treason. They can whip me as much as they like." Marcus flung the remains of his wine into the sand.

Poet licked his lips as he watched the precious ruddy nectar of the gods soak into the earth. Boy knew Poet believed a waste of wine to be an affront to Bacchus and good manners, but Poet knew not to challenge Marcus when his family's massacre was the topic of conversation. He wondered if Poet raised the topic to test Marcus's stoicism, or because Poet feared the emperor still intended to slay the last living Decia.

"If it is so written, let the gods kill us tomorrow," Marcus said. "There'll be no Tali tonight."

Boy was disappointed. He liked the game of rolling numbered sheep bones. They played before sleeping for fun or for the middle watch, the least advantageous watch. However, Boy was relieved that Marcus didn't consider the camp to be at risk and thus didn't require a night watch.

Marcus lay down and propped his saddle behind his neck. Boy draped a thin wool blanket over him before settling onto his own carpet bedding. Poet remained seated for a few minutes, perhaps pondering Pilate's plot, or the wasted last sips of his fine Greek wine.

"Let it rest, Poet," Marcus said in a soothing voice as Boy slipped into slumber. "Sleep now, and tomorrow in Jerusalem we'll find out if we live or die."

CHAPTER 3
Pilate's Praetorium

"NOTHING EVER CHANGES in Jerusalem," Poet said, "except there are even more statues of our Caesars."

Three imperial sentries met Poet and Marcus in front of the grand palace doors. The soldiers were dressed in full battle regalia—shields, swords, and golden metal armor emblazoned with the black Roman eagle. They knew Tribune Marcus Decia and permitted them entrance to the praetorium, where Pilate resided while in Jerusalem. Boy wasn't permitted to attend the audience.

Jerusalem, the City of Peace, was sunburnt and roiling with rebellion, requiring a fortress-like palace to protect the oppressors from the oppressed; the Roman crown sat uneasily atop the mad hub of festering religious fervor. Less an oasis and more seething desert volcano, Jerusalem made Poet think of the Greek oracle Sibyl's prediction: "*a city of peace will rise up in a sandstorm cyclone and destroy empires.*" Apparently, the time of upheaval was yet to come.

The praetorium's diplomatic chambers were a sanctuary at the center of this simmering political cauldron. Despite the welcoming promise extended by the peaceful ambience, Poet's stomach revolted. Poet hated politics and feared Pilate's snide condescension might make Marcus lose his patience in a place where Pilate alone determined life and death.

In the central chamber, Pilate stood elegantly dressed, like a senator about to dine with Caesar in the Casa di Augusto in Rome. A white tunic draped his slender body. A gold belt was cinched around his waist and a red sash crossed from his right shoulder to his left hip. A gold headband circled the top of his patrician head. With a chiseled face, lily-skinned Pilate could pass as the inspiration for one of the Greek marble statues that Poet so admired. Though Poet was loath to admit it, Pilate was a good-looking man.

Pilate commenced talking in his usual sanctimonious tones, directing his speech to no one in particular.

"Jew-rue-solemn! Herod built us a little Jewish Rome in this unwelcoming land, making me—forced by imperial edict to meet here and not in my comfortable villa in Caesarea—miss the real Rome all the more. I hate this city and all the conniving Semitic people using religion to enrich themselves. Damn the Jews. They whisper about rebellion, but it is the last thing their rabbis really want. They live like fat cream on top of the sour multitude, using Rome to maintain their privilege and as the enemy to hate. Such dour people . . ."

Half listening to Pilate's political monologue, Poet attempted to relax by focusing on the cool morning breeze, as the sight and sound of Pilate pontificating nauseated him even more. He took deep breaths of the fragrant chamber air that was filled with the calming floral notes of the ivy that wrapped around the pillars and windowsills. Six large planters filled with desert blooms, three in each row, adorned the wide path to Pilate's throne, adding a sweet highlight to the room's pleasing aroma. Six large windows that opened onto a balcony carried in fresh air that was circulated by six large fans waved by six large, well-oiled eunuchs, one standing before each planter. The eunuchs were like pillars or furniture, betraying no emotion or opinion. The song of a tinkling fountain, like a harp being plucked, sprang up from the courtyard below.

An imposing witness to the scene who stood by the large windows distracted Poet from his soothing musings on the scene. He was as big as two eunuchs, but stylishly dressed in an embroidered linen tunic and closely shaved. Thick, curly, reddish-orange hair bounced upon his shoulders in the breeze created by the eunuchs and the fresh air coming in the windows. *Throw two hungry lions into the colosseum against him, and smart money would bet on that beast of a man,* Poet thought. Next to him was a man he could easily fold unnoticed into his tunic. The small imp was bald and wide-eyed with a hunched back and a thin smile curling his cracked lips.

"My wife hasn't shared my bed since the Passover celebration of their liberation from Egypt," the effeminate Pilate said. "They can leave here too for all I care. She objected to the crucifixion of that damnable man who escaped his tomb, a magician who enchanted men into believing he could perform miracles, leading his followers' whispers to fly all the way to Rome. And some of those whispers sing more loudly now." Pilate shifted to a sarcastic, singsong voice while gesturing his hands in front of his face like two birds about to peck his eyes out. "Ony! Ony! He has risen! Hallelujah-jah. Son of god. Jesus the Christ has denied death. His body risen up by God. Ha-la-li-la-li-la . . ." Returning to his practiced politician's voice and dropping his sparrow hands back to his sides, he added, "Caesar Augustus is the only son of a god I recognize. And, of course, the man's followers removed his body from the tomb to prove some supposed prophecy. *And* the Pharisees are protecting the drunken guards who claim they were poisoned with some sleeping potion. The entire business smells more than three-day-old pig meat rotting in these sun-crazed streets."

Concluding his speech, Pilate rubbed his hands together, studying his manicured nails before grabbing a towel from the bowl of flowers and water beside him. He diligently wiped the palm of one hand before throwing the towel back into the basin, splashing two of the floating flowers onto the tile floor.

Poet returned his attention to the oversized man by the window. *Perhaps he is a rich Roman merchant or official but certainly a former soldier,* he thought. Despite his nice dress, the man stood like a sentry, never moving his yoke-like shoulders or shifting his feet. Only his striking fiery hair moved in the breeze. He was a refined beast who could knock down a gladiator with either hand.

Pilate, pretending to notice his guests for the first time, opened his arms wide, saying, "But Marcus Decia, I haven't offered my hand in greeting."

Poet noted that Pilate didn't use the title *tribune* and still did not offer his hand or embrace. "I see you brought your scribe and balatro," he said, waving his hand dismissively.

Poet bowed low and a loud burst burped from his backside, fouling Pilate's fragrant air. It surprised even himself. He would tell Marcus later that it was a brave rebellious act and not a nervous reflex. Marcus shoved him aside in swift punishment, causing Poet to stumble toward the window and the herculean man and the old goat beside him. He steadied himself on the sill and hoped that he wouldn't be tossed out the window for his offense. But Pilate didn't react, opting to pretend he didn't hear the noise or smell its aftermath.

Close to the beast, Poet studied the massive man's richly embroidered tunic, and the melon-sized purses clasped at his waist. A rich man. Perhaps a slave trader. "You've got enormous balls. Silver or gold?" Poet asked in a whisper.

Patting the hilt of his sword with a bulbous hand, the giant grinned broadly. The other man, resembling a slender and crooked midday shadow, leered at Poet's indiscretion. Poet made note of his simple red tunic; his long, knotted fingers; and his well-polished, knife-like nails. Since he was no soldier, he wore red to honor Mars, the god of bloodlust. The ghoul was somewhere between forty and sixty years old, his bent body likely contorted since birth. His master was much younger and very much in his prime.

Poet looked back to Pilate and Marcus, who stood a cold six feet from one another.

"That crucified and now-missing body—or that fugitive Jew—is why I summoned you from Alexandria," Pilate said. He tossed Marcus a scroll bearing the imperial seal, which he had pulled from his sash like a magician. "Read it later. Tiberius has agreed to my plan and authorized his stamp to be placed upon the order."

Poet knew that meant Pilate was following the command of Emperor Tiberius Julius Caesar Augustus. With Rome officially involved, Marcus would have limited options. *They* would have limited options. Poet bent slightly forward with his hand on his thighs and clenched his gluteus maximus, succeeding at suppressing another raucous rumble.

"You are hereby commissioned," Pilate went on, "to find the purloined body of this dead man and bring it back for display, to quash this talk of the son of a god leading the way to a new kingdom—how did the confounded man speaking Greek as well as an educated Roman put it?—'not of this earth.'" Tapping his lip, Pilate silently contemplated the ceiling that displayed shapely nymphs bathing one another. He sighed and turned to

Marcus. "And for that simple task, the emperor will show his mercy and generosity. You will be invited to Rome to kiss his ring and pledge your allegiance once again, and he will restore your good name, allowing you to fill your treasonous father's vacant senate seat and home. From there, you can rebuild the House of Decia and lift it from disgrace." Pilate raised his eyebrows, awaiting Marcus's response.

Poet held his breath and his tongue. This was no simple task. Pilate and the emperor would not have summoned them all the way from Alexandria or offered to restore Marcus's honor for anything less than a grave charge worthy an imperial decree. As a hero of military campaigns, and still holding his title of tribune because of his continued popularity in Rome, Marcus remained a force to be reckoned with. As a tribune, he would normally have the power to overrule Pilate's command, but the emperor's seal on the order would make Marcus's refusal to accept the writ a treasonous act. Still, Poet feared the typical reaction of the epic hero who always initially rejected the call to action.

Pilate turned his back to Marcus, placed his hands behind his back, and casually strolled toward the two men at the window. Poet observed the volatile scene with grave concern. Marcus, calm and resigned, stole a look at the giant, who appeared to have been invited for Pilate's protection.

Marcus pounded his chest with a Roman salute, startling Pilate, who jerked his head around as if he were under attack. "I'll locate the body unless it's been cremated," Marcus said. "If it has been burned, I'll bring back the ashes unless they've been scattered over sea or sand." Marcus's agreeable words and even tone allowed Poet to breathe. In Jerusalem, Marcus might fall to poison or lose his head if he didn't show Pilate more respect than he deserved. And truth be told, Poet could see nothing unreasonable in Pilate's orders.

After inspecting the giant standing guard by the window, Pilate twirled fully around to face Marcus and press his advantage. "Ash is no good and won't fulfill your duty. If you fail to produce the body, you'll be banished from the empire and face death if seen or heard from again. You have six months, no more, and the body, or at least the face or death mask, must be recognizable."

Poet should have anticipated that along with the reward for success, there would be a punishment for failure. The stakes were high for Rome and for Marcus, who was pragmatic in his political transactions but sometimes would erupt to intimidate his opponent or to right an injustice. Poet feared his reaction to the threat of banishment and death.

"The power to exile a Roman citizen should rest with the Senate not Caesar," Marcus said.

Poet was relieved that the political precept was expressed in a stoic monotone.

"But it doesn't, tsk, tsk" Pilate said, making Poet cringe. Pilate was against republican rule and a well-known imperialist in favor of an all-powerful dictator. That stand put him at odds with Marcus. "In six months, during the Ludi Victoriae Sullae, the emperor will either declare the body found and put this messiah nonsense to rest, or he will persuade the Senate to proclaim this Jesus a god." Pilate shook his head and adjusted his red sash nervously. "The emperor himself is impressed by the Jesus of Nazareth stories and the rumors of his being raised up like Romulus from the dead and walking alive out of his tomb after three days, tales which have lit a fire beneath the illiterate rabble. And I . . . I will be guilty of deicide if the Senate allows the proclamation of a new god. It is easier to proclaim yet one more god than to fight those who call him god."

Poet dared not meet Marcus's eyes. He didn't want him to see he was gobsmacked. But talk of gods and dead men returning to life was not just another rebel hunt but something more. Something extraordinary.

Pilate lifted a wistful gaze to the bathing nymphs. "They're the only deities I need." To Marcus, he said, "Get moving. We've been searching since his tomb was found empty. Hopefully, they've embalmed the rotting corpse, or six months may be too long. Based on multiple reported sightings of the man after the tomb was opened, the emperor believes Jesus is alive." Pilate waved one hand freely above his head. "Oh yes, his spies watch me and report on me, using his fleet of carrier pigeons—faster than mine—to feed him stories of the rebel's victory over death. That's why he gave you six months." Pilate laughed. "The emperor thinks this risen Jesus has godlike powers and will be difficult to catch. And he may already dine with Jupiter and Juno. If not, he might prefer you bring the god-man back alive. But I don't."

"Will Caesar proclaim him a god if he still lives, or only if he—what was it?—was raised up in his body by the gods like Romulus?" Marcus asked.

Poet studied the nearest eunuch's face to see if the man betrayed any interest in the miraculous drama being discussed. He did not. Poet felt sad for the passionless being, hoping that the still and silent statues had not lost their psyches and souls along with their manhood.

"Good question," Pilate answered Marcus. "He'll probably do whatever his new commander of the Praetorian Guard suggests as he idles in Capri, ruling in absentia by homing pigeons. A head is all I want; I don't want to have to crucify him again. Or have him proclaimed a god that I ordered crucified."

Poet was always eager to hear the imperial political gossip, news that among the Roman elite traveled faster than water along the aqueducts to all corners of the empire. Tiberius, who had been a brave soldier, was a weak ruler, letting others lead him—first his mother, then the traitor Sejanus, and now the new Praetorian Guard commander, Naevius Macro, a man in league with Tiberius's nephew and adopted son, the young Caligula.

"Just imagine," Pilate said, glided to an ornate wood box emblazoned with the silver and gold eagle of the empire, "a son of the one god to become a god among many gods." Shaking his head in disgust, he removed two silk purses from the little treasure chest. He tossed the first purse to Marcus. "Three hundred silver denari." He tossed the second purse. "And three hundred gold coins for your trouble, provisions, and to buy information. That's a lot of sesterces—a small mountain of brass coin there in two little purses. And I'll give you another mountain if you succeed."

Poet managed not to scoff at Pilate's casual attitude toward the value of the coins. As he silently sighed instead, a strange dizziness of mind struck him. *What have I eaten to make me so queasy?* he wondered. He stretched a quivering hand to the wall and shook his head. It was as if a demon was tapping his forehead between his eyebrows, creating a spinning vortex. The world was turning around inside his skull. When the whirling settled, what remained was a deep calm and a crystalline clarity. He'd been so worried about the upheaval in his bowels and Marcus's reaction to their new mission, he'd almost missed the magnitude of the moment. What a great story he was being told! It wasn't poets who created myths. The tales themselves rose from the earth or rained down from Mount Olympus out of the collective mind. Poets merely breathed life into what was already in the minds of men as dictated by the gods. And right at that very moment, in that palatial chamber in Jerusalem—a rebellious city in a distant province of Rome—a myth was being born. His fingers twitched, wanting to grasp a stylus. *Oh Virgil, Horace, and Ovid, let me heed the call.*

A son of a god. A crucifixion of a man. A body coming back to life and then walking once again among men. And his master was called to find the god-man. Poet was all at once ecstatic and horrified. Yet Marcus, a man previously tasked to conquer barbarians, seemed unmoved by the momentous opening of the spiritus mundi. Poet sighed again. Marcus was a brilliant commander and a generous master, but the man lacked poetic appreciation and never gave his imagination free rein.

"If he cheated death and wants to escape another crucifixion," Pilate added, "he will head east, leaving the empire."

Marcus placed the purses in a leather pouch that hung at his side. "I won't comment on your suggested penalty for failure," he said, waving the imperial scroll around like he might fling it at Pilate. He'd donned his warrior face, and his eyes flashed a dangerous look that Poet had seen before, a look of cold steel that said, *If I am banished, you'll be dead.* "But since I won't fail, you'll release the centurion in charge of the crucifixion and tomb watch so that I may question him." Marcus added the scroll to the contents of his pouch.

"I'll send word for his release into your care. I had him flogged for his failure. On that damnable day, I questioned how a man nailed midday could die well before sunset. I curse Caiaphas for forcing my hand, making me crucify an innocent man, and I doubly curse the centurion for not getting the dark deed done. The rushed crucifixion may have let him walk out of the tomb. Or maybe he was the son of a god." Pilate laughed with forced lightness. "For his part in this, the centurion lost his sanity. He is confined to barracks. He deserves Rome's wrath, not its mercy." Pilate whirled away, turning his back to Marcus again. "I admit I'm more than a bit distracted by this matter too." He lifted his hands and studied them before plunging them into the flower and water basin and then drying them on the loin cloth skirt of the nearest eunuch.

As Poet watched Pilate, he allowed his mind to wax poetic, *Trembling before me is a man obsessed. Imagining his own hands nailing this Jesus to a cross. Inspecting his palms for blood that he cannot wash off.*

"Bring me the fugitive or his head; either will be displayed and his mortality exposed. Bring one to me," Pilate repeated, "but preferably just the head. To commence your quest, I will release the simpleton centurion to you; flog him if he causes you offense. I place the mess he has made into your hands."

Poet knew Pilate was quick to order a flogging, and a death to him was always distant and, outside of the case of this Jesus, usually of little consequence. His hands never held the hammer, whip, or sword, but his words were poison. Poet kept his gaze from Marcus, not wanting to prompt an exhibition of his outrage. Marcus was not fond of Pilate and hated politicians rendering judgment and inflicting punishment on soldiers, acts which should be the purview of the military command.

"You know the old adage," Pilate said, " 'seize the mother to the find son'. His mother is missing too. She was at the crucifixion, and we believe she may have had a hand in this empty-tomb business, perhaps even overseeing his escape or the theft of his body. A little maternal torture, the threat of her being stoned, and this Jesus may rise mysteriously from the hole he's hiding in." Pilate smiled at the image his dark mind painted.

"We are all mothers' sons," Marcus said, arms crossed and eyes fixed on Pilate. "I hope the holy mother, Cybele, doesn't hear your words and see your smirk, or you'll be cursed." Marcus would not let the sacrilege pass.

"Ah, a sensitive tribune," Pilate responded. "Have you lost your sense of humor along with your good—" Marcus raised his hand and stopped Pilate one word short of making Marcus erupt. Pilate smiled and instead said, "You have your own methods of finding rebel leaders. But I wouldn't rule out torture in this case, not with all you have at stake. Your job is to find him, but make no mistake, then it will be my job to send in my guard to kill all who provided him refuge and protection. With their leader's head on a spike, the headless chickens will cluck, and we'll have them mother and all. This nonsense will end here where it began."

The casual cruelty of the Roman governor disgusted Poet. If he were of higher rank, he would chastise Pilate. The poor mother would be grief-stricken after watching her son nailed to a cross; she was likely in seclusion. He thought of his own sweet mother and how she'd have taken his place rather than watch him suffer. Unlike many military men, Marcus would never torture a mother to get to her son and would stop anyone who tried, including Pilate.

Pilate gestured toward the man towering over Poet. "Saltaurius, you bull, come introduce yourself and tell Marcus how he won't be alone on his mission. The *Pharisees* are providing him a much bigger purse than I gave you and all their eyes and ears to help find the rebel Jew's body. *He* won't shrink from taking all measures necessary to collect his bounty. Marcus, your reward remains unchanged, regardless of how or by whom the man or body is found," Pilate said with a sweep of his hand toward Saltaurius. "Don't let his fine clothes and presentation fool you. He's no gentle giant." Pilate's approving eyes and wide grin evidenced his admiration of the man. "After consulting with my wife's astrologer, a man of some great powers of divination," Pilate continued, "I summoned Saltaurius here today so you two might meet. The old man foretold that Saltaurius cannot be killed by any foe in battle and that he will kill you, Marcus, if you stray from your mission."

Saltaurius marched forward and clasped Marcus's forearm with his hand in a show of strength. His grip impressed Poet even at a distance. Marcus refused to grimace, but Poet held his breath. Though it was unclear if the giant would prove friend or foe, Poet's instincts, and Pilate's prophecy, told him that Marcus had come face-to-face with a freakishly large nemesis.

"We should work together," the giant boomed. "The Pharisees have engaged me to track down their criminals, but never before have they offered such riches and their full support. I've seen this Jesus and can help you identify him or his body."

Marcus didn't blink. "You can report, at intervals, any new information you receive, but otherwise keep a distance. I work alone. Simpler that way."

Poet cleared his throat to note his approval. All ignored him but the old imp, who put his crooked index finger to dry lips in a gesture suggesting that Poet hush.

"He'd be better as an ally than a foe," Pilate said. "Marcus, your reputation as a rebel hunter is unsurpassed even by our friend Saltaurius, but don't be pigheaded. You have a lot at stake. But it is ultimately your command to treat as you see best."

"I give little credence to astrologers who fall short as oracles and often tell those what they want to hear," Marcus said. Poet believed some astrologers could read the stars, and the flights of birds, but he also knew Pilate may have made the story up to suit his purposes. Still, the prophecy bothered him deeply. "I will maintain my own counsel and with my men will work alone as we always have. But he should report anything he finds to me."

"I am at your service, Tribune," Saltaurius answered. "I will go my way as well, sharing information as you request. Perhaps I'll put your house in order by finding the rebel first. Let's make it a competition between us men," Saltaurius said, turning and nodding toward the crooked man who'd remained at the window. "My cunning advisor in all things. He speaks many tongues but rarely uses his own. A philosophical scholar, *Diobla* is his name. Diobla Ignius plus other names that I'll spare you. He calls himself *Dio* for short and for god. He is a demigod." Saltaurius let loose a loud snort at the playful and sacrilegious nomenclature of his small companion. "He doesn't look like much, but I advise you to never cross him. He's good with a knife. And he has a good nose for human flesh and can smell a man hiding under the floorboards or in the rafters. Once he smelled a traitor ensconced in a one of twenty wine barrels. All knife and nose, my Dio." He laughed and bowed to his creepy companion.

The imp-like half man halfheartedly bowed back, straightening his back upon rising. Not a true hunchback, but a bent man, nonetheless. Saltaurius continued, "Like Rome, the Pharisees will pay for the body or the head alone. My search so far has failed to find his close followers, though they have spread crazy stories—extraordinary tales that have enthralled the people and our dear emperor."

"What stories?" Marcus asked.

Poet lifted his eyebrows, wondering what could be more extraordinary than what they'd already heard.

"Incredible stories, but to people steeped in Jewish prophecy and tales of our Roman gods who suffer a brutal death before ascending to the gods, they sound true."

Poet closed his eyes, listening to the whispering voice in his mind: *The stories we stole from the great Greeks hold sway over the minds of men, stories bearing some deeper truth embedded in our psyche. Heroes leave human remains while a god's body must vanish.*

"After escaping the tomb, Jesus supposedly showed himself to his supporters, both men and women, who were hiding together. One of their group wasn't with them, and according to the rumors, this man, named

Thomas, wouldn't believe that his master had cheated death until Jesus appeared in front of him and let Thomas touch his wounds."

Nice ploy, making men feel shame for reasonable doubts, Poet thought. *Who could blame this man for doubting? I will doubt too until we find this god or this man.*

"And you believe these stories?" Marcus asked.

"Others do," Saltaurius said, clearing his throat and turning to spit before stopping himself. After swallowing hard, he said, "They and I have witnessed the man's miracles. I don't rule out that this miracle worker still walks the earth, eating and drinking like any man. And if he does, he is a fraud and deserves to die."

Poet wanted to ask, *If he is a miracle worker who survived a crucifixion, where's the fraud?*

"Stop this nonsense!" Pilate shouted, shaking his head in disgust. "The emperor believes these stories of a once-dead man who is alive again, of a taunting ghost appearing and vanishing at will. And the emperor's infallibility gives credence to the myth that this Jesus was a god walking among the people rather than dwelling in a temple carved in stone. I am not a religious man—there is too much religion in this zealous city for the entire world, even without a son of god stepping into the menagerie. My men nailed a man to the cross. And that man bled." He laughed off his loss of composure and continued, "We have finished here. Bring me this man, dead or alive!"

Chapter 4
Bhakti

"I'LL BE GLAD to get back to Pali and off these donkeys when our pilgrimage is done," Swami Bhakti said after a long stretch of silence along the barren road. "Persia is a never-ending land of sand and mountains, beggars and thieves." He immediately regretted his whining and the fearful words spoken to Ma, a holy woman who never complained and knew no fear, while she enjoyed deep meditation on her swaying donkey's back. But they *had* encountered many beggars and the great sultan's well-trained thieves soon after they left India.

"Beautiful, isn't it?" Ma said looking up from the road to the distant mountains and basking in the late afternoon sun. "You forget the spiritual seekers and the good people we have met. All we have encountered along our path is goodwill, even from the beggars and the thieves. But I, too, look forward to returning home—to Aja and the children. Jaya Bhagavan!" Ma was always praising god, giving thanks, and celebrating his name by chanting, *Jaya Bhagavan.*

"It is true, Ma," Bhakti said. "Your divine presence shields us from harm and calamity. Tell me how you know this prophet we travel so far to meet." Bhakti would follow Ma anywhere. She was his guru, and he had surrendered to her. His only remaining desires were to serve her and obtain union with Krishna, as taught in the Bhagavad Gita—the great spiritual text Ma loved and sang to him by and from her heart.

"I knew him as Issa years ago. I called him father, but these days he is called Jesus and ministers in Judaea. If he is the same man, he saved my life."

"Saved you, Divine Mother who needs no saving? How?" Bhakti's donkey brayed, as if it too desired to hear the answer.

"He saved this body in this life," she said, letting a laugh ripple through her lithe frame. "And now he performs miracles, even raising one man from the dead, as he teaches of the divine love we all share. The man we seek has been proclaimed the Hebrew Messiah, a son of God. In our Vedic tradition, he is a living avatar."

She dismounted from her donkey just as a poor old woman heading east approached them. Bhakti dismounted also, and Ma handed him her reins. He smiled at her pleasing scent of fresh-cut wood and flowers; she was still fragrant even after riding a donkey over crusty dirt for a full day. The scent reminded him of how they met *before* they had met. He'd been living in a cave and practicing meditation and silence. After a couple of months of isolation, during deep meditations on *Shakti*, an unexplained fragrance of sandalwood and jasmine entered the cave.

One night, following the scent's arrival, a vision of Ma appeared to him. She placed her hand on his head and invited him to her ashram in the village of Pali. He set out from the cave the next day to find her. She was exactly as he had envisioned, and he had been with her ever since.

Ma walked in sweet flowing steps over the rocky road carved deep by iron and wooden wheels to greet an old lady that Bhakti assumed was a wandering beggar or impoverished pilgrim—if one could distinguish the two. They met with hands raised to their hearts. Without a word, the old woman dropped her pack and fell to her knees, prostrating herself and grasping Ma's bare feet. The woman then bent down farther to touch the holy feet with her forehead. Ma leaned low to lay her hands on the gray hair and temples of the prostrate pilgrim and whispered a blessing in her ear.

Despite Ma's clear aura of divinity, Bhakti marveled at the number of passing strangers who immediately recognized her grace and offered their humble respect. Ma raised the beggar up so she could gaze deeply into the woman's glittering eyes.

Bhakti knew his role and was already digging in his pack, preparing to share half of their remaining food. Fighting the carnal urge to hoard the last of their rations, he knew that with Ma there would always be more—he placed a swath of cloth filled with flatbread and dried dates into the old woman's outstretched hands. Bhakti felt a surge of compassion at seeing up close the skeletal frame covered loosely by translucent skin. How had she survived for so long, alone and begging, traveling the treacherous Silk Road on foot?

"Do you need water too?" Ma asked as the woman bowed after accepting the food. Bhakti grimaced as his compassion gave way to self-preservation. They had less than two days' worth of water and weren't sure how close they were to the next well or stream. Both donkeys this time brayed in protest, or so it sounded to Bhakti.

The old lady laughed, pointing to a jug hanging from her pack. "Just filled at Bactra. You should make it there before nightfall."

Both Ma and Bhakti smiled at the welcome news. They humbly bowed to their new friend, who then continued east.

After they remounted, Bhakti said, "So tell me more about your time with Issa. When and how did you meet? It seems I've known you forever but still know so little about you before we met. Each day with you is a new miracle. The past seems not to exist, yet now it rises again before us."

"Every moment of creation is a miracle," Ma said. "It was about twelve years ago—I was a simple spiritual girl who loved Bhagavan, Krishna, Kali, and God in all forms."

Ma never claimed to be an avatar or goddess or even an enlightened master. Bhakti, however, knew she was an avatar, a god in human form, and he only hoped to become an enlightened mortal through his devotion to her.

"At our home in Pali?" he asked.

"Yes, the same place, but there was no ashram back then. I was meditating, practicing japa, and chanting praise to the Lord. Samadhi came naturally to this little girl, and people took notice."

Though Bhakti hadn't known Ma as a young girl, her devoted practice and innate gifts, her ability to dip into samadhi in meditation, even as a child, were all well known in her hometown province of Pali.

"My spiritual father, Issa, was one who noticed. He was studying in a nearby temple, learning Vedic texts and practicing on his own. Babaji sent him to see me so that we might meditate and drink tea together. All my blessings and wisdom come from Babaji." She dropped her reins, pressed her palms together, and bowed her head, pressing her forehead against her donkey's bobbing neck.

Mahavatar Babaji, Ma's guru, was an ageless avatar. Ma said he could live forever if he chose to. For her, Babaji was an immortal spiritual and physical presence in her life, showering her with Bhagavan's omnipotence, love, and bliss so she might share those blessings with others. Bhakti had never met Babaji, but knowing Ma would never lie, he believed he was, in fact, her teacher.

"There was such joy in silence and in the few words we could share," Ma said, shutting her eyes in contemplation until her donkey gently brayed. "Ha! Patience, Pali, my friend," she said to the beast, who was named for their home, while stroking its mane. "I was eighteen, and Issa a few years older; spiritual lights and visions danced between us." As she spoke, she nudged Pali forward. A few minutes later, they passed tents and camps being set up by fellow travelers along the Silk Road. They would reach Bactra by sundown, so they pushed on.

"One day Issa warned me of priests coming to attack me," Ma said, continuing her story. "They claimed a woman was not supposed to practice the Vedic ways with such devotion and on her own. They accused me of pretending to be an initiated priest and practicing witchcraft. I am no priest, and by their definition, I was a witch. This Hindu sect, or maybe just their old priests, must have never heard of Shakti," she said with a laugh. "They judged my joyful practice and love of God as blasphemous. Can you imagine the mind's contortion to conceive that God is only for men? The old priests sent young priests to escort this little girl to the head priest for judgment."

She laughed again, and Bhakti marveled at how she could tell such a story as if it were an amusing anecdote. He wondered if they'd intended to stone her.

"Issa was with me when they arrived. They saw in him a genuine spirit and light. Though they saw a *man,* they should have seen a god in human form. He stood between me and my would-be tormentors, saying he would offer himself for whatever they had come to do to me. They marched him to the temple, and I never saw him again."

"But he wasn't put to death, or we wouldn't be searching for him," Bhakti said.

"There's no death, not really. Though later I heard that his compassion and courage toward me nearly cost him his life. One of the young priests told me that Issa had put the fear of divine retribution into the old priests. That should they ever harm me—" She clapped her hands like she was closing a book. "They forced him to leave, and he headed north for Kashmir and Tibet. The morning he left I found a priceless gift hanging from my door. The one that now hangs around my neck." She placed both her hands over her heart.

Bhakti had never heard the story of how she came into possession of her sacred treasure and was thrilled to hear it now, even as his bottom longed to be freed from the donkey's bare back.

"My heart believes we may find Issa in Jerusalem," Ma told him. "Word came to me of a messiah, and Issa was a Hebrew from Judaea and likely returned there. We go to give thanks. Even if it is not him, the Issa of my youth, this joyful pilgrimage takes us to an avatar."

Bhakti thought about Ma's words for the remainder of their journey. When they entered Bactra before sunset, they dismounted and quickly found level ground for their camp. While Bhakti pitched their tents, Ma fed and watered the donkeys. Afterward, she sat cross-legged and removed a necklace—a precious strand of 108 lapis lazuli prayer beads strung on silk thread—from her neck and held it reverently in her right hand. It was her one possession. Bhakti sat for japa meditation too, loving the sound of Ma's voice rejoicing in the twilight. They invoked divine peace before Ma blissfully chanted bead by bead, "Jaya Bhagavan!"

Bhakti prayed silently along with her song of praise, thinking about the long distance ahead and all the bad men they might meet. *May Bhagavan protect us and especially Ma. Protect her holiness, her virginity, and her life.*

April 23, 2029 – Day 22 at the Monastery

It was the night of my first *book club for two*. My new good friend Lama Chinchinanaga had invited me to his private study to share my combined translation and compilation of the first twenty scrolls. I was eager to hear the words I had chosen to tell the story read aloud for the first time, and to observe the reaction of Lama Chin. Lama Chin was the name I called him in my thoughts, but which I kept to myself. Though he was extremely humble and may have enjoyed his nickname, the lama was deserving of great respect.

My work is behind schedule, as I have completed less than a scroll per day. I'd intended to read the scrolls from start to finish before putting pen to paper, but soon determined that this read-through would consume too much of my ninety days. And truth be told, I feared where the story was heading. Or maybe I simply didn't want to spoil the ending. Delaying the payoff would inspire me to complete the long work by marching steadfastly forward, not skipping directly to the mountaintop.

Much like Marcus, when set to a task, I am a stoic who focuses on the task at hand and controls my instinctive questions and visceral reactions when they bubble up inside me.

I wonder if Marcus will prove to be a hero or the vilest of anti-heroes, performing his duty as dictated by Roman authority. The story has yet to assault my faith. But that a search for Jesus was undertaken—if the search was real and not a fiction—that would be incredible.

It is a profound honor, and a blessing, to be chosen for such a task—to be the first to read the text since the literal time of Christ. That first night at the monastery, I kept replaying the secretary's message from my archbishop, wondering if the wording required me to seek further approval before proceeding. As I'd jumped on the plane to Kashmir, I told myself this was my calling by Christ. And my duty was to travel whenever and wherever I am called to serve. Perhaps subconsciously I feared the archbishop would have assigned some more conservative cardinal to this glorious mission—to take my place as the Church's advocate for our Lord's portrayal in the manuscript. I realize I had not played this *by the book* and might be punished and perhaps defrocked by my conservative archbishop. Too late for that now. Now I absolutely must fulfill *my* duty with divine love and saintly devotion. I am answering a calling.

Three men, one a Roman tribune in name only, had likewise been tasked with searching for Jesus and by none other than Pontius Pilate and the Roman emperor. I am hooked. If real, what I am translating is a freshly unearthed chapter of Christian history. If fiction, I am reading a major fiction about Jesus dating to the time of the resurrection. Both options are fantastic. I've had trouble sleeping most nights, wanting to be sure my scholarship was sound and my understanding clear.

And my imagination had been like a horse biting at the bit in the starting gate, impatient to get on with the steeplechase.

I can clearly see the characters grappling with their more dangerous and exigent spiritual world. When I meditate, I have an even clearer picture of Jesus, a living Jesus, and not only a fixed image or words on a page. My work has deepened my spiritual practices, often leading me to an elation bordering on ecstasy—states I hadn't experienced since seminary days, if then.

Time constraints have prevented me from including details about Boy's tender care for their overtaxed horses, Poet's metaphysical musing and readings, and his songs of praise of Marcus's quiet dignity and bravery. I have become quite familiar with these three men searching for Jesus—their quirks and admiration for one another—and hope I have made that clear in my translation despite the omissions to the text.

The scrolls also contain copious detours into Roman history and military custom that I have had to omit as well. My time is short, and I need to move through the scrolls to get my answers. At first, I attempted to keep a notebook of significant omissions, but again, that took up too much precious time. I hope the scrolls survive, and if the pope agrees, are made available for further study. If they don't survive, I hope that posterity, the Church, and historians the world over would forgive my necessary decision to omit details that would have had them salivating for decades.

Despite my hopes and uncertainties, I have taken strange comfort and inspiration from my cathedral-inferno dream, debating whether it was a past life informing the present or simply a prescient synchronicity. Either way, *this* abbot had to work as hard as the apostle Paul to determine which words to save and as expiditiously as that medieval abbot racing to preserve the Church's treasures. I am not being threatened with persecution by the Roman Empire or a raging fire intent on destroying the holy relics of a medieval cathedral, but I am hounded by the flipping pages of a very short calendar as I toil away on an incredible ancient manuscript within a medieval monastery in a repressive police state.

Both Saint Paul and that saintly, selfless abbot gave all in the service of the Lord. How could they not inspire me?

I was appreciative that, unlike Homer, the author allowed the characters to speak to one another rather than make speeches, a technique which has allowed me to present the story in a more modern fashion. The unnamed author's use of third-person narration from multiple points of view made the narrator seem omnipotent while letting the characters reveal themselves.

Lama Chin, the only English speaker in the monastery, has been kind enough to sit by me each morning for 4 a.m. prayers and meditation, and after that, over breakfast, we speak of our work. I have come to admire him for his religious scholarship, joyful spirit, and generosity. My friend has provided me with a maroon monk robe like his, but a size larger, that I wear with humble pride around the monastery. Humble, in the modest, simple dress of my hosts. Proud, they had accepted me as a spiritual brother into their foreign religious order.

Weeks ago we agreed to meet in his private study after an early dinner so I could read the initial pages to him. I have been looking forward to our date, wanting his honest response to both the text and to my work. That and for the companionship. While my work has been engrossing—I have never been so challenged mentally and emotionally—I miss my colleagues and my students. At first, I missed the easy access to 24/7 news, but I have adjusted to the lonely solitude and the rhythms of the monastic life and have found I enjoy working with only the text, my mind, and my spirit in order to make sense of the remarkable story reaching out to me from antiquity—from the time Christianity was born into the world.

My "date" opened the door, wearing, as ever, his matching burgundy robe and offering his welcoming smile. We bowed to one another, and Lama Chin gestured for me to come inside.

His study walls were bookshelves loaded with books and manuscripts. It looked like a small library. It was less Hogwarts and a little more *Lord of the Rings*. My wise friend appeared to me to be an academic wizard. I wanted to prove myself worthy of his wizardry with my rendition of the ancient text, a story I knew he was so eager to hear.

Lama Chin poured us tea, and we sat cross-legged on cushions for my first public reading of the text. It felt like stepping up to the pulpit for my first sermon. That was how nervous and excited I was. His peaceful presence put me at sufficient ease to read aloud the beginning of the incredible events that had been buried for two thousand years. When I reached the place where Bhakti prays for Ma to be protected from evil men on the Silk Road, I realized the depth of my confusion and wondered about the unfolding story that had just been given voice.

Had I been a faithful translator? Was I doing the story justice, and who was my audience besides the smiling monk in front of me? I lowered my head to pray to Jesus for guidance. I felt his blessing, and in a moment of pure absolution and deep connection, it was his tears I felt on my cheeks.

Lama Chin and I sat in silent contemplation, a moment of brotherhood that I imagine secluded, celibate, and devotional monks sometimes shared. A Catholic priest and Buddhist lama. West had met East, and in that meeting, both were kindred spirits. My friend let out a deep, long breath and turned his moist eyes to mine, waiting for me to speak first.

"Lama Chin . . . chinananga," I said, "thank you for listening so attentively. I see now that the work has inhabited me, has taken up residence in my mind, and this reading has allowed me some distance and brought up some questions I hadn't considered before. But before we turn to those questions, what do you think of the story so far?"

"I am enjoying it immensely," Lama Chin said, "but am of two minds: one that wants them to find Jesus, and another that fears they will take his head if they do."

"That's the challenge to my faith as well. Either way, this story might upend it. The only ending that might suit my faith is one that ends in failure."

"I would not fear the story. A wise Buddhist sage once said that 'a story about a saint will not be revealed unless it has the saint's blessing.'"

His words struck like lightning. "Thank you. I do feel Jesus behind me as I work, guiding and directing the process and the pen to paper, and yet there is still a long and winding road ahead, one that may take us into blasphemous territory. I pray not to become an accomplice to the devil's work," I said with a nervous laugh. My companion nodded his head, too agreeable to disagree.

"And what of Ma suggesting she may have met him in her youth?" I asked. "She admits it may not have been the same Jesus, a common name at the time. Incredibly, no one knows where he was or what he did from age thirteen to thirty. This has always been a burning question for me—where was Jesus for half of his life on earth?"

"I cannot know," Lama Chin said, "but revered Hindu and Buddhist teachers believe he traveled east along the Silk Road meeting yogis and priests during those years. If we have time on another Sunday, I can read to you some of those accounts." He pointed to a place high on the bookshelf.

"I've heard that too," I said, "and if it's true that he spent time with sages in the East, that is not inconsistent with my Catholic faith. And perhaps that's what Luke was referring to in the Bible when he wrote in Luke 2:52 the only words about those lost years: *And Jesus grew in wisdom and stature, and in favor of God and man.* But the Hindu Ma's presence and views are a conundrum for me. How does the author know about her travels? And she refers to Jesus as an *avatar*. What exactly does she mean by that?"

Lama Chin sipped his tea playfully before saying, "An avatar is a god who takes human form, perhaps as distinguished from a man who comes to fully realize his Buddha nature or soul." He looked to the same area of the bookshelf that he'd pointed to earlier, and as if he performed a magic trick, a book fell from its perch there but was caught one-handed by Lama Chin like a can of corn. "Ah, the Bhagavad Gita, a great Hindu text. About an avatar too. I read all the best works of literature and scriptures."

We shared the moment of synchronicity, paying homage to the book genie and his all-star catch with slight bows of reverence.

"And what about Pilate's claim that the emperor considered making Jesus a god in the Roman pantheon?" I asked. "It sounds plausible, and what would have become of Christianity if that was ordained? Would the persecution of Christians have been avoided? Would the Roman Catholic Church have been formed? Would the Roman Empire have avoided the cruel and decadent excesses of Caligula and Nero? Almost four hundred years later, Catholicism became the official religion of the Roman Empire, and all the other gods of Rome were banished. And within another hundred years, the empire fell, but the Church continued to flourish. I wonder if Tiberius would have proclaimed him a god like Julius Caesar or a son of a god like Caesar Augustus?" There were so many possibilities presented by this historical fork in the road.

"Jesus is a son of God, no?"

I paused to parse his words. He used the word *is* rather than *was*. But he also used the indefinite article *a*. "Well," I said, "that is certainly a critical question for Christianity, and I may find myself in the minority within the Church regarding my opinion on the matter." He tilted the chestnut-colored dome of his head and raised his brows, so I added, "The difference rests on whether he was *a* son of God or *the* son of God. What a difference a word makes." My friend grinned at my use of the cliché. I admired his smile, his emotive eyes, and the aura-like light surrounding his shiny head.

I leaned forward, eager to state my position. "In the original Greek, I believe he was described as *a* son of God. That was written later in Latin and English versions as *the* son of God. So not just one in a line of avatars over the centuries, but the one and only. In Psalms 82, which Jesus quoted in his defense against a charge of blasphemy, the Bible states *I have said, Ye are gods; and all of you are children of the most high*. So I think he was *a* son of God—only more so—with his virgin birth and resurrection."

"Well, perhaps there has been more than one Christ or one Christ in many forms," Lama Chin suggested with a mischievous smile as he walked to the bookshelf and raised up on his toes to return the Hindu scripture to its place. Without him seeing, I made the sign of the cross; I didn't want to contradict his taking my thought a bit too far for me. I was quite fond of him and the bond we had formed, and I wanted book club to continue in harmony and brotherly love.

"It seems to me you are blessed with a sacred mission," he said when he returned to his seat. "What do you seek from all your hard work here?"

"A Missio Dei, yes." I was glad he shared my excitement if not my trepidation about my mission from God. "I seek the truth and will do my work to the best of my abilities within the time allotted and present my manuscript to the pope. He will be the one to decide if the story should be told. Not my glory but God's glory."

Lama Chin nodded. "Our records regarding the lives of saints are always a blend of truth and fiction, a product of imperfect memory using arcane words to recount an incomplete history of miraculous lives and their esoteric teachings. A safe question to ask as we seek to bring those stories of saints to life is always, What would Christ do?"

He was a wise and discerning wizard who had also spent hours transcribing ancient manuscripts.

"Exactly!" I clapped. He truly understood. "That question is a soft refrain in the back of my mind as I toil away with the scrolls. I know Jesus is guiding me, even suggesting a turn of phrase here and there." I smiled like I might be joking, but I wasn't.

At eight o'clock the monastery's bells started chiming, indicating the nightly curfew calling all monks to their chambers. Eight sounds early for bed, but felt late after being up at 4 a.m. for prayers. As we said our goodbyes, we agreed to meet again when I was halfway through the scrolls. As he hugged me goodnight and his bald head lay affectionately upon my shoulder, I heard a voice deep inside me say: *I am the way and the truth and the life. No one comes to the Father except through me.* The familiar passage from John 14 was followed by the unfamiliar: *Would you take this to mean that my Father or I would deny your friend who pursues the way, the truth, and the life with such humble diligence?* I felt the grace of the Holy Spirit come over us there and believed he felt it too.

We said goodnight, and I began to look forward to our next faith sharing book club, only thirty-four scrolls away.

CHAPTER 5
Investigative Plan

AFTER RECEIVING HIS manhunt writ from Pilate, Marcus marched back to their quarters in a guest house and tavern, Poet by his side. Marcus no longer enjoyed the ribald company of the officers' barracks and Boy having to sleep in a stable. Playing the tribune's son, Boy would be treated like royalty in this Roman-friendly part of Jerusalem. Marcus and Boy were comfortable in their roles as father and son. That relationship was based on a true loving bond of affection, while Marcus's role as master and commander was based on birth and power. Although stripped of his power, he still, by birthright, was a master and commander.

Poet was unusually silent. Perhaps he too was contemplating their next moves on what was a life-or-death mission to find a rebel or a saint in six months. Marcus labored to control his thoughts that turned bitter when he thought of Rome, and serving a Caesar that had put his family to death.

Something about Pilate, Saltaurius, and the new mission had unsettled the unshakeable tribune. The guest house was squeezed into a brick row on a crooked, dark, and narrow street. Boy, who had been busy tending to the horses and preparing the room with food and drink, greeted them at the threshold and took their swords to hang on the wall. The sparse room that had two small windows barred by wooden slat hatches required candlelight, even during the day. In the oddly lopsided rectangular space, there were two cots, a mat on the floor, and a small table with two chairs.

They regrouped in the poorly constructed but adequate room. They were accustomed to working this way to locate rebels who, like rats, could hide in a hole—though they had never searched for a dead man before who might be buried in one. Marcus started crafting their plan by telling Boy every detail of their meeting with Pilate. Boy deserved to hear the story, and it would serve as a record of the meeting, as Poet took notes. They all laughed at Poet's gaseous eruption and Marcus's shoving him aside, but Marcus did not allow the merriment to continue. He was sharpening his mind to focus on their momentous mission.

"If half of Jerusalem and the Emperor think this Jesus is a god," he said, hitting his chest with his fist to be sure his men were paying close attention, "then this is not just another rebel manhunt. People become deadly serious about their faith when food is scarce and pestilence is near. As a miracle worker raised from the dead, people will fear and respect him more than a Roman tribune without a legion. And if he descended from the cross and escaped to the east, we need to establish that and commence our pursuit."

"He's probably reburied or scattered to the wind as dust. But just imagine if—" Poet stopped himself, as if he was imagining it being true that a son of God had risen from the dead.

"Not necessarily," Marcus said. "His body may have been moved from tomb to tomb. But what about all the post-tomb sightings? You think they were all suffering mass hysteria or deluded by false news and, if so, to what end? We better pray to the gods he is still alive, or we may never find him. Boy, go around town proclaiming your devotion to Jesus, joyfully celebrating his being risen from the dead. You are driven by the gods—no, I mean *the* God—to serve him. Whisper to those who seem stricken by this Jesus things like 'Praise the Lord' or 'The prophecy is fulfilled.' Here are some coins of silver, in case you need it for valuable information." Marcus pulled a few coins from the purse and tossed them on the small table. "And keep the horses and our packs ready to ride."

Boy nodded. He jumped up and slid the coins off the table and into a pouch sewn onto his tunic.

"Any questions before you go into the sheep's den?" Marcus asked. "That's guarded by wolfs," he added, and Poet laughed.

Boy shook his head bravely. "You know Sahara and your horses will be ready to ride," he said. "And I am this Jesus's biggest devotee. Just look into my moist eyes. Perhaps I'll find a girl who loves him half as much and knows where he is hiding. I wonder how Sahara would react if I fell in love with such a girl."

"Boy, I love your enthusiasm, but don't mix love with deception in your work. You are a charming man. Let that be your hook. There's enough deception in our spying without betraying the feelings of some young lady." Seeing Boy looking down at his feet like a candlewick snuffed out, Marcus added, "You are our best man at this dangerous work." The light returned to Boy's sunny, dark eyes. Marcus marveled at how irises that appeared almost black could shine so brightly.

Marcus grabbed him by the shoulders, and locking eyes said, "So enjoy yourself, but be careful. Religious zealots can be as dangerous as barbarians . . . and more devious." Marcus released Boy and continued, "I doubt he'll be lurking about here with all the greedy eyes looking for his ghost. But see what you can find and any leads we might follow. And arrange for anyone with useful information to meet me here to testify, and I will pay them well for helping us find the body or the man." Marcus rattled Pilate's bags of silver and gold. "Also, gather information about the Roman named Saltaurius—the big bounty hunter I told you was at the meeting. The Pharisees hired him to find this Jesus of Nazareth. He knows more than we do, as he's been on the case longer. Say he boxed you about the ears for your faith. Wait, on second thought, better you do not mention him. They may think you are one of his spies. Keep a keen ear of any talk about him and where his investigation takes him."

Poet added, "If this giant Saltaurius stumbles upon you, keep a distance from his little ashen imp, an assistant he calls Dio."

"Poet," Marcus said, "when you go on and on about your poetry being inspired by a daemon, I picture a curious little man like Dio." Poet's *daemon* was a poetic spirit he stole from Homer the Greek.

"Not at all like him. My daemon—or muse, rather—is a fickle, incorporeal guide who shows me things unseen and directs my creativity and words at times of his choosing. Dio is a poor likeness of human form, though he guides the ox. I don't suppose that Saltaurius is an artist of any type. Boy, just be on the watch for his bulging eyes, thin crusty lips, and bald head . . . all atop a sloped back, one notch short of hunched."

As Boy shifted toward the door, eager to start his mission, Marcus said, "Remember—"

"I know," said Boy. "Do not believe everything I hear. Their eyes will avert mine when they lie."

"I'll see you here tonight for dinner," Marcus said. "Bring us some cured fish to go with this bread and cheese. And more candles for this dank room. Leave the sword. You are a simple slave seeking a man of God for your deliverance from Roman oppression. Show reverence for this crucified miracle worker we seek."

"That won't be hard to do. He sounds like a living, breathing oracle. Or was one," Boy responded. He placed his sword on a hook hanging from the crooked wall and then bowed and left in a hurry.

Marcus turned to Poet, who offered him some wine. "No drink," Marcus said. "We need to stay clearheaded. Our lives are at stake."

Poet turned up his nose after tasting the wine. "That shouldn't be hard. This wine tastes like a vinegar and smells like a stable." Poet pinched the bridge of his prominent nose, which meant he was becoming serious. "And to your point," he said, "this new mission may have more at stake than our lives. My muses tell me we are being cast as players in some grand drama being written by the gods."

"That is every man's lot in life. Let us do our best to play our part," Marcus replied. "But you are right to not miss the mark of the critical nature of our mission." He stood to face Poet and issue his command: "Go, find the centurion overseeing the crucifixion and who is in charge of the guards who failed to protect the tomb. He will have heard from Pilate and be willing to talk to us. Let's meet him here this afternoon. I need time to plan and think. Bring him to me."

Marcus lay back on his wooden cot and interlaced his fingers behind his head. He needed to slow the turning wheels of his mind and focus on their logical procession from here to there. From Jesus lost to Jesus found. He heard the door quietly closing as Poet left to find their first witness.

CHAPTER 6
Interrogation

WHEN POET RETURNED with the disgraced centurion, Marcus had reconfigured the sparse, lopsided room with the cots and mats bunched in the far corner and a small table occupying the room's center. The two small, cockeyed windows provided a hazy stream of gray light that pooled around the square candle-lit table flanked by two chairs. The room's asymmetry was disorienting. An ominous ambience was a military tactic Marcus used to make one talk.

The Roman soldier's uniform was soiled and disheveled, which offended Marcus's sense of legionary dignity. He had not been following any disciplined regiment for weeks. The ape's matted hair interlocked with his unkempt beard and thick sideburns, forming a helmet. He once might have met Marcus on *almost* equal footing, but not anymore.

"You are badly in need of a bath," Marcus told him, setting the mood for the interrogation. "You smell like a soldier after a three-day march over desert sands."

The centurion bowed his head in shame. Marcus didn't like the kinship he shared with this fallen soldier. Marcus too had fallen, but with dignity.

"Centurion, have a seat so we may talk with truth and honor," Marcus said to the beaten man.

"Call me Cornelius. I left my title and honor on a skull-shaped hill," he said, as if from a strange distance. The centurion would soon, absent a miracle, be stripped of his officer's rank and livelihood.

"All right Cornelius it is. Hands on table, please. Palms up." This submissive, self-restrained pose put Marcus at the advantage. By being able to examine the palms and eyes, he could discern the truthfulness of his witnesses.

He acquiesced, but Cornelius's eyes were swimming in his skull. His mind was clearly in shambles, unfocused and distracted. Marcus wondered how far it had wandered. The man was in a visible state of terror.

Marcus motioned for Poet to stand sentry by the door. He then took the seat across the table from his witness and moved one of the lit candles between them, so the flame flickered just beneath eye level. "Thank you for coming on such short notice. I'm not Pilate's hand of death and mean you no harm. I will file a good report and grant clemency for your telling me all, honestly. Understood?"

The soldier's hands steadied slightly, and his eyes seemed to relax as Marcus spoke in the slow, deep cadence of a physician calming his patient.

"Yes," he said in a deflated but eager voice.

"Do you know me?" Marcus asked.

"Everyone knows you and your family, Decia—"

Marcus raised a finger, cautioning him to stay silent about that. "I trust my cohort was not unkind in urging you to come and meet me? We have just a few questions," Marcus said. He had taken to calling Poet his *cohort* to remind people of his best friend's prior status as a military leader and to remind Poet he was his most loyal companion.

"Yesterday, I refused to give testimony to a Roman bounty hunter as big as three pillars and strong as marble," the man blurted out. "He offered to pay me to testify to the miracles of the crucifixion and resurrection. I didn't trust him and his slouching ward. That little bald man wanted me dead for my refusal, and I could see he was ready for the big man to do it." Marcus noticed the first sign of sweat on Cornelius's temples and palms. His body was rigid as he kept his hands on the table as though they were in shackles and being pulled taught by chains.

"Look at me," Marcus said. "I assure you they won't harm you if you help me."

"I wasn't sure to whom he paid allegiance. Was he there to torment me for Rome? The Jews? He demanded to know if I helped the man escape the cross—the man I was ordered to execute. That would be treason. I follow my orders. I did my damned duty that day. That is what I told him. Luckily, we were being watched by my guards, or the giant would have held me down while the little one slit my throat with the knife he kept fondling in its sheath." He swallowed hard and rubbed his neck like he was checking to see it was still attached to his head. "You are a brave tribune and a man of duty. At least I know who I am talking to here." Cornelius dropped his hand from inspecting his neck down by his side to hold his chair. He started shaking, and Marcus feared they might erupt into a full fit of convulsions.

"Please place your hands on the table, palms up. You did well not to share your story with that man and his ghoulish advisor," Marcus said. The witness returned his hands to the table. The bone-shaking shiver passed. Marcus placed his hands palms up on the table as well to level the playing field and put his subject at ease. "I only want the facts about Jesus's crucifixion and the events that transpired at the tomb. And for that, you have a friend who will speak well of you into Pilate's ear. All right?"

"It is all I can think about since it all happened," Cornelius said. "But I haven't been able to make sense of the horror and the mystery. I feel possessed like Dis Pater himself is throttling me. The tormenting images are too unbearably painful to put into words." His eyes again began dancing about. "May I scratch my beard?"

"Of course."

Cornelius scratched at his body and then his ratty beard, causing crumbs or dirt to come trickling out. He had fallen far from proud centurion to one step up from mad beggar. Marcus gestured for Poet to open the windows to air the room of the man's stink, but the ill-fitted wooden window hatches wouldn't budge. After scratching his beard and rubbing his nose—perhaps Cornelius smelled himself—he put his hands back on the table, palms up and looked around the room from left to right before locking on Marcus's calm gaze.

Marcus reached across the table and took the witness's filthy hands in his own muscular hands and squeezed just hard enough to be reassuring, but one hard squeeze away from threatening. "You have no choice but to talk to me," he said. "And I bet once you tell the story you will feel relieved. You are speaking to a comrade and friend, a soldier who has seen, and done, unspeakable horrors, as my friend there can attest." He loosened his grip of the man's hands, and looked over at Poet standing sentry again by the door after failing to crack open the windows. "He pours me wine and makes me speak of everything I would rather bury. Poet! that's what we need—some wine for our fellow soldier."

Poet filled three goblets, placing two on the table, and returned to his post. Marcus released the man's hands and grabbed his goblet, motioning with his head for his witness to take up the other goblet for a toast. "To better days. In vino veritas!"

The disgraced man drank his goblet in one gulp, and Poet moved to fill it again. Marcus had made a friend. Cornelius seemed relieved his hands were permitted to clench the goblet. Marcus realized the man did not have any trouble with the truth but rather with giving that truth voice.

"Now forget Pilate, the spiteful politician. We are soldiers and must stick together despite all the slings and arrows politicians make us endure. I have also endured flogging, courtesy of vicious Roman virtue. Begin wherever you prefer and share all that you observed."

The soldier took a big gulp of the wine and cleared his throat of a sizable chunk of phlegm. He looked about for a spittoon, but not finding one in the sparse room, he swallowed. Marcus never liked the collection of spit in a bucket. If there had been a spit bucket, he would have had it removed. "That's just it," Cornelius said. "I saw it with my own eyes, and still do not believe it."

The door to the interrogation chamber burst open. Boy appeared, flinging a man into the room. The stranger scurried to the far wall and cowered in anticipation of a beating. "He had his ear pressed to the door and with all the cracks must have heard every word," Boy reported.

"Poet, take him down to the tavern and either buy him an ale or cut off his ear, depending on how forthcoming he is," Marcus commanded. "Boy, go with him in case he tries to run. No one will outrun you. If he runs, clip both ears. And instruct the innkeeper that we are not to be disturbed again."

Marcus had measured the boot-shaking man as a coward in an instant. He knew the eavesdropper would talk and that no ears would be clipped. Poet and Boy left with the sniveling man choking on his fear.

"Well, back to our business. Nothing harmful was said, and now rest assured we will not be overheard." Marcus toasted his witness again. It was critical to get him to refocus and to forget the intrusion. He wondered if the spy was working for the giant and his imp, the mercenaries his witness so feared. He smiled at the half-crazed man across the table and kept smiling as it appeared to put his witness at ease. "Just tell me what you saw, and I'll reward you. Seeing is believing. Start from when you first saw the man."

"He was savagely beaten. Whipped without mercy by Pilate's house guard. They thought it funny to adorn the bloodied man's head with a garland of thorns and jeered, 'Here is the King of the Jews!' They delivered him to me to be crucified on the skull-shaped hill they call Golgotha. Men dying in battle doesn't bother me, but an unarmed man nailed to a cross was a horror to witness. I rode on ahead, leaving my men to bring this Jesus and his cross to the hill where two thieves were already hanging on crosses and wanting an end to their suffering."

Marcus got up to refill the man's cup. "What was your impression of the man upon seeing him?" he asked. "Anything unique? Had you heard his claims to be a messiah? Did he strike you as something more than human?" Marcus knew better than to string questions together, but he found himself strangely drawn to the story of a son of God hung upon a cross.

"Yes, as Passover approached, the city was abuzz with messiah mania. Some believed in him, while others dismissed him as a blasphemous magician. He was no ordinary man. Based on what I witnessed, Jesus might have been, or be, both man and God. Our own hearts determine which we see." Cornelius's eyes became wide and glassy, but he appeared to be looking within and not at Marcus. "He bore his lashing like a proud soldier who could endure almost any pain. Then, he gazed upon me as if I were the beaten one requiring *his* comfort and aid. His eyes bored into my soul. Upon the cross, naked and bleeding, he was a sight to see. A simple man bearing such indignity with such dignity—greater than any soldier or gladiator I've ever seen. And—" He planted his hands in his face, sobbing soundlessly behind them.

"And?"

"His mother. She was there, seeing her son hung upon the cross. Something no mother should witness. Her face. Her eyes held to his with such sweet tenderness, love, and grace. I can't live with it." The poor man's tear ducts had run dry. On the battlefield, Marcus would slap a soldier across his helmet for showing such weakness, but here he felt compassion for what the man had seen and done.

"Yet you live. A witness to a spectacle men will speak of for years to come. Do you know where we might find his mother?"

"No. I never saw her before or after. Just there upon that skull-shaped hill. Her face will be with me forever though, as will his. Pilate and the Jews are looking for the mother. They'll stone that saintly woman too. They think that will bring her boy, or at least his disciples, out of hiding." He again lifted his hands to cover his swollen eyes.

Marcus poured him more wine to ease his pain. Cornelius lowered his hands and looked into Marcus's soul for solace. "How long did you watch him suffer . . . on the cross?" Marcus struggled to ask, unable to shake the powerful gaze of his witness.

Suddenly, time seemed to stop as a vision appeared. Marcus shut his eyes for a moment. Through some power of their interactive imaginations, when he opened them, he saw the stark scene appear over the interrogation table in the candlelight. The hill, the man on the cross, a thief hanging on either side of him. The image of Jesus was clear despite his never having laid eyes upon the man. He felt the nailed man's suffering as pain turned to ecstasy as he released all resistance to his fate. Marcus shut his eyes to experience the strange, magnetic, beautiful, and horrifying vision.

Marcus opened his eyes as Cornelius answered, "About three hours."

Though thoroughly shaken by the momentary vision, Marcus never lost his composure. He attributed the hallucination to some rancid food, though his stomach felt fine. "That is short, no? I've heard men last nine hours, or even a day or more, before taking their last breath upon the cross."

"It was my first crucifixion, and it was short. We cut it short. After he called to God to forgive us, he died."

"Tell me about the moment of his death."

"He took some vinegar wine with gall to dull his senses, from a sponge that he'd earlier refused. He then spoke of forgiveness and died."

"Interesting, gall will ease the pain. Who gave him this drink?" Gall was used for dying soldiers to numb the pain and injured soldiers to help them sleep.

"Earlier we had offered it to him, and he refused. This time, one of his followers gave it. I don't know his name." Marcus wondered about this potion, who gave it, and what was in it.

"How did you determine he was dead?"

"He hung there, no longer breathing. The sky churned as dark clouds swirled above the crosses. The gods were angry as we heard what sounded like swords scraping across a lyre made of metal strings. The earth beneath our feet trembled. I ordered the men to break the thieves' legs, which brings so much pressure to the chest, it causes immediate suffocation. And it did. Jesus, who had so impressed me, was already dead. I had one guard thrust him with a spear to make sure. He didn't scream or flinch. He was dead." Cornelius hung his own head down like a dead man.

"Did he bleed where the spear entered his flesh?"

"Yes, blood gushed from the wound like it would from any man."

"Maybe, but I've witnessed men being speared after battle to ensure they were dead. And only those who moved or cried out bled."

"That is true. But I told you the truth. It was as I said. I don't trust what I saw that day. He didn't move. Didn't cry out. Didn't breathe for a long time. He was dead."

"And what happened next?"

"Many who witnessed the spectacle fled the dark skies and shaking land, except for two men. They had received Pilate's approval to have Jesus's body removed from the cross before the sun went down."

"What were their names? These body grabbers?"

"They moved fast. Joseph of Arimathea, a wealthy Jewish merchant who'd been granted Roman citizenship, and Nicodemus, a rich Roman lawyer. Both sympathized with Jesus. That was the last time I saw the body. Four of my men escorted them to a new tomb. After they finished the last rites, they sealed the tomb with a great rock. They needed all four men with wooden beams as leverage to position the barrier. Two stayed behind to keep watch. The Pharisee fretted about some prophecy and insisted we guard the tomb. They thought grave robbers might come for the body."

Marcus noticed his witness becoming more coherent as the interview proceeded and following his sharing of the graphic vision of the crucifixion.

"Why the rush for the body by this Joseph and Nicodemus?"

"Something to do with Jewish custom and sundown and sabbath coming, followed by Passover. I wonder—"

"Wonder what?" Marcus asked.

"Why were Romans so concerned with the Hebrew burial? May I speak my heart without retribution?" Cornelius's eyes pleaded with Marcus, like a man about to make his confession. Like many witnesses before him, his testimony unburdened him, and he wanted to fully bear witness.

Marcus leaned forward. "If it is true, you will only have my gratitude."

"I wonder. I heard sometime later that the prophecy the Pharisee feared was that this crucified man would rise in three days. After seeing his face, his eyes, his actions that day, maybe he was more than a magician. His face, so full of glory and grace, haunts my eyes when closed. Maybe he was a god. Our religion has many gods who have taken human form. Maybe I saw that. But where does that leave me?"

"Sitting here drinking wine with me," Marcus said as he raised his goblet and waited until his witness took a drink. "But let us get back to the facts and out of your imagination. Let go of your guilt. Did you not just say he forgave you right before he died?"

The fallen soldier hesitated, then nodded.

"Do you know where I can find Joseph and Nicodemus?"

"No. But they are prominent men and shouldn't be hard to find. I am sure they've already been interrogated."

"We will check their stories. I was told your two tomb guards slept through the tomb being opened and the body removed?"

"Yes, on the third night. There was a full moon. They say they had something to drink, but it is likely that someone also drugged them."

"Drugged?"

"By the wine delivered by some local women to the tomb."

"Can they describe these women?"

"No. They say the Hebrew women all look the same in their dark, hooded cloaks." Marcus shook his head at this common trait of Roman soldiers to not really see their imperial subjects as individuals but as impersonal chattel.

"What else can you tell me?" Marcus asked as he leaned back in his chair and folded his arms across his chest. "What else have you heard?"

"A lady, one of his followers, saw him outside the tomb."

"Her name?"

"Mary Magdalene. A companion of Jesus."

"She would testify to this?"

"If she could be found, but it's known she revealed this sighting to his disciples. She told them Jesus told her he was ascending into heaven to sit beside his father."

"There you have it. Our case is closed. He told her, and she told them." Marcus clapped his hands together, startling his witness. "No sense looking for Jesus then, unless you have a stairway to the heavens." Cornelius didn't laugh.

"Has there been a comet seen streaking across the sky like the one that took Julius Caesar to the gods?"

"No," Cornelius answered.

The door opened again as Poet and Boy returned. They were not carrying any severed ears. They waited by the door to give their report on the eavesdropper.

"Any additional information to assist me in locating the man or his body?" Marcus asked.

Choking back tears again, the soldier said, "Perhaps my men are tormenting me back at the barracks where I'm confined, simply having fun with me. But, every day, they come back with the reports that his disciples and others have seen him. That he is still alive in all his glory."

"Poet, get some parchment and ink, so he can write the names of all the disciples. Do you know all of them and where we will find them?"

Poet brought the pen and paper to the interrogation table, then returned to his post by the door.

"Yes. There were twelve disciples," Cornelius said, "but one—Judas, who betrayed Jesus—is already dead. They say he killed himself. I don't know where the others are hiding, but I can give you their names. My guards tell me they are deep underground for fear of crucifixion."

Cornelius started scribbling the names painfully slowly. Marcus told Poet, "Take the pen and write the names down for him." He turned back to his witness and said, "After he records the names, sketch a simple map for me to find the tomb. He can help you with that task too."

Once Poet and Cornelius had done their work, Marcus returned to his questioning. "How about Mary, the woman at the tomb, is she in hiding too?" he asked.

"Yes. And she was perhaps more of a disciple than the others. Always in his company."

Marcus turned to the door. "Boy, what did you discover on the streets?"

"Much to confirm his story and sightings. People only whispered to me as I started repeating the stories. But all second and third hand. They, the *followers of the way*, as they call themselves, say his new body, they call it glorified, is bathed in light, and his robes are brighter than white. They say his glorified body can pass through walls. You should see their eyes when they speak of Jesus, of his light and message of love." Boy's eyes became glassy and moist with either reverence or fear.

"Metamorphoses," Poet mumbled to himself.

"Religious hysteria is like a whirling wind that picks up all the unmoored leaves," Marcus said. "Boy, keep your horse sense tethered to the stake. What of the witnesses, the disciples, have you heard?"

"The disciples are nowhere to be found. One story of an elder, an Essene named Abraham," Boy reported. "They say he knows more about Jesus as a boy and his burial site than anyone else. The old man inspected the tomb on behalf of that Jew hunter, Saltaurius. That Roman is enriching some and scaring everyone else with his ruthless ways."

"Do you know where we can find this Abraham?" Marcus asked Cornelius.

"Yes," he answered. "The Essenes are an austere group that reject worldly things, including Rome and other Jews. They keep to themselves and are settled southeast of us, in the desert near the sea."

"Poet and I will ride out to meet this man tomorrow after we see if we can scare up any information from our own, knocking down doors in the Jewish Quarter. Boy, you will prepare the horses and look for Joseph of Arimathea, Nicodemus, and Mary, the mother, and Mary, the Magdalene."

Marcus stood to address his fallen comrade, "You told me you had gotten a good look at his face. Here are a few coins." He placed three pieces of silver into Cornelius's hand. "Go find an artist to draw me a recognizable portrait. Look for one that has seen Jesus himself. As long as you work for me, you're free from the barracks and Pilate's wrath. And thank you for your true testimony. Look for information about his followers. And report back tomorrow with his face on parchment or papyrus."

The soldier stood more erect and alert than before, but a little unsteady from all the wine.

"And start caring for yourself like a proud Roman. A bath would be a good start. And stop wracking yourself with guilt. You said he forgave you. Do you really think the gods judge you for doing your duty? Man is but their plaything, bound to a wheel of destiny. No man can escape. When we finish, my report will prevent Pilate from taking any further action against you. He has flogged you for the last time. I am in charge now and on this matter your debts will be settled."

Marcus held up his hand, calling for a moment to think. He felt moved by Cornelius's story and sorrow. The centurion had played his part in this passionate drama—of first crucifying Jesus and then in the disappearance of his body—events that set Marcus on his mission. "And I'll see to it that you maintain your officer's rank. Don't let me down." Marcus's tribune title still allowed him to execute this act of mercy for his fallen comrade.

Cornelius gave Marcus the Roman salute by thudding his chest so hard it must have hurt, as it brought tears to his eyes. He then bowed and left. Marcus turned to Boy and Poet. "Open the windows. We need some fresh air. Only beating hearts bleed. Now, tell me about the ear to our door."

Despite the four strong hands struggling, the window hatches still would not budge from their crooked frames.

"He was hired by a man that fits Dio's description, which is not very nondescript," Poet said. "They have spies crawling all over town. Saltaurius pays well. That rat listening at our door agreed to go spy on the giant and Dio for us, but I don't think we will see him again. He'll want to keep out of our sight and earshot. But we better be on our guard for other bats hanging about the rafters."

"I knew that beast and his monkey were going to cause us trouble," Marcus said. "Tomorrow, while Boy continues to work the streets to locate them, we'll look to interview Mary Magdalene and Joseph of Arimathea and this Nicodemus—all are associated with the tomb and seeing Jesus and his body there. And then we'll ride out to see the old Essene Jew who inspected the tomb with Saltaurius."

"What about the mother?" Poet asked.

"She'll be with her son."

"How can you be so certain."

"Mothers and son— the mother will want to be with her child crucified on our cross. And the son will want to protect the mother from Roman torture." Marcus only then realized the insensitivity of his words. He looked to Boy and tilted his head apologetically. Boy grinned back at him, reminding Marcus he enjoyed his work. "The bigger the challenge, the greater the reward." He motioned to his men. "Sit and let's eat, and I will fill you in on the cruel crucifixion and swift burial of Jesus. Poet, get your pen and maps so you can take some notes and plot our course of action."

CHAPTER 7

Jesus, Mary, Mary, Joseph, and Nicodemus

THE FOLLOWING DAY, Boy was hurrying to meet Marcus and Poet in the heart of the Jewish Quarter, where they had spent the morning and early afternoon making their separate inquiries. Boy was dejected after not finding anything new of value to assist in their search. Everyone had told the same stories of miracles and of the son of god's appearances and vanishing acts following his return from the dead. Everyone was either looking for Jesus or protecting him with their silence. He was downcast that he might have missed his chance to meet this Jesus. And he wanted to find Jesus for Marcus. He never wanted to fail in his service of the great man.

Boy arrived at the prearranged spot in the cardo.

"Hey, boy, come here! What's your name? I hear you are looking for Jesus of Nazareth," Marcus shouted. Boy turned to run, but Poet caught him roughly by his tunic. Both men laughed as Boy pretended to struggle to gain his freedom. Poet dragged the boy into a nearby near-empty establishment and forced him down onto a wooden bench. Marcus ordered three plates of food for the would-be interrogation.

Boy knew he was to look sullen and only speak when others could not hear. It was not a hard act, since he had nothing new to report. After the meal of stringy meat and soggy flatbread was served, they compared notes on their morning search for witnesses and information. Marcus and Poet were also finding nothing new. Boy eyed his plate and pushed around the contents with a wooden fork.

"It's goat," Marcus said. Boy thought it was more likely horse meat and Marcus only said it was goat to get him to eat.

Marcus pounded the table, spinning their tin plates. He leered at Boy, making it appear to any observers like he wasn't cooperating before saying, "That bull, Saltaurius, is strangling our investigation at each turn. He's always one step ahead. And now he's scared off Joseph and Nicodemus. The big man comes knocking and our witnesses all disappear."

"Men of means and wealth rarely hide, other than from Roman taxes or axes. The giant might have fed them to the hogs," Poet said. Boy pushed his rusty plate of horse, goat, or pig meat—whatever it was—away in disgust.

"I thought the same thing," Marcus replied, now speaking softly, though the few men in the establishment knew better than to eavesdrop on a Roman officer questioning a slave boy. "But if they helped Jesus to live and feared for their lives and being discovered like the disciples, they may still be in hiding. And Mary Magdalene was last seen being led by John the disciple north out of Palestine. They go to preach the good news of Jesus in some foreign land. No one has seen his mother, Mary, since he disappeared. I hate to admit it but Pilate is probably right. If we find her, we find him. It's no wonder they would all run for cover."

Marcus grabbed Boy by the shoulders to appear to speak menacingly. "Boy, go back to the streets this afternoon. Find out everything you can as a bereaved follower being abused by us Romans. And keep your cat-eyes focused. Something will turn up. Find me one disciple who saw Jesus after the tomb." He ruffled Boy's full head of dark hair roughly with his powerful hand, which could be seen as punishment by outsiders. He then lowered his voice to say, "And snap out of it. We are not dead yet."

Boy looked at the man he loved, his mentor and father.

"Poet, you and I, however distasteful—" Marcus said, as he also pushed away his plate. "It's no wonder everyone is having visions and seeing miracles with this food. But, as I was saying, however distasteful, we must go to find out what Saltaurius knows. I hope the old Essene hasn't been buried in the sand or turned to salt before we have a chance to question him."

"Or become hog dung," Poet crudely joked.

As Marcus and Poet rose abruptly to make a show of leaving their scared prey behind, Marcus barked at Boy, "You should go back to where you came from, or go into hiding with the rest of your Jesus lovers. Next time I see you, you'll be feed for Roman pigs."

Boy buried his face between his arms on the table. He knew that his heaving torso would look to be crying when really he was suppressing a hearty laugh that hurt his solar plexus.

CHAPTER 8
Parley

POET WAS NOT looking forward to confronting the giant and his rodent named Dio. Saltaurius, like an elephant in a tent, was easy to locate. Everyone feared him, but they also wanted to be near his impressive display of wealth and power. He was quick to share either the sparkle of his coin or the crack of his whip. It was a risk worth taking. They had learned that he held court at a notorious tavern in the Jewish Quarter, famed for its gaming and religious debates that sometimes turned deadly. Here, Saltaurius's informants came and left after whispering in his ear.

Before they entered the tavern doors, Poet once again reminded Marcus of Pilate's prophecy that the giant was invincible and was likely to become Marcus's assassin. Marcus said, "Fearing such predictions, taking them to heart, only makes them more likely to come to fruition."

Marcus and Poet entered the vast, dark, cavernous place. As Poet's eyes adjusted, he scanned the tavern room that smelled of ale-soaked floorboards and men too drunk to make it to the latrine. Dio was nowhere to be seen. Poet actually feared the little man more than the giant. And Poet believed in his muses and instincts.

Saltaurius slammed his knife into the wooden table, upending a candle, and stood with arms outstretched, almost tumbling the table and knocking over a man on the chair next to him—adding more ale to the saw-dusted floorboards. "The once great Tribune Marcus Decia pays us a visit," he called out. "Make way and bring ale or wine, or whatever they please."

Poet grasped the hilt of his sword in reaction to the insult. Marcus put his hand on Poet's shoulder to calm his nerves. The giant would easily defeat him in a sword fight. A proprietor righted the fallen candle before it scorched the table and looked to take their drink orders. Candles and wood were a combustible duo that took more lives than swords. Why fight a foe when you could just burn down their fort or village? And there always seemed to be some beneficiary of "accidental" fires.

"Better to be once great, and perhaps great once more, than never to rise above our base nature. Wine for him and ale for me," Marcus said, gesturing toward Poet. Poet feared Marcus and Saltaurius were another combustible duo, and Pilate had lit the match.

Saltaurius laughed, accepting his lot by defiantly grabbing the bulge in his crotch.

They all sat after they took measure of each other's manhood. The air was heavy with the smell of sweat, piss, spilled ale, and frankincense-scented candle wax. Poet welcomed the wine, watching as Marcus sampled the ale, before downing half the mug. Both drinks were kosher, and the wine was better than Poet expected from such an establishment.

"You are impeding my investigation," Marcus told Saltaurius. Poet wondered if Marcus would mention the eavesdropping spy. He probably would not, in case the man might honor his pledge to betray the beast and become their spy. More likely, the coward was hiding like everyone else until this oversized bounty hunter had left town.

"How's that? I offered to work together. You're on my turf here. The Jews either love me or fear me, and I am an asset to you in that regard."

"Asset? Stop driving underground all those that have information about where we might find our man," Marcus said.

"You have me wrong; you are making an enemy where there is none. I'm just doing my job. Come off your high horse, mighty tribune, unless you'd like to draw swords with me. Our great empire that has stood for seven hundred fifty years will fall because we fight one another instead of the rebel Jew Jesus and the slaves."

Poet wondered if he was referring to the tragedy that befell the House of Decia and if he was trying to get Marcus to rise and fight. It seemed so, as Marcus replied tersely, "Dangerous words to throw around. Speaking of a sword fight often leads to one. And it may come to that if you don't answer my questions." Marcus was treading a fine line. Poet was afraid. Though he had never seen a man who could beat Marcus in a battle of swords before, this monster of a man certainly stood more than a fighting chance. Smart money in the arena would be on the gladiator and not on the tribune.

"Dangerous words? That's the difference between you and me, Marcus. I'm not afraid of words and what people say about me. But let's not speak of differences of opinion and politics. I'm an open vessel for you. Let me fill your cup with my intelligence." He called for another round of drinks.

Poet noticed everyone had given them a lot of room so they could speak privately, and the tavern had grown quiet. The closest person to them was a small man who sat alone three feet away, hunched over a table under his hood with his bent back to the giant and their table. A familiar silent figure and another eavesdropper.

"The mother? Mary? What have you learned of her?" Marcus asked.

"Found nothing of the mother. I have half of Judaea looking for her, with a nice bounty on her head. She was a devoted mother, and he was a rebel son. Perhaps by cheating death he is looking to make amends, protecting her from Roman justice and Jewish revenge."

"Revenge?"

"For being a false messiah. Their true messiah would target the downfall of Roman oppression and not be spreading love like a puppy dog who ends up beaten and naked upon a Roman cross." He turned around to where the proprietor stood in waiting and ordered, "Light! I want to see my friends and fellow Romans." The proprietor brought an oil lamp to the table and removed the candles.

"The two men you met with, the ones that placed Jesus in the tomb," Marcus said. "They're now missing."

"Yes. I think I know who you mean."

"Stop playing games and tell me all you have learned."

"So, do you want to work together now?"

Marcus was a professional, but Poet could see behind his stoic face a desire to thrash the bull for his arrogance. Since he wouldn't win a fistfight or a wrestling match, and would have little chance in a sword fight, Poet was glad Marcus held his tongue and smiled.

"What did Joseph and Nicodemus say about that day and the burial itself?" Marcus asked. Poet saw he strained to control his tone and his facial expression. Marcus was a practiced stoic, but he also was used to respect.

"They were Jesus lovers. I know them well. I have seen them with him before. They, too, had witnessed miracles. Little Jo Jo and Naughty Nico— that's what I call them—claimed only to offer the man respect in death and a decent burial before the sabbath. They lied."

"And then?" Marcus was an experienced interrogator and was prodding the bull like a hostile witness.

"They stuck to their lie. Dio and I left them with the sound suggestion that they reconsider and tell us the whole truth. We gave them an hour to remember. When Dio returned for their answer before summoning me— he scares men even more than I do, believe it or not—they were gone. They ran like rats. My informants haven't found hide nor hair of them, and my network is full of rats and snakes that know all the hiding places. I will tell you if we find them. They have a lot to lose here, too much to risk disappearing."

Poet shifted in his chair. He hated rats almost as much as snakes. He glanced over Saltaurius's shoulder. The hooded man was bobbing in agreement, and from behind he resembled either a rabbi at prayer or a swine at the trough. Poet knew it was neither a rabbi nor a pig, but the devil himself.

They planned to ride out to see the Essene rabbi, Abraham, after their meeting with Saltaurius. Poet hoped they'd find the old man alive.

"Have you found any of his disciples or Mary Magdalene?" Marcus asked.

"No disciples. They may have left the city. And I want to meet this Mary of Magdala," Saltaurius said with a leer. "She's from a fishing village where they all love rebels and hate Roman rule. Jesus supposedly cured her of demonic possession, and she paid his way as he went from village to village with her as his cohort." Poet never liked that suggestive use of the word *cohort*. Especially since Marcus had taken to affectionately calling Poet his cohort, evoking the double meaning and suggesting he was as good as the five hundred men he used to command. "Fish, demons, and money—I smell a harlot," Saltaurius bellowed as he grabbed himself between the legs again. "She was with the men at the burial. I hear she can make a fallen tree stand erect again. Maybe she did some Egyptian necromancy sex on the dead god-man to bring him back to life."

"Wait. She was at the crucifixion and the burial?" Marcus asked.

"Yes, and she claims to have seen Jesus just outside the tomb," Saltaurius said, licking ale foam off his thick lips.

"Being at all three events makes her the most important witness," Marcus said, while weighing how much intelligence to share with the brute to keep him talking. Saltaurius clearly had more information to barter, and Marcus disliked being less informed than his rival.

"You forget the law and common sense," Saltaurius scoffed. "A woman is not a credible witness. Her testimony would not be admissible in court."

"That makes it even more reliable," Marcus mumbled to himself before adding, "Just because she is a woman of means doesn't mean she's a harlot. If she is, point me to her brothel. Where is she now?"

Poet scanned the tavern, observing the absence of women, as was customary at that hour. By law, only professional women were allowed in taverns after dark, so they wouldn't distract the men from their work and drinking during daylight.

"Still, I want to meet her. I imagine the attractive son of God had his pick of *cohorts*," Saltaurius said, winking at Poet. "I'm told she fled north with the disciple John. I've sent men to track them. And the one named Thomas set off for the east. The other disciples have also either fled or are underground, burying themselves, perhaps with the body of Jesus, in the catacombs. These tombs are being searched by my bravest and most well-paid spies. Those caverns and tunnels are only fit for worms and snakes," he said, making Poet shudder. Saltaurius continued. "If Jesus still walks, I believe he is heading east, maybe with his dear old mother and his disciple Thomas."

"What's next for you? Do you intend to scare away more of my witnesses?" Marcus said with a congenial grin.

"I have horses and an ox and cart ready to set off once my men return and report. I'd welcome your company, if you care to join us?"

"Ox and cart?" Marcus asked. "Are you launching a military campaign or traveling with women?"

"A man of my age and stature"—he pounded his chest as if they needed to be reminded of his size—"gets used to a certain amount of luxury. And

I don't suppose he'll move too fast on a donkey. If I find he's fleeing on horseback, I'll leave my cart behind. Like you, I get paid whether you find him or I do—I got the Pharisees to match that terms Pilate decreed for you. So you ride on ahead as fast as you can to bring back his head, but first we have to know where he's going and if he has already left."

Marcus stood, followed by Poet, as they were ready to go. Poet looked at the hunched and hooded man behind Saltaurius and believed he was listening to every word and not an innocent stranger. He approached from behind and yanked the hood off the eavesdropper's head. The old toothless man turned to look while yelping at being so rudely dealt with. His eyes were blank and innocent. Poet offered his apologies to the man for mistaking his identity.

Saltaurius laughed and said, "Dio does hear everything, but if he wants to hide, you won't find him."

≈ ≈ ≈

Poet was glad to be riding with Marcus out of Jerusalem and away from Saltaurius and Dio. As they trotted out of the city, the buildings went from Roman marble to local brick and then groupings of hovels—most of them not much more than permanent tents. The rolling hills filled with sporadic vegetation flattened as the earth became more barren. Dusty stone-laid streets turned to rock and sand. They paused at the last green hill overlooking the orange desert that fanned out before the Dead Sea. There, they found a sheep herder who directed them to the Essene camp.

Arriving at the camp, the heat was dry and oppressive except for the faint and fleeting kisses of a sea breeze. Poet envied Marcus, who only might break a sweat in the heat of battle—his own tunic was moist and clinging to his back and chest. They found water for themselves and the horses. The Essene camp had not changed since the time of Romulus and Remus. At the first cluster of tents and hovels, they received instructions to go to a central hut belonging to the man who they called the Great Rabbi.

They found Abraham inside the warm and arid but hospitable hut, saying prayers in Hebrew in front of a strange altar. He had salt and pepper whiskers, and his long, black, curly hair came down from under a black migbahat. The rabbi's robe was as black as his cone-shaped hat. His face was ruddy from the sun and stretched by the years. His eyes were big, black, and penetrating. He looked like a dead man praying with his eyes open, an immortal man that time and fashion would never alter. He interspersed his nodding prayers with periods of silence.

The hut was simply furnished with rugs and cushions and smelled of the musty old man seated inside. He was sitting in front of a small altar covered with an Arabian rug. On the rug were some candles and a pan filled with water and aromatic spices. Above the altar hung a large animal tusk, a horn as big as Marcus's thigh. Poet admired the cornucopia, one that Zeus himself might blow. He couldn't imagine the old rabbi, with his old lungs, being able to use it to announce morning prayers. Poet used to have such a horn attached to his saddle, which he would blow to announce an enemy's approach, or the charge of Marcus's calvary. But there was no looking back to their glory days.

Marcus and Poet sat waiting for Abraham to emerge from his trance, as it seemed they were called to do. Most Roman soldiers would have knocked the old man around for not rising to greet them. Marcus didn't show it, but Poet knew he was growing impatient.

After several long minutes, the devout man turned to face the Romans. All fear had been drained out of the old man's saggy face. He studied his guests with skeptical kindness. "More Romans than I've seen for years. I am Abraham. And you?"

Marcus and Poet introduced themselves and expressed an interest in the life and death of Jesus of Nazareth. "We are also interested in learning of your experience with the other Roman, Saltaurius, who accompanied you to the Nazarian's tomb," Marcus said with a respectful tone and tilt of the head.

"Yes," Abraham said, removing his black hat for a moment to rub the round bald spot on top of his head. "The big man was all muscle, but the small, silent man held the invisible harness and whip. The big man was only interested in Jesus's death and rising. He didn't give a fig for his life and teachings. I accompanied them to the tomb, but he refused to listen to me, though his little man did. Some hot posca?"

Poet nodded to show deference to his master and was glad to receive a Roman drink in an Essenes camp.

Abraham poured them three mugs with the sour infusion, but which Poet found to be warm and satisfying. The hut's shade protected them from the sun and blowing sand, but did little to diminish the heat or smell of sweat. Poet wished to be back in Pilate's fragrant and breezy chamber—without Pilate flitting about like an animated Venus de Milo, of course.

"What did you discover at the tomb?" Marcus asked.

"Your fellow Roman carted me into town to show him the tomb. He ordered me—*threatened* me—not to speak to anyone about the tomb. The crude man threw silver coins at my feet and left me to walk back home. He did not know I recognize no authority other than God," the old man said flatly. It was clear he had no fear of Roman retribution. Poet appreciated the bravery of simple men who didn't need a sword to speak their truth, but he hoped the rabbi, for his own sake, would show Marcus the respect he deserved.

"He's a mercenary," Marcus said. "I am the official Roman emissary in this matter and not aligned with him. Would you tell us what you saw? We will see no harm befalls you for your testimony."

"No promises, please. Only God can protect us from such truly wicked men. I will share what I witnessed. Nothing about the rushed burial of Jesus before Passover was according to strict Jewish rights. In fact, they didn't really bury him; they only entombed him."

"What do you mean by that?" Marcus asked.

"None of the Jewish customs of Mosaic law seemed to be followed. He was laid out on the sacred center stone, which is where one is embalmed. However, they never placed him in one of the small burial crypts that surround the tomb, that are dug out to face east to west. We found no scent or evidence of embalming material. I was told he was wrapped in linen treated with balms of aloes and myrrh. He would not have been lying on that center stone, facing north and south, if he were departing for the afterlife. There were other small signs of a rushed or unorthodox burial."

"Tell us about Saltaurius and his reaction in the tomb," Marcus said.

"He is a larger-than-life man, inspired by the dark energy blown in his ear by the little man. Like most Romans and Jews, I guess he wanted the messiah dead and did not appreciate any unresolved mystery. But strangely, he feared and revered Jesus like one should fear and revere a crucified son of God. He told me that, to his knowledge, Jesus was dead and ascended into heaven. He didn't believe the witnesses to his resurrected body here on Earth. This Saltaurius is a conflicted man, desperate for peace, and only able to move forward thanks to the quiet, calculating nature of the other man—the imp with cold protruding eyes." The rabbi swayed back and forth as if praying silently.

He studied Marcus. "I can see the light in your eyes, tribune." Then he turned to Poet. "And you they call Poet—true poets are God's messengers, scribes of his words."

"Yes, it is good to meet someone who understands the true nature of poetry," Poet replied and turning to Marcus said, "More so than—"

Marcus held up his hand to stop him. It was true—Poet always wanted to speak about poetry, even here, in a steamy hut with an old Jew.

Marcus said to Abraham, "Please tell us more about this Jesus and his life."

"Exactly—to the point! It is his presence in our lives that truly matters," the rabbi said, his face giving an almost youthful appearance. *Jesus is his poetry*, Poet mused. "Why focus on a man's death," the rabbi continued, "when it is his life that counts? He lives still. Our Savior, our Lord. We knew from the beginning. It's a story few know, but you are important men for whom time is precious. Tell me what you truly want to know."

Marcus laughed. "Other people's long stories are short to me. You haven't traveled with my friend here," he said, gesturing toward Poet. "He loves a good drawn-out tale."

Poet twirled his hand twice before giving a slight bow of acknowledgment.

"Tell us everything you know—all your reasons for believing he is the son of God and has risen from the tomb," Marcus said.

"I will tell you what I know to be *true*," Abraham said, jabbing his temple with a long, bony finger. "I am old enough to have instructed his mother as a girl. His mother Mary was Essene and gave a miraculous birth, according to the prophecy of the coming messiah. Can you imagine this young girl's bravery? Joseph was already engaged to be her husband and thought she had been unfaithful. She could have been stoned, yet she remained courageous and faithful in the midst of the accusations. Joseph eventually came to believe and took Mary as his wife, despite the slings and arrows of doubt and innuendo. The miraculous birth and her courage afterward were a tremendous moment in history that I was fortunate to witness. These critical historical moments are easiest for prophets to foresee. This is how the three sages found Jesus. After their arrival from the East on the

Silk Road, they consulted with me, Mary, and Joseph. These wise men had foreseen his holy birth. I was present, and despite translation difficulties, I grasped the important message they bore. Some of it came directly from their minds. They prophesied this boy, an *avatar of God* as they called him, would show miraculous powers of spirit when he approached manhood at the age of twelve. This put him in danger here from Roman and Jew alike. They instructed Joseph to take his family east, where the boy might survive in relative safety and learn more of God and his own godliness. He returned to Palestine at the age of thirty to fulfill his destiny and ministry. He performed great miracles and taught the love of God and man. And they crucified him because of it. He died for us as the lamb of God, only to rise again, to fulfill another prophecy." The old rabbi looked up as if there was a divine light above him, pressing prayer hands to his heart after delivering his sermon.

Poet observed nothing so poetic and saw only the hut's mud, straw, and wood ceiling.

"You believe this?" Marcus asked.

"Yes," Abraham said. Poet admired Marcus's penetrating gaze into the rabbi's intense eyes. Marcus seemed satisfied that Abraham did not lie. He didn't demand to see the palms of his hands. "But men now speak of him and his death," Abraham continued, "forgetting the mother and the miraculous birth. She is the mother who gave birth to the messiah and kept him from harm."

"Where can I find her?" Marcus asked.

"With her son," the rabbi answered. "Maybe grieving over his body. Or she saw the horror of her son on the cross and then nursed him back from death to life once more—"

"Watch it!" Poet shouted, jumping up to his feet, causing Marcus to draw his knife. "A snake!" He pointed to a large venomous golden viper with black bands. The snake had found its way to the hut wall, where it hit the dirt and paused, flicking its tongue at the obstacle.

Abraham didn't move but behaved as if it were a pet, freely coming and going. Poet's screeching caused the snake to scurry out through the hole where it likely had entered. He was almost dead from the fright. He would fight a barbarian with a club without breaking a sweat, but ever since being bitten as a child, snakes had been his Achilles' heel. Poet believed he somehow attracted snakes and that they would someday take his life. His friend Ovid, may the gods rest his soul, another Roman poet, had told him this was a curse from a prior life, one where he may have been a Dio-like mongoose, or otherwise treated snakes cruelly. For the foreseeable future, Poet would check his bedding and place a horsehair rope around him before sleep when they camped.

Marcus grinned and sheathed his knife. "All we have to do to ensure someone stays awake while camping is to simply mention snakes in front of Poet before bed." He clearly didn't realize it was a deadly serious matter. "Poet," he said, "sit. It is gone. What more questions do we have for Abraham?"

"You ought to plug that hole. Those vipers are killers," Poet said to Abraham, reclaiming his seat and wiping the sweat from his brow with a piece of cloth he carried in his satchel. He had shamed himself by acting like a frightened child. "The obvious question then, Marcus," Poet said, finally answering the question, "is what do you believe happened to his body?"

"That's the question everyone asks now," Abraham said, making Poet feel common as well as a coward. "One possibility is that someone stole his body after he died on the cross so that people would believe the prophecy and proclaim him the Christ. Or, the prophecy was accurate, and he has risen. That accounts for the many witnesses claiming he had returned to life. You are the educated men of Rome." He paused, looking at Marcus and then at Poet. "What do you believe?"

"Marcus?" Poet asked, standing to get off the snake-infested floor. He found the air was thicker and hotter when he stood, so he reclaimed his seat after checking for vipers. The temperature didn't seem to bother the eighty-year-old Essene.

"Based on the testimony thus far," Marcus answered, "it is most likely he never actually died but instead almost died and was revived and walked out of his own accord. This accounts for him being seen afterward."

"What do you think?" Abraham asked Poet.

"I think his body was stolen," Poet said. "It took four men to move the tombstone in place, so there's no way this beaten and crucified man who was dead or left for dead could have had the strength to move the stone. And how could he—the most wanted body in all the empire—vanish and materialize at his own discretion?"

"We've discussed this," Marcus said. "He must have had help from the outside. The guards were drugged."

Poet nodded. Still, he wondered about Boy's reports that people saw Jesus come and go like a ghost moving through walls.

"Please, Abraham," Marcus said, "as a mentor and sage to this Jesus, tell us what you believe happened."

"What I believe does not matter," Abraham replied. "If a man can part seas with divine intervention, what is rising from the dead and moving a stone? I cannot know, and regarding my faith, it is of no matter."

"Sir, I don't understand," Marcus said. "Please speak plain, and we will go."

"He was a son of God and told us we all are children of God in our love, charity, and service to others. He defined divine service as love in action. Miracles came naturally to one so advanced in spirit. He prophesied his resurrection, and he was a truthful man. And now he allows himself to be witnessed in his transfigured body. Whether he lived or died, rose or didn't, or someone stole him from the tomb, is of no matter, but men like your fellow citizen Saltaurius will argue this meaningless point as the foundation of belief or disbelief. Though he was hired by the Pharisee to find the body, that seems like the last thing he desires. And now, some of Jesus's followers are spreading the word that he will, or has, risen into heaven. Nobody— not Jews nor Romans nor even those calling themselves followers of Jesus Christ—want a god who merely goes on living after escaping death. But his holy life is enough for me, a man who has always believed in God and awaited the coming of the Lord."

"Where would you look for his resurrected body?" Marcus asked.

"In heaven," he said with a laugh. "If he lives and wishes to continue residing in his glorified body here on Earth, and this is God's will, he will head east. He would not live long around here with all of Rome and Judaea looking to put him to death . . . again. And you are Roman military. You must be able to imagine the massacres and mayhem that would fall upon his family and followers if he were found around here. He cannot die, but they all can, unless . . ." The old Essene's voice trailed off as he looked upward in deep concentration that looked to Poet like rapture or terror. "Unless he is able to incarnate back into his body at will and can never be captured or put to death again," the rabbi continued. "There are stories . . ." The rabbi held up his hands and started shaking. He called out in a booming voice: "A vision is descending upon me." His face grew serious, and he proclaimed:

"Now, I will tell you what I believe. What I am shown to believe." His voice was so altered that Poet couldn't be sure who they were listening to. "Though a god," the rabbi trumpeted in a powerful voice, "he was buried in his skull when he took human form. And he emerged reborn from that skull that was his true tomb. Awakened fully to the dream. A resurrected god. Remembering fully who he was. Out of his mind. No more doubt. No more fear. No more suffering or struggle. In this stateless state, it would be impossible for him to return to the world of dreams surrounding him here in Jerusalem. And he will then, after his ministry, honor his mother. The three wise men prophesied this to me thirty-three years ago." The old Essene's eyes rolled up and were buried behind his bushy eyebrows as he continued, "He now must vanish, or the seed will not take. His followers need time to spread the message before the persecution comes. And it will come. And when he comes again—if you find him and bring him back—his return will crumble the pillars of the empire and oppression of men. The days are numbered and will come to an end. It might take over two thousand years, but a match will be relit in Jerusalem, and the Greek *atomos*, no longer indivisible, will split and split over and over again. Another moment in history our prophets have seen. You must find grace before you will find him and see his exalted body."

The rabbi stopped his emphatic rambling about empires falling, took a deep breath, and lowered his gaze, returning to himself.

"How can something indivisible be—" Poet began, but stopped when Marcus placed his hand on his shoulder and gave him a sideways glance.

Marcus then turned to face the old man. "Abraham, thank you for your time and wisdom," he said. "We will visit the tomb now and keep an open mind about whether it's a grave-snatching crime scene or a place of miracles. Perhaps it still holds the answer." Marcus stood.

"Watch out for snakes. The catacombs are crawling with them," Abraham said.

Marcus laughed, but Poet could only grunt.

As they rode out of camp, Poet heard the loud horn resounding like a giant's trumpet emitting a deep resonant note amplifying Abraham's shriveled lungs and reaching all the way to Jerusalem—*om, om, om . . .*

"You think he's calling the community to prayers? Or perhaps it's his benediction to bless us on our way?" Poet asked Marcus.

"Or he's heralding the end of the world. But maybe it's just to scare the snakes away."

⌇ ⌇ ⌇

When they reached the tomb, Poet pretended to move the massive stone that was rolled aside from the mouth of the cavern. He feigned straining and grunted, then mimed giving up and panting. "It would take three of you and five of me to move this thing. Perhaps Saltaurius is the body snatcher," Poet said. The empty tomb burrowed into the rocky earth like a gaping wound. "Wait before we enter," Poet added, picking up a handful of small stones and throwing them into the tomb.

"Afraid of spirits?" Marcus asked.

"Snakes," Poet replied.

As they entered the pleasantly cool but foul smelling and ominously dark tomb, Marcus lit a makeshift torch of sagebrush, which provided a heavenly scent and illuminated the roughly square cave. A large limestone slab was in the middle. Around the circumference were four empty niches built for corpses. Marcus handed the torch to Poet so he could keep watch while he studied the scene with his great powers of perception. Poet couldn't see anything that would shed light on the mystery.

"The tomb is in a garden owned by Joseph of Arimathea, who is now in hiding or dead like the rest of our witnesses. Look here," Marcus said, twisting a twig he found on the slab between his thumb and forefinger before smelling the tips. "This center slab still bears some herbs and stains. Roman boots have trampled any footprints since the resurrection." Marcus picked up a small branch of an herb that lay beside the slab, as well as a bud of flattened aloe, and put them to his nose. "Shine the light here. Abraham said there was no smell or evidence of embalming agents. These are herbs used for healing. And see this? This is his dried blood. He still bled, even here."

Poet wondered if it was a god's blood or just a man's. "Are you saying he didn't die?" he asked, trying to mask his shivering from the cold and fear.

"No. But perhaps they attempted to revive him," Marcus said. "Remember Aloysius, who perished on the battlefield only to awaken on a pile of bodies the next night just as the flames ignited? He clambered down the pyre only to be burned to death."

"How could I ever forget his screams?" Poet said. "And the image is seared into my mind forever."

A cold wind, on a warm day, blew into the tomb, filling Poet with fear. He realized it wasn't the memory of poor Aloysius burning alive causing his trepidation but rather the magnitude of their mission that chilled his bones—finding this holy ghost, Jesus, god or man, dead or alive—was more critical than any battle with barbarians and would determine their fate. And it would test their faith and beliefs like nothing that had come before. It was even possible that the House of Decia could be redeemed and resurrected, if only they could solve the mystery of what had become of Jesus.

"Resuscitation or resurrection—not so different," Marcus said, rousing Poet from his thoughts. "I've seen mystics in Egypt that can walk on burning coals without flinching. I've seen a man healed from a deadly poison by sorcerers. And an old priest who lay without breathing for hours only to be awakened, smiling at the sound of a bell. You know what Zeno said about miracles?"

"To allow for one small miracle opens the door to all miracles, great and small," Poet answered, gathering his courage.

"Correct!"

Marcus studied the small crypts that were still waiting to be filled with a corpse. "This must be a recently dug tomb. There are no dead buried here yet to witness what happened."

"Perhaps he took them with him," Poet said.

"Funny, but this is a freshly dug tomb within a limestone cave that still smells like old eggs. Our sage torch saves us from the worst of the stench. No wonder he didn't want to stay here," Marcus joked. "Joseph, the owner of the land, must really have loved Jesus to use his own family tomb for him. And where better to hide and tend to a body? Would you leave a dead man here to rot and stink rather than put him in one of the crypts and seal it? Perhaps he knew Jesus was just here for a visit." Marcus lay back on the slab, looking up at the rock ceiling. "Imagine being crucified, set down upon this cold limestone, rising through the grace of the gods, and then having the gods remove the rock from the entrance."

Poet was not sure if Marcus was joking, but knew enough to stay silent and not interrupt his chain of thought.

Marcus sat up on the slab and continued, "Suppose this miracle worker could mimic death and then revive himself hours later, like poor Aloysius, but was fortunate they chose burial and not cremation. Even if he were dead, if he could cure the sick and raise the dead, why wouldn't he be able to resurrect himself and walk this earth again . . . and fulfill the prophecy of his rising?" Marcus asked with exuberance. Poet watched as Marcus pondered his own question.

After a minute, Marcus jumped from the slab to his feet to kick the dirt. Turning to face Poet, he said, "Or his disciples stole his dead body and are making sure it never will be found. And I'll never get to Rome to determine the truth of what happened to my family and have my revenge. Poet, I'm letting my desire and imagination taint my reasoning."

"Truth often follows the imagination," Poet said, hurrying Marcus to the exit before the torch burned out. Another dead end had Poet praying for divine intervention.

CHAPTER 9
Jesus in Galilee

ON THEIR RIDE back to their lodging in Jerusalem, Marcus worried about Boy. Witnesses were disappearing, and Saltaurius—or even the Jesus followers—might beat or kill Boy if they found out he was a spy.

Boy was doing man's work and doing it well. Marcus smiled to think Boy would never want to be reined in and, like one of his horses, he needed to be able to run free. The magnitude of the mission required they all be bold. Poet had confessed some trepidation about their future and what it might mean to find, or not find, Jesus. Marcus knew both his men would rally when destiny called. He could still hear the old rabbi's horn calling him to action.

Upon their return to the inn, Boy wasn't there, but they found a portrait of Jesus's face left by Centurion Cornelius. The artist had paid attention to detail, adding a golden orb around the otherwise black, brown, and beige visage with a beard. The eyes were moist and doe-like. Marcus and Poet studied the picture in silence. Mesmerized. Impossible as it seemed, Marcus recognized the face of a man he'd never seen before. *Who was this man with such captivating eyes, this man who resisted Judaea's power and the Roman Empire, dying humbly and honorably before vanishing and reappearing like a holy ghost? And was he to be found by the most earnest of seekers?* Marcus thought. *And where is my earnest young seeker? I'd rather be hung naked upon a cross than discover Boy had died serving me.*

Marcus focused on the portrait again, and was astonished as he realized he had seen Jesus before, upon the cross, in the vision he shared with the fallen centurion. He had written that experience off as a reaction to rotten meat or fungus.

— — —

It was well after nightfall when Boy returned to the inn, breathless and with the news. "Many of his followers sighted him two days ago, in Galilee!" Boy said. "They said he was eating and talking like any man. We that believe this man to be the son of God are all very excited." Boy smiled, as though still playing the part of a zealot. Or had Marcus's adopted son become a true believer? "No one knows where Joseph, Nicodemus, and Mary Magdalene are," Boy continued. "Perhaps in Galilee with Jesus? From all I have learned of him, he sounds like a god to love, not fear."

"Good work, Boy," Marcus said, giving him a military salute. Marcus considered correcting Boy's exuberance, but let it pass. He had done well and was excited to deliver the good news. "Eat and drink and we'll sleep a couple of hours. We'll rise before dawn and ride to Galilee."

As Marcus lay on his mat, he wondered if the others could sleep. His mind was too busy for sleep, imagining the morning ride and confronting the rebel Jesus in the flesh. And then what?

— — —

Packed and ready the following morning, Marcus waited for Boy to saddle and feed the horses. Boy brought them to the inn as the sunlight started to peer down the dreary streets and into the city.

On well-rested horses, the trio rode like Mercury along the road to Galilee, scattering the early-rising, foot-dragging pilgrims and peddlers. Boy was full of boundless joy as he galloped on Sahara next to Marcus. Poet trailed behind, riding in their dust. Boy looked like a young god about to discover the mystery of mysteries with his two Roman war hero companions. Boy was becoming a man, and Marcus was proud of the man he was becoming. He wondered if Boy was just pretending to be a Jesus lover or if he had fallen in love with the god-man they soon would meet face to face.

When they arrived at Galilee, they discovered they were too late. Jesus was already gone. Those that had been with Jesus had scattered back into hiding—except for one simple shepherd girl. "At dawn," she told them, "while his friends slept on the ground, he walked up a hill and bathed in golden light he rose like Icarus into the rising sun." Her mother thought this sighting was merely a dream of a girl who loved Greek stories. Those who recognized the man in the picture said that they had seen Jesus before he was crucified. Otherwise, the only current sighting in Galilee was reported by his disciples before they too all disappeared. One thing was certain, Jesus had moved on.

Despite failing to find Jesus, they held fast to the mission. The six moons Pilate had given them to find the body had sounded like a lifetime, but now, with no leads, it felt like a looming death sentence. But what really bothered Marcus was that Saltaurius had been there first, throwing coins around before heading off in haste with his terrifying little man and small caravan. Nobody knew, or would tell them, the direction Saltaurius took, except for one old lady, who said she saw the big and little man heading north toward Turkey and Greece. Poet was ready to accept her testimony. He loved Greece. But she was not a credible witness, as her eyes were unwilling to hold Marcus's gaze. When Marcus asked her if she lied, her cheek twitched when she denied it. When Marcus asked if she was paid by Saltaurius to send them in the wrong direction, she protested far too much before storming off. Even Greek-loving Poet had to admit she was not a good actress.

Marcus detested Saltaurius and loathed being in his dust. Was he searching for Jesus or shadow-fencing with the giant gladiator?

￼ ￼ ￼

That night, they sat around a fire on the beach of Galilee, eating some fresh fish and figs. Poet had brought the remaining wine from the inn. As usual, Boy tended the horses and fire; Poet played cook and wine steward; and Marcus whittled and thought. It was a delightful night to feel so dejected. The scent of the sea and fire was intoxicating. Poet and Boy patiently and silently waited for the next steps, until Marcus finally said, "Let me sleep on it."

The next morning, Marcus woke before the others. He dressed and restarted the fire to warm some posca and bread, and to cook three small fish. He was cheerful and restless to get moving. The gloom from the night before had risen.

"Boy, eat and drink," he said when they awoke, "and then go into the village to buy provisions for at least two weeks on horseback. Poet and I will feed and ready the horses this morning."

Upon hearing this, Poet ran clumsily over the sand to get his two empty pig stomach wine pouches, which he then handed to Boy.

"The fisherman who caught our fish told me Saltaurius rode east with his caravan. Along the Silk Road. He spoke the truth," Marcus said, handing out the cooked fish garnished with stewed olives. "They won't be hard to overtake, and we'll find out what more this bounty hunter knows. He won't outsmart me or beat me to the mark again."

He watched as they ate the food he had carefully prepared. Boy especially seemed to enjoy licking his fingers to needle Poet, whose cooking was never as good. Under the circumstances, all was as good as could be within the small, tight band of three. Marcus found it ironic that his hunt for the rebel Jesus was taking him out of the Roman Empire, which might prove fortuitous if he should fail to find Jesus and be banished from the empire under threat of execution.

～ ～ ～

A day later, they left the Roman Empire and crossed an imaginary border into Persia. Marcus thought there should be some gate or wall, or at least a stone marker for those that didn't have maps. They now would travel through the birthplace of the Hebrew Bible and the Garden of Eden, previously known as Mesopotamia or the land between two rivers, the Tigris and the Euphrates.

Two other great rivers, the Rhine running north to south and the Danube running west to east, also bound the empire. To the north was Armenia, a loosely held part of the Roman Empire. And farther north, in Germania, were the blond-haired, blue-eyed barbarians. Marcus and Poet had fought those fearless savages before. All of Rome had nightmares of the barbarians ransacking the emperor's palace on Palatine Hill. The Parthian Empire, a frequent adversary of Rome but now in a relative state of peace, lay to the southeast.

Marcus considered himself an extension of the empire that followed him wherever he went: *vis Romanus sum*. His father had instilled in him a sense of pride in being a Roman citizen and taught him to conduct himself honorably in all his affairs as a man of duty. Most men lost all civility when outside civilization's constraints, but he demanded the same discipline and decorum of his men, however far they roamed from Rome. Still, they had passed over some invisible Rubicon.

Proudly bearing the Roman eagle in their hearts, this company of three rode their horses hard along the rough Silk Road, through the untamed lands, following the ruts of the iron wheels of innumerable caravans. At last, they reached the civilization of the Persian city called Babylon, a city that God had destroyed once before for its sins before being resurrected. Babylon occupied a strategic position along the east side of the Euphrates river.

They checked with the ferrymen, who confirmed Saltaurius and his caravan had arrived the previous day. "He is a memorable figure," one of the men told them, "and not soon forgotten."

For another coin, the ferrymen also looked at the lovely drawing they carried of Jesus. "Yes, that is the semblance of the man, I think. His eyes were full of . . . light. And around his head I saw the golden glow," one of the younger men said. "They called him Issa. He entered weeks ago with an older lady and a younger man on donkeys."

They had not seen him depart. For that information, they referred Marcus to the ferrymen over the Tigris. "Our brothers," one of the men explained, "they will be able to tell you more."

Babylon looked to Marcus like a healthy Jerusalem, with even more bustling streets and markets. Absent was the animosity of the oppressed that hung over Jerusalem, where entrenched religious tradition clashed with the Roman Empire's modern imperial design.

The older ferryman had pontificated about the good governance of Babylon. "Five hundred years ago, Cyrus the Great gave us a bill of rights granting religious freedom and abolishing slavery. To this day, though the Zoroastrians worshipped one God, they don't force their views on others of different faiths." The ferryman was still speaking to his captive audience—Poet and Boy. Marcus's eyes were fixed ahead on the home of the mythical hanging gardens. "There is again slave trade in Babylon for those seized in battle, but the focus is on commerce and the arts and not the oppression of men by men. This city of many tongues houses people from all over the world. Sorry, no hanging gardens. Not anymore . . ."

After the sad note about the gardens, Marcus lost interest in the ferryman's political discourse as he focused on the giant named Saltaurius and the man called Issa, who looked a lot like Jesus.

CHAPTER 10
Babylon

AFTER SETTLING INTO their rooms at an Arabian guesthouse frequented by merchants traveling the Silk Road, Marcus sent Boy to find Saltaurius to arrange a meeting. Boy found his way to the dusty town square where all the men and livestock were milling about in the hazy afternoon sun. Saltaurius was not hard to spot. He cast a big shadow over the little man named Dio.

Saltaurius also spotted him as he approached. The giant turned his back to Boy, saying to Dio, "Tell Marcus's slave boy he should not masquerade in Roman dress, carrying a sword and riding a fine horse unless he has the Decia name. But he doesn't have that, does he?" Saltaurius asked. He left them to take a large seat by his caravan. Boy didn't know how they knew who he was. They had never met. *Good spies,* he guessed.

Poet had told Boy they likely would dismiss him and to play the humble servant. So, Boy apologized to Dio for any offense and politely requested the two camps meet.

Dio agreed to this and said, "Marcus and Poet should be our guests for dinner. We celebrate tonight. And then, they should sleep in one of our fine tents with a girl of their choosing. But we cannot invite a slave to share in a Roman feast, even here in Babylon. Being a slave is an ignoble, juvenile state of being."

The loathing in Dio's serpent-like eyes as he issued the invitation and insult through his dry, cracked lips made Boy shiver. As he turned to leave,

Dio grabbed him by the wrist. Boy shook free of the clammy and bony hand and attempted to look at the devil who called himself god without fear.

"Please wait," Dio said. "Do you realize how lost they would be without you? Their horses wouldn't be fit for riding; their camp would be a mess; their clothes would stink, and they'd rot away with pestilence." Boy heard some truth in these words and felt unable to run away, though he knew he should. "You should know your worth. And my master will pay for you to leave them. We are no longer in the Roman Empire here. Be free, child."

"You don't know me," Boy said. "And I must be going now."

"Play a game with me. What harm could come from that? Tell me what it would take? A hundred silver? Gold? And I met a fine Nubian goddess here, your age and with a body of Venus. Fit fruit for an emperor's dessert. She could make you a man this evening and for half your gold be your wife."

"Not all the gold and fine women in the world would make me break my bond to Tribune Marcus Decia."

"Slave. You deceive yourself. Every man has something he would sacrifice everything for. Perhaps you are not man enough to admit it. Or smart enough to realize what I am offering. Imagine. What if I could make you a deity? Well, you see my point. Consider this a game. What's your price to leave your master?"

Boy knew he should run from this evil, but his pride and desire held his feet in place. He knew his price, but could he name it?

"It's just a game. Out with it, Boy. Words are not actions and are of no consequence."

"You couldn't pay my price."

"Try me."

"Find my mother so that I may free her."

Dio threw up his skeletal arms in triumph. "See?" he exclaimed. "I won!"

Boy ran all the way back to the guesthouse with Dio's cackling stuck in his ears. He reported everything about his meeting with the ghoul to Marcus and Poet, except his weakness in revealing his desire to find his mother.

CHAPTER 11
Saltaurius's Theater

As evening approached, Marcus and Poet made their way to the decadent, torch-lit carnival. Poet was apprehensive along the way and kept pressing him to be patient with their brute host. Marcus knew he wanted to, but Poet didn't mention Pilate's prophecy. As they weaved their way through the caravans, women danced naked from the waist up with bells on their feet and men charmed snakes and drank. Saltaurius was at the center of the spectacle, sitting on a raised platform. Dio sat near his master on the stage. Men dressed in a colorful array of clothes and skin tones came forward to whisper in the big man's ear and then exited the scene.

Marcus took in the sights, sounds, and smells—all of it a grand illusion. Like Rome and his life there, this Babylon carnival would last for an instant and then be gone. Nothing, good or bad, would remain after its brief time of play. He had two missions: to find the truth about his family and to discover what had become of Jesus. This and his love of his men were all that mattered.

As they entered the festivities of the square and approached its center stage, Saltaurius rose in greeting, stretching out his arms to encompass the scene. "All this for some Hebrew gold and silver. Please be my guests. We shall eat, drink, and talk and then please have your pick of the women, Marcus. They dance for our pleasure. If you've never experienced a belly dance while performing the bone dance, well, it's a singular treat," Saltaurius said as he gyrated his hips and thrust his pelvis in an obscene gesture.

Since his wife's death, Marcus had not engaged in any sexual relationship. No woman could compare to his Beatrice, and any lovemaking would be hollow with a harlot.

Sitting down, Marcus accepted the big man's food and drink, eager to learn about Issa. He now believed he might be the Jesus they sought, who might be a son of God. His and Poet's wine cups were filled and their plates heaped with lamb and vegetables stewed in cumin and other Eastern spices. Saltaurius held a large leg of roasted mutton.

"Saltaurius, thank you for your generosity," Marcus said. "But after we finish talking and eating, we'll return to our room. Can you tell me what you've learned of the man we both hunt? And why you hasten east?"

"Here, outside the confines of Roman law, we sit as equals," Saltaurius said while chewing the mutton and licking his greasy, fat lips.

"Roman law follows its citizens wherever they go," Marcus said in an authoritative tone that wasn't conducive to gaining information, so he shifted it. "I'm not here to debate the law but to discover what you know about the man we seek, perhaps the one called Issa. You seem to be one step ahead of me."

Poet fidgeted in his seat. This confused Marcus, who thought his cohort would appreciate his humble words and courteous manner. He was following Poet's advice and doing whatever it took to obtain information.

"You are all business, Marcus, but business here is best conducted by drink and coin and cold steel when needed. The ferrymen on the Tigris told me that Issa passed over the river and is still heading east. This Issa and his donkeys travel without rest, up to thirty leagues a day. He trades his tired donkeys for fresh ones at every opportunity, or so I'm told. He apparently looks like Jesus, though he runs like a coward," Saltaurius said. Marcus wondered if his adversary also had a drawing of the man or was going on just a description. *How would one describe Jesus's visage and those enchanting eyes?* "Ox and cart move too slowly to overtake his flying donkeys, so I sold my caravan and slaves today, exchanging them for horses. Dio advised me to do this, but agreed we might celebrate tonight. What is one more night?"

Dio sat staring at Poet while listening to every word. Marcus thought, *That must be why Poet keeps shifting uncomfortably in his seat.* Dio, perhaps realizing all eyes were on him, turned to watch the debaucheries that surrounded their raised dais. He sipped his wine and nibbled his flatbread with a hunk of fig-flavored cheese on top, looking like a rat enjoying a baby mouse.

"My spies tell me you met the dusty old Essene rabbi," Saltaurius went on. "A dead end there with that Abraham. Shortly after our last meeting, I learned Jesus returned to Galilee, only to ascend back into heaven, his rightful place. I confess some strong sympathy for the man. Please leave that out of your report to Pilate. I saw Jesus perform a miracle before he died. Just by touching a crippled man's head, he made him walk. And my own brother, who died by this hand," he said, raising his strong giant hand holding the mutton leg bone, as if to reprimand the appendage. "My brother appeared to me in a vision, saying, 'Jesus is the Christ and died for your sins, brother. He has forgiven you for what you did to me. I forgive you too. See, he stands by me, here in Elysium.' " Saltaurius sighed like a man after a rotten tooth is pulled out. "Oh, the peace that came over me, seeing them together in heaven and hearing those words from my fallen brother after all these years of torment. I am guilty of killing my brother but now am forgiven." He looked upward, a half-crazed smile on his face. "Thank you, Jesus, for this vision," Saltaurius sang out in his deep bass voice. "Thank you, Christ, who has risen!"

Marcus thought he must have been drinking a lot of wine with his mutton.

Marcus knew of people who had visions caused by eating the wrong plants or fungus or otherwise suffering from a mild poisoning by food or drink, sometimes intentionally concocted by the local inhabitants for Roman consumption. But now that he had his own vision of Jesus, he wondered if some visions could be true while others were false.

Poet started to speak, but Marcus spoke first. "So you seek a man you now worship? To kill him or return him to be killed again?"

"No and yes," Saltaurius said. "I seek him only to prove to myself he died and is now in heaven with my brother. Died for my sins. I believe all else is hysterical hearsay. Seeing the man here, there, and everywhere. After my vision I know that cannot be, or perhaps he can now descend and ascend at will." Saltaurius laughed, although Marcus was reminded of something similar the old Essene had said about Jesus's appearances after the cross. "Now they say a man named Issa, or Jesus, heads east. I will find this fraud and behead him. If he bears sufficient likeness, I'll receive my payment for his head. The Jews will be happy with a head of a look-alike fraud." Saltaurius held up his goblet to the sky before putting it to his lips and drinking its contents down.

Marcus knew what Poet was dying to ask, but he thought it better if he took the risk and asked, "How and why, noble sir, did you come to slay your own brother?"

"I might have killed a man a month ago for asking that, but since my vision and the words of forgiveness from my brother—who could only know of this Jesus from the heavens—I may now tell you that story. This will be the first time I've spoken of it after burying it for so many years."

Poet straightened his back and asked for more wine. The wine was the best they'd had since Alexandria. While Saltaurius stood, Marcus gave Poet a wink. Marcus was also eager to hear what promised to be a dramatic tale. All Romans were fixated on fratricide from an early age. The founding story of Rome tells of Romulus killing his brother Remus over where to build the city. Romulus then built Rome with slaves while slaughtering the men, raping the women, and plundering the treasure of neighboring city-states. After planting the seed and columns of the empire, he ascended like a god to join Mars in heaven as his reward. No wonder Poet loved Greece.

"Leave us," Saltaurius instructed the few men and dancing women who were on the stage and within earshot. They promptly obeyed. Dio rubbed his bald head vigorously and gave Poet a creepy smile. He looked delighted to hear the story of fratricide.

Saltaurius began, "It was on my sixteenth birthday. My father, an ex-legionnaire, had become a famous gladiator trainer. He had trained us—my brother and I—from the time we could hold a sword. My brother was eighteen and his star seed. Faster and brighter than anyone I'd ever met. An Achilles that no one but a brother could kill. We often fought viciously with wooden swords for the pleasure of my father. Bashing each other about. I was always on the losing end, though my brother always showed mercy by not beating me as hard as my father wanted. Sometimes my father beat my brother for his failure to draw blood. By sixteen, I almost matched my brother's size and strength. On my birthday, my father presented me with a steel sword. Training gladiators had given my father a blood lust." He rapped his fist upon his head, knocking hard on the door of his memory. "He told my brother to pick up the steel sword he had received two years before. 'Now, you both fight as men for the first time,' my father said. I loved my brother with all my heart, but desired nothing more than to please my father."

Marcus momentarily put his head in his hands. Poet groaned.

" 'You can't mean to the death?' my brother asked, which might have landed him a blow from my father for insubordination. But he only clarified the terms of the brotherly battle. 'Not death but till one of you yields. The victor will accompany me to Rome and assist me in training gladiators at the Ludas Magnus for the fights in the arena. And we will stay to see the *munera,* where lesser men die and true warriors triumph. The losing brother will shovel shit for the horses until we return.' My brother loved me as much, or more, than I did him. But we both would rather die than yield. Years of practice fighting with the wooden swords would allow us to put on a good show for our father."

Saltaurius walked around his audience, dragging a foot in the sand and sawdust on the floor of the stage as he said, "My father made a circle around us as big as a large Bedouin tent-site, like this. And then he mounted his horse to watch us fight like two young gladiators in his makeshift ring. We put on our armor and helmets. I raised my new sword, holding it up high to glisten in the midday sun; I knew what it meant to be a man. I still remember the scent of my brother's sweat as he embraced me to whisper in my ear, 'Just make it look good and only side blows to the body or helmet.'

"Two boys playing such a deadly game," Poet interjected. Marcus wasn't sure if the tale moved him or if he was simply feigning sympathy. He found himself strangely drawn into the dark story, imagining how it had gutted the beast's young heart.

" 'No kissing!' my father commanded from his mount. 'You are men, my sons. Enter the center, and I will call out the start of the fight. Rome awaits the winner. Blood to blood!' "

A glassy look came over Saltaurius's eyes as he took his seat. He seemed entranced, as though back on that field two decades ago. He dropped the remnants of the mutton leg and picked up a dagger from the table. It seemed he was not so much threatening others as himself. Marcus, who prided himself on keeping an even keel, leaned in to hear the story with heart pounding. He was thinking of Boy, who had just turned sixteen. He stole a glance at Poet, who was too enthralled to blink or drink.

"I wanted to be his favorite. I wanted to go to Rome. I wanted to see gladiators die in the colosseum. And I was determined not to yield, no matter how long the fight took. I wanted to honor my father and my new sword. The fight started like our play with wooden swords, but now it was steel clashing instead of wood. My father's cheers turned into jeers as we weren't landing any damaging blows. My brother gave me a look, indicating we needed to make it look more real and start hitting the armor with the blade. We played this dangerous game, fiercely whacking each other's bodies. To appease my father's cheers and taunts, the ferocity grew until my brother landed the side of his sword across my helmet, knocking it off and me off my feet. Blood was streaming down my face and into my eyes. Something clicked inside me. An animal instinct. A demon arose, gripping my throat and mind. I swung blindly and wildly at my brother. Time stood still. I heard him gurgling on his own blood and then the thud as he fell beside me. Before I could clear my blood-soaked eyes, he was dead. My virgin sword had sliced him clean across the neck. He had let his guard down to come to tend to me."

Marcus knew Poet would record the story later. Since it was a consensual fight, Marcus didn't believe any Roman law had been broken, but surely the gods frowned on fratricide, though they were always killing one another.

"An instant later, my father is off his horse, rushing to kill me." Marcus wondered if it was also a story of patricide. "Swift retribution and deservedly so. I fell to my knees and lowered my head, hoping for a clean blow. But instead, he lifted me to my feet and raised my arm. 'Victor! The victor! The victor shall have no regrets,' my father cried out. 'I taught him better than to let his sword drop in the midst of a fight. You won the day and will travel with me to Rome tomorrow after we bury the loser.' That was how he last referred to my gallant brother. The loser." Saltaurius looked up to the stars and continued, "We never spoke of you again, my brother, though you haunted my dreams. It was as if my father had never had a firstborn son, or me a brother. And I had never killed you. I still love you. Thank you for coming to grant me my redemption."

He stood, shaking off the spellbinding memory. Saltaurius looked for his audience to speak. He turned to Dio. "Dio was there. He saw it. Dio advised my father before me."

Dio smiled, recalling the gruesome day and at being acknowledged as spectator to the event that had made the big boy a tortured man. Marcus sympathized with the Roman bull for his Greek tragedy. Fratricide was a heavy burden for any man, let alone a teenage boy.

Dio broke his silence and said, "And he has won every battle since, as I am his witness. And he still bears the sword and wields it in a way no foe's flesh can resist a taste of its blazing blade." He took a sip of his drink after regurgitating Pilate's prophecy in a nauseating way.

Marcus took mercy on the man and said, "So many Romans kill each other for honor and family. Your story describes you as just another victim of Roman gladiator culture. Any fault belongs to your father, or his father before him."

Saltaurius grabbed at his sword like he might raise it to fight Marcus for speaking ill of his father. He looked over at Dio, as if asking permission to add another victory to Orion's belt. Dio looked placidly back at him and shrugged his pointed shoulders. Saltaurius drank down his wine and walked a couple steps to empty his overripe bladder with his big aqueduct off the side of the stage, enjoying the stream's flow into the sands below.

After relieving himself, he returned, saying, "You can see why my brother's words of forgiveness meant so much to me. Now, if you will excuse us, I have some words to share with Marcus in private. For his ears alone. A secret Rome would not want you to know and would kill me for sharing with you." Saltaurius commanded. "You two philosophers should give us a moment. Go have some highbrow discussion." Dio was watching a snake charmer who had set up his act close to the stage. Poet was also keeping one eye on the dangerous spectacle.

"I'll warn you, Dio. He loves all things Greek," Marcus said. He knew Poet would rather be thrown to the lions than have a tête-à-tête with the lurking counselor. But it was Poet's task to assess the advice being given by this strange counselor to his master. Dio seemed reluctant but nodded his assent while fixing an entreating grin and leering eyes on Poet.

Dio pointed a long, crooked finger back to the snake, its hood now extended a mere foot in front of the flute-playing charmer's face. As soon as the flute stopped playing, the snake's hood folded, and the long body dropped back into the straw basket like a cord being cut. The turbaned flutist shut the top of the basket, ending the show.

"Poet? You can breathe now. The snake's been put to bed," Marcus called to him. "I mentioned your love of Greek culture, and you don't speak?"

Poet rose to defend his Greek fetish. "All well-educated Romans appreciate the great Greek thinkers and poets," he said. "All our art and architecture we owe to the Greeks. We even stole their gods and branded them with Roman names. There's no Rome without Greece. Our sole distinction was to promote Mars—the god of war, murder, and bloodshed—and make him protector of Rome. The great Greeks relegated their god of war and murder, Ares. His own parents loathed Ares as a hateful coward."

Dio made no speech before they moved aside to have their philosophical wrestling match, while the head men spoke of secrets that even their trusted advisors were not allowed to hear.

CHAPTER 12
The Bazaar of Babylon

WHILE MARCUS AND Poet were being entertained by Saltaurius and the goblin, Boy finished his duties at the Arabian guest house and stables. He worried whether his master and Uncle Poet would return unharmed. Dio had left him in such a state of fear that he felt unmanly. He also didn't like being excluded. He was growing out of being a boy and slave.

With all his chores complete, he walked to a bazaar in the center of town to clear his head.

As he stepped out into the great circular open-air market of Babylon, the world itself swirled around him. The Silk Road paused here, much like a spot where two mighty rivers meet, one heading west and the other heading east. His life was carrying him along the east-bound river, from his childhood Morocco to Alexandria, where he became a young man, to Jerusalem, and now into this foreign land. The course of his river was picking up speed. His full manhood approached like too much sap coursing through a blooming tree.

The bazaar was a melting pot composed of many churning pots from all over the world. A pot of commerce—people were buying and selling silk, silver, and spice alongside porcelain, ponies, and people. A pot of skin colors—all races and ethnicities from ash white to black night and everything in between gathered there. A pot of ideas—debates about life and death and good and bad. A pot of religions—some were worshipping one and others worshipping many gods. A pot of languages—the cacophony of sounds was aided by hand gestures to aid communication. A twirling pot, spinning out smells, sights, and sounds, all woven into a grand tapestry of man.

In the center of it all, in the center of this universe, in the center of the bazaar, in the center of his being—in a place along the Silk Road called Babylon—Boy decided it was his time to become a man. Innocence had served its purpose, but now he craved experience.

He observed the entire menagerie, absorbing the scene like a thirsty man in a desert downpour. He was about to pass out from the sensory overload when he was jostled by the stump of an arm that belonged to an old man who looked like he had traveled from some far distant Eastern country where people's eyes were oval and skin the color of the sun. The man had only one arm. He smiled in apology for rousing Boy from his reverie. His ancient eyes were still glittering and gay. Boy felt a rush of kinship with the disabled man who had come from the opposite direction, as if he was meeting his future self. The man's missing arm reminded him of his missing mother, which could never to be replaced. Boy suddenly was aware of the suffering he'd previously overlooked. The suffering was everywhere—in the shadows around the edges of the rich and colorful marketplace. There was an orphan girl dressed in rags and reclining in the dirt with a begging bowl. It looked like a strong wind might carry her away. A flower stunted in its growth, never able to rise from the ground that was already calling her back to dust. There was a muscular ebony slave being led by a leash around his neck to the auction block. Propped up against a clay wall was a dead or dead drunk man who may have fallen from the moon, judging by his contorted body. People gave his bare feet, which were covered in oozing sores, a wide berth. Plagues and leprosy traveled along the Silk Road too. Suffering and death were everywhere once one opened their eyes to it.

A beautiful little child of about twelve, so fair it was hard to tell whether it was a boy or girl, like Aphrodite straddling the sexes, tugged at Boy's sleeve. The child led him to a stall where billowing silk captured the twilight and made it more brilliant and brighter in the soft evening breeze. The colorful patterns were vibrant enough to make one's eyes spin. The merchant gave the child a morsel of hard cheese and sent it back out to look for more customers. Boy's Roman dress, small purse, and big sword had made him a target for peddlers.

"Come, touch," the man said, as Boy looked at the robes, scarves, and shawls swaying in the wind. He gawked at a garment whose silk was so sheer and transparent. *A lady's undergarment?* he wondered, imagining a girl's nakedness half-hidden under the shimmering silk. "Come, touch. Countless caterpillars perished for this wondrous touch of butterfly wings," the man said with a wide smile. "Come, touch. You have good taste. They call it a slip because it so easily goes on and even more easily comes off." His teeth seemed too large for his mouth. "Come, touch." He held out the silk slip that Boy had been eyeing and draped the delicate silk over Boy's outstretched hands. Boy tenderly and eagerly caressed the wisp of a fabric. His hands were accustomed to the rawhide of his reins, saddles, and horses. It felt like the smooth skin of a virgin girl, a sensation he could only imagine. Handing it back like the flash of silk had burned him, he blushed, stumbling away without a word.

Now, all he saw was the beauty of the bazaar. The wonders of humanity and its art. Arrayed before him was a pageant, people acting out parts of a play, so he might understand the intersection of passion and expression. A woman sang like a Persian nightingale, pleading for the sun's return at dawn. There were tapestries, urns, and golden copper goblets with scenes of lovemaking and the carnage of war. There was a marble statue of a winged horse with a man's head and beard. Everywhere was art and beauty and silk. There were stout, well-dressed men with big ornate knives and pearl-adorned purses accompanied by beautiful ladies behind thin veils. The feel of silk still lingered on his hands and draped his heart.

Babylon's bazaar, at the crossroads of innocence and experience, displayed suffering and death alongside beauty and life in equal measures.

A young girl with a painted face and sparkles on her nearly fully exposed breasts beckoned him from a doorway to another world. "Come and be a man with me." Tempted and terrified, Boy jerked away from her outstretched hand. He apologetically tipped his head and fled.

Black night fell fast upon Babylon as Boy ran back to their lodging to wait for Marcus and Poet, fearing they might have been bludgeoned by the giant or poisoned by the imp.

Chapter 13
Philosophy

Poet and Dio sat on opposite ends of a wobbly wooden bench. They straddled the wood, facing one another like children on a seesaw. Poet wanted to keep a safe distance from the ghoul. Dio's eyes seemed permanently bloodshot, and he had a habit of licking his dry, chapped lips until they appeared ready to bleed. He stared unblinkingly at Poet, waiting for him to start their philosophical discussion or to pass out from his withering gaze. Poet grasped the bench to avoid falling off. A splinter pierced his right index finger, and he was trying to remove it when Dio spoke. "Tell me about that slave boy that travels with you," he said in a sweet childlike voice that entered Poet's ear like another splinter.

"You gave him quite the fright earlier," Poet said. "I don't want you speaking to him. Any harm to him is harm to me and Marcus. Mistreat him, and you will be doubly mistreated."

"Are you threatening *me*? We played a game, that's all. Tell me about him."

"I'd rather not."

"What happened to his family?"

"None of your business."

"He said his mother is missing."

"He said that?"

"Yes. Couldn't Marcus, the great tribune and manhunter, find his own slave's mother? Or was he too busy to look for his precious slave-son's mother?"

"Yes, he tried! Did everything possible. But unlike a slave, who is a spoil of war, where records are kept, men impersonating Roman soldiers stole her in the night. Cowards who didn't leave any names or trace. It disturbs Marcus greatly. His one unsolved case—but no more of that."

Dio had taken him off track. His task was to understand the enigmatic man and what guidance he would supply Saltaurius. He should start with basic metaphysics. "Do you prefer Roman or Greek philosophers and culture?"

"Not to offend your love of all things Athenian and its exclusive citizenship," Dio said, "but I think Rome is much more pragmatic in its embrace of power and what it takes to keep it. Greece is now just a territory of Rome. We can claim her history and culture as our own and make their worthy men citizens of Rome. The Roman Empire is the greatest achievement of man, and I make no apologies."

Poet thought, *The lap dog might become counselor to the emperor but for his poor breeding and manners.*

"What do you think defines Roman virtue and honor?" Poet asked.

"They move in lockstep with their gods in discipline, duty, and hierarchy."

A classically trained answer.

"And Roman slavery and cruelty?"

"Greece had slaves and Spartan savagery. All men are slaves," Dio said. He sounded like Marcus. "Hierarchy governs both gods and men. Tiers upon tiers, from Heaven to Hades, with angels to demons and all levels of men in between. All either serve those above or they are cast out of good Roman society—sometimes to find their head upon a spike, which deters other rebels from causing havoc."

This man, thought Poet, *could be a senator speaking in favor of the empire and the slaves that built it.* "It sounds like you're not in favor of the republic and Greek democracy. You favor an all-powerful Caesar?"

"Of course, we need order and hierarchy. Otherwise, there will be barbarian anarchy. This is the driving force behind the empire's mission to bring order to the world. And the emperor's divine right to bring order to the empire."

He speaks of a power devoid of love, thought Poet. "Our human nature craves liberty alongside order and security," Poet said. "But let's move away from your reverence of Rome and Mars, its great protector. What do you think of this Jesus we seek, dead or alive?" Poet sat up more erectly upon the log for a height advantage over his slouched competition.

With his long, sharp-nailed fingers, Dio twisted his knife in its sheath by his side while licking his cracked lips. He still did not blink. Poet then realized what was so shocking about this man's appearance. He had no eyebrows or lashes, like a gray, hairless cat. Dio smiled and looked into Poet's eyes, seemingly glad to be seen. "This Jesus, they say, only believes in one God, like the Hebrews, but also says all men can find the kingdom within," he said. "I see scant evidence of that. Perhaps one God with many faces and temperaments. But his kingdom is above and not within men. *Within* men is his punishment. Damned by our original sin."

"Is that what you believe?" Poet asked.

"I believe in suffering and death. These are self-evident in the world. Rely on your experience not belief."

The devil was not averse to speaking partial truth when it served him. "Do you believe it is possible that Jesus still lives?" Poet asked.

"No."

"Why not?"

"He is a saint, and all saints are dead. He is not the son of God. No more than you and I are."

"You should get ointment for those chafed lips of yours."

"To moisten, so you might kiss?" Dio laughed.

"Let them bleed, for all I care," Poet said, feeling revulsed. "What would you do if you found Jesus alive before Marcus does?"

"We will do whatever my master wills us to do."

"But what will you advise him to do? He listens to you."

"As I said, a saint cannot live."

"So you would kill him?" Poet asked.

"Not me."

"Your advice would be to kill him?"

"How can one kill the dead? It is impossible. And if he lives, he is merely a man. I do not deal in hypotheticals."

"Your philosophy is the sophistry of circular reason," Poet said, feeling a little dizzy. He blamed the splinter in his finger, though he knew it was the thorn in his side.

For no apparent reason, Dio made circles with the thumb and index finger of both hands and placed over each eye like glass lenses used to magnify things. The gesture made him look like a bug-eyed bat. Its effect was more frightening than comical. With his finger-circles still around his eyes, he said, "All philosophy is the art of sophistry. Do not deceive yourself and think you will find truth with a cascade of questions, unless you ask the one question you really want to know," he said, peering into Poet's soul.

"What is that?" Poet asked, looking down at the log between their legs to avoid the silly man and his framed eyes. And he picked at the splinter in his finger that seemed to only move deeper.

"So I can see you better. I see your life leading to death." He ceased the spectacle and placed his hands back on his lap, interlacing his long, crooked fingers.

"No, *what is that*—the question I really want to know?"

"Who am I?"

"Who are you?" Poet asked. And really wondered if Dio was some dark demigod with his stunted physical appearance mated with some higher intelligence.

"No, who am I?" Dio responded.

This silly philosophical joust and the ghoul's glare of superiority irritated Poet.

"But I'll tell you who I am," Dio continued. "I am human nature that suffers and dies. In a circle of life and death, one must either kill or be killed—living in fear of death and the oblivion of one's own self. I am *every man* trapped within this skull and body."

"You know thyself very well."

"Yes, wise Socrates."

"Well, then, let's end this with your compliment to my philosophical prowess," Poet said. "It appears Marcus is ready to go."

Marcus was standing and looked impatient to leave. The bench remained horizontal to the ground, as neither side had won.

"I can get nowhere with you," Poet said, though he thought he'd learned a great deal about the icy heart and cold calculus of his nemesis.

As they returned to the inn, Poet told Marcus what he had learned. "He's a student of Cicero's skepticism, taken to new depths of depravity, and will spin that bull's head in any direction that points to narcissism and death."

Marcus nodded, but seemed to be lost in his thoughts. He refused to say what secret Saltaurius had shared, other than they would all rise early, and Boy and Poet would continue east and wait for him in Arak. He would meet them there in a week. While they continued following Issa east, Marcus would travel off their path to the north to Al Kut, where there was a small Roman presence.

That night, after having trouble falling to sleep, Poet dreamed of a horned viper snake biting him on the throat. Despite being indoors, he got up to place his horsehair rope around his matting. The room at the guest house was on the ground floor. He couldn't get back to sleep and kept thinking about Dio's dark philosophy and how Saltaurius might have distracted Marcus from their course. What could be more important than their mission to restore honor to the House of Decia by finding the self-proclaimed son of God?

CHAPTER 14
Rhagae

FARTHER EAST ALONG the Silk Road, in a town called Rhagae, Bhakti and Ma received some miraculous news. The man they sought, the Hebrew messiah named Issa, lived in the town and spoke each dawn of miracles and the giving away of worldly possessions as one's true service to God.

Bhakti was elated. What wonderful synchronicity that they should head west to meet him, not knowing he was heading east. And his master and her master would now meet in the middle. God works in such wondrous ways!

They woke while it was still dark to meditate and then rushed to the place where Issa met his devotees and pilgrims at dawn.

The man called Issa sat high on a dais, in the center square of town, to speak to a gathering crowd. When the sun was fully above the horizon, he stood to preach. At the end of his sermon, one by one the audience stepped up to make an offering in exchange for answers to their soul-searching questions.

There was a tear on Ma's face as she stood with Bhakti at a distance from the dais, observing the religious ceremony. Her reaction confused Bhakti. She was not joyful, but saddened at the end of their long, arduous journey. He knew her bliss, and this was not that. He would drink her tears like holy water, but these tears were not for him. Her aura turned shades of blue and black, as illuminated by the dawn sun. She looked like Kali, the goddess of destruction, ready to take flight and torch the town, or at least the square.

He assumed her reaction could only have been in response to hearing about Issa being brutally crucified by the Romans in Jerusalem.

Bhakti was encouraged as Ma composed herself and wiped away her tears with the sleeve of her sari. He moved to speak, but she held up her hand and gave him a smile. She was content to watch her old friend from a distance.

Issa sat crossed-legged in a golden robe near the edge of the dais. People had lined up to kneel at his feet and ask their questions. He raised his arm and spun it above him. As his hand emerged from his sleeve, Bhakti could see that he was holding something into his fist. The man at Issa's feet wore a fine plum-colored linen robe and a darker plum-colored silk belt and headscarf. Issa's sprinkled ash on the man's head, a manifestation—a small miracle and blessing—that made the crowd gasp.

The kneeling man bowed and put a coin in a donation box placed next to Issa. He asked the holy man above him, "If you are the son of God and were put to death on the cross, where are the wounds on your hands and feet, and where are the marks of the Roman lash, and spear, and spikes you claim to have endured?"

A dissenting murmur arose from the crowd. The flaxen-robed Issa raised and flapped his arms. He looked like a golden bird about to take flight from his dais perch. With silence restored, he said, "Have you not answered your own question? You all know of the miracles I have demonstrated. If I am a god, what is it to heal some wounds for one who can return from the dead?"

The crowd hummed in approval of the wise answer, but the kneeling man dared to ask another question. "Then why not show us a small miracle now, so that we may believe?"

Issa just smiled and remained still and silent until the man placed another coin in the box. "Thank you for the offering for the poor," he said. "But did I not just produce ash and place it on your head? Again, you have your own answer. If coming back to life isn't sufficient, what lesser miracle would you believe? Do you not accept the ash as one?" Issa bowed his head to the arrogant man before him. He then stood and offered the man his hand, guiding him onto the dais. "By returning to this body, I henceforth renounce all miracles, so you may focus on the living God, the miracle of miracles, and not on simple magic tricks. Your Eastern yogis can walk on water, but a boat is faster."

Bhakti wondered why Ma had not yet approached her old friend. And tears again fell down her cheek. He imagined an olive tree growing from the sacred water on that holy ground where they landed. *The news of Jesus's death on the cross and resurrection was new to them and had upset Ma greatly,* he thought.

Ma abruptly turned to leave, saying simply with a sad smile, "It's not him."

CHAPTER 15
Al Kut

AFTER A LONG, hard ride, Marcus arrived before sunset in the small village of Al Kut. He removed his tribune ring and put it in his pocket. He found the Roman officer he sought drinking alone in a small, dilapidated establishment made of stone and with a thatched roof that was more hovel than tavern. The Roman soldier looked glad to see Marcus. There were four tables placed around a dry dirt floor. Small windows barely let light in, so candles already were lit. The ceiling was just high enough for Marcus to stand up straight without hitting his head. He considered leaving his helmet on for this meeting.

"Welcome fellow Roman officer!" the soldier and sole patron of the establishment said. "What brings you so far from Rome to this godforsaken place? I was sent here to be as far from our glorious home, forgotten, as my reward for serving my emperor. But I piss and moan. May you buy me a drink? The ale tastes like hops wrung out of a dirty loincloth, but the wine's spice overpowers its poor taste. I recommend it."

Marcus pointed to the Roman's mug, raising two fingers to the proprietor who sat squat on a mat, performing his pagan prayers. The man, with his head wrapped in cloth, brought a jug and another clay mug to their table, filling both mugs.

Marcus removed his helmet as he sat. Grinning, he asked, "Flavius? Where are your men?"

"Yes, I am Flavius. Once of Caesar's noble imperial guard now scouting for riches in the hinterlands. All but banished for doing my duty. Just three of my men accompany me, but I demand they stay sober, at least during the day, even in this godless place. They encamp down the road, and are probably playing Tali, with one always standing guard, in case of trouble. And you are?"

"A truth-seeker and wine-buyer."

Flavius nodded energetically, glad to have Marcus, a high-ranking Roman legionnaire buying him drinks.

"I may know of you. You mentioned being part of the emperor's guard in Rome before, is that right?" Marcus asked.

"That I was! And now, for my loyal service, I am trolling around this barren, sand-blasted Mesopotamian countryside with my small band of men, mapping and spying for the empire, risking getting our throats cut if we ever sleep all at once. Al Kut is as good as any place around here to rest and refresh oneself." He saluted Marcus with his drink, and Marcus signaled for another. "But what brings you an officer here and all alone? May I know your name and rank?" Flavius's tone and face were starting to show concern.

As the proprietor poured more spiced wine, Marcus asked, "May I show you something, the real reason I came to Al Kut?"

Flavius nodded his head, but furrowed his brow. "Sure. The person who buys can speak as much as he likes. But what is your name, friend?"

Marcus stood, drew his freshly sharpened sword, and held it to Flavius's throat. Flavius didn't flinch.

"You must be wondering why you are about to die?"

"Yes," Flavius said, "don't all men fear a pointless death?" He still didn't blink. Marcus wished he was a coward and begging for mercy, as that would make his job easier.

"I am Tribune Marcus Antonius Augustus Decia. I think you knew my family in Rome before you slaughtered them?" Marcus reached his left hand into his pocket and slipped his tribune ring back on. He held it out to Flavius, but he didn't kiss the symbol of his authority.

Instead, Flavius threw his hands up in the air, causing Marcus to grip on his sword tightly with both hands. "I surrender. But I was only doing my duty. They attempted to assassinate Caesar. They were harboring two slaves they had paid to do the deed. The slaves managed to murder two of my emperor's guards in a failed coup attempt. I was sent with my men to track them and followed the trail of blood and money to your family's home. The slaves confessed to Senator Decia's plot before they were all put to death by the emperor's orders. In a post-mortem trial, they condemned your family for treason. Since you were abroad, fighting bravely for the empire, they spared you. And I understood you may have been innocent of the conspiracy—until now."

"You lie. Good, that will make it easier to kill you. I've heard that story. That is what the world believes. If my family wanted to attempt a coup, they would have fared better to wait until I had returned to Rome with my legion of men. But it is all a lie. I knew my father, mother, and wife. They may have disagreed with the emperor on his slave policy and his demagoguery in the Senate, but they would never commit treason. Place your palms face up on the table. To tell the truth or die."

Flavius hesitated, and Marcus moved the tip of the sword a few inches closer to his neck. "Listen," he said, "if you tell the truth, there is a way you may still live."

Flavius placed his palm upturned on the table as instructed.

"Halt!" Marcus commanded the proprietor, who was shuffling toward the hovel's door. "Sit!" Marcus demanded, pointing to the mat. He didn't want the man escaping to warn Flavius's men.

The man sat and started weeping.

"Silence!" Marcus ordered. The man kept bobbing his head, still crying or praying, but silently.

"Now, Flavius, tell me the truth. It's hard for dishonorable liars to believe others tell the truth as a matter of honor. But here we are. Perhaps you are unfamiliar with my skill in detecting lies. But the choice is simple. You will tell the truth or die lying. I will let you draw your sword and fight for your life, if you tell me the truth of how and why my family was murdered." Flavius looked confused, so Marcus explained further the benefits of his deal. "If you slay me, then your secret will die with me. Or, having told the truth, you will die with honor in battle," Marcus said. "The decision is yours."

Marcus then nodded for him to return his hands to their palm-up position.

"I will be put to death for the truth," Flavius said.

"Not if you kill me. No one will know. That man on the floor doesn't understand us and doesn't look like he'll be in Rome anytime soon."

"I was just following orders," Flavius repeated. He swallowed hard and pursed his lips. Marcus could see the truth coming from him. "I've told the other story so many times. I almost came to believe it is true. History will so record it. Facing this truth is difficult, especially in your presence. When duty calls for the killing of innocents . . . the horror of it."

"Truth will set you free. Come now and ease your mind," Marcus said, offering encouragement. "I'm here for truth not judgment."

"May the gods forgive me. The emperor's secretary caught two guards under my command in a compromising situation. The location, an imperial study, was more damning than the act itself. You're a soldier. You know its commonness in the field, but not in the imperial palace. My men were caught with their pricks out and couldn't deny it. My orders were to behead them. Still, I begged for mercy for them from the emperor's praetorian commander, Naevius Macro, who consulted that wicked pup Caligula. He concocted a plan to turn their illicit fornication into his gain. He's a cunning and conniving politician. Caligula was not a fan of your father. He didn't like hearing about the need to free slaves and a return to a republic. Since his controlling mother, Livia, died and Sejanus betrayed him, Tiberius Caesar, while lounging in Capri, allowed Caligula free rein to take care of anyone, or anything, that threatened their imperial agenda."

Marcus had admired Tiberius as a military leader, but as emperor, he had proved weak and easily led astray by others.

Flavius continued, "I was instructed to arm two strong eunuch slaves so they could kill the offending guards, who were bound and gagged. And then the unwitting slaves were told to report to your family home to be reassigned and rewarded by your family for their service. They carried a sealed message from the emperor himself to give to your father in order to gain entry. Macro and Caligula had seen to this. How much Tiberius Caesar knew is not clear."

"He is responsible for his actions," Marcus said, "and cannot hide behind Macro's and Caligula's twisted robes. But when this hypocritical Caesar pays his debt, they shall too. May I or the gods see to it," he declared, pounding his fist into his chest.

"I doubt that," Flavius said. "Caligula will be the next emperor, and the story of your family's treason will be etched in stone. Soldiers and slaves don't write histories." Marcus glared at Flavius, who added, "But perhaps you will find a way to right the wrong."

"And then the slaves went to the House of Decia?" Marcus asked.

"Yes, and I followed, accompanied by four men with orders to kill the slaves that had murdered two of the imperial guards but failed to gain access to kill Caesar. And then, my orders were to kill the traitorous cell of your family who had planned the coup—to nip the rebellion in the bud. In just two hours Caligula's plan played out like a bad dream. I assure you; I was just following orders. I have always done my duty. There you have it. That is the whole truth, and may you go to Hades and be buggered by Vulcan there if you don't honor your promise to fight me like a Roman officer."

Marcus stood from the table to render his judgment of whether the story was fact or fiction. "You have no reason to tell that story if it was a lie. Stand and fight."

As Flavius pushed back from the table, the proprietor darted out of the hovel. Marcus calculated he had just a couple of minutes before Flavius's men would reach the door. No time to wear down his foe with a long fight.

They already wore light mesh metal armor over their tunics, but they both grabbed their helmets from the table and covered their heads. A Roman officer sword fight was really a quite civilized affair with strictly established codes of conduct.

Flavius held up his hand and said, "Wait. I owe you this much for not killing me without a fight." It seemed like he was stalling to give his men time to come to his rescue. Flavius reached into his tunic and took out a small square of folded parchment. Marcus recognized the Emperor's broken seal. "I swore I burned this at the scene, but I kept it here by my breast with me all these years in case they changed their story and tried to blame me for your family's deaths. But rather than blame me, they made me disappear— sent by Macro to these foreign lands to die in obscurity. Some poetic justice, eh, you finding me here? This is the letter announcing the slaves and commanding them into the safekeeping of Senator Decia. Caligula loved the irony of sending your father slaves with blood still on their hands to become the evidence of your family's treason. This is that letter, signed and sealed by Caesar." He placed it on the table in front of him and drew his sword.

"To the death," Flavius said

"To the death," Marcus repeated.

They both swung their swords to clash. The fight was on. The low ceiling made overhand swings impossible. All Marcus's training was now limited to thrusts and swinging sideways. After several thrusts and ineffectual swings met by Flavius's sword, Flavius hid behind the center beam. He shifted left to right to counter Marcus's movements. They circled the wooden post for thirty seconds. Flavius was buying time for his men to arrive.

"Fight like a man!" Marcus commanded. "Or let's move this fight outside." Running out of time, Marcus hacked his way around the beam, swinging his sword left and right at his opponent and blocking his opponent's jabs. Hunks of wood flew from the beam as both swords struck it. Marcus felt only elation—no fear. With death so near, there was only a single-minded desire to kill and live. Flavius's men entered the tavern just as Marcus hacked fully through the beam protecting Flavius. Time slowed as Marcus watched the men draw their swords. Despite the odds, he was not prepared to die in a hovel in Al Kut.

But what happened next took Marcus by surprise.

"Stop! Stand by," Flavius commanded his men. "This is not your fight."

"You're an honorable man," Marcus said to the man that had massacred his family and unborn child.

"To the death!" Flavius shouted.

Marcus answered with a mighty chop of his sword. Flavius blocked it with his weapon. A large plank of the ceiling above the fallen support beam cracked down on Marcus's helmet, making him stumble backward. Flavius charged. Marcus dropped to his knees and held out his sword. Flavius's momentum took him right into Marcus's sword, clear through his mesh and into his heart. He died in an instant.

Marcus stood to confront the men at the door. He assumed command as the ranking officer. "He died with honor." The tribune pulled his sword out of the dead man's chest, which made the familiar sucking sound finished by a smack. A sound Roman soldiers called the giant's wet kiss. "See he gets a proper burial. Say only that he bravely fought to the death with another Roman officer following the military code." He waved his bloody sword in front of them as he spoke, hoping they would not notice his tribune's ring on the other hand. "None of you saw or heard the cause of the quarrel."

He picked up his damaged helmet and the letter with the broken imperial seal and left, brushing past the men. Breathing heavily, Marcus took his horse to water, resting his bruised head a few moments before riding off. Nightfall was near, and he had no time to waste.

The letter he now bore was held by his father shortly before his death. They would deny it as a forgery back in Rome. The letter alone would not bring the emperor and his conniving partners to justice, but it would go a long way in clearing his family's name. He would have to challenge Caesar to a duel to get to Macro and Caligula for his full measure of revenge. But Caesar would probably not accept the challenge and sentence him to death. Rome rarely crucified Romans, but they just might make an exception in his case.

CHAPTER 16
Arak

POET COULD FINALLY draw a deep breath when he saw Marcus on his horse, galloping up to their tidy camp inside the Arak village walls just as the horizon swallowed the sun. Boy took the reins of his master's exhausted horse. Poet was ready for Boy to chastise Marcus for riding his horse too hard, but Boy only shook his head and smiled. "I'm glad you've made it back," he said, leading the horse away to cool it down.

"The House of Decia returns to us," Poet said, also grateful to see Marcus again. Poet knew the wild look in Marcus's eyes. He had come from a fight. But there was more. Those eyes had purpose again. "Now you must confess your desertion to us," he said, "and let us judge if it was justified."

"When we are all settled around the fire, you will hear the story of the return of the House of Decia."

"Sounds like an epic. While you make me wait," Poet said, "I too have news to share with you. Issa is ministering in a town called Rhagae. It's a three-days ride from where we stand."

"Good fortune has found us. Some wine to celebrate!" Marcus said in joyful proclamation.

Poet was eager to celebrate Marcus's return and filled three cups. They seated themselves by the campfire and waited for Boy to join them.

"Boy is light enough," Marcus said. "We could send him ahead. If he rides Sahara into the dark, he could make it there in just two days not three. Where is this Rhagae? Show me on the map."

Marcus was back in command of himself and his men. Heartened, Poet unrolled the map. "Here it is, some ninety miles east of here."

Boy returned from tending to Marcus's horse and stoked the fire. "Boy," Marcus said, "I've got an important mission for you to assure our magician doesn't disappear again. Before dawn, I'll wake you up, and you'll ride for twelve hours each day to Rhagae. Your job is to ensure the miracle man doesn't escape."

"Sahara will be hard pressed on such a ride. Your horse was only a couple more miles of hard riding from death today. Your horse needs to recover. My apologies, it is not my place to question an order and the honor of a mission. And I too want to see this Jesus. But what if I arrive, and he moves to leave? Do I try to stop him?" Boy's eyes were lit too. They had caught Marcus's fire. Poet's heart was singing, and he didn't know why.

"You will think of something. Don't let him see you in a Roman tunic and carrying that sword, or he will run for sure. Perhaps scatter his donkeys, or tell him you need to be cured of the wasting disease. You're thin enough and his biggest devotee. You're sharp and will think of something. If nothing works, follow him and leave word and signs as you go, so we can pick up your trail. We will find this Issa, and if he is Jesus, we will rebuild the House of Decia!"

They showed Boy the route and ate dinner as they waited for Marcus's story. Poet knew Boy was as eager as he was to hear about Marcus's ride to Al Kut and what happened there and why he was suddenly so inspired, like the day they had won the field from a barbarian club-and-axe wielding horde.

"Boy, you must rest, but first, I will tell my story. Poet, fetch my helmet. It's in need of mending."

Poet returned to his seat by the fire, shaking his head. "Now I understand that welt upon your forehead. I'm no blacksmith, but I'll do my best. It looks like Hercules took a club to your head. Do we also need to bathe your sword?"

"No, I've already seen to that," Marcus said, pulling out the near completed sandalwood horse from his pack to whittle while he spoke. Poet and Boy sat back to enjoy the story of family redemption with their wine.

At the end of the tale, Poet was confused. He felt he should revel in the victory, but instead was baffled by how this discovery of the imperial treachery would alter their destiny. The empire they served had betrayed the House of Decia, but there was no way to right the wrong. Any attempt would be suicide.

"What, no slaps on the back for a job well done in proving my family's innocence?" Marcus asked. "No worries, my good men. We all die in the end," he said, seeming to enjoy his audience's dumbfounded reaction.

"I'd like to live some first," Boy said, pacing around the fire. "It's a wonderful story, but I have so many questions. Poet?" He turned to Poet for help.

"I'm confused by what this means for you and our mission," Poet said. "You still want to hunt this rebel god for an emperor who slaughtered your innocent family—but why?" Though he seemed inspired by his sword fight and confirming his family's innocence, Poet wondered if, with the blow to his head, Marcus wasn't thinking clearly.

"Why did he commit the outrageous treachery? Or why would I have us continue to follow our mission and do the empire's bidding?" Marcus asked.

"No, you told us the treachery was in response to your family's views on slavery and the republic," Poet said. "I'm asking why we will continue to serve this Caesar?"

"Boy, what do you think of that? Slaughtered just for suggesting an end to slavery?" Marcus said, ignoring Poet's question. And not waiting for Boy to answer, he proceeded to tell Boy in great detail how his father fought valiantly in the senate for the abolition of slavery. "Boy, what do you think of that?" he asked.

"I've heard your family's views on slavery before, and I like them. If I discovered my mother was alive and knew where, I'd ask for my freedom to free her and take revenge. Whoever stole her also caused my father's death." Boy clasped at his family breastplate hidden over his heart under his tunic. "I live better than most men and women we meet. Also, I love the two of you." Boy smiled compassionately at his master and uncle.

Marcus, rubbing his still swollen head, said, "Am I becoming that doddering old man who repeats himself? Sorry, but it bears repeating. I need some sleep after a hard fight and ride. We are one small, loyal contubernium, and I love you like my son. And you are free to go. Just give me a couple days' notice as we'd be hard pressed to survive without you."

Marcus tossed to Boy the now finished whittled horse. "For you. She looks a bit like Sahara?"

"Very good likeness. I will treasure it. Thank you, master." Boy bowed and sat next to Marcus to inspect the carved horse.

"May I remind you that a *contubernium* consists of ten legionaries, and we are only three," Poet, ever the wordsmith, said while he worked on Marcus's helmet as the blacksmith. "But still the point stands—our small band's loving bond is undeniably true. But you haven't answered why we would continue to serve this Caesar?"

"It is my duty. And my way back to Rome. And it is my means to get near enough to the emperor —"

"You weren't kidding," Poet interrupted. "We will all die," he said between gulps of wine.

"You are always free too, my friend. My good, loyal friend."

"I'm with you," Poet said, taking another quick drink.

"Me too!" Boy said, mimicking Poet's drinking too fast. Poet sneered at him for his mockery.

"I will submit my evidence to the Senate and challenge the emperor, or his stand-in, to a fight to restore my family's honor. The one who survives will determine the truth for history."

"That's a losing proposition," Poet said. "He'll pick a gladiator as big as Saltaurius to fight for him."

"It will be in the gods' hands, and I will have done my duty. The two of you need to live to sing my praises when I am gone," Marcus said, smiling at Boy.

Poet looked up to the night stars. The lights of many campfires. The fire Prometheus had stolen to light man's world before daily enduring a giant eagle eating his liver, only to have that liver grow back each night. Romans had their suffering saints and regenerative miracles too.

"The gods have already rolled the dice. It is all already written, and I need only to find the words to put into song," Poet said half to himself before adding, "How about a poem before we ride east to capture or kill a god and then back to Rome for our revenge on an emperor?"

"No!" both Marcus and Boy replied at once. Marcus added, "We need to get up early." Boy and Marcus moved to their mats and lay down. Poet knew they only pretended to be already sleeping peacefully as he sang an old Greek song of love and glory.

Chapter 17

Sahara

THREE DAYS LATER, Marcus rode into the village of Rhagae to find Boy in the stables, lying beside Sahara. Poet, following just behind him, entered the stables as well and squatted down next to the horse, which was wheezing as it lay on one side. The stall stunk of horse sweat, piss, and dung. It was hard to tell who was in more pain, Boy or his horse. Marcus sighed—perhaps it was him. After all, he was the one who issued the order that was now causing Boy so much pain. The blame lay squarely on his shoulders.

"I rode her too hard," Boy said as he struggled to stand to give his report. Marcus moved to sit down next to him. "And all for nothing. The man they call Issa is still here and not planning to go anywhere. He holds court in the market square most days at dawn. I'm sorry . . ." Boy's voice trailed off and he sobbed, "She's dying."

Marcus draped his arms around Boy, pulling him into his chest. He could feel Boy's pain in his own heart. Marcus understood military missions often resulted in nothing gained, or, as in this case, a catastrophic loss. He had been responsible for so many of these losses, but he couldn't remember one that hurt more than this one. And it was the innocent horse of his adopted son and not a soldier that lay shuddering with death rattles in that unkempt stall.

He looked at Poet, who was never at a loss for words, squatting helplessly on the other side of Boy. Poet tried to no avail to comfort Boy with Roman religion. "Sahara, a winged Pegasus, will return to Epona. Her goddess calls her home. She has served you well and you must let her fly now without fear." His words fell short of the mark. He stroked Boy's long, dark hair.

"You need sleep," Marcus said. Boy was as undone as the stall where he must have spent the night and half the day. "Would you like me to send her to the green pastures in Elysium, where you can join her when the gods see fit? I made you ride her here without rest. The fault is mine. You told me more than once we weren't riding in the cool forests of Germany but an arid, unforgiving land—that we shouldn't push our beloved horses beyond their limits."

"She's been with me since we met, and you gave her to me. One of my happiest days and this is—after my parent's loss and the day you were flogged—my worst. It is my duty to be the one to show her the mercy of a quick death." Boy stroked and kissed Sahara's long brown cheek, which was drenched in sweat. The horse lying there beside him seemed to realize the end was near and closed her bloodshot eye.

Boy stood unsteadily. Marcus handed him his sword so he wouldn't have to use his own. "You have seen it done, but it is different in the doing. Down over the shoulder blade and clean through the arteries above the heart. I will help you aim but you must not hesitate at the last minute. Are you sure?"

Boy nodded and raised the sword over the half dead horse. Marcus adjusted the angle and direction. And with one clean thrust, the horse was dead. Boy collapsed onto his steed as if to ride her into the heavens.

"You were following orders and Sahara was following her destiny. Blessed by the gods with your love. Most beasts die a cruel, slow death and never have such care and affection during their lives. You have done well. I am proud of you." Marcus kept talking until Boy finally rolled off the horse covered in hay and sweat, exhausted from the pain.

Marcus waited until Poet took Boy to camp before removing his sword. After saying a prayer over the horse's corpse, he found two young men to take Sahara to feed the poor in the village.

The loss of a soldier's horse was like losing an arm. And Boy was young with a heart still tender. Marcus wondered if this was an omen. He was uncertain if he would kill a corrupt magician or the only son of God in the morning. Bringing the man back alive to Pilate would cost time and put his men at risk. So far, they had only lost a horse. But it would be the noble course to bring the prisoner back alive to plead his case, and he always followed the noble course. Perhaps he would ignore Pilate's orders and stir the empire by marching the rebel directly to Rome.

CHAPTER 18
Issa's Sermon

MA WATCHED ISSA'S sermon for a third day. Each day, he was back on his stage for another show. Bhakti looked pained and disgusted as he stood by her side. Before the lucrative question-and-answer period, Issa spoke about God and love as if he were the real Issa and real Jesus. Perhaps he had heard the real Jesus speak before being hung upon the cross. Ma knew there was no death, not really. In her heart she knew the story of Jesus's resurrection was true.

Each morning, Ma marveled at the spectacle and had to restrain Bhakti from confronting the man and boxing his ears. Ma did this as a way to meditate on God, love, and truth. *Were the people worse off after listening to secondhand wisdom espoused by a fraud?* she wondered. One thing was for certain: their purses were poorer for it, as his teachings were not free.

Before their return to India, Ma needed to convince the imposter to stop his fraud, or otherwise she would expose him. But how and when? And how had he come by the name of Issa? She meditated and prayed for answers to these questions. She trusted God would supply the answer at the right time.

The answer came on that third day as two Roman soldiers and a slave boy, also carrying a sword, entered the square and moved into the crowd in front of the stage. She feared there might be bloodshed. This phony Issa had spoken at length about his cruel Roman crucifixion and how he rose from the dead. He warned his followers to watch out for Romans coming to murder him once more.

Ma could sense the poor Nubian boy carried a great burden and was in tremendous pain. She felt moved to come to his aid, but before she could approach him, Issa stood, pointed his golden arm, and called out, "Look! My tormentors have followed me here. Don't they know they cannot kill me? Not here, amongst my honest flock of protection and retribution."

Chapter 19
An Exotic Lady

Boy realized they all might soon follow Sahara into the afterlife. The crowd glared at them as Marcus nonchalantly unraveled his papyrus image of Jesus to compare it to the Issa that stood before them. Boy looked over Marcus's shoulder and thought that the shape of the face and its skin tone were like the charcoal depiction, but the eyes seemed different. Perhaps they were missing the love that everyone said they felt when looking at Jesus. He saw that in the picture but not in the eyes glaring at them from the stage. Boy had learned a great deal about Jesus and of his honesty and courage while posing as a Jesus-lover in Jerusalem. He had come to admire the true Jesus. The man on the dais reminded him of the silk merchant he met in Babylon, except that he was selling something entirely different. Jesus was known for his self-sacrifice, and this man's response to danger was an immediate leap to self-preservation. Hardly a martyr's overture.

"Be not afraid," Marcus called out. "I seek only a quiet audience with you. My men can stay behind with your humble flock as collateral." Marcus raised his hands as if in surrender and to calm the building roar of the unsettled crowd. Angry faces surrounded them. They bore no resemblance to those radiant faces of those that so loved Jesus in Jerusalem.

"Thanks for that," Poet mumbled. Boy stood tall, shaking off his grief to meet the dire moment.

"You bear a sword," Issa said.

"And you the power of a God if I—I mean you're—not mistaken. But I will leave it here with my men." He unbuckled his sheath and sword and handed it to Boy, who took the weapon that sent Sahara flying the evening before.

"And the knife on your hip," Issa said.

Marcus complied, handing his knife to Boy and saying softly, "Next he'll ask I leave my boots, so I don't stomp him to death." Boy smiled for the first time since last night.

"Well, then," Issa said. "Follow me to my private lodgings. Good people have no fear. Rome does not rule here. God will protect us." He gathered his gold robe around him and started up a path toward a nearby inn. Some of his followers scurried to line the path as the son of God and his oppressor made their way up to the inn.

Boy and Poet tried to appear relaxed as they stood back-to-back in the crowd. A beautiful lady with a lovely caramel complexion and dressed in angelic white approached Boy and stood just two feet in front of his face. Boy felt loved by her goddess-like eyes. He imagined Sahara had come back as the goddess Epona to comfort him. He had the distinct impression he had known this exotic lady his entire life.

CHAPTER 20

The Interview

Issa wore precious blue onyx bedazzled sandals on his feet, which were fit for Achilles. Marcus followed Issa to the top floor of the inn. His room was also lavish. The man claiming to be Issa offered Marcus a chair near the window to move him away from barring the door. Marcus waved off the invitation.

"What blasphemy do you intend, Roman?" Issa asked. Marcus thought this a little out of character, even if Rome had supposedly crucified him a couple of months ago. Was Jesus not supposed to love and forgive everyone?

"None. You've done well for yourself, I see," Marcus said, eyeing the luxury that draped the room like the red silk sheet covering the bed. Marcus patted a pillow and said, "Feathered." He noted a basin of water by the far windowsill, a knife and fork, bread, and a salted fish under fine Roman or Greek glass. "I heard you were a fisherman. Where does the fish come from?"

"There is a river nearby. My beloved followers provide it for me."

"While traveling the Silk Road to trade silver for silk," Marcus said. "We heard the tale of a remarkable man, a son of God, crucified in Jerusalem and then risen from the dead. I had to come to see for myself the power and mystery of the man they call Jesus of Nazareth. Is that you? I carry his picture. Cannot a Roman worship a god like any mortal man?" He pulled the drawing from his pocket to study the two faces close up. Either it was a poor drawing, or he was the wrong man.

"Yes, my son. In God's eyes, we are all his children. I forgive you."

"For what?"

"All your sins, Roman."

Marcus had met pompous priests many times who used holy words and righteous tones to cow brave soldiers. He found it laughable.

"I thought you died for my sins, or at least that's what I heard, albeit from an unreliable source," Marcus said, thinking Saltaurius had been right to say Issa was a fraud. Unfortunately for the big man, the head and face of this fraud were worthless, as they wouldn't pass for Jesus. "Did you? Die for our sins?" A well of anger began bubbling within Marcus, one that he didn't understand. Maybe it was because he and his men also assumed many roles to get men to speak candidly. And Marcus hated frauds. But that was not the cause of this deep-seated rage bubbling to the surface.

"Yes. Yet, you still commit them," Issa said. "What do you intend here? Do you mean me harm? Any harm coming to me will not play as well in Rhagae as it did in Jerusalem."

"If you tell the truth, I mean you no harm and would offer to march you in victory all the way to Rome to be crowned as a god. The emperor may anoint you as a god. Imagine the joy and pageantry of being initiated into the pantheon of the gods." Then it dawned on him. The anger was arising out of deep despondency. Since this man was not the man he sought, his mission's failure was all but certain. He forced himself to take a deep, calming breath. A man could not always control the circumstances of life, but it was essential that he control his reaction.

"The idea of going to Rome doesn't appeal to me. Why would they deify a man they tortured and crucified to death? Will you please sit?" Issa asked.

"Because he didn't die, and you will be there to bear witness. But let me hear your testimony. Let us start with the truth. And, yes, let us both be seated." Marcus motioned for Issa to sit by the window, which he did in a slow a deliberate manner befitting a holy man. Marcus moved a table between them and pulled up a second chair, keeping his back toward the door.

"Place your hands upon the table like mine. Palms up." Fake Issa shook his head. Marcus growled and made his warrior face. When Marcus found himself without a weapon in a fight, he had made his foe drop their weapons and run just with that fierce look. And his anger and disappointment were near the tipping point. The rattled Issa complied, placing his hands palms up on the table. "Yes, like that. Are you the man who was crucified in Jerusalem? Are you Jesus of Nazareth? Did you defy death to come to Rhagae and preach?"

"More or less."

"Well, is it more or less?"

"Yes," Issa said with slight hesitation and squirming like a golden toad, trying to keep his robe from bunching up beneath his buttocks.

"Your mother's name?"

"Mary."

"Correct. Your father's?"

"God."

"Have you heard of an Essene sect?"

"Yes."

"Are they your mother's people?"

"No," Issa said. Marcus raised his eyebrows. "My mother is now a follower of mine and no longer part of any sect." Marcus was impressed with his verbal footwork.

"The cross must have been painful. How long did you hang there? I see your wounds have healed. That is a miracle."

"Less than a day."

"Half a day? Or almost a whole day?"

"More than half, I believe. I didn't keep time."

"Understandable. I imagine minutes felt like hours with all the pain. What did you wear upon the cross?"

"A loincloth." Issa's palms started sweating as Marcus's eyes penetrated his.

"I heard you were naked. That's the garb of Roman crucifixion, established for maximum humiliation. But I was not there." But Marcus remembered his vision, and the real Jesus was naked there. "Would you name all your disciples for me?"

"So you may persecute them and put them to death?"

"Clever answer. But we both know you are not him. The only question that remains is if you will live or die," Marcus said again, flashing his warrior face at the fearful fraud.

"If I die, you and your friends will too," Issa said, trying to still look in control, but he couldn't even keep his flowing robe, which he kept adjusting, in a comfortable position under his seat. Marcus knew men's haunches clenched when death came near.

"That may be, but like your namesake, we are not afraid to die doing our duty. Here is my offer," Marcus said, showing a more congenial face to the quivering man as he realized there was more to the story. "Explain how you gathered such information about the man in this remote location to perform your impressive impersonation. Take your bounty and move on, never claiming to be the man who died on the cross again, or I'll slit your neck with that crude knife over there and take my chances with your fickle, defrauded flock." They both turned to check on the knife by the fish on the far side of the room.

"Please, don't kill me. I saw him preach southeast of here on his way to India."

"Ah, I thought so," Marcus said, but it really only occurred to him at that moment. The fresh breeze of hope returned to his lungs and soothed the monster inside him that was ready to kill. "Too many people have identified the man in my picture for his trail to stop with you. You're not a great likeness. How long ago and how far from here did you meet him?"

"A month ago, near Farah, where he stayed for a couple of days. I attended his talks every day. He was the most remarkable man I ever saw, sometimes almost too bright to look upon. After he vanished, I thought there was no harm in spreading his message."

"This him?" Marcus asked, showing the fraud his charcoal drawing.

"Yes. But different somehow. I can't explain it." The fake Issa covered his eyes with his hands after looking at the picture.

"Well, they say he was transfigured." Marcus said without conviction.

"Yes, transfigured might be the difference. I wear gold trying to capture the brilliance of his light and the enchantment of his eyes," fake Issa said with a hint of contrition.

"Yes, you're just an actor in a costume whose played his last show," Marcus said. He still thought if the real Issa were Jesus, he was a miracle man resuscitated and nothing more. "Do you know where he was heading in India?"

"I heard him mention Pali, a place he'd known in his youth. To see an old friend there."

"What else can you tell me? Did he travel alone?"

"He was with a woman who might have been his mother."

"Mary, and she was an Essene. Anything more you can tell me in exchange for your life?"

"A man was with them, another one of his teachers. That is all. I swear. I was only doing God's work—in his name." The defrocked man glanced to the windowsill as the sun chose that moment to spotlight the knife and glass orb over the pickled fish.

"The knife is still there. And I will let the gods judge you, but if I find you again in this lie, I will kill you. I will be back through here soon," Marcus lied. "Now, here's how we will play this." Marcus moved to the window overlooking the square, where most of the crowd remained waiting below. He opened it wide and saw his two sentries standing in the middle of the crowd as if they didn't have a care in the world, even speaking to a beautiful, young, light brown woman in a glowing white robe. *Now there is a holy sight,* he thought.

"As I walk to the square," Marcus continued, "you will lean out this window and wave at your defrauded flock to assure them that all is well. Put on a big smile. I will kill you if you cry out some lie. I'll inform them that we had a pleasant conversation and that you will speak to them tomorrow morning. Depart before sunrise, unless you desire to disclose the truth. You've done well for yourself here, but Issa, you are no more."

Marcus walked to the far end of the room and picked up the knife to inspect it. After some deliberation, he placed the knife down and lifted the glass dome over the salted fish. He used a piece of cloth from the table to wrap the fish before placing it in his leather pouch. "For our midday meal. Alms for the poor," he said.

Marcus left the bread and the golden-robed man without a name. Once outside the inn, he waved goodbye to the imposter, who was smiling and waving from the window above. He returned to his men. Boy was relieved of his grief and restored to his jovial nature. "A fake for sure," Marcus informed them, "but, gods willing, we have a destination for the real Issa. And what happened here to put a smile back on Boy's bright face?" he asked.

Poet explained, "He whined about Sahara to some lady in white who cradled his head with her hands and said a few words in Hindi he didn't understand. But it did the trick; it brought him back to his sunny disposition."

"It was her eyes, her smile, that reassured me and made me whole. She called me *son*—that I could understand. I know Sahara is happy now and will never be dead to me," Boy said. He blushed like a child at his childish words of wonder. "The lady in white, her name is Ma—can you believe it? She—I can't explain—is how I imagined Jesus would be."

"She was something," Poet said, as if searching for, but not finding, the right words.

"We may see her again before we leave," Marcus said. "We might have use of Hindi speaker. Boy, find yourself a horse and provisions for a couple of weeks of riding. One more day of rest for the horses, then we leave together. Here, this should be enough silver." He gave Boy a handful of coins. "And point me toward where the Indian woman went. Then, when done, join us for a fish lunch, courtesy of the imposter. Here take it, so I don't smell fishy for your Ma." He sniffed the wrapped fish and handed it to Boy.

"Poet can show you where she went. She invited us for a drink she called tay, whatever that is. I wish I could come with you, but I am going to pick the best new horse for me since I'm missing Ma's tay," Boy said, and held out his hand. Marcus laughed and added one gold coin to the silver. Boy almost skipped away to find the best horse.

Marcus noticed the Rhagae square had been cleared of almost all the people who had attended the morning show. "Poet, before we go for Ma's tay, let's sit and consult your maps." They found a broken-down stone wall on the edge of the square to sit upon. Poet pulled his maps from his side bag and spread them out. "For India," Marcus said, tracing his finger over the map, "we will take a southeast route to a place called Pali. Hmm, doesn't seem to be any marked caravan routes to take us all the way there. We'll be traversing the Parthian Kingdom, which has had a tumultuous relationship with Rome. The new king brings uneasy peace and has reopened the trade routes."

"Phraates the fifth spent some time studying in Rome before returning to assassinate his father and marry his mother and assume the throne," Poet said. "And we thought Rome was a vile political state."

"That's Roman education for you. It creates a patricidal, mother-fornicating head of state," Marcus joked, making Poet smile. "While at least we are not at war, they are a fierce foe. I've seen the Parthians pitted against barbarians in the arena, and they are a good match. We will pose as Roman merchants and pretend we are looking to buy silk with our remaining silver and gold—Awoll! whadathat?" A small rock had hit the back of Marcus's head.

"David!" a woman called out to the little miscreant. The projectile-throwing boy's mother grabbed her little David by the arm and hastened him away.

"Little bastard's braver than the fake Issa," Marcus said. They both laughed as he rubbed a small welt on his already bruised head. It served to remind them they weren't in the Roman Empire anymore.

"Poet, when we get to India, if we don't secure this Indian guide to Pali, can you speak some Hindi? She looked young. Let's hope she is willing and can ride. We could strap her in the saddle if needed."

"I speak a little Hindi and understood most of what she said. After reading their great text the Upanishads in Greek, I wanted to read the Hindi translated from the Sanskrit and struggled through it. So I can speak Hindi about the ineffable." It took Marcus a second to comprehend Poet's wordplay. Poet loved words and languages. "It is a foundational text of Hinduism, but she was speaking some dialect to Boy."

"Let's go find her. Hopefully, she was not a follower of this phony Jesus. She won't like that I made him leave if she is. The real Issa is heading to India, and we are too. We may find he is also a fraud—just a better one. Or we just might find the son of God."

CHAPTER 21
Saltaurius Sheds his Skin

SALTAURIUS, WITH DIO at his side, was pleased to have joined the company of wealthy Persian traders traveling east. Dio, clever as he was, was often taciturn on long journeys. The Persians rode stout Arabian horses. After a couple days of uneasy travel, they pitched their camp between Tehran and Rhagae. Saltaurius felt he had gained sufficient familiarity with the leader of the Persians, who spoke some Greek, to start asking questions. He didn't totally trust his travel companions. And Dio didn't trust anyone. The Persians didn't drink wine or ale and thought it was some sort of abomination. Saltaurius found this sobriety an affront to good society.

They were evenly matched, one extra-large man and a half man against three men, if swords were drawn over some dispute about drinking or religion. Though foreign in their customs and manner, Saltaurius admired their flowing robes, which were better suited for a big man like him than tight fitting Roman tunics.

That night, as they talked around the campfire, Saltaurius followed their custom and drank only warmed herbal water in order to make his guests comfortable and forthcoming. No wine or ale. Dio understood their Persian-Arabic dialect but pretended he didn't.

"Has word reached you of a Jesus of Nazareth? One who was crucified in Jerusalem and then raised from the dead?" Saltaurius asked, after expressing some pleasantries regarding their dress. "Perhaps he is called Issa here?"

The Greek-speaking leader of the Persians, Zamir, translated Saltaurius's words for his two travel companions. The group looked alarmed but nodded. Their strange looks made Saltaurius sense he'd hit the spike on the head. "What do you know about him?" he asked.

Zamir spoke softly, as if he didn't want anyone to overhear. "His disciples are coming out of hiding and are willing to risk their lives for him. One, a man named Thomas, escaped east for his mission. If word of Jesus is spoken too far and wide, soon Rome will persecute Christians, who are loved by neither Gentile nor Jew. The empire needs a scapegoat. They will be persecuted." This was the first time Saltaurius had heard the name *Christians*.

He dug his stick hard into the sand in front of the fire. The news disgusted him. Saltaurius turned to Dio for his reaction. The cold-hearted bastard just shrugged his shoulders, unable to conceal his thin smile. He knew Dio found the faith of his master—based on his vision of his brother with Jesus—a source of amusement. Or perhaps it merely made him gleeful to hear the prophecy of persecution. If it wasn't for their Arab company, Saltaurius would have thrown the stick at his dog.

"Only more blood can assuage Roman guilt," Saltaurius said. "Have you heard that Jesus, the Christ, may have cheated death and resurrected himself, fooling the Romans? I have heard someone claiming to be the son of god may have passed near here, heading east."

Zamir moved his seat to consult with his travel companions. The question made the Persians uneasy. Zamir returned to his seat by Saltaurius with his left hand awkwardly covering his right wrist and asked, "You're a Roman. What interest do you have in this Hebrew prophet?"

"I will trust you with my confidence. I saw the man once, and he was a sight to see—a miracle worker. They speak of his miraculous virgin birth. I saw him cure a man of his paralysis—a centurion's slave in Capernaum. He later raised a man from the dead. Miracle after miracle, until the biggest miracle of them all. After dying a cruel death on the cross for all our sins, he raised himself from the dead, body and soul, to join his father in heaven. I had a vision of him with my brother, who is also in heaven." Saltaurius glanced at Dio, who did a better job of masking any cynical reaction and even managed to look supportive of his declaration of faith.

"And being Roman, you wouldn't kill him again, if he still lived?" Zamir asked.

"Not as a Roman . . ." Saltaurius became lost in his own dark thoughts before speaking again. "If he lives, that will deny his last and greatest miracle,"

"Why is that? Isn't his rising and living after being crucified and dead the greatest miracle?" Zamir asked.

"Not as great as rising body and soul into heaven," Saltaurius said. He had never expressed aloud his new faith based on his vision of brotherly forgiveness. "And now that you tell me of the courage of his followers and the dangers they face in his name, I'd like to ask him how he can run from his people and not call down an army of angels to protect us." Dio shot Saltaurius a look of warning and contempt, perhaps signaling he should not be challenging their beliefs if he wanted to gain information. "But I love this Jesus, as I loved my brother," Saltaurius declared to comfort the Persians, letting it be known that he was a good Christian. "The son of God should have no fear of me. I just fear there are imposters pretending they are him."

Saltaurius stood to stretch. The confession he just made to these heathens, that he was a newborn Christian, made him uneasy. His whole new world of forgiveness hinged on the Jesus being with his brother. Otherwise, his vision of his brother's forgiveness was a delusion. He loved the Christ in heaven but would be betrayed by a Jesus who still walked the earth.

Zamir consulted at some length in Arabic with his fellow travelers before returning to speak to Saltaurius with his simple Greek. Mesopotamia was still the land of Babel. The exception was Dio, who comprehended everything that was spoken.

"I have good news," Zamir said. "The man you seek, we seek, some call Issa, but we call Yuz Asaf. He is near here. We will take you to see him, tomorrow. We are on our way there to worship and protect the prophet. He resides in Rhagae and has recently had trouble from a Roman tribune." Zamir raised his bushy eyebrows as he awaited Saltaurius's reaction, while constantly covering his right wrist with his left hand.

"A Roman tribune? Now we're the ones who follow," Saltaurius said to Dio, who cocked an eye to urge him to say no more. Saltaurius had learned to read his right-hand man's subtle signals. Sometimes he felt he could hear Dio speaking in his head. Turning back to Zamir, he said, "That tribune is a bounty hunter and is seeking to kill Issa. We all should rush to his protection. Would you sell me some of your clothes so that I might join you? If I am a Christian, I cannot be Roman anymore."

Saltaurius was gleeful at soon overtaking the illusive Issa, and played the part of a big buffoon for everyone's amusement, as he slipped into the loose-fitting Arab robe and the dashing red turban headdress. The robe's sleeves were too short, but he nonetheless was free from all Roman restraint. And his religious and fashion statements pleased both Zamir and Dio.

Dio came near and whispered in Saltaurius's ear, "Tomorrow, I will enter Rhagae just before you, dressed as a wandering Roman outcast in a simple tunic," he said. "That way, I will draw attention away from you as you go about your duty."

As he fell asleep alongside his Persian brothers, Saltaurius wondered if he was lying to himself. Either way, he would be better suited to meet his savior and demand answers as a Persian merchant. His understanding of his duty, as Dio put it, was unclear, but he knew he had to be cautious not to offend Zamir and his travel companions. They loved Yuz Asaf, the fraud they would all meet in person the next day.

Saltaurius awakened at first light, still in his Arab dress. He looked over at Dio, who sat watching the Persians lying by the still smoldering fire. A sticky pool of blood circled the head of each Persian. Their throats had been slit in the night.

"Dio, what have you done?" Saltaurius asked.

"Protected you, master," Dio said. "I understood their words last night. They didn't trust you and were plotting against you. They would have prevented you from doing what must be done in Rhagae today."

"What must be done? Not this! Now, what do we do with three dead bodies?" He began pacing about the camp, making sure they were not being watched. He wished they had camped farther from the road.

Saltaurius looked down at himself and said, "I wear their clothes. And awake to this bloody dawn."

"And own all their possessions. Master, please calm yourself. We are far from Rome and civilization. I will make a pyre. What is not seen, not known, never happened. All men die and are soon forgotten. Man killing man, there's no end to it once it was started. But better to kill than be killed."

"Make your pyre while I think. My duty, 'what must be done,' you said . . ." His voice trailed off, still unsure of his course of action.

"Is for you to decide. Free will. I have made it easier for you by removing a triumvirate of human interference."

"There's nothing triumphant in this. Have you no pride or shame?"

"No, they are weaknesses. I only did what had to be done to serve you."

The big man was still weighing right and wrong. He wondered if Dio was telling the truth and how to react to the cowardly killings. And if he now had to execute the man that had always served his family.

Dio folded his arms to deliver his closing argument in his defense. "You would have insisted we fight them like honorable men and one of us would have died, and that would be me, since no foe can kill you. And then who would serve you?" That was the truth. "All we have are stories to ease the suffering and forget the horror of death at the end of each of our roads. Stories of gods and lovers, stories of adventure and conquest, stories of survival despite all odds, and now the grandest story of all to comfort men's souls—the story of one man cheating death, escaping the charioteer's sure lance for a place free of all this suffering. And he washes the slate clean with the pain of his death. He paves the way for all men to follow him into heaven. True or not, this Jesus story is worth defending by all means necessary and will bring you wealth and comfort in this life. If you dare to do what must be done." Dio dangled a leather sleeve that looked like a horse's shaft and tossed it to Saltaurius. When he looked inside, he saw the sapphires and rubies.

"The one called Zamir had it sewed into the wrist of his garment, which he kept hiding with his other hand. I'll stitch it into your robe the same way, after we dispose of the bodies. Just don't fidget with it like he did."

"You could reason your way out of a lion's mouth. A snake would die if it bit you," Saltaurius said, removing his hand from the hilt of his sword.

"And don't you wonder why Issa still has his head after being found by Tribune Decia?" Dio asked his master.

"I assumed . . . I don't know what I assumed. Tell me."

"Either Issa is already well protected, or Tribune Decia is betraying our mission and doesn't intend to show Jesus Roman justice. Or this Issa is not Jesus," Dio said.

"That doesn't really help me much. And this Issa, despite the resemblance, cannot be Jesus. Get to your pyre. You're lucky dry wood is abundant here. I will scout about to make sure no one is approaching."

As he went about circling the camp at a distance, he considered Dio's fine words. But how did those words justify killing three sleeping men? He knew himself to be a brute, but a brute who lived by an honorable code of conduct when it came to killing a man. That same code demanded he execute his lifelong advisor—adding him to the pyre as rough Roman justice.

He only killed men in honorable combat. But he had not killed these men. His conscience should be clear. And the gems Dio, his deadly assassin, had discovered were worth more than a bucket of gold.

Maybe Dio was right. He was slight and not blessed with the strength to win a fair fight. He possessed only cunning. Perhaps he had just prevented the Arabs from attempting to kill him and had thus made a preventive strike. Maybe he was a dutiful servant dispatching foes who plotted against him. He cursed his weakness and hurried back to camp to help his loyal servant move the bodies onto the pyre, praying their bones would not later rattle and rise from the ashes.

Chapter 22
Meeting Ma

MARCUS FOUND THE Indian woman and her old male attendant or guardian upon a dune nearby seated with their legs fully crossed and looking over Rhagae. There was a subtle breeze. A canopy erected over their heads provided them shade. Poet also assessed the scene as they approached the camp on foot, his hand shielding his eyes from the sun. Poet was almost always by his side, but here, neither of them would need to protect the other.

Upon seeing the seated saintly Indian woman, Marcus felt a shift within, a wave of tranquility washing over him. Studying her face from a distance, reminded him of the joy of winning the last battle after a long war—joy that didn't so much come from the victory but from the peace that followed. *Beware of enchantment,* he thought.

The man in an orange robe, hearing their approach, stood—either to greet the guests or to protect his companion. She remained seated in a stillness stiller than silence. He motioned for them to come with him to the far side of the camp. "Greetings," he offered in a wary, unsure whisper. They sat on some cushions. Observing the motionless woman, he noted, "Ma is in *samadhi*, a complete state of absorption, and is not to be disturbed. How may I help you?"

"Thank you for your hospitality. She invited us to tay," Marcus said.

"Tea? That sounds like her," the man said.

"We are setting off for India. The day after tomorrow at first light and are looking for a guide. I am Tribune Marcus Decia. This is my cohort, Poet. He speaks some Hindi," Marcus said. Poet looked lost in a peaceful daydream as he gazed at Ma. Marcus nudged Poet with his elbow to get him to focus.

"We will return to India. I am Swami Bhakti. I serve her, and she serves me. She is my guru and will determine how and when we return. India is a vast and holy land. She likes to take her time and meet people on her way and is often called to service by the gods and her guru. I'm afraid we are only fit to serve as spiritual guides."

Marcus looked over at the braying donkeys. "That's not our speed," he said. "We need to ride horseback without meandering."

"That won't work for us. I can't ride, and I'm too old to learn," the swami said.

"How about her? Does she ride?" Marcus said. They all turned to watch Ma sitting with half a smile and eyes slightly open.

"Ma does whatever she pleases. She is a fully realized being."

"Awakened?" Poet asked the swami and then turned to Marcus. "I recognize the concept from my reading of Eastern mysticism."

"Yes, an avatar, our mother, though she says she is just a little girl. She is all innocence and bliss. But wise as any sage," the swami said. "No . . . not just *any* sage. She has obtained cosmic consciousness," he added.

Marcus, studying Ma from twenty feet away, blinked his eyes as she appeared to be almost a mirage, dancing in and out of view. A golden haze surrounded her head and bare feet, which perched on top of her crossed legs. The sand and sun danced in bright colors around her. He'd heard of levitating magicians and wondered if her bottom, covered by her robe, even touched the ground. Her image seemed like a constantly shifting dream, appearing and disappearing each instant—imminent and transcendent.

Marcus shook away the spell and strange thoughts that had entered his mind. "How long can she sit there before she is reabsorbed into her body here? I have met men from the East who can sit still for hours. Grown men with no purpose or sense of destiny. They desire to leave no footprint wherever they go. This is the opposite of the Roman boot, which shakes the ground wherever it lands."

"She travels within cosmic consciousness, drinking and bathing in the sweet nectar of the gods. Ma is very much of this life too. Her sole purpose is to spread love and joy. You will see." The swami looked over to Ma and said, "See, she stirs."

Marcus and Poet turned to Ma, who, coming out of trance, now had her eyes open. Her smile was slightly more pronounced across her face. For the first time, Marcus noticed her immaculate white Indian dress and the lapis lazuli prayer beads in her hand. She seemed to be materializing right before his eyes—or at least becoming more solid in her graceful form.

"We may now approach. Gently, please, my Roman friends. We need to respect the peaceful transition back into her body. I will translate."

"Please let my friend try his hand at translating first," Marcus said. He had known translators who repeated not what they heard but what they wished had been said. They picked up their cushions and followed the swami. They sat in a semi-circle around Ma. She still had a radiant glow following her meditation and welcomed them with her eyes and smile. No one spoke. Marcus felt instant intimacy, as if he had known Ma for all of eternity. Her same graceful presence that enveloped Marcus seemed to encompass the entire scene. He felt denuded of his Roman metal, like his sword was a long blade of grass and his Roman tunic with scales of armor on his chest was transparent to her eyes. Eyes that could see into his heart.

Poet sat with a foolish grin on his face.

The silence was becoming unbearable. Marcus sensed Poet was bubbling with words he wished to express, but he would never speak first. The moment before the unbearable bubbled over, Ma dipped her head with prayer hands to her chest and said, "Jai Gurudev!"

Poet burst forth repeating, "Jai Gurudev!" mimicking her angelic voice full of mirth and good will. This made Marcus laugh a bit too loudly.

Marcus said to Ma, "Thank you for that greeting. I hope our interruption of the sermon in the square earlier and breaking up of the congregation did not disturb you, my lady." *My lady?* This was a term of endearment he'd only used for his wife. "My apologies. We meant no harm. I assure you; he is not who he claimed to be."

Ma laughed at Poet's translation as she stood to set a metal pot over a small fire she stoked. She spoke to Poet in some common Hindi dialect that sounded like poetry. *Using their voice to mesmerize was another tool of an enchantress*, Marcus thought. He would have to stay on guard to avoid falling completely under her spell. "She says I speak like Vedic scripture," Poet said.

"And she took no offense. She recognized the man as an imposter and is pleased that you prevented him from speaking anymore. And she is glad he was not harmed. She suggests her friend translates but will continue to use me if you prefer. She says he can be trusted to translate faithfully. And the swami has taught her some Latin."

Ma crumpled a handful of leaves into the heating pot and then waved her hand over the brew to take in its aroma. Marcus wondered if perhaps she were a beautiful witch making a concoction with which to beguile them. In all his travels of the world, meeting emperors and queens, he had never been so quickly stirred before. What magic was this?

Marcus settled himself and, speaking through the swami, said, "We are traveling in haste to India the day after tomorrow."

Ma prepared a clay pitcher with a small sheer cloth over the top and passed the hot liquid through it, collecting the leaves on the fabric. It smelled holy. The aroma alone, thought Marcus, might heal the sick. She didn't speak as she poured four cups from the pitcher and passed them out before she sat.

"What is this?" Marcus asked.

"Tea. Have you never had tea? It's a simple spiritual and medicinal pleasure." Ma seemed delighted to meet her Roman guests and to serve them tea. She was a constant babbling spring of delight from an unlimited source. And she shared that joy with them. Marcus had only seen such unaccounted joy in simpletons before, but her eyes were not simple. They were wise, deep wells of light and love. This harmless, unarmed, blissful girl demanded Marcus's full attention more than a barbarian charging with a swinging axe.

"Never heard of it. We will drink after our host," Marcus said. All Romans either used poison or were afraid of being poisoned. He didn't think the tea was really poison but did fear it might steal his mind and make him a blissful idiot.

Ma moved the cup like a sacred chalice to her full, smiling lips to take a pleasing sip. Marcus followed the gesture in equal measure, and he looked over to see Poet enjoying his first taste, his face full of rapture. The tea was better than good.

"Wonderful!" Poet exclaimed. "Soothing. Lovely. Mmm, better than fine wine. I imagine noblemen and women will someday sip this in the salons and baths of Rome." The tea had clearly made Poet a blissful idiot, but he was always so easily swayed by a beautiful face and voice.

Ma giggled and said, "Tea knows no hierarchy and should be enjoyed by all."

"Ah, an Indian republican. I like you already. It is pleasant," Marcus said. "We travel to India, a place called Pali. Do you know of it?"

These words brought Ma exuberant joy and contagious laughter as the wind swept the sand into their faces. Even Marcus joined in her laughter, though he didn't understand what was funny other than her reaction.

She let the laughter settle and said, "Excuse my silliness—I am such a little girl. I've known Pali since I first entered this body. Beloved Pali is the place of my birth. Why do you venture to my home, and so far from your own?"

"We seek the man that the Issa in the square pretended to be. A self-proclaimed son of God. We call him Jesus of Nazareth, if it is the same man. We believe he is headed to Pali," Marcus said. "And the gods have led us to you." Poet raised his eyebrows taking note—Marcus rarely invoked the gods.

"It does seem destined that we should cross paths," Ma said, enjoying the fortuitous meeting. "We are all children of God. Issa is an avatar. God in human form, rather than a human seeking the God within. A man of many names this Jesus, this Issa, this Yuz Asaf. Just like Babaji. Jaya Bhagavan!" She raised her arms and hands to clap them over her head. "You know this Jesus? Why do you seek him?"

"He cheated Rome of his death. I am charged with bringing him back—"

"Dead or alive" Ma said, finishing Marcus's thought. She didn't smile at these words but remained unmoved by them.

"Yes and no," Marcus said. "I would take him alive. And march him directly to Rome if he chooses, since Jerusalem treated him so badly. I am just his escort not his executioner." These words came from Marcus but struck him as strange and novel. Poet, too, looked surprised by his words. Marcus's elevated train of thought continued: *why kill him, after all, when they could strap him to a horse if necessary? And it would serve them to have a miracle maker and rebel son of god by his side, to help clear his way to the emperor, to challenge Macro and Caligula with the mass murder of his family. They rarely crucified Romans.*

The prospect excited Marcus. "Can you imagine if he is innocent, and the son of God entering Rome's gates with a Roman escort? The glory of the scene." He looked to Poet, knowing he would share in his excitement. But as their eyes met, he saw Poet was picturing the triumphant return home with some trepidation. "Know no fear," he said softly to his cohort. It was something they used to say when heading off into battle.

Poet smiled at Marcus. "You know I'd follow you into Hades."

Though simply seated in a circle on a sandy dune somewhere on the Silk Road—and the farthest he'd ever been from Rome—Ma's presence swept Marcus into a celestial realm of possibilities.

"Like Arjuna from the *Bhagavad Gita*, you have your dharma. You must follow. How may I assist you?" Ma asked, as she seemed to enjoy Marcus's epiphany.

"We could use a guide who knows the way and speaks the language better than my loyal friend." While saying that, Marcus reached over to lay his hand on his comrade's shoulder. "I understand your companion cannot ride, but you can. It won't be easy. Eight hours a day on horseback with few days of rest."

"To be clear, I said she could ride or fly if she chose to," the swami said.

Marcus took no offense at being corrected. "Yes, of course it is your choice," he said. "Will you join us? I will guarantee your safety."

The swami laughed after translating. Marcus again chose not to be offended, sensing there should be no such arrogance or animosity in front of Ma.

"God protects us all," she said. "When we surrender to him, keeping his name in our voice and hearts. Jaya Bhagavan! I too seek this Issa and believe he may be an old friend of my youth who saved me. If he travels to Pali, it might be to see me." Ma looked compassionately at her swami and said, "I see in these men a great bond of brotherly love and affection, and I met their young man earlier, the boy who so loved his horse. His heart is also pure and true. So you must trust fate and me." Ma turned to Marcus and said, "I will join you, but first, you must promise to not harm him."

The swami looked distraught and moved to speak, but held himself back. Ma looked deep into Marcus's heart, studying him for a liar. He groaned inwardly as he searched for an honest response. The master of discerning the truth of men's words had met his master.

"I will not lie. I won't harm him, but I might have to restrain him if he doesn't come willingly," Marcus said.

"Would you restrain me and force me to accompany you?" She laughed at her own serious question.

"No, of course not," Marcus said. He would never force a woman against her will.

"Perhaps you will afford him the same respect. I will join you."

The swami could no longer restrain himself. "Ma, Divine Mother, these are men of war and a cruel empire who crucify men. I am too old to travel at that pace on a horse's back. I never rode a horse before, but you know I'd die to join you if you tell me to. How can you . . . What will I . . . without you?" He looked like a child being ripped from the arms of his mother. Marcus felt sorry for him.

"Dear Bhakti," Ma said. She stood, taking his hands to pull him to his feet so she might delve into his eyes. "And what will I do without your delightful spiritual company, cooking, and service? We will abide. But imagine the synchronicity of this meeting. We all travel to Pali to find Issa and meet here in Rhagae. How can we not follow where the gods lead us? And our children, just think how happy they will be with my early return." Bhakti's pain-stricken face managed a smile at the thought of Ma returning to their children? Marcus noted they didn't seem to be a couple, and there was a significant age difference.

As Marcus pondered, Ma continued to comfort Bhakti. "I am always with you, and you are with me. Whenever you need me, I'll be there. Return to Pali at your pace, giving comfort and aid to people as you go, for Shakti and me." She laughed and added, "It sounds like our cavalry will not be stopping to smell the desert flowers or enjoy the cool mountain air. You must do this for both of us. I will be at peace, as I always am. Krishna will protect you as you hold fast to your faith. Kali calls, bidding me to ride alongside these warriors of empire. Bhagavan moves in such strange and wondrous ways. Jaya Bhagavan!"

May 15, 2029 – Day 45 at the Monastery

After one and a half months I, Thomas Mann, translator and editor, am still toiling away in my monastery cell in the Himalayas. Another Sunday night celebration has arrived. I am much more eager to meet, read, and discuss the story with my good friend, Lama Chin, than I would be with my archbishop, a realization that troubles me.

The jolly old lama, in a matching maroon robe, will soon be seated casually on a cushion across from me. He will be delighted to hear the story as written and then engage with me in an inspired discussion about the text as a launching pad into related spiritual matters. But the archbishop, I imagined, would be seated on a chair larger than mine to reign above me. His tight white collar and red cloak would be immaculate, and he'd eye me closely, one furrowed brow arched high, and his arms crossed tightly over his large well-polished crucifix, stopping me after each sentence to demand a footnote, correction, insertion, or deletion, as if we were ghostwriting the account to suit his personal theology.

Some version of that scenario might eventually play out with a Vatican cardinal, playing gatekeeper before my audience with the current wise and liberal pope. I'd aim high and start with the dean of cardinals as the archbishop had suggested. But today I'd meet with the lama, a man of understanding and curiosity, a man with sensibilities closer to the pope's than to my archbishop's.

I am midway through the scrolls and keeping pace at day forty-five of my ninety days of rice and vegetable curry with yak-milk tea. I have lost ten pounds, and my mind is playing tricks on me. My mind is much more present in the world of Jesus's resurrection than it is in the world of 2029, subjecting me to a passionate enchantment that consumes and enthralls me—one I don't want to escape. Some of my disorientation is likely a result of living by candlelight amid monks chanting day and night. Whatever the cause, the monastery and the manuscript have created a bridge back in time for me. When I am not working, my mind is mostly still; I looked forward to my friend's comforting guidance to question my work and the story being told. So I wouldn't forget, I took notes about what I thought we should discuss in our book club for two.

The work itself possesses me, placing me inside the hearts and minds of people whose lives were so intertwined that they knew each other almost as well as they knew themselves. They loved one another too—the respect and concern they displayed was heartfelt and authentic—possibly because theirs was an age when death, visions, and faith were much dearer and nearer, even for the reprehensible characters. I'd become immersed in a time when faith was recognized as the only true antidote to suffering other than, perhaps, Ma's tea and Poet's wine.

As I walked along the long dark corridors to Lama Chin's library study, I thought about the journey that the characters were on, a journey that spanned months on donkey and horseback. The ordeal must have been transformative, even for those used to such travel, and they were only halfway to India. Today, tourists travel with a water bottle and snacks always at hand while boarding air-conditioned tour buses and posting pictures of the Taj Mahal to their social media accounts. I could only imagine the hardship and exultation, the search for Jesus from Jerusalem to India over two thousand years ago produced.

At my host's study door, ample light from many candles and the smell of sage wafted out between the cracks. My solitary candle seemed inadequate. Lama Chin wasn't a Christian, but he was a wise man and full of light and love. I wanted to be no less a spiritual wizard and not just a scribe. Hot candle wax dripped onto my sore right hand, which ached from writing and rewriting. I smiled, thinking of all the hard work that I'd done in the service of the Lord, before knocking gently on the door.

Same as always came the lama's humble and hearty greeting. He embraced me and poured our reading-time tea. Knowing he was eager to resume the story, I began to read, starting with the final section of the earlier text to remind him where we'd left off. I read with dramatic feeling, as if I were auditioning to narrate the audiobook.

When I concluded, I joked, "So East has finally met West. Don't Marcus and Ma make quite the pair traveling together in search of Issa, who may be Jesus? If you believe," I added, not wanting to color his reaction with my doubts and hopes for what had and would transpire within the story.

"It is a grand story!" Lama Chin said with infectious joy.

It struck me that he was an older male version of the holy Ma. More than once I'd wished I could meet her; spending time with him proved as delightful as I imagined speaking with her would be. Ma had this old priest's heart praising the Lord with Jaya Bhagavan! Though Ma was a Hindu, she conjured the image of the Divine Mother. And though Lama Chin was Buddhist and looked like a Buddha, I saw the light of Jesus in his radiant eyes.

"I've been studying your Bible," the lama told me while pointing to an old ornate Bible sitting on his study table. "I know you to be quite literal," he said, "so maybe this part of the story may trouble you?"

I shook my head, not in consternation but with wonder. "Yes, there is a discrepancy that troubles me, but may I ask what you think it might be?"

"There is reference to Jesus ascending to be with God after forty days, and we are past that point in the story." With my hands pressed to my knees, I nodded in admiration, and he continued to read my mind, adding, "Like me, you must in your heart hope they find the real Jesus, but your head says that cannot be or what will that mean for your faith."

"You know me well, dear friend," I told Lama Chin. "But hours of prayer, toil, and conversations with you have opened my mind—or perhaps my heart—and made me less 'by the book' as my friend Miles would say. Yet, there's another discrepancy that still troubles me. The Gospel of John is the only one to report the Romans spearing Jesus on the cross. John also wrote that he bled, but blood *and water*. Even modern skeptics who argue he may not have died on the cross struggle to explain how water coming from the wound would indicate anything but death by asphyxiation." Hearing myself discuss Christ's crucifixion like a clinical coroner analyzing a cold case unsettled me.

"But if they actually find Jesus," I said, "that would be the biggest discrepancy of all, and a faith-affirming or faith-shaking discovery. And what will they do if they find him? I shudder to think."

"Men like Saltaurius and Dio still exist in our world," he said, for the first time looking downcast. I recalled that the para-military government shot protesting monks dead in broad daylight in the streets of Srinagar, so I imagined that was what he meant. We put our hands to our hearts in unison.

"Yes, but not here in your wonderful monastery of divine spirit," I said, wanting to cheer him up. "And wait, before I forget, *Centurion Cornelius*? Could he be the same Centurion Cornelius who, according to the book of Acts, was the first Gentile converted to Christianity by Peter? Until that point, Christianity was exclusively for Jews. And all this came about thanks to Marcus showing mercy to the fallen centurion?"

Lama Chin shared my excitement and responded to my rhetorical questions. "I don't know. I will have to read the Acts account!" My friend was a spiritual scholar.

"Tell me about your work transcribing texts—work that fills you with such joy—a joy I now understand after hours of toil and meditation on my manuscript."

Lama Chin beamed. "Yes, I've worked with many ancient stories, histories, teachings, and, ah, the poetry," he said, kissing his thumb and two forefingers as a chef declaring a masterpiece. "Mostly, the writings are Buddhist, some are Hindu, and some are non-denominational. Whatever the religion and language, the one great spirit shines through the poetry. There's a lot of beautiful poetry in the Bible." We both gazed reverently at his lovely Bible. Like Poet, Lama Chin loved poetry.

He stood either out of excitement or to stretch his legs and continued, saying, "Reading the perennial wisdom of the ancients is a spiritual practice for me. I imagine that the author, thousands of years ago, was writing for me. They wrote of the most important matters for posterity, and I search to recover those buried gems of wisdom. Since most people at that time were illiterate, and without a printing press, they would reach more people by telling their stories around campfires than by spending long hours painstakingly inscribing them with crude instruments onto precious paper. But instead, they still wrote with a passionate fire for those they loved *and* for future generations. They wrote for immortality. Only the best—" he said, looking admiringly at the books arrayed along his bookshelf. I imagined he had painstakingly translated more than a few of the works there, translations that had become as dear as children to him. He continued, "—wrote for you and me, the ones charged with transcribing their words and worlds into our current words and worlds. Perhaps they envisioned monks laboring to make copies or some new invention to preserve their stories and poems, making them easier to share with others."

He rejoined me on the cushions. The light in his eyes dimmed slightly as he looked deeply into my eyes. "It would be a tragedy if your pope buried your work out of fear of the past and the story it tells, like burning down an ancient forest." Though he said *forest*, I imagined that medieval cathedral going up in flames around me. He licked his thumb and index finger to snuff out a candle that was burning low beside us. "Thwarting creativity and extinguishing the life force that seeks to be heard after all these years." He bowed in conclusion, as though apologizing to both the pope and me for getting animated about the potential we would suppress the story and incinerate the scrolls. "But back to your story!" he said like a child not wanting to go to bed. "You must hope Marcus and Ma find Jesus, or would you rather they fail?"

"Well, we'll know it's fiction if Marcus finds Jesus and succeeds in marching him back to Rome for them both to be vindicated or put to death. There would have been a record of that," I said. "But you asked if I hope they find Jesus and not just another pious fraud using his story. Yes, I do, but let me explain." He stopped me with an outstretched hand and poured more tea. We both sipped; I was thankful for the moments of contemplation he'd given me.

I picked up my handwritten pages and waved them overhead, saying, "My breaks are spent reading the biblical accounts of the resurrection and the limited accounts of the ascension. Mark's reference to the ascension perplexed me. Inserted between Mark 16:8 and 16:9 in the English Standard Version of my Bible was one of the few commentaries that noted, 'Some of the earliest manuscripts do not include 16:9-20.' "

He held up his hand again, went to his desk to write down the passage numbers, and returned to his seat, where he nodded eagerly for me to continue.

"Most Christian scholars believe Mark did not write those passages but think they were added later. But why? That question led me to debate with myself about whether Jesus's *final* ascension after forty days, as stated in the book of Acts, is critical to my faith today. Maybe it was critical at the outset of Christianity—there's no correct way of saying—to believe that Jesus ascended once and for all into heaven. Our Saint Aquinas believed that his post-resurrection glorified body could ascend and descend at will—so perhaps if he went on teaching in his glorified body that would be faith affirming." I slumped to the side, chin resting on my palm. "I imagine my archbishop would not agree," I said.

"Or it's just a beautiful story of a child of God saving his saintly mother," he said. I recalled my magnum opus about the importance of the Holy Mother to Christian faith—an unfinished manuscript left behind in New York. But this journey, this story, would change everything. My own work felt minor and uninspired in comparison—reflecting an immature desire for the comfort of the Mother without fully confronting the life, death, and resurrection of our Lord. This was a true magnum opus—not mine, yet mine to bring to life.

"Maybe," I said. "Alone for hours with the manuscript, I confess to wanting Jesus Christ to be found alive by our heroes and not Saltaurius and the homicidal Dio. Is that blasphemy? As a good Catholic, I said. "priest, it is my duty to bow to the pope's prerogative and allow him to decide if this story should be told. Though I'd hate to see an old growth forest destroyed." We both smiled sadly.

"We don't yet know what they will find," Lama Chin said, "but I hope we will meet again in a couple weeks and learn more. Let us pray," he said, and we knelt in front of his stone Buddha. I pictured Jesus's living face in place of the stone one.

We prayed until the eight bells of curfew sounded, and I returned to my chamber, chastened and humbled. Book club with my good friend had renewed my determination to offer another ten pounds of flesh to finish my mission, scroll by scroll, before submitting myself and the manuscript to the wisdom of the Holy See in Rome.

CHAPTER 23
Another Horse

POET AND MARCUS marched back to their camp after meeting Ma like nothing had changed. They didn't speak. Poet was embarrassed at feeling like a schoolboy who had just climbed the highest tree. In camp, Boy was preparing their bundles of provisions, but dropped what he was doing to grab the reins of his new horse. He led the majestic animal over to introduce him to the men. "Charger," Boy said. "Have you ever seen such a black beauty? He's Arabian and almost as sweet-tempered as . . . Thank you so much for Charger, master Marcus and Uncle Poet. He will be well cared for." Boy didn't have to thank him, as they both served Marcus—nevertheless, it was a nice gesture.

"Boy, I know he'll be loved," Marcus said, and stroked the long, well-groomed neck of the horse. "And he's well named. A black beauty, ready for long rides with you. As we press forward, I will heed your advice on when the horses need to rest." Poet saw true penitence on his master's face as he spoke the words. "And now we need another horse. One that can travel long and hard like Charger, but with a featherweight rider. Make it a low mount or you'll be helping her on and off the horse ten times a day. That Indian woman has agreed to travel as our guide. Where she learned to ride is a mystery. We shall see. But she knows the man we seek, speaks the language, and knows the way."

"The Jaya Bhagavan woman?" Boy asked. "Ma? The beautiful lady who so lifted my spirits and smelled like the whittled horse you gave me? It was like she had bathed in sandalwood and jasmine." Boy was so delighted he jumped up and down, performing some Moroccan dance. They all shared a laugh.

"I am looking forward to finding more about her Hindu practices and beliefs," Poet said and turned to Marcus to get his assessment.

"I must confess, I admire her radiant countenance," Marcus said, looking down at his feet, shaking his head. Poet thought he might be blushing.

"Marcus is sweet on her," Boy teased his master, and was rewarded by a shove.

"Go get the girl a horse," Marcus said.

⌐ ⌐ ⌐

Two mornings later, Poet watched as Ma approached her horse to look it in the eye. The horse dipped its head for their foreheads to touch as she stroked its neck. "Kali," she said, naming her mare. Then Ma grabbed one horn of the saddle and swung herself up like an Olympic equestrian. The little girl could ride, though it may have been her first time on top of a horse.

The brothers and their newfound little sister and mother set off on their journey to Pali, seeking Issa and hopefully Jesus, with only mountains and deserts, bandits and warlords standing between them and their destiny.

Chapter 24

Unholy Redemption

Saltaurius arrived in Rhagae three days after Marcus and his travel companions departed for India. They'd come for Issa. He had sent Dio ahead to enter first, posing as a Roman merchant looking to sell the Persians' horses—all but one, Zamir's large Arabian. Saltaurius required an extra horse to carry the extra coins and gems and supplies, and Zamir's mount was a stout one for him to ride while resting the other horse. Saltaurius felt like a force of nature that no man, or men, should cross while riding that tall mount with Persian gold and silver around his waist, and a bracelet of gems stitched around his wrist.

He'd forgiven Dio the over exuberance of his rash, unsanctioned actions. Dio was right—Zamir and his men would have tried to prevent him from seizing his bounty. Their charred bones were left behind in the pyre and were now buried in his mind. He gave Dio his own fine bronze Roman necklace to wear over his tunic to make him appear more the wealthy seller of horses. The large medallion, the size of the giant's two fists, was meant to protect the heart in battle. It was engraved with a black Roman eagle framed by garlands, above the initials S.P.Q.R. The small breastplate covered Dio's entire gaunt chest, making him look somewhat ridiculous. Saltaurius had assured Dio, "Do not fret, Rhagae is not current on Roman fashion. You can keep it for all the gems you brought me. Maybe you'll grow into it."

Saltaurius still wore Zamir's Arab clothes. He was in fine spirits on a beautiful day. He'd finally meet the fraud named Issa and find out why Marcus had already left town empty-handed. Saltaurius wondered about Pilate's prophecy that he would kill Marcus if Marcus strayed from his duty.

Riding into town, Saltaurius spied a simply dressed man who looked Mediterranean, and might speak Latin or Greek. The man wore a crude wooden cross around his neck. He hadn't seen this symbol before but thought it must have something to do with Jesus and his crucifixion.

"Fine day, my friend. Where do you hail from? And what brings you here?" Saltaurius asked.

"Greece." The man didn't seem to want to engage cordially, despite Saltaurius's kindly salutation and imposing size.

"What's that you wear around your neck?" Saltaurius asked, and thought, *And you better stop walking away while I'm talking to you.*

"Two sticks bound together," the man said and continued to walk toward the square.

"A cross? Are you, like me, a lover of Jesus?" Saltaurius said. "Do they call him Issa here? And do you know where I might find him?"

"Everyone is wary of strangers, stranger," the man said.

If I wasn't in such a good mood, I'd be throttling you. Dio's pyre is still smoldering, Saltaurius thought. He'd said a soldier's prayer in front of the blazing pyre just a couple hours ago, as Dio pretended to bow his head, though it may just have been his normal slump.

"Issa is now well guarded after being threatened by a Roman tribune who said he would kill us all if Issa didn't leave town," the stranger said. "So the holy man left—for our sake. But now with the Romans gone, he has returned and will resume his sermons tomorrow in the square there." He pointed a short distance down the lane ahead.

"I have also come to protect his holiness. Where will I find him?" Saltaurius asked.

"At the inn, there," the Greek man said, pointing up a hill a short distance from the square. "But you'll have to wait till dawn tomorrow to see him preach. And see there," the Greek said, raising his finger to point to the square, "another Roman has come, but he doesn't look like he could beat one guard, let alone three." In the square, Saltaurius saw his cut-throat advisor with the Arabian horses he was selling.

The Greek walked on into the square as Saltaurius amused himself, calling after him, "Unless they were asleep."

Dio had successfully drawn significant attention from the devout followers of Issa, who didn't trust any Roman, even a small one armed only with a knife. Dio had a large crowd around him and most of his audience didn't look like they could afford a horse. The farther east they roamed, the more they stuck out as strangers, even while still on the Silk Road.

Waiting until the next morning was not an option for Saltaurius. He dismounted his horse and found a stick. He broke the wood in two and used a thin strip of leather to bind them together into the semblance of a cross. Saltaurius found a stable to hold his new horse before walking up the lane to the inn, where he was met by three guards with curved swords. Clutching his cross, he requested an immediate audience with Issa. There was a lot of back and forth with one guard shuttling in and out of the inn. Saltaurius assumed he was consulting with Issa. He'd offered to send up a bag of silver coins. They required him to hand over his sword and knife, along with the silver, which had been accepted to gain his audience with the holy man.

As Saltaurius entered the room, Issa gestured toward the window seat. "So you are Greek?" Issa said. "And you speak Latin and dress like a local, but you carry a straight sword? I hope you are not a Trojan horse. You certainly are as big as one. But I am glad to see you carry a cross. The symbol of my persecution."

"I do carry it," Saltaurius said, kissing his rustic cross. The man didn't look sufficiently like the real Jesus to bother with taking his head, but Saltaurius would have fun with him in any event. "I am a man of the world and call no place home. Are you Jesus, the Christ who performed miracles and was resurrected from the dead? I worship that man. My Persian friends call you Yuz Asaf."

In a less wary voice, Issa said, "That's what they say. I simply say I am not a man of this world. Though men have given the son of God many names, call me Issa here. And yes, I resurrected myself from the cross."

"What about your disciples and followers you left behind in Judaea to be slaughtered?" Saltaurius asked.

"They will be at peace with my father, having accepted me," Issa said, bowing his head before looking up at his large wayward practitioner. "My son, I see you are a tortured soul. Do not trouble yourself with others' suffering until you heal yourself in my name. Please come and kneel that I might touch your forehead and bless you. Then you may go on your way in peace."

"And may my peace be with you when I go," Saltaurius said, enjoying his devout role, kneeling down with reverence, amused that he was still shoulder high to the charlatan. Issa pulled back his golden sleeves to pray over his head. Then Issa picked up a scented oil vial from a tray to sprinkle the oil on two of his fingertips. As Issa bent over to touch the giant's forehead with the anointing fingers, Saltaurius grabbed him by the neck, whipping him around into in a full headlock with the crook of his arm holding the fraud's jaw shut. His wrestling lessons served him well. He twisted Issa like a small branch over his knee, so his face looked up into his. The fraud looked comically frightened, like he was staring into the mouth of the hound of Hades. Saltaurius opened his own mouth wide, threatening to swallow him with one big bite.

"You're no son of God. I know him, met him, saw him perform miracles. He would not allow his disciples and believers to suffer so. You are a fraud. Jesus died on the cross for my sins and ascended to his father. And you tarnish his mystery and glory." He now understood what Dio meant. He knew his duty.

Dragging his small prey by the neck, he headed toward the other end of the room, in case there was an ear at the door. Issa flapped his arms and legs like a golden calf headed to slaughter. With utter horror behind his eyes, the fake Issa stared up at the rafters.

"I have some questions. If you scream, I will break your neck before anyone can help you," Saltaurius said with his thick arm still around Issa's neck. "You saw three Romans. The head man was a tribune. They met with you. And now where are they going?"

"Yesssssss," he hissed through a half-collapsed windpipe. "I'll tell you if you let me live."

"Be quick about it." A fork pierced the dried salted pork under a glass dome on the cupboard. Saltaurius removed the dome with his free hand and picked up the pork by the fork to take a bite. "Ah, a knife," he exclaimed as he discovered a small blade hidden beneath the pork.

Issa's eyes bulged, and he started struggling.

"Don't worry about the knife. I could just ring your neck or fork you to death. Quietly, now, tell me where they went." He stabbed a large chunk of pork that he devoured in one bite.

"They are following the real Issa to India," Issa gasped like a man eager to not to be sucked into the belly of the beast.

"Where? You see? You still can breathe." Saltaurius loosened his grip further.

"To Pali in India."

"I know you want to live." He gave the man's slim neck a little wiggle room. "What else can you tell me about them?"

"They rode out on horses with an Indian holy woman three mornings ago to find the real Issa."

"What do they want with this woman?"

"I don't know. Please let me go." The fraud was too scared to lie.

"Sure, I will dispatch you. You are God. The great resurrector cannot be killed." With his free hand, Saltaurius pulled the knife from the plate. "Holy pig eater—die!" he said as he plunged the knife deep into the bulging jugular vein. He watched the man writhe, drowning in his own blood, flopping his body about like a goldfish on a hook until, twenty seconds later, he was dead and not coming back to life anytime soon.

Saltaurius used a pitcher of water to wash the blood off his arm and into a basin. He then put the remaining hunk of pork into his satchel and picked up the bag of silver he had sent up. He paused and then placed the silver back down. "A deal's a deal," he said to the dead man and laughed, and then considered removing the blood-streaked golden robe as a trophy for Dio, but that would cause him trouble with the men guarding the inn door. Saltaurius met them with a devout smile on his way out and held up his cross, so they'd let him pass. They returned his sword and knife, and he headed on down the lane, whistling a marching tune.

Saltaurius had only walked twenty paces from the inn before the shouting started. He saw Dio crouching behind a cart to his left, pretending to relace his boot. From behind, he could hear the three armed men from the inn were rushing him, but as they got closer, he slowly turned, still whistling. With raised Arabian scimitars, they shuffled their feet as they approached, none of them wanting to be the first to arrive at the foot of the bear. Raising his own Roman sword, he faced them. Just out of sword's reach, they stopped, bracing themselves for a fight. Saltaurius knew such men. It was plain they hoped to use each other as shields when the fighting started. Though Dio was now in hiding, Saltaurius was grateful to him. If Dio hadn't slit the Persian men's throats, he'd be facing six men and not three. Zamir alone would have been a formidable force.

The three guards looked terrified, and this made Saltaurius feel fearless. They feared his size, but they had no inkling of his true power. Saltaurius never failed to take his foes by surprise, his sword an extension of his will, flowing seamlessly from one hand to the other with lethal precision. Each strike came from an unpredictable angle, a dance of steel that none had lived to bear witness. Now, as he faced his hapless challengers, his equipoised assault itched to be unleashed after a long fallow season. But he would grant them one final chance to walk away—if they were wise enough to take it. He stopped whistling to say, "He was a fraud. And did you forget my silver? And all his other possessions and coins? Your new inheritance. Thank me and go, or die. Your choice."

They saw the logic in his reasoning, but the ingrates offered no gratitude. Instead, they shuffled back toward the inn, keeping an eye on the giant. Saltaurius turned and started whistling again as he moved in the opposite direction.

CHAPTER 25
Tali

ON MA'S FIRST day of riding with the men, they set up camp by sundown. Boy was grateful that Marcus had avoided pushing the horses or Ma. She looked quite comfortable on Kali and had no trouble keeping up with the leisurely pace. Boy reflected on what he believed to be a miracle he had witnessed that day. As they rode, he saw Kali's four-legged shadow upon the ground, but her rider, Ma, cast no shadow. As he was about to point this out to Marcus and Poet, a large cloud appeared suddenly in the otherwise clear blue sky to block the sun. He took this as an omen to never speak of the shadowless Ma, but his spirit stirred as never before. She made him feel . . . whole. Ma was a wonderful addition to their small company.

The camp was secure and at little risk of bandits, so they would play Tali for fun, not for the order of the night watch. Poet showed Ma the sheep bones they would use to play.

Boy foraged for a large piece of bark to serve as the dice board. He liked his sheep bones kept clean and not rolling on the dirt. Looking around the forest for the Tali board, Boy wondered if he was too sensitive to be a man like Marcus. He'd already noticed a seismic shift of energy with Ma now a part of their quest—a balancing of polar opposites and smoothing of rough edges. He already felt love for Ma the way the worshippers of Jesus loved him, he imagined.

Each time she affectionately called him "son" in her sweet voice, the single word plucked a string in his heart, sending ripples through his core.

Returning to camp, he heard Poet instructing Ma. "There are four sides, see: one, three, four, and six. The two ends, two and five, are too pointy to land face up. There are four dice rolled. The best score is all four producing different numbers. Next, three different numbers, followed by two. All the same number and you lose. You'll soon catch on. We'll play just for fun." He rattled the bones in his hand.

"That's good. I have no money," Ma said.

"Neither does Boy, and he loves to play. When we play for stakes, it is for who gets which watch that night. No one wants the second watch, in the middle of the night," Poet said. "But it is said that the stakes are always high, with nothing short of our entire lives being determined by each roll. Dice is a game we Romans infuse with superstition. We believe the gods play along."

"Wow! High stakes! But how does the game impact our *entire* lives?" Ma asked, brimming with excitement.

"Based on what we roll, the gods change our fate," Poet said.

Ma smiled. She was always smiling, just more or less. "I didn't know the gods played dice," she said. "But of course they do. They are immanent in all things, and transcendent too, of course," she added with a laugh.

"We'll roll first and then you. So you can learn," Poet said.

The three of them rolled the Tali as Ma watched. Boy got three different numbers, Poet two, and Marcus the coveted four.

"Now it's your turn, Ma. You now have to match Marcus's roll, or he wins the first round." Poet handed her the dice ceremoniously.

She put them between her hands, which she placed to her heart and closed her eyes before she rattled the dice and rolled—a four. Boy could almost feel her peace and fullness of heart when she emptied her mind.

"Beginner's luck," Poet said. "You and Marcus roll for the winner of the first game."

Marcus rolled another perfect score of four. "Auspicious is the day!" Poet exclaimed.

Ma performed her same mind-clearing play before she rolled. She, too, rolled another perfect four.

The men exchanged glances with Boy. They looked unnerved. It's very rare to land a back-to-back pair of four rolls by two people. Boy was thrilled with Ma's first game of Tali and the magic of the rolls.

"Logic tells us the chances of this coincidence are very unlikely. The Greek Pythagoras could calculate the odds. But it is very odd," Poet said.

Marcus mimicked Ma's gestures in jest, dramatically cupping his hands to his chest and closing his eyes momentarily. This pleased Ma. But he rolled all sixes, receiving the lowest score. Boy remembered he once suggested they invert the game where all sixes would be the best score, but Marcus and Poet had dismissed his suggestion. All true Romans played Tali as the gods had decreed.

Ma showed Marcus how to perform her mummery and rolled. They all sat looking at the roll in disbelief as she rolled another four. Boy scooped up the dice and put them away, doing it joyfully, not fearfully. In all the games of Tali he had ever played and seen, he had never witnessed this. Seeing was believing.

Ma giggled. "Is the game over so soon?"

"The Oracle's Roll," Marcus said, using the Roman expression for three perfect rolls in a row. Boy knew Marcus was not a sore loser, but he appeared shaken by the Oracle's Roll. He had picked up his whittling, which he used to settle his thoughts.

Poet explained, "It is said that when a person rolls three perfect scores in a row, the gods have intervened, entering that person. It is beyond coincidence, and the game must end immediately."

Boy was glad Marcus did not believe in witchcraft—or, at least, that all witches were bad. He had heard Poet tell the story of superstitious Roman soldiers who met a seer in the black forest of Germania. She bet the men a large, antlered buck that they had just shot with an arrow against her life that she could roll the Oracle's Roll on her first three rolls. And she did. The soldiers beheaded her for witchcraft but buried the bloody buck by her side.

"The gods are always with us," Ma said. "There are no coincidences. I simply imagined what I would roll and let the gods provide it. Jaya Bhagavan!"

CHAPTER 26
The Calm

POET WAS INSPIRED and began writing poetry again. He had never experienced such ease on a long, arduous journey before. The band of brothers and sister—as he liked to consider the four of them—enjoyed a challenging but uneventful two weeks of riding about eight hours a day. A mountain range appeared on the horizon, which gave Poet a point of reference. India was still at least two weeks of deserts and mountains away. Ma knew a pass through the mountains that led into the large Indus valley. Marcus and Boy also appeared lighthearted as their horses trotted along in the fair weather. Ma never tired or let her joyful spirit drop. Poet knew the three of them would not be outdone and matched their spirits to hers. They played Tali to pass the time. Ma didn't always allow herself to win. Poet thought he could tell when she was being gracious by the soft smile that played on her lips.

Poet and Boy were learning seated meditation, and Marcus would lie still in what Ma called the dead man's pose. Poet drank less wine and more of Ma's tea. He found that after long days on horseback, the wine would dull the pain of his aching of joints and stiff muscles, but the tea refreshed and soothed them. Ma's cooking complimented Poet's staple of boiled, fried, or pickled fish and salted animal flesh, which Ma did not eat. For breakfast she made a simple but delicious *kanji*—wet rice with nuts and Indian spices. For dinner, she mixed grains with lentils and any vegetable

Boy could find—accented by spicy peppers and turmeric that Poet had never tasted before.

Gone were the rip-roarious farts around the campfire the men used to compete with for maximum sound, duration, and foulness of odor. Poet found a kindred spirit in Ma, who was able and wanting to speak of soaring philosophical concepts and sublime poetry. He was teaching her to speak, read, and write Latin like a Roman. She was a voracious learner.

"Tell me of your own poetry," Ma said to Poet as they traveled a pleasant, flat stretch of road.

"I am a poet only when the spirit moves me. Greek and Roman poets are like minor prophets or demi-oracles. We wait for the muses to come to sing our songs. We are mere instruments to these higher powers that play us like a lyre. When we sing, it is with their voice, not our own. Only they can express truth and beauty through us."

"Ah," she said with a laugh. "Truth *is* beauty. Then you must quiet the mind so the divine grace may come—just like me. Genuine passion and poetry please God. Tell me, do they let women sing and write poetry in Greece and Rome?"

"Yes," Poet responded. "The mother of lyrical poetry was a Greek woman named Sappho. May her words of love never be lost." Poet made prayer hands to Ma and almost fell off his horse in doing so.

"Let that be a lesson to you," Marcus said to Poet, as he had been listening to the conversation. "The great poets are Roman men who sing of the glories of war. Poet, you should write Ma a song about her quest with Roman soldiers."

They all had a laugh.

"Ah, I'll do that," Poet said, "if she can answer this riddle posed by Pythia, the Oracle of Delphi. If she can, she will have answered all questions."

Ma was beaming again, awaiting the challenge.

"Where and when does east meet west?" Poet asked.

Ma didn't miss a beat. "Here and now, of course!"

Poet and Ma laughed, but he wondered if she had just solved the question that had stumped the great intellects of Greece and Rome.

CHAPTER 27
The Gathering Storm

MARCUS WAS WELL aware of the gathering storm. Despite the jolly esprit de corps, an incorporeal demon followed them day by day and slipped into the camp each night, fanning unholy desire. Perhaps it was Ma's ability to ride and camp with delightful presence and her luminous olive skin that drove him to distraction. His admiration and physical attraction had become an unexpressed obsession. His desire was bolstered by the heat of the days and Ma's rhythmic bobbing up and down in her saddle. Marcus's horse was now falling in behind hers for long stretches.

Poet had caught on. He must have recognized the look in Marcus's eyes when he gazed upon Ma. One didn't have to be a doctor to diagnose the fever spreading from his loins to infect his mind. Poet warned Marcus that he feared disaster would follow. "Nothing sinks camp camaraderie faster than sexual relations between two members of camp," he had reminded Marcus. Poet saw a potential desecration of Marcus's nobility should he take what he so desperately desired.

Marcus rationalized the matter by noting to himself that gods and goddesses were always taking worthy mortals to mate. She was Diana on this hunt and Epona of the horses, but she also was flesh and blood. Her flesh could barely hold her buoyant grace. Her blood was pulsing with vibrant life. She was also human, though she ate like a bird. Her scent of sandalwood and jasmine surrounded him like a delicate fog, even when she was riding far ahead or behind him. And her girlish laugh intoxicated him like tiny bubbles running up and down his spine. Ma was always quick with that laugh and the singing of praises to gods he didn't know. At times, it almost overwhelmed him like a full bladder of wine in the morning when the cock crows. There was a time for mirth and singing and a time for passion and its glorious fruition.

Wasn't he worthy of an Indian mystic, even if she was some sort of goddess? Or did his family's fall mean he could not have her as an equal? He was still a tribune of the Roman Empire. His mind raced, and his body ached for a taste of forbidden Indian fruit.

Her dark and mesmerizing brown eyes, which she locked readily with his, opened vast vistas of pleasure in him. Other than looking into her blissful eyes, so joyful and wise, she gave him no sign of passion. He would wait for her invitation or initiate the coupling at the point when he could no longer bear the torture of restraining his animal desire. Between the heat of the day and the fire that burned inside, he thought, like Heracles, he might suffer self-immolation.

The summer heat required water not wine. Lots of water for the horses and their riders. Water was heavy and they could not carry too much on the overtaxed horses. And donkeys would slow down their progress too much. Ma led them from one watering hole to another, with minimal hardship. If they missed one of these sources of water, it would have meant misery or death before they reached the next.

At one of the many streams that Ma had led them to, in the shade of a big old banyan tree, Marcus and Ma idled with their feet in the stream. The goddess turned her gaze from the endless hypnotic current of rushing water and asked the Roman tribune, "What is the meaning you search for, from this Issa or Jesus?"

"To restore my family's honor."

"Is honor more important than meaning?" she asked, raising her dripping-wet feet, and pointing her perfect toes. Marcus reflected on those beautiful feet that men and women who didn't know her would prostrate themselves to touch while Ma giggled and told them to rise to meet her eyes.

Ma continued to flex her feet and point her toes. As she dipped them back into the stream to join his feet, Marcus had the sneaking thought that perhaps this was the spiritual foreplay of Indian courtship. He brushed his foot against hers in the water, feeling a rush of elation. As she gazed into the stream, she turned taciturn for a split second before regaining her joyful countenance. The water, too, seemed to ripple around their feet before returning to its calm flow.

"There is no meaning unless we live with honor," he said.

"Agreed," Ma said and let out a gentle laugh. "But meaning dictates what honor is. What is the meaning of our lives?"

"To survive, so we may protect and provide for those under our care and those we love." Marcus pounded his leg, thinking about his failure to meet his own standard. He'd let his family be massacred while he was gallantly fighting in Egypt for their killer.

"Sometimes it is impossible to protect those we love. And that too is God's will," Ma said. Marcus had reprimanded Poet for telling Ma about the treachery and slaughter of the House of Decia in Rome, though he knew she could be trusted with the confidence. "You take on great responsibility."

"*Responsible!*" Marcus exclaimed. "That is the word for me."

"Then you approach realization. Our actions become responsible once we realize who we truly are. Responsible service to others is worthy action, but what gives that service and our lives meaning?" she asked again with those dark brown eyes fixed upon him.

"You tell me," he said.

"Love!" she exclaimed, clapping her hands and laughing. Her face, the picture of holy love, confused Marcus and his all-too-human desire. "Now, once again, why should we continue our search for Issa?"

"Because it is my duty?" Marcus asked, becoming impatient with her questions and his answers. He realized his answer was only slightly different from before.

But Ma was patient with him, like he imagined she would be with any young student. "Is your duty aligned with love?" she asked.

It was his turn to laugh. "Not always. If you ever fought barbarians, you'd understand."

"Even going into battle a warrior can be aligned with divine love. There's a good Vedic book about that. I'll tell you all about that Song of the Lord around the campfire tonight. You'll like the story. It's about a warrior like you."

They both removed their feet from the icy water to warm them in the sun. Ma lay back to take full measure of the sun. Marcus again wondered if this was a subtle eastern sign, but it wasn't enough of an invitation to act upon.

"But here we are searching for a master magician or the son of God," Marcus said, "to bring the fraud to justice or to discover the God for ourselves. I can't imagine a more important duty. Seems to me to be aligned with love. But Ma, to be clear—so I am aligned with you and thereby with love—if we find him, I will not hurt him but demand he accompany me to Rome, where we will both meet our fate and seek justice for our wrongs."

"Only a master can make demands on a slave. He is no slave. You are free to ask, even if you make your request in the form of a demand. I will lead you to him, so you may *ask* him to go to Rome. But let us focus on the journey and our search for divine love wherever we find it." He wondered if she was implying to love the one you're with. And then she added, "Home is when our hearts are in perfect alignment with God. May you find that again."

"Rome is, or was, my home. My father was a brilliant statesman and senator for the people. My wife was the epitome of grace and beauty."

"How about your mother?" Ma asked.

"Kind, sweet, nurturing, and loving—qualities I pushed away as weakness." Marcus rarely spoke of his unassailable mother. The Decia family villa in Rome held a shrine to goddess Cybele, making it home to two great mothers, with his wife about to make it three, before his entire ancestorial lineage had been so brutally cut down.

"Why resist the tears now? Allow those qualities of the Divine Mother to come alive."

"I never got to say goodbye or thank her for her . . ." Marcus choked back tears. His unmanly display of emotion, which he feared might break forth in full force, unsettled him. If he just grabbed Ma and kissed her hard and long enough, perhaps he could stem the flow and self-loathing. But the thought of his dead mother reined him in.

"Sacrifice?" Ma asked.

"Yes," he said, while trying to gather his thoughts, which swung wildly from passionate action to maternal love.

"She wouldn't consider it a sacrifice to have a child like you. A good mother you honor by your gratitude and openness to her love in your life."

"How do you know so much about motherhood?"

"My name is Ma, and I have a hundred children," she said as she smiled with her eyes and lips. Marcus didn't want to be just another child to Ma. "When mothers rule the world, there will be no dictators, slavery, castes, or war. And every child will be cherished." She bent down and scooped some water from the stream into her hands to take a small drink and then dipped down again and offered Marcus a drink from the water cupped between her precious hands. He surprised himself and lowered his face to her hands, feeling like a child and less like the suitor and lover he wanted to be.

"A dictator destroyed my home and slayed my mother, so that day might be too late for me. But I can still wish for it for all humanity," Marcus said, mimicking her frequent gesture by placing his palms together in front of his heart. He wondered who now led them forward and if he had just relinquished his command.

"Our home is here and now," she said.

"And a wonderful home it is by a stream, on a sunny day, somewhere in Parthia with you." He reached for her hand, but she picked it up before he could consummate the touch. Ma closed her eyes and adjusted her seat to a crossed leg position, signaling she needed a moment of peace and meditation. Marcus stayed beside her as one moment passed into many moments. He waited in silence for her to signal the time of refreshment had ended.

"Om, shanti, shanti, shanti," Ma intoned with a deep and resonant voice. "Let's move on," she said while standing, offering Marcus her hand. He took it and was stunned by her strength as she pulled him up. "There is another stream we can reach before nightfall."

Ma would always exclaim, "Jaya Bhagavan!" before she drank at a new watering spot. Soon Boy and Poet were doing the same. Despite being a leader, not a follower, Marcus couldn't escape the refrain in his head. Ma had no fear of dying of thirst. She had no fear. He wondered how she did not even fear him. If she could see his thoughts and knew his thirst for their lips and flesh to coalesce, she might fear him. But perhaps she already knew. She was very intuitive.

CHAPTER 28
Casual Cruelty

BHAKTI WAS HALF asleep when he heard the threatening sound of horses cantering up from behind him. He didn't have to turn around to feel their dark energy.

"Look, Dio!" Saltaurius yelled. "Asses up ahead. An orange ass riding a little red donkey." The big man laughed, and the stunted man snickered at the childish humor. They overtook Bhakti, the big man slowing next to Bhakti's slow-moving donkey while the little man and horse fell in behind.

"Greetings, friends," Bhakti said, but they ignored him and kept riding along with him as if he wasn't there. Bhakti was not going to put up with being flanked by the intimidating marauders, so he dismounted and pulled his donkey aside, off the dirt path, to see what they wanted. They too stopped, no doubt to menace him further. Bhakti assumed they were well aware of the fear they induced in people. He noted the extra-large man was clearly not Parthian or Persian even though he wore an Arab robe. But it was the other man that scared him. As a spiritual adept, Bhakti was sensitive to energy fields. He had seen brilliant energy fields dancing with light and color, none brighter than Ma's, but this little man's field was black and devoid of light and color, a negative vortex sucking light in and allowing no light to escape.

"How may I help you?" Bhakti asked.

"How kind of you to offer," the big man said as he dismounted his enormous horse. As he hovered over the holy man he said, "First, we seek information. Did you see three Romans and a holy woman—one of your kind dressed in white—pass you along the way?"

This question posed an ethical dilemma for Bhakti. He had vowed to always tell the truth, but he suspected these men had malicious intentions toward Ma and her companions. "No one fitting that description has passed me." This was true and satisfied his conscience because technically they did not pass him; they left him behind. "What are they to you?" he asked.

"They are fellow travelers like you, my friend, unless you lie to me and then you are my mortal enemy. I am Saltaurius, the great fraud hunter. And this is Dio, also quite skilled in the art of deciphering deception."

"You take the truth quite seriously, as do I," Bhakti said.

Dio, still mounted, moved his horse up behind Bhakti, close enough that its hot breath was moistening the back of Bhakti's neck.

"My friend," Saltaurius said, pointing to Dio, "is a classically educated Roman and not enamored by Eastern mysticism, which he thinks is all sorcery and witchcraft. You are not a sorcerer, are you? Or a witch with sour sack bosoms hiding under those bright orange robes?"

"No."

Dio pointed to the donkey, which had a long staff strapped to it. Bhakti used it for walking long distances when his donkey needed to rest.

"You carry a staff like one," Saltaurius said.

"I am not a sorcerer."

Dio rolled his eyes and murmured.

"What are you then, in those robes?" Saltaurius demanded.

"A simple monk."

"In such bright robes? No riches?"

"No. A poor and simple monk."

Saltaurius nodded to Dio, who then dismounted and began to rifle through the donkey's packs.

"Hey, stop that. This is beyond rude. I have nothing of value."

But Dio didn't stop. He dug until he found the bag of grain that Bhakti used to make simple flatbread and to feed his donkey. Dio let a significant amount drop from his hands, falling into a heap on the dirt.

"My apologies," the man named Saltaurius said. "He doesn't think you are telling the entire truth. Neither do I. Let me ask again. Do you know some holy lady?"

"I know a holy lady . . . or two."

"Could she be the one that rides with my friends? And who your tracks have been following since Rhagae?"

"Could be. But I cannot see what is ahead of me any more than you can."

"Let's assume she is the one with my Roman friends."

"All right . . . Stop that!" Bhakti shouted at Dio, who was taking all his scrolls of holy text and bowls and cups and tossing them onto the dirt road. Dio answered by taking a long drink from Bhakti's water pouch while puckering his thin, cracked lips.

"Dio," scolded the big man, "show some manners. He's cooperating now."

Dio, having found nothing of value, led Bhakti's donkey away and tethered the reins to his horse. Bhakti's fears were now confirmed. *If they didn't kill him outright, they planned on leaving him for dead fifty miles from the last village without food or water. And the next village was fifty or more miles ahead. Without his donkey and water, his life was lost.*

"That's just to prevent the ass from wandering off," Saltaurius said, as if reading Bhakti's thoughts. "Again, if you don't lie to me, we mean you no harm." Dio sneered at the promise of no harm. "So let's say it is your friend. Why would she ride with Romans?"

"Maybe they are looking for spiritual guidance?"

"Maybe, but not likely. I've been told by others that have been more forthcoming with me that she is from Pali, India, and is leading them that way. You, with your leathered brown skin, look like you might be from there. If they were not so easy to follow, we might ask you to join us. Is the holy lady you know from Pali?"

"Yes."

"What a coincidence. Before meeting the Romans, she traveled with an orange-robed swami, someone who sounds a great deal like you, by the description others have provided. Was this swami, by any chance, you?"

"Yes," he said proudly, "I am Swami Bhakti." The declaration of his true self brought him some modicum of courage.

"Well, my Swami Bhakti, can you tell me anything useful about the Issa they seek, perhaps?"

"No," Bhakti said. "It seems you know more than I do about these matters."

Saltaurius moved back to his horse held by Dio, but returned to Bhakti to finish his humiliation. Merely leaving him without his donkey, food, and water was apparently not sufficiently cruel. "I think you lied or didn't *not* lie. Either way, we defrock lying priests in Rome. You'll remove that nice orange robe. It'll make a nice blanket for our donkey."

"No," Bhakti said as he backed away. He tripped on the uneven earth as he did but managed to keep himself from falling, though his legs remained unsteady beneath him. His last vestige of his relationship to Ma was his orange robe.

Dio pulled his knife, and Saltaurius laughed. "That won't be necessary. We don't kill without reason. Even though you lied, I don't think you are a spiritual fraud. We do kill those. But we must enforce Roman law wherever we go." Saltaurius grabbed the back of Bhakti's robe and yanked it over his head, knocking the holy man to his knees. "On second thought, Dio, catch. You can wear it to bed at night." He balled up the robe and threw it to Dio, who stuffed it in a saddle pouch. "Now, stay put and pray for your life."

As the horses led Bhakti's enslaved donkey away, Saltaurius reached down to the donkey's side and untied Bhakti's walking stick. "Here, keep your sorcerer's rod. It's too small for me and too big for him." He threw it like a javelin. It stuck in the soft ground inches in front of where Bhakti knelt. And there he was, a once proud swami. He lowered his head in shame—lost and alone.

Bhakti knelt there for a long time until his knees were sore, and his thigh muscles burned. He reasoned he must have deserved the pain and humiliation he'd just suffered at the hands of his fellow man. With Ma, everything came when needed and all calamity was averted. Without Ma, where was his faith? Doubts and fear filled his mind. How could his guru abandon him and allow this cruel fate to follow? Without clothes, food, or water, and only a loincloth and a walking stick, he was sure to die. If he just sat there, he would survive longer without food and water than he would scrambling down the road with foolish hope. He looked down at his raisin-like skin further shriveling in the sun. This dirty, barren place was far from auspicious for him. It was the spot of his fall from Ma's grace.

Ma's grace. A giggling breeze of sandalwood and jasmine was tickling his nostrils and whispering in his ears. *His grace, our grace, Jaya Bhagavan!* He looked up at the blue sky and golden sun. It was a loving, smiling face—a gift for him. Ma's radiant face! Ma's beautiful voice! She was still with him.

What a blessing, he thought, *being stripped of all trappings to test my faith.* He used his walking stick to get back up on his spindly but sturdy legs. He reached down to gather the handful of grains from the dirt where Dio had dumped them and walked forward. His heart brimmed with praise, gratitude for life, Ma, and divine grace. If death should come, he'd be ready.

The next day, he found a small desert oasis with a well and some cactus fruit. And by divine providence there was a gourd left there that he filled with water and fruit. Three days later, with the gourd down to its last drops of water and a single berry, he reached an enclave in need of a cook. A month later, he joined a caravan of good people traveling to Pali, India, serving as their cook and spiritual guide.

CHAPTER 29

Camels

By the third week of their journey to Pali, the landscape shifted from wooded terrain to sandy desert stretches, with mountains in the horizon. Marcus's desire was still straining his loincloth and clouding his mind. The incessant rays of the sun beat down baking the sand beneath their horses' hoofs. It was good that Ma knew where to find shade as well as water. Boy did his best to keep the horses from overheating. They made slow progress, stopping for long stretches in the shade to avoid the midday sun. Still, they had felt close to death at many points during that week. Though Ma now led the way, Marcus still felt responsible for his troops' lives, and he'd seen enough to know death was always near.

Near the end of one long, insufferable ride, nine armed men on camels shadowed their steps. They didn't look friendly and there were too many to confront head on. *How was he to defend his men and Ma from an attack?* He didn't have a good answer.

Poet said, "Should we outrun them? How fast can camels with two humps gallop?" The bandits, traveling in luxury, sat between the two humps. The second hump provided a pleasant backrest.

"On soft sand, for any distance, the camels will overtake horses, who may stumble," Marcus answered.

"Best we pay them no mind, like a passing dream," Ma said.

"Like a mirage?" Boy asked.

"Exactly!" Ma exclaimed, laughing despite their deadly serious situation.

Marcus held up his hand to signal silence as he searched his mind for their best strategic option.

They rode on in silence with the bandits only a good javelin throw behind them over their left shoulders. Marcus looked for an opportune place to camp before sunset. "They may be waiting to charge when the setting sun will be in in our eyes," he said. But they still did not attack. Marcus located a spot to camp against the face of a rock cliff, preventing them from being encircled. He motioned to Boy and Poet. They knew the drill and started roping the horses five to ten paces apart and positioning boulders in between to prevent a frontal assault on their camp. It would be three against nine, unless Ma proved to be a warrior as well. Ma, for the time being, went about feeding and watering their horses while they continued to fortify their position.

The bandits, who until then had been watching at a safe distance, started their deliberate approach. Marcus, Poet, and Boy sat sharpening their swords, hoping to dissuade the foe. They noticed the bandits were dressed like Turks in their white sheets and yellow rope belts for strangling, and self-assured in their posture. They rode right up to the horse line to make their demands. Their leather and fur saddles made it clear to Marcus that they were not straggly bandits as Marcus had hoped but successful ones who hailed from a land of extreme temperatures, probably dwelling in the mountains and patrolling the desert valley. Several of them carried arrows and bows. The cliff behind them no longer served as a tactical advantage. Their archers could be repositioned there after climbing the long ridge to their right. If they shifted their archers to the ridge, Marcus would strike the remaining men before they could secure their position above them.

The leader was tall and strong with scars on both cheeks. "I serve the sultan, and you must pay a toll for crossing his lands," he demanded in a local dialect Ma understood and translated. Marcus had the remaining silver and gold from Pilate's purses and some of his own. He was weighing whether to negotiate or fight. Always negotiate first was what his father had taught him.

Then Ma stepped forward and addressed the bandits. Marcus disapproved of Ma speaking out of turn in this critical situation, but he also didn't want to undermine her—and himself—by pulling her back or correcting her. Their foe would perceive such an exchange as a weakness of his command. Poet, who had been learning her language faster than Marcus, translated under his breath. "She says, tell the sultan that Ma sends her blessing and gratitude for safe passage."

The leader of the bandit party called back to her, "You are Ma? The revered mother from India who recently visited the sultan with a swami? If you lie, you all die. Come see the sultan with me. He will know if it is really you."

Ma slid under the rope line and past the horses. Marcus restrained Boy as he moved to pull her back. She was their best bet to escape with their lives. And he needed Boy for the fight if she failed in appeasing the bandits. The bandits drew their swords to protect themselves from the unarmed *little girl*, as she liked to call herself. Marcus held up his hand calling for his men to continue to stand back. They all were ready to spring to Ma's defense.

Ma moved to the leader's camel to stroke its long face, admiring the beauty of the beast. She had a way with animals just like Boy. Marcus hoped she'd also pacify the bandits. "Please tell the wise sultan," she said, "that Ma is traveling at Kali's request and in haste. I will enter into his dreams and give him a darshan blessing there. His eyes will be closed, but he will see mine there looking into his—awakening him within his dream. Please camp with us or go for we need to eat and rest now." Ma stood intently smiling at the camel or its rider—it was hard for Marcus to tell from where he stood behind her. It was ignoble, standing behind a woman like her little boy, but he would suffer through it if it meant saving their lives. He would speak to her later about their respective roles.

Without another word, the bandits rode off, likely to report to the sultan. Marcus, Poet, and Boy all saluted Ma as she reentered the camp. She giggled at the gesture and bowed, saying, "Namaste." Boy returned her bow and said, "Namaste," followed by Poet. Marcus was last to bow and express gratitude in the Hindu way. She deserved any salute she preferred. Ma the fearless was even more luminous in the twilight.

"Promise me one thing, Ma," Marcus said. "If it comes to a fight down the road, you will stand back and let me take charge."

Ma considered the bargain and said simply, "Agreed."

"We must be on our guard to assure they don't return during the night," Marcus said.

"They won't," Ma said with authority.

"I see now why Bhakti laughed when I promised to protect you," Marcus said. "What was that?" He thought heard someone stalking or slipping into their camp. He felt a shadow come over him like a black cloak of night. Marcus tried to shake it off saying, "We must play dice to see who will stand each watch tonight."

"Tali!" Ma exclaimed.

"Not tonight. Tonight, only the men play for one of the three night watches. You have already saved us, so you are excused from standing watch." He didn't like disappointing Ma and knew she would have gladly taken her watch, but he had to reassert his command. If it came to an actual fight, she would not bear a sword and would not lead his men in battle.

That night, Marcus felt an incubus attempting to possess him. As he stared at the fire, a battle raged within. The wine was oil on the fire and the demon within was thirsty. Poet no longer pushed the wine and was mixing lots of water into their remaining pig belly. An energetic discord hung over the camp like an electrical storm brewing.

"Boy, get the dice," Marcus said.

They rolled the dice. Marcus won but selected the least desired middle watch, a magnanimous gesture that Ma surely notice. He watched Poet through half closed eyes, as Poet sat first watch. Poet was also watching him. *Is he suspicious of me?* Marcus wondered.

Boy tossed and turned on his mat. Only Ma slept soundly. Marcus waited for Poet at the end of the first watch, but he didn't come to rouse him. After it became clear that Poet would let Marcus sleep through his watch, Marcus got up and insisted Poet get to his bedding. He paced while keeping watch and waiting for Poet to fall asleep. His mind raced while debating the demon of desire. He'd heard his fellow officers boast—*that a man makes the first move in lovemaking or he'll never know a woman's true desire.*

The incubus persuaded Marcus to move his bedding by Ma. Unshackled, he found his body now next to hers. *Time to embrace her as my lady, as my equal,* he thought or was prompted, hoping she would yield, roll over, and make him her lord and master. He had not slept with a woman since his wife, and he yearned for this simple, fearless, beautiful lady to desire him as his wife had. He was at risk of the incubus taking full possession of his body and wits.

Ma's body was a soft and warm shimmering light. He struggled to maintain his virtuous self-control and wakefulness of his watch. His thoughts were not his own: *Follow the audacious heroes of old who were fortunate enough to bed a goddess. Be a bold Roman conqueror, daring the gods and testing the fates.* Still, something held him back from the first touch the incubus demanded. But he couldn't take the irresistible longing a moment longer—he had to know.

Closing his eyes before crossing the Rubicon, a vision of Ma rose in his mind as a blue deity with many arms and skulls about her neck, poised to strike him dead with a sword raised high above her head. *I am Kali! Even as we dream, we serve somebody. It may be the devil, or it may be the Lord. Demon be gone!* Marcus heard the fearful goddess say. And with a *hiss* that sounded like a blacksmith putting a red-hot blade into an icy bucket, he felt the incubus flee his body and mind.

When he opened his eyes, there was the gentle, saintly Ma, breathing her sweet, rhythmic breath. *Had he dozed off on his watch?* Her lips did not move, but he heard her loud and clear say: *This is not what you want for your mother and sister. I am destined to be a virgin woman. You are the protector of my dharma. I offer you the unconditional, unlimited love of God, not from my body, but from my soul.*

He sighed deep and long and then raised his head above hers. Her eyes were still closed but fluttering. She was a goddess, a warrior, and a little girl. Both mother and sister to him. "You could have just said 'no,'" Marcus whispered in her ear. A soft smile crossed her lips. He placed a tender kiss on her forehead and moved his bedding back to its rightful place. And stood up to keep watch.

The storm had passed, and all but Marcus fell asleep for the second and third watch.

CHAPTER 30
Saltaurius and the Sultan

SALTAURIUS WOKE TO see an imposing man with a black beard grinning at him from across a table in a grand hall. The teak table was as big as the deck of a small ship. He did not know who the nobleman was or how he got in this hall.

Saltaurius looked about to assess his situation. He struggled against the thick ropes that bound his wrists like Hercules. His head hurt, but he wasn't gagged. The great lord, with his long jet-black beard and hair, sat on a throne made of bone as some bearded men enjoyed a feast around the table. Their leader wore a leather vest with black fur over his shoulders. Behind his seat, there was a roaring fire, and propped against his seat was a massive club.

There was sand on the stone floor beneath his own feet. This was a land of extremes: snowy mountains above and burning desert sands below. The last thing he could remember was lying down to sleep on a warm bed of sand. *Where is Dio?* he wondered.

All eyes fell on him as he stirred and tried to make sense of his situation. The surrounding voices became silent as the fire continued to hiss and crackle. The leader picked up his club for no apparent reason, other than to show his now-conscious guest the spikes facing out from the fat end.

Saltaurius's money belt lay like a prize centerpiece in the middle of the magnificent table. He went to grab his right wrist, but the restraints prevented him. He stole a look instead. The gems remained sewn around the wristband of his robe. Even if robbed of his belt and all its coins, he would still be a wealthy man. And he expected to leave alive, since *no foe can defeat him* as Governor Pilate had prophesized.

The great hall where they dined was a monument to hunting. An African lion head faced a Bengal tiger head across the room. Their skin rugs lay stretched out in between. Those that traveled the Silk Road through his patch of towering mountains and valley sands were required to pay the lord tribute with these trophies from faraway lands. Local goats and elk heads filled every remaining area of the walls. Thirty-three candles burned overhead in a large candelabra. Two balconies flanked the hall where archers stood watch, protecting the private rooms above. Saltaurius imagined a wife preening and lounging in each of the rooms, awaiting their lord of the castle.

Slave women milled about the round table, serving the men.

"Welcome back!" the leader said. "My men, like jackals, jumped you while you slept. They were afraid to seize you while you were awake like real men. You are quite a man, dressed like an Arab but wielding a Roman sword, riding two horses with a fat coin belt fastened to his waist that my men were too afraid to remove, so I had to do it myself." He motioned to the money-belt centerpiece. "They feared the sleeping giant might awake and snap their necks." The nobleman scowled at his men around the table. "You are my guest high upon a mountain peak. My humble fortress is impenetrable," the black beard said to him, as if he might have a small army coming to save him.

"If I am your guest, unbind me and let me eat and drink," Saltaurius said, still groggy from the lump on his head and more hungry than scared. His throbbing skull reminded him of the crushing guilt over his brother's death that used to tighten like screws upon his temples.

"Yes, but let's be clear you will act as a guest and not ruin our feast. You might kill some of my jackals before you die." The black beard looked up to the balconies where the archers raised their bows, drawn with arrows ready to fly.

Saltaurius nodded and coughed due to the smoke in the room. His eyes were stinging from the smoke as well, but he couldn't wipe them.

"Cut him free and get him food and wine," the black beard ordered, and it was done. "I am the sultan here," he added.

"I am Saltaurius. A man of the world." He rubbed his eyes and looked about the hall, but did not see Dio.

"Are you looking for your travel companion? My men tell me he scampered like a goat up the rocks and disappeared. A colorful story they tell of his flight, like that of a flying monkey with burnt yellow wings. It must have been something he was sleeping in."

Saltaurius laughed at the image. "The orange robe of a monk. He gave it to my monkey for his good service to him. My man might never die. I believe he will outrun death."

"My men couldn't find him. I think they were more scared of him than you—as men fear snakes more than an ox. He can't be far, as we took his horse. In a way, my men paid you great respect. They feared your colossal physique. You had to be captured in your sleep, knocked unconscious, just to play it safe. How cowardly of them." The sultan again scowled at his men and wagged his black beard by twisting his jaw back and forth rendering his judgment. His men sheepishly ate and drank in relative silence. "They have been told to only speak when spoken to during our talk. After the way they seized you, and let your companion escape into the night. I should have sent my slaves with sticks and whips to capture the bull and his monkey." The fire cracked loudly behind him, and two slave women scurried over to brush burning embers out of the sultan's fur cape with their hands—hands that long ago, Saltaurius noted, had become numb to fire.

"Now, Saltaurius, some simple questions and a pleasant negotiation to go with our meal. Tell me your story?"

"I ride to catch three men and a woman who must have traveled near here. I was on their route to India."

"Are they your friends or foes?" the sultan asked.

"We share the same mission, so more friends than foes, but I wouldn't die for them if they offended you. Have you seen them?" Saltaurius attempted to play it straight down the middle.

"What is your mission?" the sultan asked, ignoring Saltaurius's question.

"We seek a rebel outlaw in India."

"Whose law has he broken? And what great crime has he committed that you ride so far from Rome, risking death?" He picked up Saltaurius's sword and placed it in front of him.

"The man we seek was crucified for insurrection against the Roman Empire and is wanted for cheating death."

"Cheating death? So he cheated God's law too, or God may have granted him special dispensation. Ha! I am God here. I may have heard of this man. Issa?"

"He goes by many names. Issa, Yuz Asaf, and maybe Jesus," Saltaurius said.

The sultan held up his wine goblet for a table toast, and said, "To Issa." They all drank. "Ma told me Issa is like Babaji!"

Saltaurius, sensing they held Ma, Issa, and Babaji in high regard, pivoted. "I am a Roman Christian," he said, "and my mission is not just finding the man, but also protecting the holy crucified man from the Roman tribune who likely passed by here with the woman, another Roman, and a slave."

"Why would you protect a rebel?" the sultan asked.

"I saw him perform a miracle," Saltaurius said, scowling at the surrounding men to prevent anyone from smirking.

"Did he walk on water?" the sultan asked. "I bet Ma could levitate if she wanted."

"I witnessed him heal a man. But only heard he walked on water." Saltaurius pulled out his makeshift cross that now hung around his neck and kissed it. He hoped they would recognize the power of the symbol, but by the look on the sultan's face and from the snickers around the table, the gesture seemed to only make him look weak and superstitious.

"Silence!" the sultan called out, reprimanding his men for their reaction. "And do you know the Ma I have mentioned and who travels with the Romans?"

Saltaurius realized he was one wrong answer away from being quilled like a porcupine by arrows. "I've not met her, but I believe they may hold her captive as a guide," he explained.

"She had a chance to escape and didn't take it. Doesn't sound like she's held against her will to me."

Saltaurius sighed. The sultan seemed wary of his guest and enamored of the woman called Ma. "I'm glad to hear that," Saltaurius said as pleasantly as he could. "Is she really a holy woman? A friend?" he asked.

"Ma is like a mother to me. She is my spiritual guide. I only met her once on her way west, but it was as if I had known her forever. She, too, was my guest for three nights." He smiled and sighed at the memory. "Those were days of peace in a life of violence. She showed me a miracle on her first night. But perhaps I should not speak of that as no one would believe it."

"Please do," Saltaurius said. "I told you I saw this Jesus perform a miracle and came to me in a vision. So I believe in miracles."

The sultan looked at his men. "These swine couldn't understand but perhaps you can. She came to me in my sleep last night to bless me as she did on that first night she stayed here. Just by looking into my eyes, she stirred me to my core. Ma is beautiful and radiant. So, on her first night here with me, I went to lay with her as a man and to offer her to become my wife. For her, I would have forsaken all others. But before I could roll her over, she became twice your size in the form of a ferocious black and blue goddess with many arms and a sword dripping with the blood of a severed head. I bowed down and retreated to my own bed. We never spoke of it. And now, I wish to say no more about it." All of his men looked wide-eyed in wonder.

Saltaurius also pretended to be impressed, but he was incredulous. He knew better than to tell the man at the head of the table that he'd been bewitched.

"Now she heads east to her home and without stopping to see me," the sultan guffawed, as if this was hilarious. "She told me to only fight in self-defense and to free my slaves. I promised I would when I was old and gray. She told me not to wait. Maybe I will travel with you to see her and ensure her safety."

Saltaurius, thinking quickly and sizing up his position, said, "The great sultan is more than welcome, but I travel in haste before it might be too late."

"That is why you travel with two horses?" the sultan asked.

"My weight. Twice a man." He spread his arms to show their length.

"Yes, and lots of coins are adding to your load. I can lighten that load before you go." He looked at the coin belt in the center of the table.

Saltaurius laughed at the all too predictable predicament. "Ah, I see we are onto the negotiations. Why not just put four arrows in me and take it all?" he asked. The men gazed up at the archers, who once more readied their bows. "Still, I might manage to kill one or two, maybe you, before I die," he said. He didn't want to test Pilate's prophecy against these odds. The men beside him placed their goblets on the table and squirmed, rocking their chairs away as if to prepare themselves. Flight, not fight, would be their first response.

"No threats, or your blood might spill out faster than you can control. Perhaps I'll hang your beast head on my wall." The sultan pointed to one of the few spaces left on his wall for another animal's head to hang and laughed. "Before meeting Ma, I would have killed you and had all your wealth, but Ma has changed me. All my trophies disgusted her. She cried when she looked into the tiger's eyes. Burning eyes that see right through you. Not the tiger's—Ma's."

He motioned for one of the older slave women to come to him. "I hereby free you," he said. "You are no longer my slave." He dipped a greasy finger into his wine and dripped it on her forehead. "I anoint you in freedom." She smiled with her remaining teeth and refilled his goblet before returning to her place at the side of the room. "See? Like I told Ma, a bird grows to love its cage, and an ox would die when the yoke is lifted without the barn and hay. The real sacrifice would be not to replace the old slaves with the new." He looked leeringly at a younger slave girl whose apron was swelled with child. "Still, I'll free them all before I die, unless one of these jackals slits my throat before I do."

Each man picked another man at the table to glare at, as if he would be the one that might slay the king. As they eyed each other, the sultan took note of the winner seated next to Saltaurius. The man had a scar on both his cheeks. *So much for turning the other cheek*, he thought.

"For love of Ma, I now only take what I need and what I'm owed."

"And what is that?" Saltaurius asked.

"Respect for starters. And an allowance to pass over my land—Roman coins: three hundred silver or fifty gold."

"A hundred silver," Saltaurius said. He treasured his gold coins. They were less weight for more value.

"Two hundred and you can leave sooner rather than later. With your head intact and your body not stuck with arrows."

"With or without you at my side?" Saltaurius asked. "If you come, I don't want to keep paying as we go."

"Without. I have business here, but I will go see Ma as soon as I can. No harm better befall her, or don't pass back this way. Tell her I love her when you meet and ask that she pray for a wretch like me. Do you know what she will answer?"

"No, how could I?"

"She'll sing out in the sweetest of voices—Jaya Bhagavan!"

"I'll deliver your message and protect her, but we won't meet again," Saltaurius said. "I plan to sail home with the spice trade when my mission is done. Silk Road be gone. My ass is sore." He shifted from cheek to cheek on his chair, grunting from the pain in his buttocks and the lightening of his belt. "Two hundred silver and our deal is done." Saltaurius really had little leverage to negotiate. Dio was not about to ride with an army to rescue—or avenge—him, though the threat of rescue or revenge may have been keeping the sultan from taking all his coins and his life. He knew men who believed in violence and revenge—fear, violence, and revenge.

The sultan used his large, spiked club to push the money belt over to Saltaurius. With the ransom agreed upon, the sultan waved his hand in the air and reanimated his men. They all began laughing, drinking, and speaking in their strange tongue. There would be no fight. Saltaurius painfully counted out large handfuls of silver, as if pulling them from his spleen.

Once he finished making a pile of two hundred silver coins, a tall, slim man shuffled in from the wings, clanging his shackled feet. He cleared the coins from the table onto a tray for counting and left the room.

"My silver and gold slave," the sultan said. "The only one I can trust not to run off. He doesn't fight, but no coin slips between his fingers."

"Tell me about my man and his escape," Saltaurius said, still amused by the image.

"They tell me it was a magic trick," the sultan said. "My men surrounded him, but as soon as the blow struck your hard head, he was onto the rocks and out of reach like a spirit of the night, with a sun-kissed robe flowing behind him like a serpent's skin."

"That's my loyal Dis Pater. He has unmanly talents that protect him from death." Saltaurius smiled, imagining Dio scampering up the rocks to avoid capture. He surely would explain, without shame, why his survival was for their mutual benefit and that the ransom for two men would have been twice as painful. Saltaurius laughed aloud at the thought of his retort to his stunted comrade, *No, only one and a half times as painful.*

CHAPTER 31
Into India

As THEY CROSSED over an invisible border into India, Marcus shared Ma's joy as she smelled the spiced breeze and raised her arms in celebration. "Mother India, sweet Kali, holy Ganga, your child is home!" she sang out. Poet and Boy mimicked her, also raising their arms in the air.

The twilight yellows, oranges, and purples danced across the big sky above the vast expanse of green. Cool air from the sea carried to where they were setting up camp on a hill in a wooded area in that fertile valley. Marcus, Poet, and Boy had taken to wearing thin, white linen clothing, which Boy had secured for them. Marcus thought the white linen was in tribute to Ma and the heat but not the best look for intimidating other men. He still had a long sword swinging by his side for that.

They transversed many terrains and were fortunate to avoid the highest of the mountains and the longest stretches of desert along their route to India—thanks to Ma and not their maps. Ma led them along less trodden paths, away from the heavily traveled roads.

They were also fortunate it was a mild summer thus far, and they had experienced no monsoons, which were common at that time of year. The weather had been hot but not unbearable.

"Hard rains are sure to come," Ma said. "We and the earth could use a bath." She laughed. Marcus marveled at Ma's scent, which always smelled sweet like moist wood and flowers. Even her fine beads of sweat were fragrant dew, like she had just bathed in holy water.

Boy tended to the horses and set the fire as Ma prepared the food. She was a better cook than Poet. Marcus and Poet were in deep conversation studying a large map in anticipation of finally catching the elusive Issa. As the food cooked high over the fire, Boy and Ma sat for evening meditation. Before settling into their silent practice, Marcus heard Boy ask Ma, "How did Jesus save you from the Hindu priests?"

"He was called Issa then, but I called him father. I cannot be sure that it is the same man. Though I have been receiving intuition and messages from him. Back when we practiced together, he used a Vedic tradition of spiritual debate to resolve the matter of life or death in my favor. Usually, the losing debater would become the follower of the winner, but the head priest decreed this debate was to determine whether I should live and be able to maintain my practice. If Issa lost, I was to be killed as a witch."

"What was the topic of the debate?" Boy asked.

"Just that—the ability of women to seek divinity, to be divine and follow yogic practices and read the scriptures. The elder priest had local custom and dogma on his side. He could even find some textual support. Yet Issa had God and the truth as allies. I heard later that it was a very lopsided debate and Issa's words sang out like a simple, harmonious heavenly choir while the priest's words tied themselves up in knots of a metaphysical bramble. After winning the debate, they threw Issa out and forbade his return. He was lucky that he didn't get killed after embarrassing the high priest. No one bothered me again. Issa went north and may have trained with some Buddhist monks."

"That makes me mad. It's bad enough in battle, but threatening to kill people for their beliefs is . . . maddening," Boy said, raising his fists playfully to the heavens.

"Don't be mad. Rejoice! We're here now together in this beautiful spot because of everything that came before," Ma said to her newest devotee.

Marcus called over to the lotus sitters. "You sound like Seneca, the great Roman philosopher," he said. "Our destiny comes from everything that fell before it. But how did you get here?" he asked. "You traveled the long and treacherous route we found you on by donkey with no map."

"Sweet Bhakti provided company and aid. And I always have Kali to protect me," Ma said as she gazed up at the pure blue sky. "And I have the sun and stars and my guru, and now you, to lead me to water, to food, and to Pali. Wonders of wonders are the play of maya." Marcus had learned Kali was the name of Ma's favorite deity and her horse, that her guru's name was Babaji, and that *maya* was the term she used for the grand illusion perceived by all our senses. "Magical India welcomes us, its joyful weary travelers, to the miracle of God's creation. How blessed are we by our journey together," she said, making prayer hands and bowing down until her forehead touched the earth.

"Jaya Bhagavan!" Boy joyfully sang out.

Marcus looked at Boy and shook his head. He then asked Ma, "Is there slavery in India?"

"Not the outright ownership of man by man," she replied. Then her peaceful countenance became stern and thoughtful. "But oppression comes in many forms. I was just telling my son," Ma smiled at Boy, "about the patriarchy in India, which will be the last form of oppression to disappear from the world. Until it does, there will be war and hierarchy based on power. In India, we have castes—a structure derived from men who read and translate the scriptures to their liking. And guess who is on top of that institutionalized social and occupational hierarchy? The Brahmin— the priests who read the scriptures. One's caste is handed down through the generations and is very hard to break free of. And at the bottom are the untouchables, or Dalits, human outcasts. Being born into a Brahmin family, the priests targeted me as a little girl." She laughed to break from her diatribe.

"Like a horse hearing our clucking sound—" She clicked her tongue off the roof of her mouth the way Boy had taught her to get their horses to move along at a faster pace. Boy and Ma never used the whip, but Marcus still believed a gentle swat to the strong flank of a disobeying or lollygagging horse was a perfectly acceptable discipline. "—My mind ran off at the mention of slaves and castes. You rattled my monkey mind, Marcus. Now we need to meditate." She smiled at Marcus and turned to Boy, saying, "Om, shanti, shanti, shanti."

Marcus again shook his head at the mysterious Ma and her intrepid nature. He returned his attention to Poet and the map as Boy and Ma meditated.

"Have you found our best route home?" Marcus asked.

"Three moons have passed of Pilate's six, and we have one more week to get to Pali," Poet said. "We could make it back to Jerusalem just in time but not to Rome. Sorry."

"Damn Pilate and his sundial," Marcus said. "I'd like to smash them both. We have been driving these horses on too many long rides. Boy has done a great job keeping them moving, but he is cautioning me again. We must pause here for another day."

"They can rest in Pali," Poet said. "We should sail back. After traveling out on the Silk Road, we'll travel home on the Spice Road, moving more swiftly on the back of the sea breeze carrying us over the Erythraean Sea and up the Arabian Gulf." Poet traced his finger over the route on the map. "With eight weeks and strong wind, we could make it back to Jerusalem within Pilate's six-month deadline. I've been thinking we might take back some of Ma's tea leaves and plants. She tells me she grows the plants at her place in Pali."

"We are not merchants and have only one mission. Stay focused on resurrecting the House of Decia, if you please," Marcus said. "How about Alexandria? We have friends there."

"It's shorter over land once we have landed at the tip of the Arabian Gulf." Poet pointed to a spot on the map called the Port of Captos. "But what are you thinking? Those are not Pilate's orders, and six months will pass without completing our mission."

"We could send word from Alexandria by carrier birds to Pilate and the emperor that we have our man and are sailing across the great Roman lake directly to Rome to deliver him. Let Rome show Roman justice to this man. Even Pilate said he was innocent. But Pilate would kill him again to avoid the appearance of failure. The emperor is treacherous and superstitious. The old man has lots of blood on his hands and may want to proclaim our miracle man a god and receive his blessings, and that may get me close to him for my revenge."

"Sounds like a plan where we all die," Poet said. "Let's catch the god-man first to ensure he's not an imposter before deciding. We'll have time during the long journey back to finalize a plan. But what will you do if we don't find him in time?"

"Well, you can't take Pilate at his word. If failure means death, better it be in Rome. I will sail back, contact some allies of my father—powerful men and senators—make the truth known about my family, and die with glory trying to challenge the emperor. Again, you will have to leave me on that suicide mission after we get to Rome."

"I can't do that. I've pledged my loyalty and life to you and need to be there at the end. Boy, however . . ." He called Marcus's attention to Ma and Boy, who sat across from each other, Ma in blissful samadhi and Boy not far from it. "Perhaps he should be free to continue his training with Ma."

"He will be. I think he's found his mother." They smiled at the familial bond between the pair of lotus-seated meditators.

"These Hindus break up the divine into many deities," Poet said. "Unique aspects of the same godhead. It's similar to the way the Roman gods are personified, but the Hindu way seems more devout and spiritually profound. I believe our gods and their stories hold poetic truth. And our elite, those in the Senate, use our gods to maintain order and hierarchy. I've often wondered if Julius and Augustus truly believed they were gods. And now we skeptical Romans, speaking for us both, let us not forget, seek the son of God, risen from the dead. Let that be our goal."

Poet's words inspired Marcus. He stood and pulled Poet up to face him. "Well stated, Poet. That is precisely the mark of our liberty. We should not let others set our path, tell our time, or determine our goals, lest we become no better than slaves to that oppression. Pilate be damned! The gods have already blessed us with a goddess. If we find the son of God, let us be content with that and trust our fate to be whatever comes next."

"Of one thing we can be sure. If we find God's own son . . ." Poet waited for a response with a wide-eyed grin.

"What's that?" Marcus asked.

"It's God's will."

CHAPTER 32
The Abode of God

BOY'S HEART WAS singing as their weary horses and backsides arrived in Pali. Everyone along the long, straight dirt road to Ma's humble ashram prostrated themselves. Boy thought someone along the path would point out that Ma cast no shadow, but no one else seemed to notice. Maybe they took it for granted, or maybe everyone else saw her shadow. They did all cry out, "Jaya Bhagavan!" He wondered what they thought of her Roman military escort wearing white linen but carrying swords. No one looked concerned. The tiny hamlets along the way came alive in celebration. Of course, it was a sunny day to welcome Ma home.

As they approached her spiritual sanctuary, Poet read aloud the Hindu inscription above the gate: "The Abode of Bhagavan."

Boy looked to Ma. Always quick to laugh, she responded in Latin, "Everywhere is God's abode. We just like the reminder." As she rang a large bell hanging down from the gate, she sang out, "Jaya Bhagavan!"

During the long days on horseback and nights by the fire, Boy had observed how thoroughly they had learned each other's way of speaking and thinking. Ma's joyful way turned the language lessons into play. The men had become proficient in simple Hindi. It had come easily to Boy, as the youngest of the men. Ma was speaking Latin like a Roman, but with a soft, smooth voice rather than a sharp dictatorial edge. Poet had told Boy that Ma was a savant—she learned to read and write in Latin so quickly. The horses had even learned to accept commands in either tongue. Hearing songs and stories in Hindi enthralled Poet. Even Marcus marveled at how old patterns of mind shifted when thinking and dreaming in Hindi. Boy knew Ma's teaching did not stop at sleep's door.

After passing through the gate, a narrow path climbed up a hill overlooking Pali, where Ma's small spiritual abode sat serenely on top. The rolling hills farther up became mountains. Ma's ashram consisted of several small white dwellings and two larger ones, each with a burnt-orange roof made of tile. The roofes had little windmills resembling daisies with long white petals. The men and the horses eyed a pool of clean water within the courtyard garden. As they pulled their horses to a stop in the center of the well-manicured garden-like compound, Boy eyed a young girl about his age drawing water from a well. She wore a brilliant yellow robe, and he imagined the colorful, sheer Babylon silk slip underneath, trembling on her smooth skin like fluttering butterfly wings.

She was the most alluring angel he had ever seen. Delicate and strong. The virgin goddess gracefully set down the water jug, which was half her size, and ran like a gazelle to Ma's horse to assist her in dismounting. Boy noticed as she ran the robe clung tight to her blossoming form, but it was her blessed face and emerald eyes he had instantly fallen in love with.

The Abode of God, full of wild and abundant gardens, was heaven on earth. The twenty attendants, mostly yellow-robed females, rushed out, singing Ma's song. No one matching their picture of Jesus came forward. The devotees formed a procession, one after another, falling to their knees to place their foreheads on Ma's feet. Ma, laughing her little girl laugh, pulled them up to meet her blissful eyes full of gratitude and love for their devotion, not to her but to God above. The men were glad to watch the outpouring of affection and the bliss Ma experienced in receiving it, but Boy's eyes kept darting back to the girl from the well. She had returned to finish filling the jug before balancing it on her head and walking away. Boy watched until she turned a corner, and the last thread of her yellow robe was out of sight. An invisible silk thread connected her to his heart.

When the greetings gradually ended, Ma showed the men to one of the smaller dwellings. She said, "This is your home now, as long as you care to stay. Please bathe and enjoy. I have some business to tend to and then will inquire about Issa. I will arrange massages for your sore backsides. Later, I will meet you for dinner in the ashram's dining hall."

Boy was too shy to inquire about the girl, but he was determined to meet her, touch her, kiss her, and wed her, if the gods were willing. There was something about *her* and the Abode of God that made him feel a sense of destiny, that he too had come home.

"After Boy waters the horses, may we bathe in the beautiful pool of water in the center of the compound—ashram?" Marcus asked.

"Of course! The pool is fed from a spring and mountain snow so that you may enjoy it. Ask anyone here for anything you need. Now, I need to go to my room for a meeting and then quickly go see to my children."

"You have children, Ma?" Marcus asked.

"I told you, a hundred," she said with a laugh and clapped her hands. "We run an orphanage just down the lane. We all serve each other here. No castes. You are our honored guests. Please, enjoy."

Ma was full of delight, and Boy shared her joy of homecoming after their long journey.

But what of Issa? Where was he? And why hadn't he greeted them? Boy thought. He feared they'd be back on the tired horses before he could meet that girl in the yellow robe.

CHAPTER 33
Ma's Reunion with Aja

MA'S NATURALLY LIT room was sparsely furnished with a rolled mat, cushions, a low teak tea table, and a small altar. On the altar sat a natural-stone buddha-like figure seated in meditation. Juxtaposed to that figure was an incongruously larger blue-and-black figure of a fearsome Kali, the Hindu goddess, with her red tongue sticking out. In her many blue arms, she was holding a trident, a bloody sword, a man's freshly severed head, with another arm and hand below holding a bowl collecting the head's blood. Kali completed her attire with a necklace of skulls. She guarded innocence and divinity by destroying evil.

Ma was excited to go to greet her children but wanted to meet with Aja first. Ma lit a candle upon the altar and said a prayer of gratitude to Kali just before a young woman entered with two cups of tea. Aja was the same young woman that had brought Boy to rapture as they entered the Abode of God. Even while being greeted, Ma had observed Boy's fixation on her young protégé and devotee. Aja bowed, and Ma embraced her. Then they both sat on cushions facing each other to drink the tea.

"Ah, sweet Aja, my little sister, so long these eyes beheld you only by looking inward. And here you are now for my outbound eyes to see." The young woman's eyes reflected the light of the white-robed Ma, who was almost twice her age. Their eyes locked in a darshan gaze for one hundred and eight beats of Ma's heart. "Om, shanti, shanti, shanti," Ma intoned with Aja joining in.

Aja made a long forward bow before she said, "Blissful mother, we have so longed for your presence, though it never left this place or our hearts. But here you are!"

"How are the children?" Ma asked.

"The children are thriving but have been longing for their mother's return. They will be so thrilled to see you. We . . . they didn't expect you back so soon." She repeated the deep bow of spiritual connection and affection, ending with her forehead in Ma's lap. Ma stroked her fine black hair. Then, Aja raised her head and asked, "But where is Swami Bhakti, and who are these men with swords?"

"He follows on donkey and foot. Some misfortune befell him, but now he rejoices and will return in a couple of months. You know no distance separates me from him, or any of my devotees and children."

Aja smiled knowingly. "Yes," she said, "and thank you for entering my dreams while you were away. We miss the swami's cooking." Aja licked her ample lips, not yet kissed by boy or man.

"Its absence will make it taste even better when he returns. These men who arrived with me hail from Rome, and the young one, who we call Boy, is from Morocco." Ma noticed Aja's eyes dart downward. "Boy is good, kind, and brave. He is my student now. Did you notice how he looked at you?"

Aja blushed. They both laugh.

"We traveled like centaurs fleeing a demon army. It feels as though my backside is still saddled to my horse." Ma rose to stretch her legs while Aja remained seated, looking up with reverence at her guru. Ma pulled a ruby red flower from her sari sleeve and positioned it behind Aja's ear. The girl smiled in love and gratitude. In an instant, Ma saw the girl's future, and she was glad. But as the vision of the future continued, she also saw a battle of men that might take her own life and alter Aja's bright future with Boy. Ma saw the deadly scene set ahead of her, but not where or when—or how it would end.

Aja's look of concern interrupted her vision. Ma shook off her third-eye sight and said, "We made such haste to find a man who may have been coming here to see me. Did a holy man come to Pali during my absence? Perhaps to see me?"

"A holy man visited with his mother and another man. They camped by the stream in the foothills about a mile from here. He came and asked that we call him Issa. He said you were a dear friend. Issa waited a week here, then he had to travel north. We did not know when you would return. He was a most remarkable and memorable man. Like you, sweet Ma, so full of radiant light."

"He is more than a man. Did he say where he would go?" Ma asked.

"He said you'd find him in the land of Jammu and Kashmir. He would show you the way." Ma smiled, though she worried about Marcus and his disappointment at not finding Issa here. She did not fully understand what he intended to do should Issa be the Jesus he sought. Rather, she understood Marcus did not fully understand what he would do. She took refuge in knowing Issa would only be found if it was God's will. Ma looked up to the black and blue statue and said a silent prayer to the Kali in her heart: *Thank you for all your protection and guidance. Please allow Marcus to perform his dharma and come to his aid when it is needed.*

She then turned to Aja and said, "Now join me in samadhi, so we may recharge and reconnect with the divine. And then let's go see the children. I want to spend some time with each and every one of them. I feel in my bones that the rains are coming. And my buttocks forewarns another long journey is ahead." Ma playfully rubbed her haunches. "But now, let our meditation begin. Jaya Bhagavan!"

CHAPTER 34
Dinner and Guidance

DESPITE FINALLY HAVING arrived in Ma's place of peace, Marcus suffered an inner turmoil. Pali sat in the uncertain center—between his tragic past and the end of his quest where he would have to face death. His men relied on him, and he felt he'd lost his way. He assumed Issa was not in Pali, as Ma would have reported that news immediately. They'd traveled a long way, hoping to find the man here. Their failure would mean the end of all prospects of meeting Pilate's six-month deadline. Still, his men deserved to enjoy the Abode of God, as Ma had encouraged.

The afternoon swim in the spring-fed pond and the fresh, exotic fruit drinks and flatbread topped with some spiced chickpea spread were refreshing and nourishing. They were constantly refreshed with another cup of tea. The highlight was a spiritually uplifting massage. The yellow-robed sannyasinis provided them with light, white linen robes to wear before and after the healing. Marcus had never experienced such a medicinal massage before. And unlike at the Roman baths, it was free from any sexual undertones or blatant provocation. The exotic oil-soaked hands of the yellow-robed woman expertly tapped into some great energy as she worked out his tight muscles and unlocked tiny chains of tension that slid down and out from his mind and body. Since that healing, everything seemed to dance with light.

Yet, he yearned for something more. Marcus was uneasy and reluctant to admit to himself the cause of the pangs in his solar plexus. He felt like an injured soldier being cut off abruptly from his opium. After their month of arduous travel together, he missed Ma's constant blissful company.

The dining hall at sunset was abuzz with song and laughter. Marcus found himself impatient at not seeing Ma there to greet them. He was also a bit disgruntled as he and his men were to wait in line with the yellow-robed religious zealots to be served their food in begging bowls. When it was his turn to have his bowl filled with exotic-smelling vegetables and rice stew, he looked up and into Ma's beaming eyes as she served him. "I'll join you after everyone is served and share the news of Issa."

Marcus reproached himself for his pride and impatience, in such stark contrast to Ma's humble nature and equanimity.

The meatless food was as spicy and wonderful as its aroma promised. As soon as they finished, Ma was there to join them at the table. Ma ate little during the trip, and she sat with only a cup of tea. Marcus wished she would eat more for fear she might disappear.

"I trust you are enjoying your time in God's abode," Ma said.

Marcus and Poet nodded, and then Marcus thanked her for their medicinal massages.

Marcus and Ma shared a look at Boy, who was not paying attention, and then at each other. Boy's eyes were gazing at a table of yellow-robed sannyasinis while his hands played with his bread and bowl. Everyone used their hands and flat bread to scoop their food to eat in this untamed part of the world.

Ma turned to Boy and said, "Her name is Aja. I will introduce you tomorrow. I call her little sister, though she came to me orphaned as a small child."

Boy bristled and then smiled, repeating softly and with feeling, "Aja."

"My friend Issa was here but left over a week ago for the north," Ma said, flashing eyes full of consolation and hope. "I am sorry, Marcus. I know you need to find him to see if he is your Jesus of the cross, and sooner rather than later. But we must trust God to find a way."

"Yes, sooner would be good if I am to avoid exile and to restore my family name." He didn't need to remind her, but he was also reminding himself of all he had at stake. Ma was like an opiate, dulling his focus on his mission's objective with her presence. "Not your fault, Ma. You led us here faster than we would have found it on our own." He realized, as he was saying this, that he had not given her full credit. They may not have even made it there alive without her guidance. "May we stay here for a little while to rest our horses?"

Ma made prayer hands and said, "God's abode is your home for as long as you care to stay with me." She smiled knowingly.

"And do we have any additional knowledge about his destination? Or just that he traveled north?" Marcus asked.

"Yes, to a land called Jammu and Kashmir. I'm told he will guide me when it's time," Ma said.

"How will he guide you?" Marcus asked.

"Perhaps the way God communicates with us all when our minds are silent, and our hearts are open and full."

Poet said, "Marcus, even if we are sailing back, we can't spare a week more."

"Forget Pilate and what he said. I still have the power of *ius intercessionis*."

"Yes, you can veto Pilate's commands," Poet said, looking down. "But not the emperor's."

"Let Pilate be damned. I will address the senate in Rome and plead my case. Let the moon fly around the earth a thousand times. We'll find him, if he's the one. If the man we find has wounds on his feet and hands, we will sail to Rome with him, sending courier birds ahead as soon as we can. They can only kill me once. Have you lost interest in finding the man who came down off the cross?" Marcus said, teasing Poet, who he knew was fully committed to their quest.

"Never!" Poet swore with the Roman military salute. "Only death will stop us," he said. Some of the yellow-robed devotees chortled at Poet thudding his chest. Only a month ago Marcus would have offered stern correction to the *sannyasinis*. He could now see how it might appear humorous in this abode. Poet ignored them to continue to speak to Ma and, as Marcus saw it, to embarrass his master. "That's Tribune Marcus Decia to the core," Poet said. "The man can take a knockout blow and get up to fight some more. I've seen it a thousand times on the battlefield. A dead end is merely another challenge for Roman engineering and ingenuity to overcome."

"He exaggerates," Marcus said, hoping Poet would stop.

"It's called poetic license," Poet said, and they all laughed, except Boy, whose attention remained singularly focused on the contents of a certain yellow robe.

"Will you join us? It wouldn't be the same on the road without you," Marcus asked Ma. He couldn't imagine going back to their old, crude ways of being—not to mention Boy losing another mother.

"If you seek his life and not his death," Ma said.

"I have sworn to you; no harm will come to this Issa from me. Again, I will not deceive you. I will take him to Rome, alive."

"What if Issa is not the Jesus you seek?"

"I'll leave him in peace. But you told me, though years have passed, Issa held a resemblance to my picture of the rebel Jesus." He had looked at the picture so many times that it was now easy to pull up Jesus's face onto the screen of his mind. "So, if he doesn't deny it, that's enough for him to serve as my safe passage home to Rome. And there we both will be judged."

"For the sake of some senseless revenge, you return home?" Ma asked, not having expressed this opinion before. Marcus shook his head, knowing she could not understand his way of life any more than he could hers. They all knew his return to Rome was a suicide mission that he hoped would clear his family's name.

Ma continued, "I won't leave until I receive guidance. We will not find him unless he wants to be found, and we seek him with love in our hearts. And I don't suppose there are ropes strong enough to hold him." Though the words themselves were harsh, her way of speaking and the sound of her voice was like sweet-sounding lute music.

"I love him, if he is the man you think him to be," Marcus said, hearing her music over the words. "For saving your life years ago, even if he is not the man we seek. We will wait a couple of days and rest the horses. Hopefully, one of Poet's muses will guide you by then, and you will guide us north."

～ ～ ～

Marcus was alone in Pali much of the time while they waited for Ma to receive a sign and agree to rejoin their manhunt. She had convinced them to not ride off without her, as she predicted a hard rain, and that guidance was on the way. He had a lot of time to ponder his life, the life before Ma and the life after.

Marcus grew impatient with himself and his idle men in the Abode of God. Poet studied Hindi with scholars in Pali that Ma had introduced him to. Boy and Aja performed the dance of young love. It pleased the gods and even lifted his downhearted spirits. Ma or the horses chaperoned the young lovers. Boy taught Aja to ride so the horses, who were getting some much-needed rest, could stretch their legs on short rides around Pali. And Aja had introduced Boy to Ma's children, who loved the horses and learning how to care for them.

Marcus filled his days by investigating. He tried to gather information on Issa's return from locals but learned little. The woman with him might or might not be his mother, people said. The other man might or might not be a disciple. He went south to minister in India, while Issa and the motherly figure went north. Issa blessed those he appeared to but performed no miracles. Those so blessed believed Issa was a holy man, with a body and face full of light, "transfigured," they had said, but they had no proof. And everyone thought he resembled the picture Marcus showed them, but they couldn't be sure. "He looked like Babaji!" they would say and then admit they never met Babaji other than as described by Ma. No one looked for scars on his hands and feet as they were transfixed on his face and eyes. Some of his witnesses believed Issa headed north toward Kashmir, others thought he was travelling to Tibet, thus shrinking the world of possible destinations to the size of Italia or expanding it to the expanse of a sea.

Ma was certain her friend was heading to Kashmir. How she knew certain things was a mystery, but Marcus had learned to trust her.

Ma managed all the ashram and orphanage affairs. No task was too large or too small. She had yet to receive the spiritual guidance she anticipated and could only comfort Marcus by saying, "I, we, can't demand the time or the way. But it will come." He was used to waiting patiently for winter to turn to spring to start a new military campaign, but each day in Pali seemed like a year.

CHAPTER 35
Boy and Aja

BOY WORRIED ABOUT Marcus, but his worry was overshadowed by love. He saw Aja's face basking in bright golden light every time he shut his eyes. He was transported into a state of bliss when he imagined she felt the same way as he did. And he dared to think she did. A day before the rains came, Boy and Aja pretended to meet by happenstance in the most secluded arbor of the ashram gardens. He knew, and she knew, that it was no coincidence. They both were always aware of the other's presence or absence.

She blushed, having no Ma or horses as their witness. She had no experience of boys or men—of that, he was sure—and he could almost hear her heart fluttering like a trapped bird yearning to take flight before the cage door would shut once more. His skin tingled when she was near, as the hairs on his arms stood erect. Her eyes, her mouth, the palms of her hands— every part of her glistened in his presence. She smelled like lavender tea. He loved tea and lavender. Each word they shared was laced with love, and each moment of shared silence was a communion of their spirits.

For Boy, love made him fearless and afraid. Fearless in that he would do anything to be in Aja's passionate and spiritual presence. And afraid of losing that presence. Boy saw in her emerald eyes the union of sensual grounding and spiritual heights of desire. He would rather die than lose her.

They sat inches apart speaking as he imagined long lost lovers do. The anticipation of the first kiss hovered in the no man's land between them—

like two great armies poised on the battlefield, awaiting their orders to charge. The primal energy of boy and girl, of all creation, teetering on the razor's edge of that moment and all the moments that would follow.

Then, in that secluded garden, it happened, and not by accident. Her index finger brushed against his as they sat for meditation. Her flesh and energy rested there and coiled around his—finger touching finger for thirty minutes or more. That first prolonged touch took him to new heights of spiritual ecstasy.

— — —

How had she come to love this young man with a sword from a country she'd never heard of, traveling on a big horse and with Roman soldiers? Aja was sure she had Ma's blessing, but her feelings for Boy confused her. She found the sweetest bliss of meditation in his adoring eyes. She loved his scent of leather and wood. But she'd always assumed she would follow in Ma's beautiful virgin footsteps into her full glory of divinity. And she never wanted to leave Ma's side or the peaceful Abode of Bhagavan.

After meeting in the secluded arbor—she knew Boy would follow her there—they sat on cushions of moss upon the ground sharing stories of their childhoods and everything that came before, all that somehow had led them to be together in the shade of the grandmother banyan tree and its luscious green canopy that hung in sympathy over their heads. They gazed into each other's eyes when words seemed inadequate. Boy's eyes reflected her own, which shined brighter and more lustrous than gold. She felt she could see through the reflection of her own eyes in his dark brown eyes a place of shared consciousness. A perfect spiritual union.

His moist lips were just inches away.

When they sat to meditate, Aja wanted their minds and hearts to touch. She brushed her index finger against his and felt a warm current of prana flowing between them, a current connecting their hearts that she never wanted turned off. She held her finger there and he intertwined them. She entered the bliss of samadhi with Boy by her side, touching her in this small but oh-so intimate way.

CHAPTER 36
Hold Your Horses

THE NEXT DAY, the weather turned as Ma had predicted, though Marcus had hoped she would be wrong, finally, about something. She wasn't. A late season monsoon hit Pali with a week of rain that kept them all indoors for much of the days. Except for Ma and the children who turned the mud and pelting rain into outdoor fun and bathing ritual—enjoying the most inclement conditions. Marcus marveled at the way Ma embedded life lessons into play for the children, teaching them adversity as opportunity.

Marcus was brooding like the weather, but glad Boy was in love, and Poet was receiving so much joy from his esoteric learning. Boy was moving deeper into his mediation practice and learning yoga asanas, or postures, from Aja. Love was the best inspiration and paid no heed to the weather. And Poet had his scrolls and pen and was writing poetry inspired by Eastern mysticism. Poet was enthralled by Ma's east meeting his west. Marcus watched the rain and whittled to slow the chariot wheels turning round within his head. *Perhaps he too had found love—loving Ma in some foreign asexual way? Why else would he tarry and not ride out to find Jesus or face his death?*

Hiding from the rain and Marcus's future, the band of brothers hovered around a small fireplace in their ashram common room where it was relatively dry. There were four small sleeping chambers, each only big enough for a small mat and cushion, fanning out from the common room.

The small fire and chimney removed the heat and humidity, circulating air from the open door and slat windows of their living and sleeping quarters. Something about the white clay-brick architecture and vents kept the room at a hot but livable temperature. And an ingenious fan that looked like white wings circling above them, harvesting the wind and rain passing above the enclosure, turning the little daisy windmills stationed on the roof. Without these innovative inventions, the room would have been a moist oven, and they would have been better off in the rain with Ma and the children. Marcus thought that Roman engineers could learn a thing or two from this humble Indian abode.

They were studying Poet's maps inside the small common room. Marcus thought the layout looked much like the interior of the Hebrew tomb they had visited three months before. Despite the gloom of the rain and claustrophobic space, he tried to make the best of the insufferable delay. Marcus debated with himself whether they should leave when the rain stopped or continue to wait for Ma.

"Boy, have you kissed her yet?" Marcus asked to lighten the monsoon mood. Boy always wanted to speak of Aja and her many charms. He pounced up, pacing like a bolt of lightning had struck his buttocks. "You're a stallion in a barn with a mare out in the pasture," Marcus said and laughed. Poet stifled his laugh.

"Not yet. I will kiss her when the time is right. Being with her is perfect. Isn't she the most beautiful lady in the world?" Boy asked.

"She is a virgin goddess with her emerald eyes," Poet offered.

Boy stopped pacing but his legs were still shaking as he said, "You know what Ma said when I asked for her blessing? I was worried that it all came so fast and so easy that she might think us fools. She said something like, 'Son, anyone who knows love knows it can happen at first sight. Sad people with closed hearts and entrenched minds say there must be a match based on background. That a boy and girl need time to know the other. But I imagine the cosmos as omnipotent love. It knows when to bring two entangled consciousnesses together at the perfect time and place. You and Aja are bound by lifetimes, and not just this life. True love between two pure hearts can immediately see the essence of the other and their future together. You and Aja must decide what is true for you.'"

"Sounds like she gave you her blessing. The way only Ma can," Marcus said.

"We touched," Boy said, sighing. The lovelorn look on his face showed he was recreating the touch of Aja in his mind for the thousandth time.

"How did you touch her?" Marcus asked with a knowing smile.

Boy answered with another sigh. Marcus returned to studying the map with Poet.

After a couple of minutes of leaving Boy to stew over Aja's absence, Marcus turned his attention back to his adopted son. "We will move on when this rain stops, with or without Ma. You better make the time right soon for that kiss," Marcus said, "before Poet and I finish plotting our route north. Boy, come sit by the fire with me."

Boy sighed and sat with Marcus.

"You're a slave in name only, and carry a sword and ride a horse as well as any Roman. We are your kin, and if circumstances allowed, I'd give you my name, if you'd have it." Then he added, "The Decia name may make you a target of the emperor and his henchmen as long as I still live. And it will be stripped from me when Rome thrusts me into exile. The end of the line for the House Decia is likely coming soon, when I return to Rome with or without Jesus of Nazareth."

Poet looked sadly at Marcus, who was facing the circumstances like a commander assessing a losing battle about to begin. Marcus continued, "But that is not what I want to talk about. Now, as for you and Aja, Ma and the gods bless you with this love." Boy squirmed in his seat. Marcus draped his arm over his shoulder to settle him and to keep him from running off. Marcus remembered his father, the skilled orator and senator, and felt his guiding presence. He knew his young ward to be a virgin and saw the desire Boy tried to hide bulging between his legs each morning—the torment of first love yet to be consummated.

"Do you know about the act of love?" Marcus asked, precipitating the ageless talk between father and son.

"I've seen horses do it," Boy said.

Poet laughed. Pointing to the map, he said, "Funny shape, this peninsula here."

"Horses and beasts have sex. Noble men make love," Marcus said, ignoring Poet. "The physical parts will take care of themselves when the time comes. You focus on what she wants and how to best express your love through the union of your bodies. And wait for her pleasure to release your own. And do not think. Not thinking is the key to dancing and to making love. Lead and follow in turns as the music of your heart guides you. Thought should fade away as you become one in mutual desire."

"Romantic for a Roman tribune. Perhaps you should write the poetry," Poet said. Marcus welcomed Poet's playing the fool to ease Boy's discomfort.

"Poet will be the one to write you an ode to love for your wedding day. But back to making love. Don't rush things. Hold your horses. Let nature take its course. And for the gods' sake, kiss the girl. Any questions?" Marcus asked.

"How do we end this talk?" Boy said, though Marcus believed he was glad to have received his guidance and blessing. Marcus led men into battle, but had never guided them in the ways of love before. He had given the matter some forethought and thought the talk had gone well.

The bell at the front gate of the ashram rang out, announcing an intrepid traveler had arrived, soldiering through the driving rain. Marcus and his men moved to the small porch of their dwelling to see a giant riding one massive horse and leading another riderless one. The beast entered the compound like Hannibal atop a wet wooly mammoth trudging through the monsoon mud.

"Boy, take the tarp and follow," Marcus said. "Don't let him see you, and come get us if he moves to see Ma, or otherwise looks to molest the devotees, or attempts to go to the orphanage."

Marcus watched as Boy grabbed the rain tarp from the porch and ran to protect his two new loves.

∽ ∽ ∽

Not long after the gate bell rang, Saltaurius ducked his head to enter the small chambers of the men, sucking all the air out of the cramped quarters. He stood the full height of the space, his crimson turban rising above his curly blood orange locks brushed the ceiling while water puddled around his freakishly large boots.

"I was told by the yellow robes that I'd find three Roman hens in this chicken coup," Saltaurius bellowed, shaking off the rain that clung to his colossal frame. "Dio, like these ladies, now has an orange robe as well. Aren't you going to offer me a seat to dry by the fire?"

Boy came in behind him. From out of his pocket, he pulled the whittled horse Marcus had given him. He showed it to Marcus and slid it into his other hand, signaling the bull had gone to the stables.

Since Saltaurius had told Marcus where he might find out the truth of his family's massacre, Marcus owed the big man a small debt of gratitude. He gestured half-heartedly for him to sit by the fire—and soon wished he had not been so hospitable, as Saltaurius started grunting while stripping off his dripping wet Arab-style clothing to lay it out by the fire. He threw his loincloth down so it covered the end of one arm of his robe, but he didn't bother to reposition it, and he left his money belt on as if daring someone to come and take it. Like a dog, he shook his long and dirty orange hair, turned blood red by the rain. His body bore well-earned scars from some past skirmishes he must have won.

The distasteful stench from his rough and hairy naked body and his loud presence offended all the senses at once.

"Where's that holy woman you were traveling with? She here?" he asked. "I'm an animal in need of a rutting." He did a naked man dance—thrusting his hips back and forth while pumping his arms up and down in the disgusting way some crude soldiers do over a fallen enemy. Marcus had disciplined men for such a display over another dead man's body. He found it even more offensive when done in the flesh and while speaking of Ma.

"Do you embrace the beast in you?" Marcus asked, though it was not a question. "What would Jesus and your brother say to such crudeness? Show some respect."

"Touchy! Just a little soldier's humor. I've been traveling alone with Dio for too long." He paused, staring hard at Marcus. "Has she become your Venus? Relax. I just asked if she was here."

"No. She had business elsewhere but provided these rooms for us to wait out the rain," Marcus lied. Ma was either twenty yards away in her chamber, meditating or speaking to her devotees, or at the orphanage. Someone— Marcus had the sinking thought—had probably already informed her of the giant's arrival, and she might soon come through the door to welcome him. Marcus didn't want Ma near the man out of concern for her safety. He couldn't imagine such ugliness and beauty could occupy the same space without his world coming to an end.

Boy mercifully brought the beast a horse blanket to cover himself. Boy must have been afraid that if Aja came to visit, she'd never want to see another man's body. And she'd embrace everlasting virginity like Ma.

"Where's your shadow?" Marcus asked. "Dio?"

"He's in town asking questions and getting us well stocked for when this rain clears. We won't stay in this stark spiritual commune, though I see you have an extra room for me." He looked to the unoccupied fourth crypt.

"I don't think you'd fit in there. I'm sure Dio will find you more suitable accommodations, more befitting your stature," Marcus said.

"You are less than inviting, and after I directed you to Al Kut and—I see one of you survived." He winked at Marcus, reminding him of his debt. "Dio tells me it'll clear up tomorrow. Today's darkest skies always mean the monsoon is passing, or so he says. And he always knows these things; he never steers me wrong. You only have one horse each and an extra for the holy lady I assume. I saw them in the stables. But they look well rested. Marcus, it is time to share information and join forces. I hear Issa is heading some four hundred miles northeast to a land called Kashmir."

Poet pointed to the map hanging on the wall and said, "Maybe, but that is a big valley surrounded by mountains higher than Olympus. It's like searching for a grain of rice on a beach."

As Poet was illuminating the beast, Marcus whispered to Boy, "Go tell Aja to keep Ma away from this man. Tell her to stay away too."

Boy nodded eagerly. He rose and casually said, "I'm going to check on the horses," before darting out.

"Marcus, you surprise me. You're just going to sit here with the yellow-robed ladies? That's your plan? I thought you were a man of action, determined to fulfill your duty to put your house in order."

Marcus replied, "You will not teach me my duty. I told you before, we are not working together. You must go your way as soon as the rain stops."

"And you as well," Saltaurius said. "Because if six moons pass before you can deliver his body to Pilate, you will fail in your mission. You will lose your Roman name and citizenry—marked for death with a bounty on your head. Or do you know, as I do, that he is just another imposter?"

"What makes you so sure he is *another imposter*? And why do you still seek him if he is?" Marcus asked. He assumed Saltaurius was referring to the imposter he'd scared off in Rhagae but wasn't sure.

"We've been told that a man who bears a resemblance to the picture you had commissioned passed through here. That was smart. Carrying a picture of the man you seek should be standard operating procedure in our line of work. All I need is a lookalike to collect my reward and do *my duty* as Dio calls it."

Marcus bristled and Poet grumbled at being lumped together with Saltaurius, but it was true. They shared a vocation with Saltaurius as manhunters.

"I hope you didn't molest any of the people we interviewed. I don't like to be followed," Marcus said.

"Ha! And you don't like being led. The fraud in Rhagae we both met. You left him to continue his false preaching? I took care of him by administering Roman justice." Marcus understood what he meant, that the man who claimed to be Issa was now dead. He'd been warned not to return to his pious fraud, and there was no purpose in defending his own actions in Rhagae, or in asking any more questions, as he wanted to hasten the brute on his way. But Saltaurius wasn't done talking, "And look at you all dressed in white Indian wear." Marcus wished he was in his tunic with his light armor on top.

"Ha!" Marcus laughed off the jest. "But if you could see yourself right now, I don't think you'd be talking about how we are dressed. You looked like a Persian when you came in, and now you look like a naked ox standing on two legs."

Saltaurius laughed a bit too loudly but let the rebuttal stand. "All right then, just between us dandy-dressed Romans, the one we still track, I'll separate his head from his body and return with it in a box to Jerusalem. 'Let him return from my death if he is not a fraud,' as Dio says. No one will want to examine too closely the rotting head upon my return. But it cannot be the Jesus I saw. *That* Jesus would never desert his flock and leave all who worship him to suffer. He died and rose up to heaven by his father just as prophesied and proclaimed by my dead brother in my vision." He raised his massive arms to the heavens to proclaim: "Just like Romulus, he has risen for a new Rome to be born. What an excellent Roman god this messiah is, to not raise an army of Jews to fight the empire as they so desperately wanted. Isn't that right, Marcus, leave the fighting to us born to fight?"

"You're a . . . what one might call . . . a Christian?" Poet asked. He looked apologetically to Marcus, who smiled, giving Poet leave to speak. Marcus had heard the term whispered by those he had interviewed in Jerusalem who all claimed not to be "one of those Christian followers of the Way."

The large man stood with the horse blanket only covering half his torso, his manhood immodestly exposed and flopping about. "I saw him heal a lame man while a light, the power and glory of a God, hovered around him, defying all natural laws. So, yes, I believe the story of his crucifixion and his ascension into heaven. A man who could move mountains wouldn't run from the fight to hide."

Marcus was confused. "I thought you said he should leave the fighting to us?"

"But one must fight to save those he leads," Saltaurius said. "Marcus, what do you believe about this man we chase?"

"I think you have given this too much thought. They crucified him and then his body disappeared. We were sent to find him and now find ourselves here together, whether or not we like it," Marcus said. He was weighing how this whale of a man might scuttle his hopes of making a triumphant return to Rome with the man they both sought. He would need to find Issa before Saltaurius severed his head from his body. "His head will rot before you get out of Kashmir. He won't be recognizable," Marcus said.

"This isn't my first manhunt," Saltaurius replied. "That's what the linen and powder are for, to make plaster. If he's as pretty as your picture, he'll provide a beautiful death mask. The rotting skull will just serve as a match to the mask."

"Yes, of course," Marcus said. "We too heard he is going to Kashmir, but only on his way into Tibet." Marcus pointed to the alleged route on the map. He looked to Poet with raised eyebrows.

"An even bigger expanse of land," Poet said, though they had heard no such thing. Marcus hoped Poet had caught his subtle shift in tone and would follow the game he was now playing.

"As you note," Marcus said, "our time granted us by Pilate no longer allows more time chasing the holy ghost. It requires we give up the search and head by sea back to Rome to plead my family's case. You enabled me to obtain the means to present this case, and for that, I am grateful. You might follow him to Kashmir and you won't find him waiting for you there as he will have moved on toward Tibet," Marcus said, pointing again at the map. "But if we had time, we'd head directly here along the Ladakh river, where he is heading after Kashmir. He would have already alighted in Kashmir and will only spend a week there. This way cuts off a great distance. You may even beat him to Ladakh."

Poet must have caught on, as he hurried to gather up the map like Marcus was giving away their advantage. He rolled it up, looking at Marcus disapprovingly. They had played similar gambits before, and Poet had always enjoyed the righteous deception and playing a part like an actor on the stage.

They knew each other so very well. Marcus loved his man. "Poet, I decide what information to share here. Unfurl your map and tell him what you found out from the local priests. I command you."

Poet, shaking his head, spread out the map. Marcus imagined he was thinking about how best to make use of the legends and places the local wise men had recently taught him about. Poet sighed, contemplating the map before him. "The Hindus here tell me he is going from here in Pali to Kashmir and then to Ladakh before heading deeper into Tibet. A pilgrimage of sorts. He's retracing a prior journey, one of his youth."

"And . . ." Marcus said, pretending to prod Poet.

"And there is an old Bon religious site, now a Buddhist temple, and he is heading to that temple in Ladakh on his way to Tibet." Poet placed a finger on the map, tracing the journey as he had described it. "That is all. They wouldn't tell me the name of the temple. I had asked too many questions." He then mumbled softly, "As you do now." Poet moved from mumble to grumble, still shaking his head in disbelief that he'd been forced to share such information with the beast.

"Tell him the name of the temple!" Marcus demanded.

Poet stood at attention with a look of resolve that conveyed he would empty himself of all he knew. "Naropa Temple along the Ladakh river. And if you take the innocent man's head, may you be damned." He saluted Marcus and stormed out into the rain to wash away the stain of betraying the son of God to the god-slayer. He was so good, Marcus almost forgot that Poet was just playing a part.

"Why are you telling me all this? I thought we didn't work together," Saltaurius asked.

Marcus knew Saltaurius had only shared the information about Flavius to delay his search and perhaps hoping Flavius might kill him. But this was a good time for playing dumb. "You did me and my family a great service by suggesting I go to Al Kut to meet the emperor's imperial guard there," Marcus said. "A service I have sworn to keep secret. Poet couldn't understand that. Now we are even. And though we still are not working together—and I head to Rome after resting here for another couple of weeks—when you find him, send a carrier bird to Rome with the report. I'll tell them I led you to him, and maybe that will buy me some mercy under the terms that said I will have fulfilled my mission regardless of how he was found. Can I give you a piece of gold for your trouble?"

"Save your sesterces. They will not accept the word of some bird to spare your life, and I wouldn't go to the trouble. What will you do, failing your mission? Will you fall on your sword or plead for mercy from the emperor?" Saltaurius asked, clearly fooled by the ruse.

Marcus had to weigh his words. Saltaurius had only discovered one part of the story—that the emperor's guard that had slaughtered the House of Decia was in Al Kut. That was all he had whispered to Marcus. He didn't know of the imperial treachery behind the massacre. Saltaurius was not the type to parse the nature of revenge whether or not it was righteous. It was best not to announce his family's innocence and letter of proof, though he wanted to. Saltaurius might fear his part in uncovering the truth would become known if Marcus could return to Rome to present his evidence.

"Marcus, you couldn't have forgotten Pilate's prophecy that I might kill you if you betrayed his mission," Saltaurius said.

"Correction, he didn't say you might kill me," Marcus replied, confusing the brute. "He said you would kill me. But it wasn't his prophecy, rather a prophecy supposedly told by his wife's astrologer. And I'm not betraying my mission but charging you, as my ally, with how to fulfill it, by getting to Ladakh before Issa heads to Tibet."

"Come to think of it," Saltaurius added, "once the time is past and you are exiled, I would make even more coin returning with your head. Dio would help me concoct some story about your plan to return to Rome to revenge your family and finish their coup." Saltaurius assumed a threatening pose and looked toward his sword reclining against the wall to help make his point.

Marcus looked at his own sword. In hand-to-hand combat, he would be at a big disadvantage. Just then Boy and Poet reentered the room, taking seats by the fire and evening the playing field, yet by the relatively tranquil looks on their faces not realizing how close to a deadly fight the situation had become.

"You know what they say," Saltaurius said, pausing for effect. "Two heads are better than one."

Despite himself, Marcus had to laugh, and the laugh cut the tension. "Well, praise the gods, I still have a couple of months. Maybe there will be another miracle. I've been told to believe that one miracle opens the way to all miracles. You yourself claim to have seen one. So don't count me out. Boy, go to the canteen and get us food and drink. We will eat here tonight. Just us three. I'm sure the humble meatless food here would not suit you, Saltaurius."

Saltaurius said, "Marcus, the farther from Rome we get, the less I understand you. You do need to head home soon, even if just to die. I know when I'm not welcome." He started getting dressed. "As soon as the rain stops, I'll head out. Perhaps we'll meet again at some temple in Ladakh if you change your mind and renew the hunt. Naropa, Naropa, that shouldn't be too hard to remember. A Hebrew who claims to be divine traveling with his old mother by donkey is far from commonplace there, I'm sure. You haven't been hard to track, and he shouldn't be able to beat me and Dio on horseback to Ladakh. Dio is like a dog when he picks up a scent. He led me to this hovel. And he is as quick as his whip."

Saltaurius finished dressing and left, allowing air to reenter the room.

Marcus couldn't be sure their ploy fooled Saltaurius, but he had to congratulate Poet on his acting. Marcus let the Tali dice determine the three shifts for the night—to assure the giant did not return to the Abode of God to slay them while they slept or to molest the innocent women. Poet did not complain, though he drew the dreaded second night watch. Judging by the sour look on his face, he thought it was unnecessary after performing his role so convincingly. Marcus knew Boy would have stood all three watches to assure the giant or Dio didn't come anywhere near Aja. He loved his men.

The rain stopped just before dawn.

June 7, 2029 — Day 67 at the Monastery

My exultation has vanished and has been replaced by an equal and opposite wave of doubt and fatigue that weighs on my heart and muddles my mind. *Are my motives pure? Are my methods sound? Is my faith unassailable?* My urge to reveal the earth-shattering story wars with my fear of how the Roman history or story will end. My archbishop would have already started the process of laicization to defrock me, citing my abuse of authority in seizing the glorious opportunity of resurrecting the buried text without following Church protocols. *If you need further guidance . . . before proceeding . . .* I struggled to recall the exact wording of the archbishop's message. I realized he hadn't authorized me to move forward without further authorization. And if the archbishop knew the story I am transcribing from the scrolls, he might add the charge of heresy. He has always tolerated my more liberal social views because I had been, until now, a strict constructionist who adhered to the literal words of the Bible on matters of faith.

Unable to see the end and unmoored from my initial commitment to perform my sacred duty without desire for grandeur or fear for my faith, my way forward is now uncertain.

With only thirty-three scrolls remaining, unanswered questions demanded that I drop my pen and read to the end; I had to know whether Ma would lead them to the elusive Issa and if he would be Jesus Christ. But with the manuscript's antiquated Latin and numerous detours, I would lose about a week of my remaining time if I read to the end now. If I gave way to this compulsion to stop and just read, I wouldn't finish the painstaking, methodical transcription in time. Maybe I could write the ending from memory later, but that would mean losing the actual words and the nuanced interactions of the characters.

Torn, I knew I had to share this gnawing dilemma with my dear friend, the rightfully revered Lama Chinchinanaga.

We got comfortable on our cushions. Lama Chin's eyes were bright, and his body poised as he was clearly excited to hear more of the story. I felt unworthy of my mission and his beatific company, but managed to give voice to the story for his sake.

After the reading, we moved into our discussion about the text, both comforted that Saltaurius and Dio had been sent off in the wrong direction to seek Issa's head where it wouldn't be found. But what was most notable about this occasion was Lama Chin's unbridled exuberance—an emotion that stood in stark contrast to my wavering convictions. He'd been beaming with the bright spiritual current coursing through him throughout the reading, and that glow continued as we discussed the quest.

"Not to dampen your spirits—and no, I still don't know if any of this is true or what they will find," I said, "but I have a deep-seated fear the scrolls will be lost after my time here, deliberately mislaid—destroyed even—by the Kashmir government. They might erase all evidence that backs up my entire mission here, just as they did with the mummified body protecting the scrolls that vanished after being found by my friend."

Poor Miles must be dying with curiosity about my work and desperate to find that mummy. Surely, he was working like a madman through the university to pressure our government to pressure Kashmir to release the scrolls and find the mummy. Our friendship might be on the line if the pope decided the story was blasphemy, and I had to refuse Miles the fruits of his discovery. I didn't like the idea of being an instrument of censorship, but had to heed papal authority on such matters. If Kashmir didn't destroy the historical record, I feared Rome would.

"The manuscript is a treasure trove in a myriad of ways, and yet it could easily disappear. And that, my friend, hurts my heart. I have fallen in love with the sweet-smelling papyrus scrolls and the story they tell, though the ending will be key to Christianity. Or at least to me."

"Perhaps, if I may suggest," Lama Chin said, with a sweet smile, "you should turn that fear into love and devotion for your work and finish your task of capturing the story for posterity with the same dedication and diligence you've shown to date. It is not time to waffle or change directions. Patience and faith. Be like Marcus, who, though he will be banished and put to death, is still determined to find Jesus and march him back to Rome for the reckoning. And don't become attached to any particular outcome. We will have all our answers soon enough, I pray."

He made prayer hands and bowed his forehead to the floor by my feet. I had not posed my burning question, but he had read my mind. Was I a child who had to read ahead out of curiosity and sacrifice the work for Christ's sake?

"You're right. Like Marcus, I have a lot riding on this ending and on doing my job well. The pope may judge my work as being heretical or otherwise unworthy." I shook my head in humble dejection. How could I be worthy of such a task? Who was I, Thomas Mann, to serve the Lord in this manner, when mistakes seemed so certain and all else so uncertain? Surely another would be more qualified, more suitable.

Maybe it was a grievous error to seize this golden opportunity for myself. To show off my skills and to seek fame from my good fortune, I thought. *Maybe spiritual hubris has blinded me.*

Lama Chin maintained his child's pose in front of me. I closed my eyes, not wanting to delve any deeper into my inadequacies. But I opened them just as quickly when a question and response rushed up from my heart: Where was that brave and humble abbot who knew no fear and risked death to save the the statue of the blessed Virgin Mary from the inferno inside the cathedral? That devout ghost was with me still. *I am a servant of the Lord; let me serve according to your will.*

"But what about the apostle Paul?" my brilliant lama asked as he finally raised his head from the floor to point to the beautiful Bible centered on his desk.

"Speaking of unworthy messengers," I said half joking.

"What?" the lama asked, looking confused.

"Before Saul of Tarsus was transformed, he was the most vocal of detractors of Jesus and his fledgling followers. But then?" I raised my eyebrows, sensing he knew the answer by the way he leaned forward on his cushion and crooked his index finger.

"The resurrected Jesus appeared to him on the road to Damascus?" he asked.

I was beaming now because of his curiosity and careful reading of the Bible. He had an agile and beautiful mind. "Yes!" I said, sharing his excitement. "Paul was blinded by the light, By the vision of Christ but not like Saltaurius's because not all visions are from God." I thought about Joseph Smith's visions and how we accepted some visions and rejected others. "But that is a good point. The risen Jesus appeared as a light and a voice to Saint Paul much later than the forty-day ascension reported in Acts." We silently pondered his observation, reflecting on how it might relate to the story we were reading together.

We sat in harmony and contemplation for a long time. Then came the familiar eight bells, indicating the end of our meeting. I was disappointed with their swift arrival. We embraced by the open door, as was our custom, and I felt the comforting hum of Lama Chin's sweet spirit. But then my excitable friend held up his right hand, pointing his right index finger toward the heavens, which I read as a call to attention.

"When we next read, when you have finished your mission and we know the end of the tale, I have a secret surprise for you." He twirled the finger and rose on his toes to dip his forehead to touch mine, a sign of his affection and to seal his secret to be revealed at our next and final reading at our book club for two.

Chapter 37
On the Way to Kashmir

Marcus sent Boy to spy from a nearby hill as Saltaurius headed out of Pali the next day with his two big horses. A small shadow trailed behind him on a small horse. They headed northeast, hopefully toward Ladakh and not Kashmir.

Marcus hurried to the garden, where he was told he would find Ma. There she was, looking serene as always, enjoying the first rain-free day in a week. The air was extra rich in oxygen and the sky was crystal blue. Ma was in her usual white sari, but here at the Abode of God, she was always wearing garlands of flowers that were presented to her. She would re-gift those garlands when the spirit moved her. Marcus was glad she didn't garland him, as it was enough that he wore the white linen robes.

"Ma," Marcus said as he approached, "Good morning, holy lady. With Saltaurius setting out before us, there's no time to tarry. I have to leave and seek Issa in Kashmir. We will have to get going, with or without you. I think we sent the assassin and his demon in the wrong direction, but he may choose to follow Issa into Kashmir. That giant is looking to send your friend's head in a box to Rome. What say you?" Marcus didn't like to speak so bluntly to Ma, but he had to rouse her to action. He didn't want to leave without her.

Ma's peaceful countenance, one that always registered amusement or bliss, broke form and turned to a grimace. "That man, and the passing of the rain, were the signs I was waiting for. We must get going. I will guide you while trusting Kali to guide me. Jaya Bhagavan!"

"Jaya Bhagavan!" Marcus replied. He had heard the rallying cry many times on the trail from Rhagae, and now as a call and response at the Abode of God. Ma seemed pleased he was making an effort.

"When we celebrate the Lord and sing his name, he draws closer," Ma said.

"Then let's sing it all the way to Kashmir," he said.

"It will be done. We need to speak to Aja and Boy," Ma said. "This will be hard on them—this hasty break." Marcus nodded as Ma motioned to a nearby devotee in a yellow robe. "Ask Aja to bring Boy to join us here, please."

Despite the sense of urgency that filled him, Marcus found himself distracted by the beauty of the place. "What are those short green bushes that smell like long grass?" Marcus asked, motioning to the sloping hill in front of them, where many yellow robes and one orange robe flowed between the gentle waves of green picking the leaves.

"Tea!" Ma exclaimed. "We grow and bless it here. They are harvesting the flush for our pleasure. And the grass smell will become a heavenly aroma as soon as the leaves dry. Then they will be brought back to life by hot water."

Ma and Marcus sat in sunny silence, watching the tea being harvested. Soon, the young couple approached them in the garden clearing and sat down next to Ma on slim mats, eager to hear why they had been summoned. Boy had now mastered sitting crossed-legged. Marcus sat on a log, thinking their bottoms must be getting wet from all the rain despite their slender cushions.

Ma started out by placing garlands that had adorned her around each of their necks. And then she said, "Boy and Aja, you realize the spirit's ever-present nature you share. Two hearts that have truly touched are never apart. Marcus and I will leave at first light tomorrow." She turned to Marcus. "Marcus, do we need to rush and get a half day ride in today?"

"If it was just over the next mountain, maybe," he said, "but this venture will require a couple weeks of riding and it's best we prepare well today. We will travel faster in the long run that way." Marcus knew this was true from many campaigns and long cavalry rides.

Ma returned to addressing the lovers. "Boy's help is needed to care for the horses during the long journey to Kashmir. Aja, please arrange some warm clothes and food for our journey. It will still be cold there on some of the mountain passes." Cold sounded refreshing to Marcus as they sat in the Indian summer heat. He looked forward to dressing like a soldier again as they headed north. "And I must go to explain my leaving again so soon to the children." A shadow passed quickly over Ma's face after mentioning the children. She bowed down with her prayer hands to her forehead as the shadow lifted.

Meanwhile, the young lovers looked at each other like wild horses were dragging their chariots in opposite directions.

Aja looked forlorn. "Please don't be sad," Ma said. "We go to find my friend and teacher. To Issa and Kashmir is where Kali and Babaji now lead me. You are needed here to tend to the children in my absence. I will be back soon enough."

Marcus stood and motioned for Boy to stand at attention as a matter of regimental discipline. "Boy, this ride will take several weeks, but when we find the man or god, you may return here with Ma, if she is willing."

"But of course I am willing and wanting!" Ma said, clapping her hands. She and Aja looked jubilantly at Marcus.

Boy bowed down to his master, his face full of love and light. Marcus pulled him up to hold him by the shoulders. He spoke to him as if the women weren't present. "I believe you found your mother and wife here. Leave us now to arrange for our departure and muster the courage to kiss the girl."

Boy's bronze face darkened with embarrassment as Aja and Ma giggled. Boy reached over for Aja's hand, and they ran off.

Marcus turned to the still-giggling Ma and said, "I thought he needed a little prodding." Ma's laugh was like a babbling brook flowing over rocks in an endless stream of joy. Marcus couldn't help but join her in her mirth as they watched the bobbing yellow robes and one orange robe amidst the waves of green bushes. But he stopped laughing abruptly as a strange, amusing, and horrifying image paraded through his mind, that of Dio's ghoulish gray body swimming in an oversized orange robe.

"Ma," Marcus called out warily. He feared that his thought would unsettle her and perhaps change her mind about coming with them to Kashmir. But he had to tell her. "Just now, I am reminded of something that Saltaurius said in passing. Something about his sinister friend now having an orange robe. He followed us from Rhagae and, perhaps—"

"Swami Bhakti?" Ma finished his thought. "Yes, I have seen this, and Bhakti was challenged, but he is fine. More than fine. His heart has never been so full and overflowing. I am always in touch with my students and teachers. Don't worry. Jaya Bhagavan!" Marcus did not know what she was talking about or how she could know what had befallen Bhakti, but he was glad Ma believed the swami to be unharmed, and she would continue on with their quest.

❧ ❧ ❧

The next morning, they were set to depart the Abode of Bhagavan bound for Kashmir. Just before dawn, Boy slipped out of their chambers supposedly to tend to their horses. Marcus suspected an ulterior motive when Boy returned at sunrise with a face of a man who just tasted the bliss of a first kiss—taking all the sting out of their parting, but sure to hurt all the more within the hour. Marcus commanded they make haste. Ma was ready with the sun.

Aja arranged a celebration in honor of their departure. She marched with all the children, singing, into the ashram compound. There were only joyful faces, as Aja and the children knew the tears should wait till later. As the three horseman and the holy mother mounted their horses, the children chanted a glorious Hindu song of praise, *Om Namo Naraya-naya*, and the older children played cymbals and drums. As that simple chorus played, Ma and the Roman soldiers rode out of the Abode of God like a royal procession to find the son of God.

Marcus was not sure if Poet's disclosure of the Naropa Temple destination had convinced Saltaurius. They would soon find out. The big man was hard to miss, and they would pass people who would have seen him. Either way, there was no looking back, and he prayed Ma's guidance would get them to Issa first. And if Issa was Ma's Issa, regardless of whether he was also Jesus, he would bear a likeness, and that would be enough for Marcus to fulfill his mission. With Ma riding by his side, he believed in himself once again. And he believed he would reclaim his glory in Kashmir and his good name in Rome—be it dead or alive.

As they rode north and gained elevation, Marcus and his men exchanged their white robes for their Roman military attire. Despite that change, for the first time Marcus fully accepted that Ma was in charge of their journey.

He would take charge only if they were forced to fight some foe who fell upon them.

Ma had them stay west of the great mountain ranges as they headed north. She told them that would help them avoid potential steep and treacherous climbs in deep snow. She pointed to the snowcapped mountains and assured Marcus that if Saltaurius had taken any other route, he'd be bogged down for weeks, if not months.

With Ma in front, their small calvary galloped from monastery to monastery en route to Kashmir. The elder of each monastery invited her to speak. Hindu temples seamlessly became Buddhist temples. And those lofty Buddhist monks recognized Ma's humble divinity irrespective of her religion. The men would set up camp nearby the temples and await her return. Each monastery was about a couple days of riding from the previous one. This lent a spiritual rhythm to the pilgrimage's progress. Marcus was also feeling a shift inside him that he couldn't explain, perhaps a slowing of the wheels inside his mind. Though slower, his thoughts seemed brighter somehow and kept returning to the stillness of Ma's and Jesus's faces and eyes. Ma's smiles and gentle reassurance suggested she understood perfectly well this more peaceful state of his mind.

Ma's intuition about how she might receive messages from her friend Issa proved true in Amristar. Issa had stopped in the same monastery, leaving word for her that his next stop would be Jammu. On the road to Jammu, Marcus sidled up to Ma's horse to question her.

"Can you be sure the monks at the last monastery did not see the large Roman in Arab dress, Saltaurius? Did he make inquiries there?" Marcus asked. She had already told him as much, but he sought reassurance.

"No. No reason for them to lie—the lama I met was spiritual and truthful."

"Though I didn't want you to meet this Saltaurius, I must admit he possesses a crude intelligence. He had some notions that I wonder about too. If Jesus revived himself with God's help, wasn't his duty to his people there in Judaea?" Marcus asked his teacher.

"That assumes the people of one place are more worthy of his teachings than the people of another. And perhaps in being reborn his dharma changed, ascending one place and descending in another at will like my Babaji." She had told Marcus of her ageless guru before. He found it hard to believe in an avatar who lived forever, but he found it even more difficult not to believe Ma. "There are many ways we are called to serve. Maybe it was time for his disciples to teach. And he is with his mother, tending to her. His light, as an avatar, as a Christ, is within everyone, everywhere, at every time. Whoa, Kali!" She pulled on her reins to slow down her horse and turned to face Marcus, whose horse slowed in turn. "I am glad I can speak of these things with you."

"Thank you," he said. "And thank you for your patience with me over the long road." He felt ashamed of the night he had almost touched her with that lustful incubus inhabiting his entire being.

"All's immediately forgiven when we open our hearts to Bhagavan as you have done," Ma replied, sharing the depth of her nut-brown eyes with him. Her eyes filled him with the frequency of love that vibrated within him.

Marcus had become two men: one the Roman tribune in his tunic and armor on a mission to vindicate the House of Decia and the other a simple man that loved Ma in a purely spiritual way and was going to meet God.

The tribune asked, "Another question the brute had was how Issa could leave his followers to be persecuted and killed without a fight. He fought to save your life and risked his own, didn't he?"

"He debated to save my life." Ma laughed and brushed a fly from her horse's mane and then stroked its neck. Marcus looked over his shoulder at Boy, who was smiling as he rode behind them. Boy admired Ma and her love of the horses. Ma also looked back at Boy, smiling at him before turning back to Marcus and saying, "Isn't there persecution and oppression all over the world? With the prophecy fulfilled and his divine message delivered, to stay would just lead to more bloodshed. You think like a soldier and not a man of God, though your heart is true. I imagine his presence and love live even more there now in his absence. And from there it will spread over time and space. Even here and now we speak of him and his love."

"Without a leader, his followers will fight among themselves, and then his name will fade into obscurity," Marcus said, following conventional Roman political wisdom.

"Maybe, or maybe being without a leader will afford his followers the time to allow the message of love to take root and flourish before persecution comes to stamp it out," Ma said, expressing an alternative wisdom.

Marcus knew firsthand this was true. Boy had reported on the great wellspring of love for Jesus, which Marcus had also found on the streets of

Jerusalem, where those he questioned would rather die than cooperate. Even Saltaurius loved Jesus—as long as he was in heaven.

"You are right," Marcus said. "If he'd stayed in Jerusalem, the governor, Pilate, would have brutally ended it then and there by removing his head and all the heads of those that followed him. Avoiding a losing battle is often the best course for your men and cause." Ma never ceased to amaze him. "However, Saltaurius believes the man we will find is not him and will be yet another imposter. He was right about the fraud in Rhagae. And even if he is the Jesus that survived the cross and then deserted his post and the chosen people, Saltaurius thinks he deserves to die for violating his gladiator code of conduct." Marcus was still grappling with the shadow of the giant and his twisted way of thinking.

"This is a corrosive thought, that some people are chosen and others are not," Ma said. "God's mind does not work like that. Is it possible that those who love Jesus do not want him to live?" she asked.

"Saltaurius does not. Hopefully, we will never see him again. Either way, as long as that giant lives, your friend is not safe in Jammu, Kashmir, or anywhere."

Ma started clicking her tongue, coaxing Kali to move to a trot, canter, and then gallop along the dirt path. Marcus and his men chased behind her.

CHAPTER 38
Soothing Waters

POET WAS HEARTENED to see Marcus so at ease and enjoying Ma's company as she provided him guidance on their journey. As a poet, he wondered about all the faces of love. Even as their horses trod through mud, the surrounding scenery was the most spectacular he had ever seen. He too was seeing through Ma's eyes the majesty of God's love.

They traveled through a pass between some Olympus-sized mountains. Jammu was less than a two-day ride ahead of them. No one had seen the giant and his imp, which allowed them all to relax. Their deception had worked. Poet imagined running into Saltaurius and Dio years later, which at first struck him as amusing, but then caused him to fear that it might be a deadly encounter for him.

Their muddy morning ride had Ma almost falling off her horse with laughter as she transformed their misfortune into a comical source of joy. As midday approached, the sun was high and strong. The mud paths would harden by the next day. The surrounding air was fresh from the melting snows in the peaks of mountains that towered above them.

Ma pulled up her reins and stopped her horse at a spot along a small river coming down from the mountains. The rocks that guided the water on its run provided cascading waterfalls that ran into deep, sparkling pools. The vegetation and wildflowers along the banks were lush and emitted a honeysuckle scent. It was a secluded slice of Eden basking in the sunlight.

Marcus rode up beside Ma. They led their horses to the water, and then their horses led them into the water, which stopped halfway up their mud-caked legs. In unison, the magnificent animals dipped their long necks and faces down to drink. Marcus consulted with Ma before they announced to Poet and Boy that they'd have a short holiday. They all dismounted for the day after only a half day's ride. Boy had warned them earlier that the mud was tiring the horses and advised against a full day's ride.

Poet was happy with the respite, as his backside and saddle pleaded for a divorce. He was slightly older than his companions and squeezing his legs against the sides of the horse as they bucked over often rough terrain and unpaved roads for ten hours a day was becoming more challenging by the day. He missed the smooth Roman roads of flat rock set in concrete where he didn't have to squeeze the horse's flanks to keep from falling into the mud. Clever Boy had suggested someone should invent a way to secure the feet by the horse's side. Poet thought that Boy's invention sure would make riding a lot easier.

Perhaps it was Ma's stories and songs, but Poet—used to hard campaigns of conquest on horseback—saw the challenging days of riding and camping as a heroic quest of discovery and mastery of oneself. He saw a change in Marcus too. His old friend was still his master and commander, but now he had unguarded moments of connection and reflection. He saw it in his eyes and the tone of his words with Ma and his men. They were all sensing the great logos alive and vibrating in them and through everything, manifesting their destiny right before their eyes. Their goal, which was nothing less than meeting God, was sure and true. And Marcus's certainty that their end was near had been passed on to Poet.

Poet's lyrical heart was soaring. And his buttocks were humming, glad to be free of the saddle. The horses were watered and then tethered, and it was time for the goddess and men to rest and refresh.

Ma went first into the rushing stream, wearing the white Indian sari robe she always wore. She was giggling like a little girl as the cool stream danced round her body and over her head. Ma sat under a falling stream that provided a massage to all areas of her body. She stood and waved for the men along the bank to join her. Out of respect for Ma, the men hesitated to bathe naked, despite that being their usual practice. Poet thought Ma would just laugh if they did. Following Marcus's lead, the men stripped down to their loincloths. Poet noted that slender Boy had become a young Adonis along the way. Dressed liked slaves, they entered the freezing water to enjoy its cleansing and healing power. The bracing chill of the rushing mountain waters took Poet's breath away for an instant, before he took quick gasps of air and enjoyed the water chutes massaging his aching muscles. Poet marveled at the scene—a Moroccan slave, a Roman tribune, and a poet bathing with a divine Indian woman. *It must be a first*, he thought. *All as equals, with God the only witness.* He imagined how Homer might write the scene, or how the great Greek artists would memorialize it in marble or paint it on an urn.

Ma playfully splashed about, going deep under the pools of water and challenging the largest of the small waterfalls to knock her down. She was teaching the men to once again experience a bath as child's play.

Ma led them all to a large slab of rock between the forking stream to dry their newly born bodies in the sun. As they lay down on the flat-topped rock, an eagle soared overhead in ever higher loops of flight. Poet no longer saw the eagle as a symbol of a predatory empire but as a deity of nature, gliding on the wind and celebrating the blissful bathers below.

They all followed Ma's lead and lay back on the smooth rock with arms stretched out and legs separated to drink in the sun. They could sense Ma beginning to enter the deep meditative state she called samadhi, a stateless state which would encompass the entire scene.

Staring up at the sky as the eagle was sailing out of sight, before Ma became fully absorbed into the ethereal source beyond this world, Poet asked her, "What is your secret?"

"It is not mine, and it is not a secret. But I will tell." Ma, already in a trance-like state, spoke like a spirit was speaking through her. "Realize that in each moment we have a choice. Call it free will. Why not choose peace, light, and love over and over, until you walk with God on his path?" With that, they all became silent as the grace enveloping Ma enveloped them.

CHAPTER 39
Samadhi

As THEY ALL lay there spread out like corpses on the large slab of rock, with rushing waters beside them, something was holding Marcus back. He saw his fear of losing control. His practical mind was deeply rutted, as it should be; it had served him well. He paused the chariot wheels of thought to hear Ma's voice say inside his head, *Let go! I am with you. There's nothing to lose.*

With that, Marcus experienced an exaltation like he had never felt before, even after a victorious battle. Grace like waves of sunshine passed through him as he lay upon the holy rock in Kashmir in the company of all he loved. He felt his body and awareness being drawn toward the sun dancing upon his flickering eyelids. He saw his wife smiling at him, taking him by the hand, and leading him down a perfect sunny row of olive trees to an even brighter light that welcomed them. *How could a light be brighter than the sun and still be gazed upon?* At the height of his reverie, the dazzling light became Jesus's face, so well-known to him by now, smiling and inviting him to embrace his divinity and grace. His eyes were like Ma's eyes, the same windows shining the light of infinite and eternal life. The peace, light, and love of Elysium flowed through him uninhibited.

He realized that experience would change his life. Ma was divine, and he now believed in his own divinity, and in a personal god. That god was not just some invisible force of logos but very real and inside of him—and lying next to him in the form of Ma, Poet, and Boy.

CHAPTER 40
An Omen

THAT NIGHT, THEY camped by the holy site of rushing waters. As they slept, Poet was startled from his sleep by a rustling in the camp, a sound like an animal searching for food, or one that had already stolen their food and was fleeing. Whatever it was, it scurried away after Poet had opened his eyes and sat up. Or so he thought.

As Poet lay back and closed his eyes, he felt a slithering around his bare leg. He was too scared to call out, afraid he might startle the large, cold, muscular mass moving up toward his manhood. Terrified, he sat up slowly and carefully within this waking nightmare. He pulled down the blanket over him revealing a huge sand-colored cobra that reared its head, bringing them eye to eye. He was no snake charmer and had no flute and basket. The hood opened wide as the snake twitched its tongue, ready to strike.

Poet had the fleeting thought it might be a lucid nightmare. But no, this was real, and he was only a flick of fangs away from death. He said a quick prayer in his head—*God help me!* Just then a small hand grabbed the snake by the neck and lifted it up to her face. *Ma!*

She looked ready to laugh but must have seen that Poet was in mortal fear. "Nothing to worry about now," she said. "I will dispose of him."

"Kill it!" Poet pleaded. The others awoke at the noise and drew their daggers. When they saw Poet terrified and scurrying across the sand like a crab to get away from the snake, they sheathed their daggers and laughed.

"No need to kill him," Ma replied, to Poet's great dissatisfaction. The snake curled itself around Ma's arm. She twirled to untwist it and said, "I'll take him deep into the forest before I release him. Don't worry, I will talk to him, and he will not return."

Knowing the righteousness of Ma, of her powers and her honesty, Poet nodded in reluctant agreement with her plan to allow the serpent to live.

"Boy, go with her. And toss it over the small cliff we passed. I don't want you too far from camp. That way it won't die but won't be able to climb back up to . . ." Marcus stopped mid-sentence, but Poet could finish the thought. "We all need to get back to sleep," Marcus said, but Poet knew he would not be getting back to sleep that night.

Poet thought it a great irony that Greeks and Romans used snakes to symbolize rebirth and protection. He pulled his horsehair rope from his bag and started laying it down around his mat. This was more than a coincidence, perhaps a sign or an omen. Since he didn't have an oracle to consult, he would ask Ma in the morning.

As they broke camp at dawn, Marcus posed his question for him about the portent of a snake coming into camp at night. Ma laughed in response and said, "Our fears follow us, until we turn our thoughts entirely toward the love of God."

CHAPTER 41
Jammu

TWO DAYS LATER, as they trotted into Jammu full of anticipation, Boy was posting on his horse like a peacock. Though each stride forward took him farther from Aja, he knew it brought him closer to their reunion. He believed their long journey would soon end. And for the rest of his life, he would have the delightful Aja as his love and the shadowless Ma as his guru. Ma had overheard his thoughts about why she cast no shadow, and had explained, "Son, as a follower of the way, you only see the light in me. Those that focus on my body see me cast a shadow."

The men set up camp as they waited for Ma to return from the nearby monastery. Marcus roused Boy from his thoughts. "Where's our fire?" he said. "How will Ma find us in the dark? Get the fire lit and then you can daydream about Aja's emerald eyes burning there." Boy saw Aja's body and her light.

"She is Boy's Cleopatra, and he would die for her like Marc Antony. But would you die for us, Boy?" Poet teased, and Boy didn't answer. "We are fortunate we have met no one who has seen a giant riding two horses."

"We would have heard of the beast. It's impossible to miss him. The gods willing, he's headed more east toward Ladakh and is now crossing icy peaks to get there," Marcus said. "Ma assured me the message left in Amristar was just for her and would not have been shared with Saltaurius."

They helped Boy arrange the seating and bedding around the fire.

Poet held up a stick to pontificate, "We have moved out of Hindu land, and now the monks are Buddha worshipers, but Ma seems equally content and knowledgeable in Lord Buddha's teachings. The teachings are so different and yet so much the same. One seeks to find the self, and the other says there is no self. One has many gods, and the other is silent on a single god. But they both include meditation and the goal of reaching an elevated state of divine consciousness. Each man must follow his own path to Elysium. Boy!" Poet threw the stick playfully at Boy whose mind had wandered back to Aja. "Listen here to what the great Cicero had to say on the matter, and I paraphrase, 'You cannot expect the gods to go by our names in foreign lands.' Ma could hold her own with Plato and show him the sun that casts the shadow on the cave wall. The sun itself casts no shadow."

Boy repeated to himself, *the sun itself casts no shadow.*

To Boy's amazement, they discussed openly how their cadre of three had all, more or less, become students of Ma. Boy was wholeheartedly practicing Ma's teachings. Marcus said he now understood what Ma meant by an elevated state of grace. Poet was becoming a master of their Eastern mysticism and its metaphysical texts and tenets. The change that had come over them all pleased Boy. And they were still on their way to meet their teacher's teacher. Boy prayed Issa was the Jesus that the people he'd met in Jerusalem so revered. He wanted to meet the man-god, whose beautiful face was now etched upon his mind.

"Jaya Bhagavan!" Ma called out as she appeared in the circle cast by the firelight. Boy, Marcus, and Poet jumped to their feet.

"Jaya Bhagavan!" Boy sang in response to Ma's rallying cry.

"Men, we were caught off guard," Marcus said with relief in his voice. "Jaya Bhagavan to you too, Ma. I'm glad you were not barbarians come to slay us."

"My apologies, master, for not being more vigilant," Poet said, bowing his head. "But I think barbarians would make a little more noise. Ma's feet barely touch the ground as she walks."

Boy was relieved as Marcus and Ma laughed at Poet's apology. They'd all been lost in their conversation about Ma and Jesus. Ma began singing her "Jaya Bhagavan!" as she clapped her hands above her head and danced around the fire. Boy followed her around, singing for three loops. Poet clapped and Marcus smiled. As their joyful dance concluded, Ma sat to deliver her news.

"Issa left one last message for me," she said with a smile. "We continue north, outside of Srinagar, to a place called Rauza Bal at Khanyar. He will wait for me there. And it's less than week's ride from here. There is no doubt we will find him there." She then shared her delightful eyes by looking at each of them, one by one, eye to eye.

"We may find the son of God after all," Marcus said. "I'm actually grateful that Pilate pressed us into such a difficult challenge—even if it allowed him to wash his hands of crucifying an innocent man of God." He bowed to Ma with great gratitude and respect. Boy thought Ma must be braver and wiser than all the senators and nobles in all the world to be shown such respect by his master, Tribune Marcus Decia. He loved Marcus and Ma with all his heart, but each so differently. And his love for Uncle Poet was undeniable too. He pondered the different kinds of love. His love for Aja was the most different with its longing for physical union. But there was something common too in all his loves. He would die for any of them.

"Love is love. Just love. God's love is always with you," Ma said after reading Boy's thoughts.

Poet said, "The journey home will soon begin. Our hero, flanked by the son of God and his loyal cohort, riding into Rome to redeem the House of Decia and proclaim a new God."

Boy would miss that journey, but not even that glorious event could keep him from returning to Aja.

They were all jubilant, but Boy was beside himself. Not only would they get to see if this man was Jesus the Christ and Ma reunite with her old friend and the horses get a rest, but he would soon return to Aja a free man. That one kiss they had shared would become one unending kiss of bliss in the sanctuary called the Abode of God.

They all ate and drank their fill that night. Ma took a sip of the spiced wine, or perhaps just pretended to, and actually ate a couple bites of food. They finished with a cup of Ma's tea. The aroma and singular taste of sun, earth, and dew sent them off into dreams of God's love and glory.

CHAPTER 42

The Garden of Salomon

As MA AND her companions rode into Srinagar at midday their spirits were high, and the sun was shining with anticipation on their path ahead. Everyone greeted them with smiles and without fear, despite the men carrying swords. As in India, the simple people of Kashmir recognized her as a spiritual master. She smiled, knowing that all that made her a spiritual adept was a little girl's unwavering love and devotion to her guru and Bhagavan.

Ma pulled up her reins and dismounted to question a wandering aesthetic, *sadhu* was the word people used. She asked Marcus to hold up the picture of Issa's face yet again to a prospective witness.

The emaciated sadhu lived a hard life. The dirt caked on his face and his matted, twisted, long black hair provided great contrast to the luster of his eyes and smile. Despite the early summer chill of the mountain air, he was nearly naked, wearing only a disheveled loincloth—kept warm by austere spiritual practices.

After she had asked her question and he had replied, Ma turned to the group and told them, "He says Yuz Asaf accepted an invitation by Vedic priests to meditate and dwell in the Shankaracharya Temple, also known as the Garden of Salomon. It is high on a nearby hill."

"Yuz Asaf?" Poet asked.

"It means 'the healer' or 'the shepherd.' But he looks like the man in our picture. Issa will be here, just as promised. The locals call him Yuz Asaf."

Ma thanked the sadhu and placed one of the many garlands that she had received along the way over the dried mud of his neck and hairless chest. The sadhu whispered in a solemn tone into Ma's ear. They bowed to one another in parting.

As she remounted, Poet asked, "What did he say?"

"It is rather esoteric, but you love metaphysics. The temple celebrates the union of Shiva and Shakti, the divine masculine and feminine. Duality, the world of opposites. He spoke of this phenomenon, then said, 'Life and death will meet us there. The divine play of creation and destruction and creation again.' His words may have been a warning or a wry spiritual jest." Ma didn't tell the men of her own precognition of a deadly confrontation. She could not disturb the delicate balance of the coming dance between Shiva and Shakti without interfering with God's will.

After they watered their horses and themselves, they began their ascent up a low mountain. Ma surveyed each of her dear travel companions as the bittersweet end of their long, arduous journey approached. Her eyes filled with tears. Boy caught her in this moment, his eyes full of extreme tenderness. Ma raised a finger to her lips and then blessed him with her smile, letting the moment pass.

At the base of the majestic, pyramid-like temple, wide and steep stone steps led the way up to grand golden doors—the entrance to the carved stone temple. "A hundred and eight," Ma said of the great stone stairway. She didn't have to count. Two monks in red robes stood guard in front of the doors at the top. They held brooms for clearing away debris and swishing away the begging monkeys when they became too aggressive.

She noticed Marcus surveying the temple and grounds and said in jest, "Yes, neither the monks nor the monkeys are a match for Roman steel."

"You caught me. It's a fortress, but unprotected," Marcus said. "I'll have to watch my thoughts." Marcus was easy to read.

"I'm glad you are an ally and not a foe. Wait here and I will inquire." Ma bowed before ascending the steep steps to speak to the two sentries.

CHAPTER 43
The Legion and the Legend

MARCUS FELT OVERWHELMED by his responsibilities—to his men, to Ma, to his slaughtered family, and to the gods. Rome was formerly on the top of this list. What would happen if he met the true son of God? Nothing was clear to him. His military mind, which marched in straight lines, could not see his future or his duty. Would he truly force a man of God to ride to Rome, hog-tied and strapped to a horse? For the time being, he would follow Ma's lead. She had not misled him thus far.

Poet asked, "So, if he will not leave with us for Rome? Then what? We storm the temple and bind this holy man, and then strap him over a horse? There are bound to be more monks inside. It will be a bloodbath."

"Is everyone able to read my thoughts? Boy, make camp here," Marcus said. The peak where they and their horses stood was on a level clearing amongst tall trees, looking up at the temple. "One thing is clear. We will not set off for Rome today. Let us rest here and wait for the temple oracle to speak, to see if he's our son of God. I'm eager to meet him."

Ma returned from speaking to the two doormen. "There is a ceremony being conducted within, but we were expected," she said. "Temple rules allow only one visitor at a time and by invitation only from one within. I am invited by my friend, my father, Issa. I wanted to inform you first, before entering."

"Then, once within, could you invite me in?" Marcus asked.

"And then you could invite Poet and then he could invite Boy and Boy could invite Aja. We could call the entire world to worship in that way." Ma laughed, and Poet joined her. "If I can invite you to enter, Marcus, I will. But you must leave your sword here in camp."

"I mean him no harm," Marcus said. "I need to confirm if he is Jesus of Nazareth, who came down from the cross and rose from the dead, and ask that he return in honor and glory with me to Rome. Either way, I pray he is your Issa and you will enjoy a reunion after all these years."

"He is. His messages and visions have been clear. I will see him for myself soon enough," Ma said. "The only honor and glory he will seek is God's, but perhaps it is God's will for him to go to Rome with you and Poet. Boy and I will return to my home and Aja. But, first, I will visit with my old friend. I can finally give him my thanks. Jaya Bhagavan!"

Ma ascended the monumental steps again and entered the pyramid-shaped temple.

In the camp below, hours passed slowly in uncertainty and anticipation. Marcus was eager for his answer. Boy's grin suggested he was meditating on Ma, Jesus, and Aja.

Poet, who had been lost listening to his muse, writing lines of poetry, stood ceremoniously to recite a poem. He cleared his throat and said, "It's still a work in progress." Boy opened his eyes to listen.

"The Legion and the Legend of our Tribune," he began.

"The Legion—is strong and united, though cut down to three.
The brave, the honorable, and the true.
Through many trials and tribulations
Their hearts, forged in fire, were renewed.

The Legend—as east meets west, in the shade of Salomon's garden,
Awaiting a god-man, a goddess has brought them to.
Whether they make it back to Rome is uncertain.
But sure is their love and devotion,
And knowing, the House of Decia, was tragically tested,
So it now may be resurrected."

Marcus felt a deep, almost divine love for his men as Poet spoke his fine words. He saluted Poet before bowing with prayer hands to Poet and Boy, as Ma had taught him.

As twilight fell upon their camp, a monk descended the steep steps. He pointed to Marcus and waved for him to follow. Marcus handed Boy his sword and followed the monk up the steep steps to enter the temple as a humble man and not as a tribune of Rome.

CHAPTER 44

Unwelcomed Guests

POET'S EYES POPPED open. The fire embers were the only light under the moonless sky. Horse hoofs clamoring up to the mountain peak had awakened him, and Boy as well. Poet stood to see a lit torch leading the horsemen. Beneath its light sat one gargantuan man, straddling a gigantic horse and leading another. Eclipsed in his shadow was a third, smaller horse whose rider could not be seen in the dark. Poet and Boy scrambled for their swords to welcome the unwelcomed guests.

The giant's reddish-orange hair streamed down from underneath his blood-red turban. It looked like it had been set on fire from his torch. "Hail, old friends," Saltaurius called out. "I guess they're right—all roads *do* lead to Rome, but I thought you were sailing there. You don't need those swords. We're fellow citizens of Rome. We mean you no immediate harm even though you lied to me." He dismounted and handed Boy the two sets of reins.

As they had little choice in the matter, Poet gave Boy a nod, signaling that it was all right for him to tether their horses. They sheathed their swords. Poet could see that Boy was shaking his head but holding his tongue as he felt the horses' haunches, where the welts of overused whips protruded. Boy firmly believed a man's goodness could be judged by how well he treated his horse.

"Where are Marcus and the holy woman?" Saltaurius demanded. "Do they make separate camp or is he plowing that virgin field up in the high temple?"

Dio also dismounted and tossed his reins to Boy. The imp circumnavigated the camp like a dog marking his territory before squatting down and hunching over the embers. He nodded to Saltaurius, as if the hound from hell was giving the earthbound bull silent orders.

Poet moved in to face the giant, his eyes at chest level. With his hand on the hilt of his sword he said, "Marcus will return soon. Should we relight the fire or do you want to sleep?"

"Being so near the goal, how could any soldier sleep?"

Poet took this as a minor reproach for their being startled from their sleep a few minutes before. "I hear it is hard to sleep when one is followed by ghosts," he said.

Saltaurius growled a threatening laugh at the affront. "The great actor who tried to send me to Tibet via some temple in Ladakh. Naropa Temple was it? I checked with a local monk, who got to keep his robe, and you didn't make the place up. But what a show you put on. Only . . . Dio saw through it. So, no harm done, other than to your reputation as a reputable man and a reliable storyteller. But bygones—let's have a fire."

The giant held up his torch to cast light off the stairs of the temple. The light faded as it reached the monks sleeping on the top step. They appeared like two hazy heaps of red laundry. "What a fortress. I wonder if even Hercules could demolish this temple?" He flexed his arms as if pushing down pillars on either side of his gigantic frame.

"I think you mean Samson," Poet said.

"Here, Boy," Saltaurius said, handing Boy the torch, "for the fire. I have some salted lamb for us to eat while we wait. And you'll tell me where Marcus is, or I'll go search the temple tonight. I hear a Yuz Asaf, who fits our man's description, is within. The imposter goes by many names, it seems."

"One can only enter with an invitation. Lots of monks guard the place. Marcus was invited in, but we were not," Poet said.

"Good, he can kill this Yuz Asaf and bring him here for me. He does my work for me. Better than killing a lot of little brown monks already dressed in red."

Dio threw a burning stick at some monkeys hovering outside the firelight. They raced up into the trees, chattering as they went.

"Good eating," Dio said in a withering whisper, perhaps so only Poet could hear.

Their talk of slaughter, deicide, and burning and eating monkeys disgusted Poet—Saltaurius and his imp had cast off all semblance of civility, but he and Boy would have to restrain themselves to avoid a losing confrontation. Boy was a good soldier and knew Poet was in charge when Marcus was away. Poet also knew Boy was probably even more offended, having never met barbarians before.

They settled in for an uneasy peace around the campfire that Boy had stoked back up into a blaze. Dio rose and left to ramble around the temple, likely looking for monkeys to torment or other ways to enter, or escape, the temple along the pyramid's base. The beast's rumbling stomach was almost as loud and noxious as his words as he gnawed the rancid-looking lamb leg down to the bone. When the flesh and fat were all gone, the giant began sucking every inch of the marrow. He belched between bites and sucks.

To top it all off, as he tossed the remnants of the bone into the fire, he let loose a horn-like eruption from his backside. The trumpet's roaring stench assaulted the senses. Poet couldn't hold his breath long enough. Through his rudeness, Saltaurius was making it clear that he was not impressed with his lowly company that posed no threat to him.

After displaying the full range of his lack of manners, the giant passed the time by telling them of his and Dio's adventures along the Silk Road, which included killing the Issa imposter in Rhagae, humiliating Swami Bhakti, and escaping from the sultan's hall. He then amused himself with a story of how he and Dio watched from afar the ridiculous scene of Roman soldiers bathing with a slave outside Jammu. "Like slaves in your loincloths, playing splishy-splashy with a sexy Indian girly, and then taking a nap on a rock."

Poet was glad when he finished mocking them about how easy they were to follow.

"Poet, a song!" Saltaurius demanded. "To pass the time. Or should I go knocking at the temple door?"

"I am not your minstrel," Poet said, and immediately wanted to backtrack, thinking it might keep him from talking about matters of mayhem, slaughter, and sexy Indian girls. "But how about a story?" He hoped that one of Ma's stories would put the beast to sleep.

"A story will do. And here comes Dio, back to camp. I hope you didn't impregnate a chimp," he said with a gruff laugh. Poet had a passing thought that it could be true. Dio's red tunic was covered with leaves, perhaps from scrambling through thickets, looking for a hidden door into the temple.

"Boy, get some rest," Poet said. "You've heard this story from Ma before. Only one man is needed to keep watch." Boy lay back down on his bedding, though Poet knew he only pretended to sleep—or more likely, he was meditating. Either way, Poet knew he too was on high alert and always at the ready.

Saltaurius stretched out on his mat as well. "Dio can keep watch for me. Any monkey who attempts to steal our food will become a meal for him. He can throw his knife with artistry and precision," he said, and then motioned with his hand for Poet to begin the story.

"Our hero is a warrior prince—"

"I like it already," Saltaurius said.

"A great battle is about to ensue—envision the battles of Caesar and Pompey of our regrettable civil war."

"Better and better," interjected the giant. He might not fall asleep, thought Poet, but he also wouldn't be leaving his matting to storm the temple.

"Two great armies are assembled for battle. Brother facing brother."

Saltaurius raised his colossal head to see if Poet was mocking him, but Poet pretended he didn't see the threatening face of the bull. "The prince and his charioteer, a god, engage in a beautiful dialogue at the precipice of war."

"Less talk and more battle," the giant bellowed.

"Families and friends face family and friends. Both sides are on the verge of dying or killing loved ones. The prince, upon seeing his old comrades across the field, refuses to fight, like Achilles did at Troy."

"A coward with a cowardly god?"

"The god Krishna counseled him to do his duty and fight," Poet answered.

"That's a true god. He doesn't run from a fight but serves as charioteer and rides into battle! What's his name again?"

Under the current circumstances, Poet was regretting his story's plot and was failing to impart its spiritual essence. "Krishna," he said flatly.

"Sounds foreign. Still, he has Roman virtue. Get to the good part. Who lives, who dies, and how well did they die?"

Circumstances aside, or perhaps because of the circumstances, Poet was still struggling to convey the beauty and spiritual essence of Ma's story. "Yes, there is his duty, life and death, but there is also divine love. Boy . . ."

Poet stopped, spying a candle in a swinging lantern as someone descended the stone stairs above. They all rose to greet the light. Boy was ready with Marcus's sword.

CHAPTER 45
Marcus Negotiates with Saltaurius

BOY RACED UP the last few stairs to hand Marcus his sword. Seeing the uninvited guests, Marcus felt his bliss draining from his veins. He had to assume command of the situation.

"Thank you," Marcus said to Boy as he stepped into camp, turning his attention to the colossal figure that blocked the firelight. He felt like Janus, the two-headed god, with one face reflecting the vulgar man in front of him and one still radiant from the holiness he had encountered in the temple above.

His dark face seemed to speak automatically as it said, "Saltaurius, I see you're not so stupid. Appearances can deceive. Or was it your ghoul here that saw through our ruse and enabled you to follow us?" Dio was lurking at the edge of the firelight.

Saltaurius shook his bulbous head and orange locks. "Marcus, my friend," he said, "what a rude greeting."

"Rude? It is you who have followed me when I told you I wanted nothing to do with you." Marcus felt like he was suffering from whiplash, going from perfect, joyful love with Issa and Ma—descending one hundred and eight steps—straight into the eve of war with Saltaurius and Dio.

"Who deceived who?" Saltaurius asked. "You'd have me traversing rivers in Ladakh and mountains in Tibet. I knew the great Tribune Marcus from the disgraced House of Decia would not so easily give up his mission. Your only path to redemption was to bring back the man in the tower's head. You didn't want to share the glory with me? Is it done? Have you killed him? Where's his head?"

"Don't you even care to know if he was the son of God, the Jesus of Nazareth? And don't speak ill of my family in my camp or you'll be asked to leave." *Asked?* The softness of his words to the brute, half crazed by the two faces of his present state of mind, bewildered Marcus.

Poet handed Marcus a cup of water to drink, giving him a wary look that told him to be on his guard. Despite the gravity of their situation, Marcus couldn't help beaming at Poet. He was eager to tell his men of his temple meeting. "Let us all sit and I will reveal all. Boy, get that fire stoked. It's still an hour before dawn. And Boy, don't worry, Ma will stay a while longer with her friend and then return with you to the Pali and Aja."

"Your Ma is here? The Indian goddess you travel with?" the giant asked, now pacing in long steps to the stone steps and back.

Marcus didn't like Ma's name coming from Saltaurius's ruddy and greasy lips. "A holy woman, yes," he said. He then turned to Poet and said, "Wait until you hear! You won't want to miss a word." Marcus could only hope his story and enthusiasm would sway the giant from his hostile predisposition and impatience. "Luckily, you remember everything anyone says and can repeat it word for word. Saltaurius, look sharp. This man can make us immortal. He is no ordinary man. We have all succeeded. The man in the tower is Issa, and maybe Jesus, but it does not matter. His eyes . . . the light. At first I was afraid, but then came the peace and joy of his presence. If it is, or isn't, Jesus, he's more than a dead man come back to life." Marcus saw the joy on the faces of Poet and Boy, but Saltaurius looked disturbed and turned toward Dio for guidance. Dio, loyal pet that he was, came over to whisper in his master's ear.

"There'll be no secrets in my camp," Marcus commanded. "Jesus, I mean Issa, is such a man to see, with no anger toward or fear of me, a Roman tribune sent to bring him back after we crucified him. And he *was* crucified, of that I'm sure. He bears the marks of the cross." Marcus looked up the steps, trying to recall what he'd seen and experienced there, and he became uncertain. The marks he thought he saw on Issa's hands were faint and all but healed. *Could it have been just wishful thinking?* He wondered. It was possible he had imagined them. One thing was certain: he wished he could return to the peace in the temple. "Stillness and silence, and peace and love surround the holy man. And Ma adds her exuberant bliss! A palpable presence of . . . just love."

Marcus was speaking to Poet and Boy, who after their long, hard journey with him deserved this moment, compelling him to share the ecstatic experience he had in the temple with them. "He and Ma together make a remarkable sight. The joy still vibrates through me. The pyramid temple is a vortex of their loving energy." A transformed Marcus was unwilling to transition fully into the dire and deadly situation that surrounded him.

"Like Shiva and Shakti," Poet mused.

"Yes, such a sight—worth a lifetime to see. Two good and awakened beings. And then to come here and see you all with swords half drawn. And this one whispering his conspiracies," he said, motioning to Dio, who had returned to the periphery of the camp.

Saltaurius stood and adjusted his coin belt around his waist under his Arab robes. He twisted his torso like he was shaking off a spell cast by Marcus's high intensity. Marcus wondered if the giant's money belt might protect him from any sword to his midsection. He took note and decided if it came to a fight, he'd go for the arms, to prune the tree before cutting it down.

"Marcus, have you gone native and fallen in love with this Hindi woman and the imposter, who cannot be him . . . the man . . ." Being tongue-tied made the beast angry. "The Jesus, the Christ, the Issa, the Yuz Asaf—whatever name you give him. We may never know, but if he dies here, at my hand, he is just a man."

"A godly man," Marcus corrected. "And he fits the picture's depiction, which is etched upon my mind. Though no proof is necessary beyond his eyes. On his hands—"

"Enough of this! You said it only *may* be him. He is another imposter! Of course, an imposter would bear signs of the cross. A real god would heal his own wounds, the same way he came back to life. There is no wound greater than death!" Saltaurius huffed and kicked a smoldering log back into the fire.

"Saltaurius, calm yourself. And we both may fulfill our mission. He says he will return with me to Rome, 'in the fullness of time.' That was what he said. I'm hoping it's sooner than later, but we will wait. Rome may judge if he is Jesus."

"I must see him sooner rather than later," Saltaurius said, with clenched hands and jutted jaw. "And what did he say? Didn't you bother to ask him, 'Are you Jesus of Nazareth?'"

"I asked, but his answer will not satisfy you." Marcus struggled to recall the exact words as they were cryptic, but they had been clear as glass in Issa's glorified presence. "He said something like, 'I am a son of God. We are all the Christ once we find and follow him. The Holy Spirit guided you here.' He looked into my heart and said, 'You have found me—have you not?' It wasn't his words so much as his presence, his love and peace. I can't express it—"

"Really?" Saltaurius snorted, "And that satisfied you as an answer? Are you a slave to accept such an answer? The man spoke in parables and paradoxes. Let him speak clearly and say, 'I am Jesus, the one and only son of God!' If not, I will kill him."

"I am still tribune here. You are a mercenary and citizen of Rome. If you swear fidelity, I will let you join our march to Rome and see you're paid. I am not fit to judge him, but I can see he is holy," Marcus said, still hoping he could negotiate a peace.

"This imposter must die," Saltaurius said, grabbing the hilt of his sword. "If you will not do your duty, I will. Treason runs in your family. Of course, you would love a rebel, real or not." He moved toward Marcus and said, "And if you try to stop me, I'll take your head too. Since you are alive here, I imagine there is a dead imperial guard in Al Kut. The emperor will be glad you are dead. When I return, Pilate won't inspect your head for freshness. It will be in a box beside the head of that man in the temple with matching death masks."

"Don't lose your head, Saltaurius," Marcus said, not really believing humor would divert the volatile Saltaurius from his desire to kill. "You're in no position to make threats."

"Why? Because of them," he said, pointing to Poet and Boy who had slowly surrounded Saltaurius, awaiting Marcus's orders. He had trained them well.

Saltaurius surveyed the battlefield and said, "Might give you a fighting chance. My father trained me like a gladiator to beat the odds. And I've heard it said, *no foe can defeat me.*" He looked about the camp, but Dio had moved out of the light. "Dio is no threat. He scampers away when danger draws near. Still, he may get one of you with his dagger point. Ah, but here he comes again."

Dio was rummaging in the tree line near the campfire's edge.

"I won't need any sword but my own," Marcus said. "But let us cool our heads. Boy, pour us some wine, so we may talk like civilized Romans."

Boy poured the cups and Marcus sat to establish his command position over the scene.

Dio, like a phantom, emerged from the trees and briefly consulted with Saltaurius who then sat down too. Poet and Boy remained standing guard and watching the enigmatic Dio. The old goat, with his sinister sneer, was a treacherous advisor, but at least for the time being, he had counseled the bull to peace.

"Here's my most generous proposition," Marcus said. "We all march to Rome, and just before we enter her gates, I will surrender my sword to you. If the emperor wants my head for arriving after the festival of Ludi Victoriae Sullae, you may offer him two heads on the platter. Let Rome be our judge. Perhaps he will decide Issa is Jesus and declare him a god. You, yourself said he was a Roman worthy god. Then, you will be the god-bearer who brought him to Rome." Marcus paused to let the image ripen in Saltaurius's prideful imagination. "Either way, you'll collect your reward."

Saltaurius didn't jump at the offer but sat back and studied the fire while considering his options. He looked at Dio, who gave a noncommittal shrug.

"That's an interesting proposition," Saltaurius finally said. "As an honorable man, you will pledge this and let Poet record it prior to our departure. I still want to confirm that we will present a viable imposter."

"How can you be so certain it is not him?" Marcus asked. "I told you; he bears the wounds and the likeness."

"You must be drunk on ambrosia. He is an imposter. Maybe he mutilated himself or hung on some cross. We Romans use so many crosses. In Jerusalem, a woman suffered similar wounds and called it a stigmata. I saw the wounds bleeding on the palms of this true believer. She never hung on a cross but still bore the marks. Wounds or not, he is still an imposter. Jesus is in heaven with my brother never to be seen on Earth again. The man who died for my sins would not abandon his followers to suffer. If he did, he was an imposter the whole time. No son of God runs and hides. Either way, he must receive Roman justice. I do fancy the idea of riding into Rome to deliver a rebel and a traitor to the emperor. Eh, Dio?"

Saltaurius stood to look about the camp for Dio, who again had disappeared into the trees. "Damn man can't sit still. Before our deal is done, I must see the man in the temple and have it in writing."

"Poet will memorialize it, and I will sign it with my seal. But you'll need an invitation to enter the temple," Marcus said. He looked at Poet, and even though he was not grumbling, Marcus knew he dreaded traveling to Rome with the bull and Dio. Poet looked nauseous. After their journey with Ma, what starkly different travel companions they would make.

"This is all the invitation I need," Saltaurius declared while rattling his sword by his side. "The Hindi goddess can invite me in the morning. Can't wait to meet her. I came a long way, hearing of her saintly beauty by everyone who saw her traveling with you as you led us on our journey here."

"Why? She is nothing to you. Unless you want to learn to sit quietly for hours, or dance and sing. And you have my word, and my sword when we reach Rome, and no trouble from my men," Marcus said fearing his two faces would meet in the middle, and he would lose both his warrior edge and spiritual ecstasy. He slapped his own cheek like a bug was on it.

"Maybe you can sweeten the deal by giving the Indian goddess to me as my slave?"

"She is no one's slave and no part of this bargain. She will return south with Boy." Marcus was disturbed to think of his two worlds clashing. Roman brute force and transcendent spirit were about to meet, and he was powerless to prevent it.

"Such a tenderness in you," Saltaurius said, seemingly pleased to discover this weakness in Marcus. "I hope she can tell us more about this 'fullness of time' Issa mentioned. I'd like to rest my horses and be off on our long journey. The sooner we leave, the sooner I can be garlanded with glory and riches back in Roman civilization. Dio and I grow increasingly . . ." he paused while searching for the word, "uncivilized."

Marcus was concerned that Saltaurius hadn't sought assurances about the amount of his reward money and who would pay it. Was he serious about accepting the deal? He seemed to be playing the part of relishing returning to Rome as the conquering hero. Maybe he didn't realize that as a man of humble birth, without a title, he'd get nowhere near the emperor. By the time the emperor decided what to do with Tribune Marcus Decia and the god or rebel Jesus, the giant bounty hunter would already be relegated to obscurity with a fat purse.

"And I still need to see the man before our deal is done," the giant repeated, again scanning the camp for the missing Dio.

Marcus studied the big bounty hunter. He realized the man they had sought meant more than duty and money to both of them—after meeting this Issa in the temple, he understood that. If there were no risk, Saltaurius would leave the next day with two heads in a box. Marcus's offer provided him with most of what he sought, including men to safeguard his bounty during the long journey back to Rome. But in the end Saltaurius wanted Issa dead not alive.

"I will ask Ma if we can arrange for you to see him and press her on when he might leave with us—without being bound and dragged from the temple." The prospect of forcing Issa from the temple was no longer an option for Marcus. "Saltaurius, just imagine you leading the rebel Jesus and exiled Marcus Decia into Rome, like Alexander the Great returning from the East with unimaginable treasures. They will write songs in your honor. For now, patience. Let's sit in peace. Boy, meditate. Poet, speak—you have never been dumb for so long."

"Saltaurius, something I do not understand," Poet said, after a quiet moment. "If the man in the temple survived the crucifixion, did the miracles you saw with your own eyes, and may be the son of God, how is it you seem so eager to see him dead? Even with all that, would you still turn thumbs down and condemn him to death?"

"You are blind to my vision. If he didn't die on the cross, he didn't die for my sins, and therefore I am not forgiven for killing my brother, as promised me in my vision. All our gods ascend or stand and fight. It is as Roman as Jupiter and Mars. He is nothing to me if he betrays that vision."

This is why men should not be trusted to create their own religions, Marcus thought.

"So you play Pluto, bound by the story and a dream you had to murder the son of God?" Marcus shot Poet a look, fearing he was becoming too aggressive with his questions.

Deicide is only rare because homicidal, fratricidal men rarely get to meet a god, Marcus thought.

"Poet, you tempt the fates to mention the name of the god of death and Hades," Saltaurius said. Superstitious Romans believed if one mentioned Pluto, death would soon follow. "But you have a lawyer's logic and tongue.

When I see the man, he can explain his desertion and deception to me. Perhaps you can be there to defend him."

Poet bowed to conclude his questioning and then sat next to Boy.

"After he returns to the living," Marcus said, "he either stays in Judaea to be crucified again or he saves his own life, along with his mother, to continue teaching his message of love here in the East. I find it hard to find fault with that—a son that sacrifices for his mother and perhaps left the empire to save his followers from being slaughtered." Marcus thought that saving his mother from Roman persecution in Judaea was a sufficiently noble reason to make their escape, but he also recalled something Ma had said about his absence, giving his message time to flourish.

"The son of God should have the power to prevent all that. He has ascended and that is that," Saltaurius said. He yawned to show he was done with the discussion.

"A *son* of God is not all powerful. And perhaps he ascended and came back? That would allow for your vision," Marcus offered. "What do we know about the gods and their powers? Each one has unique strengths. Only one god can be all powerful. Jesus was born of human flesh. And now I believe, despite my stoic logic, that his reanimated body is transfigured—full of light." Marcus fought back tears and went to look into the smoke of the fire to create his excuse. He rubbed his eyes, but it was his heart that cried out for all that was holy and that he just witnessed in the tower above.

Saltaurius scoffed, "Marcus, you confound yourself, justifying your dereliction of duty. Pilate said to find him dead or alive. He didn't mean to bring him back alive. You can't possibly believe that. Let's sit quiet now with our thoughts like Boy over there."

Boy appeared to be sitting in meditation, but Marcus knew he was listening to every word and ready to draw his sword.

It didn't matter if the man in the temple was Jesus, even though Marcus believed he was. He looked just like Jesus and that was enough for the mission. And he had met Ma and Issa, a holy woman and holy man, and no longer had any doubt about God or fear of death. He did fear Saltaurius, however. He was responsible for protecting his men, Ma, and Issa from the homicidal giant and his demonic advisor.

CHAPTER 46
Two Worlds Collide

NO ONE SLEPT—EXCEPT maybe Dio, in a tree with his monkeys. At first light, Ma descended the tower steps. Light silhouetted her as she floated down the steps, her bare feet barely touching stone. Saltaurius's presence in camp did not offend or surprise her. Ma expected the scene she was about to enter. She was exalted from her time with her "father" Issa after so many years apart. Her spirit and spiritual powers elevated from the reunion.

Her powers of precognition and perception allowed her to see from all perspectives—the ignorant and fearful points of views as well as the loving and wise. She had seen this stage before, like a familiar Greek tragedy, though she could not foresee the ending. Here there were too many strong currents of history, karma, destiny, and free will colliding for her to see clearly what was about to unfold.

"What an angel in white," Saltaurius said with a slight bow. "You are more beautiful than I've been told. I've seen you once before, but from some distance. Stay away from the ladies in Rome. They'll rip your amber eyes out for their beauty."

Ma noted his brutish attempt at chivalry as he avoided looking into her eyes and got their color wrong. She had heard the men speak of this giant who sought Jesus, or any facsimile, for his head.

"You make the Roman women sound like tigers. Tigers are beautiful too. True beauty is the divine nature we all share," Ma responded in her usual playful and level tone.

"Does this divinity even lurk in me? Within this tall, broad frame?" Saltaurius said gracefully spinning around.

Marcus held up his hand as Ma said, "Yes . . ."

"Ah, but you're yet to meet my man, Dio. That man has no soul. Where has he gone?" The little man Ma had also heard so much about was missing from the camp.

Marcus spoke sternly to Saltaurius, "We have stated our business terms. Go explore the gardens and search the trees for your man, so I can talk to Ma and my men in private."

"Oh, but we haven't discussed the most important part, my bounty," Saltaurius said.

"Whatever the Pharisees promised you. Double that," Marcus said. "Now leave us in peace for a while."

"Seems a small price for producing a god. Besides the lady and I just met. I will not argue in front of her. I'll be back soon, so we can get better acquainted." He made a shallow but courtly bow as he backed away.

"Take him with you," Marcus said pointing to a squatting Dio, who had slipped back into camp and was so quiet that he might easily be forgotten.

After they left camp, Marcus spoke to Ma. "It may be hard for you to fathom a man like him," he said. "But believe nothing he says. If we cannot convince Issa to come with us to Rome soon, we need to buy time to protect him from this man. You should get back into the temple as soon as you can to warn him and alert the monks to be on guard."

Ma said, "They don't have any weapons."

"I'd hoped they had their swords stored somewhere. I saw four monks. Are there more? Will they fight?" Marcus asked. He was preparing for war, and Ma was still praying for peace.

"Swords are forbidden in the temple, Marcus," Ma said. "Two old priests and two young monks accompany Issa, and the two monk guards you have seen at the door. Issa's mother is being tended to in the town, following their long journey. Issa will tell them not to put up a fight. And he may choose to go unseen by those not ready to see his light."

She turned to address Poet and Boy. "Issa joyfully anticipates meeting the two of you," she said. "I will stay here a week with him and then return with you, Boy, to Aja and the Abode of Bhagavan."

"I am grateful," Boy said. "But with Saltaurius and the little one with him, I fear for Marcus and Poet when I leave."

"Don't worry, Boy. If Saltaurius waits a week, that will be a miracle," Marcus said. "We will miss you. But you must go. My heart sings, imagining how happy you will be there."

Poet said, "I am thrilled to meet Issa but not looking forward to traveling with those two wretches all the way to Rome. I can't imagine Issa will enjoy their company, either."

Marcus sighed and said, "Even their darkness cannot snuff out his light, but the contrast will make for an interesting journey. Look how well Ma has transformed us," he said, and Poet laughed. Marcus turned to Boy and said, "We've all shared the long journey. And we couldn't leave without you seeing that familiar face of Jesus."

"With Ma, they seemed like quick jaunts around a ring. And I believe it is him without even having laid eyes upon him," Boy said.

Ma smiled and said, "Blessed are those that believe without seeing. 'Not that which the eye can see, but that whereby the eye can see: know that to be Brahman the eternal. And not what people here adore.'"

"The Upanishads," Poet said. Ma loved that he recognized the verse. "Marcus, if it comes to it with Saltaurius, give the new signal and we'll be ready."

"And what signal is that, Poet?" Marcus asked.

"Jaya Bhagavan! Of course." They all laughed nervously.

The giant flippantly sang a randy soldier's song as he reentered the camp with Dio. "The buxom angels could not resist," he crooned, "the long shaft of Pegasus."

Ma knew she was to be tested. "I will return to the temple and will send for Poet and Boy, one at a time," Ma said, walking off toward the steps.

"Wait, what about me? Am I not invited? I must see this miracle man," the giant said, stretching his arms wider than the oak oars of a ship of war.

"I will ask. But no swords allowed in the temple," Ma responded.

"And if he declines? I will have to wait till he comes out."

"Yes," Ma said.

"In the fullness of time?" he laughed. "And what in Hades does he mean by that? We wait upon his whim. Is he Caesar here?"

"He is no emperor. Just a divine being following God's will." Ma omitted to mention that Issa had arrived in Srinagar with his aging mother and that it might not be God's will that he make such a trip while she still lived. The arduous trip east had sapped his mother of her saintly strength. The irony was palpable. Issa had brought his mother to the safety of his sangha in remote Kashmir, only to be discovered by opposing camps of Romans bargaining for his life—or his head.

"Saltaurius, address your questions to me. She must be going," Marcus commanded.

"In a minute. Just one more question for the lovely lady. I'm not waiting forever, and the longer we talk, the longer I wait and there will be no shedding of blood. That should please you, no?"

Both men looked ready to draw their swords in response to Saltaurius's fighting words. "And she is all that stands between you and your head in a box," Saltaurius said to Marcus, before turning to flash a broad grin at Ma.

"Marcus, thank you. But I will answer his question and go," Ma said.

"Now that's much more hospitable. Thank you, divine lady. Poet was telling me an Eastern story about a warrior prince with a god as a charioteer going into war. The brave god was telling the warrior he must do his duty and fight."

"Ah, I know the story well. The Song of the Lord! Jaya Bhagavan!" She looked at her friends to make sure they didn't think she was giving the signal to start a fight. "Let me tell you more."

"I've been hunting the man up in the high temple for over four months. Take your time, but skip to the battle and its ending. Who lives? Who dies? And did they die well? Poet never answered that." Saltaurius offered Ma his seat by the fire, and she complied with her back to his oversized saddle. He sat closely by her side, still avoiding her eyes.

Ma could almost smell the man's lust for blood. Her precognition did not show her who would live and who would die. She could not alter free will but hoped she might show the homicidal man a way to peace through the Bhagavad Gita. It was worth taking a chance.

"Ah, the battle is within men. A battlefield between good and evil. And it never ends, even in death when we transcend our physical forms. And then begins another story," Ma said in a lyrical voice.

"You are speaking in riddles," Saltaurius brooded. "Are you referring to the man we've been searching for who is now hiding nearby? He who died and supposedly came back only to run away—if it be him—cowering in the tower?"

"I'm talking about all humans. But in the Vedic holy book, the story you were being told—"

"Yes, tell the ending of the story!"

"The entire song teaches Krishna's message—"

"What message is more important than one must do his duty?" Saltaurius cut in. "The warrior prince is told to fight by a god! That is all there is in life, duty and death. Isn't that right, Dio? Where did he go?" Dio was back in the trees. "Anyway, this is all the fantasy of the childlike Eastern mind."

"It is a historical account of a battle and dialogue between Krishna and his student, Prince Arjuna. Krishna is as real as that fire, but he is both immanent and transcendent."

"Cease with the philosophy. Dio is not here to debate you. On with the story." Saltaurius dipped his colossal head and huffed like a bull preparing to charge.

"The prince is told he should not refuse to fight out of fear of killing his kinsmen," Ma continued. "Any more than he should fight out of a desire for riches and glory. There were two banners represented there: one good and one evil. The prince's army represented the righteous and if he chose not to fight, he was in effect choosing evil. Whether he fought or not, there was going to be a battle. The victor and a loser was for God to decide. He is a warrior, and it is his dharma to fight. The prince's bow, which he picks up to perform his dharma, or sacred duty, represents his free will. Krishna shows him the nature of ever-present divine love and the atman, our true self, within. The prince aligns his will and love with God's will, and his foes become his allies, allowing him to perform his duty in the preordained battle. We are all called to that alignment, and to remain unattached to the outcome of our actions as we follow God's will."

"Well, this is my bow," Saltaurius said, rattling his sword.

"But which side do you choose, the devil or the Lord? You will know by whether you feel love and non-attachment. Otherwise, our actions fall short of God's will. You mistake the story for the message. The story of the man you seek may be beautiful and poetic, but it is his divine love and presence in our lives that matter." Ma's eyes opened wide, offering the cruel man her saintly love, but he refused to look.

"Now, you speak of Jesus?" Saltaurius asked. Ma's calm tone and words did not pacify him. "How can he have died for my sins if he still lives and didn't stay to lead and fight for his followers? Dio!" He cried out for his man. His face was becoming red with rage and confusion.

"Jesus is not a warrior like the prince in the story but a son of God, and you are not Krishna to tell him his duty. He knows well his duty and that was not to fight. Even God cannot remove your sin, which is ignorance. Free will prevents that. Our choice is one of love or fear." She pressed her palms together and bowed.

Saltaurius bellowed a bitter, hollow laugh and looked in all directions like a man lost in a labyrinth. His Dio still had yet to reemerge from the trees, but could be heard conducting his choir of monkeys.

"Hindu temptress," Saltaurius said with a red face and nostrils flaring. "You think you can bewitch me with those eyes and sweet voice? Like you did the great sultan? He still dreams about you." Saltaurius jumped up like Ma was a snake about to bite him. Ma stood too, holding up her hand to beseech Marcus not to come to her defense.

Saltaurius continued, "Yes. Marcus, hold back a while. A fight may be coming but not as long as she and I speak." Poet and Boy stood ready to protect Ma too. "We met your monk friend on the road. He lied to me, so we disrobed him. No longer a monk. My Dio wears his robe to bed and makes self-pleasing noises in it. Your friend was afraid and is likely dead by now. Would you like the robe back as a reminder of him?"

"No, thank you. He learned a lesson and is thriving now," Ma said.

"How can you know that? And what was the lesson? Was it his duty to eat dirt and drink his own piss? Where is Dio? He would find all of this quite funny." His eyes darted about, looking around the tree line.

"No, not that." Ma would not react to his increasing vulgarity. She knew he was testing her. "He learned it is humility and faith, and not a robe and a donkey, that makes one a monk and a swami."

Saltaurius looked rattled. "How could you know we took his donkey? You should fear me," he said to Ma and again spread his arms wide, as if she might have missed his enormous size. "How long must I wait?" he demanded to know. Ma peered into the hard muscle of his heart and was beckoning it to soften. "Stop looking at me, witch!" She realized her words of peace and compassionate innocence had only delayed the giant's eruption. He moved forward to confront her, still avoiding her eyes like they were the sun itself. "You should fear me, bitch!"

He grabbed Ma by the wrist, pressing the gems sewn into his wristband into the palm of her hand. At last, his homicidal eyes locked with her eyes. Ma knew what he was concealing, and that he knew she knew. And she knew he now intended to kill her.

Marcus bolted forward. "Saltaurius, back away from her. We will wait a week—"

"Too long!" Saltaurius cut Marcus off, and in one smooth motion he put his sword to Ma's virgin neck. Marcus didn't get there in time. He held up his hands in a gesture of surrender, hoping to pacify the beast.

"No more talking. No more stories. Take me to him! You will be my invitation, and he will be my retribution."

Looking at the tip of the blade at her neck, Ma understood she was a quick strike away from being decapitated. Poor, brave Marcus didn't dare charge or threaten the beast as he said in a calming voice, "Your fight is with me, not her."

"You are three, and I am one. She is my shield and token into the temple to see the Christ imposter, deserter, fraud . . . coward. I'll have his head in the fullness of an hour."

Ma didn't believe she could change the path of the ignorant homicidal man that held the blade to her neck, but she wanted to make sure Marcus fully understood the situation. She said to Saltaurius, "If you even see him— if he lets you see him—you can't kill him in his resurrected body."

"Then he can keep his body, and I'll take just the head. One thing is sure: you will die here, witch."

Ma turned to Marcus. "Marcus, I am not afraid to die. Though I may bleed, there is no death, not really."

"Fight only me. My men will not intervene," Marcus said, still looking at Ma, firmly and lovingly reasserting his command. She smiled to reassure him that he was on the righteous path. She had agreed that he would be the one to lead them into battle. He had on his warrior face, and this was the time for that.

"And if I win, I claim your head and then enter the temple for another, and then leave with a full bounty, without having to fight and kill the two of them?" Saltaurius asked. "Swear it. I don't kill without reason and don't want to press my luck. Dio, time to show yourself!" he shouted into the forest. "I could use a little help from your sharp knife."

Still, Dio remained unseen.

"We . . ." Poet spoke and then stop, deferring to his master while the sword was so near to taking Ma's life.

"My men will not interfere. Poet and Boy—Boy—you hear my command? I have given my word," Marcus said in a voice of a tribune issuing orders.

Ma's heart bled for Boy. She knew the story of how he had lost his father and mother and saw the blood rushing through his veins as old scars opened. She could tell that Marcus saw it too—his man ready for battle—and reissued his order. "Boy, I will not restrain you. You are a man now. But if you don't listen to my command, you will dishonor us both."

"I will do as you command out of great love and allegiance. I could never dishonor you," Boy said and gave the Roman salute. He then shouted, "Jaya Bhagavan!" and bowed to Marcus. The men didn't attack as Marcus raised his arm, commanding they hold their places. Poet and Ma repeated Boy's words of praise. Poet also bowed, but Ma chose not to bow into the sharp sword held to her neck.

"Ma," Marcus called out. He met her eyes, letting her know he'd heard her lessons, and he was now the prince in Ma's "Song of the Lord." He was a warrior called to fight without desire or fear, allowing the great logos to move through him. His action aligned with God. Ma saw all this in his eyes, and that the two men he'd become, tribune and Ma's divine lover, were becoming one in that moment of darshan. "I am ready to die," he said, "if it is God's will. Elysium and my family wait for me there. If I die here for you and the Lord, let it be! But may the big one die first."

Ma risked her life by making prayer hands and bowing her head, pushing down on Saltaurius's sword with her forehead, as he stood by in disbelief at her audacity.

Though the prince in the story won his battle, Ma knew the virtuous were not always the victors here on Earth. For every slayed Goliath, the field was littered with dead Davids.

"Now we fight, and no more speeches," Saltaurius commanded.

"You must first swear no harm will come to her or my men. Swear to it," Marcus demanded.

"On my honor. In my dead brother's name, I swear. No harm will come to any of them from my hands. I swear it. Now the deal is done?"

"Yes," Marcus replied. "Now remove the sword from the little girl's neck and fight like a man."

"A match to the death!" Saltaurius roared.

"Ma, believe it or not," Marcus said, "he can be trusted to keep his oath. The warrior's code. In gladiator tradition the match ends only in death, and the promises made are never broken. The blood oath is stronger than hate and deception. And Saltaurius, here, in his way, is an honorable gladiator."

Marcus turned from Ma back to the giant. "To the death!" Marcus repeated, sealing the oath.

Ma brushed aside the giant's sword like it was a mere branch. "Marcus, I will not stand between you and your destiny. But know if you head to heaven, I love you. Issa loves you. God himself has always loved you. And know you have embraced his love and follow his will. May the ever-righteous Kali be with you. Jaya Bhagavan!"

Marcus bowed slightly at Ma, indicating he understood what she was saying. Ma knew Marcus would need divine help to slay the giant.

"Jaya Bhagavan!" all but Saltaurius shouted.

"Nice last words for a Roman tribune. Now to destroy the only son of the House of Decia. A name to be remembered only for its infamy." Saltaurius raised his sword with his strong right hand like an unholy redeemer. The tip of his sword hovered twelve feet high and was ready to come crashing down.

CHAPTER 47

A Good Death

SWORDS CLANGED ABOVE their heads and about their torsos. Each of the giant's mighty blows demanded a defensive retreat by Marcus. Marcus would wait for an opening and then go on the offensive. His heart banged within his chest double time to the ancient dance of death. The arena was set in front of the temple steps. Ma, Poet, and Boy watched the battle with their backs to the slow dying bonfire from the night before. Dio watched from the trees.

Though they both had donned their helmets and wore the light armor scales of an armadillo over the thin tunics covering their torsos, neither Marcus nor Saltaurius held a shield, and the scales would only protect one from a glancing blow.

Saltaurius suddenly paused his onslaught, stepped back, flashed a wicked grin, puffed his chest, and let out an ungodly howl—an eerie summons of some subterranean power. Then he surged forward, his sword raining down in a relentless cascade—from the left and the right—each stroke a brutal testament to his ambidextrous mastery.

Marcus skillfully blocked and parried, but the ferocity of Saltaurius's two-handed assault stunned him and left him reeling. Saltaurius was now twice as formidable. Marcus would not be able to prune the arms that wielded the giant's sword. His only chance was that the big man would tire, but Saltaurius showed no sign of slowing down and only became more ferocious with each left, right, left, right blow.

Then, gripping his sword with both hands, Saltaurius unleashed a succession of overpowering overhead blows. Marcus staggered back to the stone steps leading up to the temple, cutting off his retreat.

Marcus attempted to hold his ground but was being beaten down. He knew the end was drawing near. The gladiator's next blow glanced down off of his sword, leaving a gash on his forearm. First blood flowed onto the ground. The giant had a manic look as he craved more blood. In a rush of adrenalin Marcus leaped up two steps, giving him a height advantage. Saltaurius lunged like a bull with wings into Marcus's waist, impaling him with his helmet. They fell back on the steps and then rolled down in a mass of clanging flesh, steel, and stone. Marcus's sword broke free from his hand as he pounded down on the last step. The beast hit his head on the rock landing, giving Marcus a moment to free himself from the dazed bull's clutches and retrieve his sword, but only to find the giant's swords being thrust deep into his solar plexus as he turned back around. Marcus knew instantly it was a deadly gouging.

Time stood still. What remained of his life trickled away—it would be seconds, minutes at best. His moment of truth was near. He tried to focus on the world that spun around him. He held up his blood-soaked hand to be sure his men and Ma did not come to his aid. Ma bowed her tearful face with hands to her heart, whispering a prayer. Poet bore witness like a pillar of stone. Boy started to charge but restrained himself, releasing a howl of agony at losing another father. The Roman code of conduct was clear: no interference until one man was dead. They made way for Marcus as he stumbled back toward the still burning fire and fell to his knees and then onto his back to die, clinging to his wound with one hand and to his sword with the other. For a Roman tribune, dying with his sword in hand is a noble way to die.

Marcus raised his head to look at Ma. He knew he must be dying soon, as she was blue with many arms, holding bloody instruments and a severed head. Her Kali! And he understood.

Saltaurius walked slowly toward his prey, whistling a Roman tune played for the dead. He was enjoying his triumph, coming in for the kill. As he stood over the fallen tribune, ready to remove his head with one clean blow, Marcus heard Kali or Ma whispering in his ear, telling him what to do. He mumbled something through the pain, words no one could understand—his last confession or curse. The victor needed to hear a dying man's last words to preserve the story. The giant ceremoniously removed his helmet before bending down to hear Marcus's dying declaration.

There would be no death, not really. Marcus long ago had accepted death but now could see beyond it. He had only to heed one last call of duty. As the large bull's head lowered down to Marcus's stammering lips, it rolled off and into the fire. Marcus's aim and sword were true.

The flames consumed the giant's head—bulbous cheeks, ruby hair and shocked eye bulbs. His body, a stump of flesh, fell over like a tall tree trunk with a thud that scattered the birds in the trees and made the monkeys chatter. The giant was dead. In the end, it was he, who lost his head.

Ma, Poet, and Boy all rushed to Marcus.

CHAPTER 48
Suffering and Death

BOY PRESSED HIS hands on the wound just above the Marcus's stomach to stop the bleeding, but he could only slow the flow. Ma sat beside Marcus, putting his head on her lap. Poet stood above Marcus, looking into his hero's dying eyes, seeking some fitting benediction, which would come but not in time.

Marcus's soft stammering was a ruse. He could still speak for a while longer. Boy kept trying to stem the rush of blood from his wound. With just minutes to live every second counted. Though Poet knew a sword thrust to the midsection to be the most painful type of battlefield blow, Marcus looked elated from his ultimate victory. His stoic smile would not allow fear to cloud his face while passing into Elysium. Poet had imagined his own death and Marcus's death so many times before. He knew this day was destined to come.

Marcus looked into Ma's eyes. He smiled like a small boy with a splinter and gazed at her with perfect love. "It's all right, Ma," he murmured. "I'm only bleeding."

Like birds at dawn, the multitude of monkeys in the trees were chattering all at once, making for a somewhat exotic, joyful sounding cacophony. Or was it a warning?

They had all forgotten Dio, who suddenly surprised Poet from behind with a long sharp knife at his throat. Boy grabbed Marcus's sword and jumped to his feet. Poet hated to die at the hand of his cowardly rival, but his biggest regret was not being able to sing the praises of Marcus Decia and how bravely he fought to protect all that was good in life—and to not return to Rome with that song. He would soon be dead, and Boy would kill Dio. Ma's healing hands now covered Marcus's gaping wound, allowing him to live to see his best friend die a senseless death by imp. All Poet could think was how inglorious and embarrassing that would be.

"Boy! Wait! Hear me," Dio pleaded, as if misunderstood. "I know who knows where your mother is to be found. They've always known but were afraid you would run away to her. Marcus is a tribune of Rome with a powerful senator father. You don't think they could find a slave taken by Rome? They've known all along."

Boy looked to Marcus to answer, who said, "He lies. We could not find her. I can now truly say this is my biggest regret, now that I am so close to being reunited with my family."

"I lie?" Dio said. "Poet told me this, the night we met in Babylon for dinner." Dio pulled the knife blade against Poet's chin and neck, making it impossible for him to speak without being cut by the sharp blade. "See, he doesn't deny it. The songbird is at a loss for words."

Dio's breath on Poet's neck was fetid and rank. His slithering words entered intimately into Poet's ear so no one else could hear. "Around my master's waist is a belt with lots of silver and gold, and into his wristband I sewed gems, enough for many opulent lifetimes. We just need Boy's help. If you get him to drop his sword, I will let you live, and I'll leave with that belt and wristband." Now, with blood on the ground and death in the air, Dio found his voice and his whisper.

Dio turned his wily words onto Boy. "Boy, if you come with me, I will lead you to her. I have lots of money that will buy us the information. Records are kept. They would record the enslavement of a chieftain's wife. Let's make Poet speak and disclose her location to us. He won't stand up to a little torture. A mother and child reunion, can you imagine that? A reunion these two denied you."

Poet could see Boy's mind was racing to keep up. Marcus's life was slipping under heaven's gate, and his uncle's life was a rancid breath away from joining him there.

Dio waited for Boy's answer.

"Of course!" Boy yelped, distraught by the magnitude of the betrayal. "They must have known all along. Poet, tell me, and we will let you live. Dio, you agree to that?"

"Yes, of course. We will bind him and leave once he tells us where to find her. You can drop the sword. My knife holds his life a horsehair from death."

"Don't drop the sword. His words can't be trusted," Poet pleaded, gasping against the blade.

Boy slowly approached Poet and Dio. He looked hard at Poet and said, "Tell me where I will find her and you will live. You have my word."

"For her beautiful nobility, she became the property of a senator in Rome," Poet confessed.

Dio must have been shocked by Poet's confession—to discover his lie was true.

"His name?" Boy demanded. "I'll bind you with your rope and we will leave."

"Senator Janus Aurelius," Poet said. "Forgive us, Boy. We feared you'd try to free her and meet a certain death, if you even made it as far as Rome."

"Boy, now we have it. Disarm him and get the rope," Dio said.

Boy moved closer and removed Poet's sword and knife as directed.

"Now drop that sword and get the rope," Dio said, taking command.

"If I drop the sword, you'll slice his neck. And mine. Drop your knife and I'll bring the rope," Boy said, as he gathered the rope before tossing it to Dio.

"Wait! It can't be . . . but is it a game you two are playing?" Dio was stamping his feet with his blade flicking up and down Poet's neck. "A slave boy strumming me like a lyre. Speaking to me like I am his equal. Playing a part with his old uncle to outsmart me? Are you simple, Boy? I offer you liberty, riches, and help to find your mother. Your master is dying and yet you refuse me?"

Poet's and Boy's ruse had been unmasked, though it was well played. Poet was proud of Boy's bold gambit—one that had almost worked. It would be the last role they would play together before Poet's throat was slit by the sharp blade pressed against it.

Poet knew Boy wanted at all costs to save his life, even if it might mean never seeing Aja again. Boy drew his own knife and said, "A fair fight. Just you and me. Poet will let you go if you prevail. I hear you are good with a knife. You have my word. I'll toss the sword once you let him loose."

"Hmm, I have no experience in fighting boys or men who are awake and not afraid to die," Dio said. He had one final decision to make—whether to kill Poet or Boy. And how to make his escape from the other.

Poet looked to his master, whose head rested in Ma's lap. Poor Marcus was a helpless witness to the deadly duel unfolding as his life kept slipping away. More treachery he was too far gone to stop. Ma was using her sari shawl to wrap around his torso. The white garment was quickly stained red from the flow. The great tribune looked like a large infant being nurtured by his saintly mother.

Dio demanded of Marcus, "Leave his body undisturbed so I may return to bury my dead. You must promise no one will touch it."

"It'll have to be a big grave, and I am happy for you to dig it. We will leave him where he lies if you go," Marcus croaked through dry, cracked lips. Drawing a shallow breath, he added, "If you leave now, you have my word, the body won't be touched, and you can pick his bones of all his wealth."

Dio eased the pressure on Poet's neck as he whispered into his ear. "I slit three innocent throats thicker than yours outside Rhagae all because you and Marcus didn't do your duty and put the Jesus imposter to death. If I let you live today to collect my master's coins and gems, I'll be back for you someday. Lots of snakes slinking about, like that cobra outside Jammu."

"Of course it was you," Poet said. "Your devotion to suffering and death has not served you or your master well."

The ghoul whispered, "Your master is as good as his word. Now, I only have to decide between your death, Boy's death, and all my master's wealth. Hmm."

"Would you shut up? Take me, you imp," Poet said, determined to grasp the hand and knife as soon as Dio started to slice. If it didn't save his life, it would buy Boy time to wield his sword.

Dio moved the knife from Poet's neck to between his shoulder blades and said, "Boy's death will cause you the most pain." He thrust Poet violently into Boy, who almost impaled him on Marcus's sword. Dio threw his knife squarely into Boy's chest before darting off into the woods quicker than his monkeys.

Dio's knife's point hit Boy in the dead center of his chest, but it clanged and fell to the ground. Boy pulled out from his tunic the breastplate underneath. His mother's artistry was undamaged except for an indentation on the black cat's chest. Its emerald eyes still sparkled. Boy kissed each emerald eye. "My mother's mystical work of art," he said.

Marcus managed a smile. They all turned to Marcus, who asked Poet, "What'd he say, before scampering off?"

Poet, thinking quickly, told his dying master, "He said, 'Marcus Decia won the day, besting a beast no man could beat.' A fine tribute if you ask me. Tribune, the giant slayer." He bowed down to his fallen leader, knowing that Marcus knew he lied, and that it did not matter. "But how did you defeat a man no foe could kill?"

"Ma's words showed me the way," Marcus said. "I aligned with love and fought not a foe but an ally in our deadly battle that was preordained by the gods. He was my redeemer, bringing me to this good death."

As Poet attempted to parse Marcus's words, Boy offered his master his sword

"Keep it. It is yours now," Marcus said. "I no longer have need of it."

"Please get Issa," Boy pleaded with Ma. "He can heal him."

"He may be able. I will go ask, if . . . Marcus?" Ma said, looking down at Marcus.

"No, Ma, stay with me," he said. "Your touch and sari wrap are all that hold me to this life now. I don't *know* if he's Jesus. I do not need to know. My heart tells me he is God. And that you are God. And God is love. Thus, I am released from all fear of death."

"That is a divine realization," Ma said. "You saved my life and other lives here today."

"Then this will be the best of all deaths for me. How could I fear such a death? Jesus's disciples must feel this too, being ready to sacrifice their lives for his teachings. Promise I will have your blessed company for the rest of my life," Marcus said, managing to smile at Ma.

Ma smiled back. "I'm not going anywhere," she said.

Their eyes joined in mutual appreciation and holy union. And there truly was no time to get Issa. Poet watched as the curtain slowly descended on the great Tribune Marcus Decia's life. Marcus was determined to be stoic and pragmatic to the end, rising above the pain to meet the magnitude of his final, fleeting moments on Earth. Poet always knew that when death came for Marcus he would look right through it—into Elysium.

"Ma," Marcus said, "it is my surety that I have seen divinity through you. I am ready to join my family in heaven.

Ma said, "Yes, life is everlasting. Light and love are all that abides. Nothing real is lost. When the moment comes, let the light pass consciously, without fear, through the crown of your head."

"Yes, know no fear!" Marcus said, looking to his comrades, issuing his last command.

"Ma, hold me till the end and take my hand. You give me strength and slow the seeping of my vital force. That I may speak my last words to each of you and then pass . . . from this life. My love for you all will not die with this body." Turning to Poet Marcus said, "Poet, you first." Poet knelt in front of Marcus, whose head was still propped up on Ma's lap. "Take half the silver and gold for yourself. Give the rest to Ma and Boy."

"The creature whispered to me that wrapped around the giant's waist and wrist are a fortune in silver, gold, and gems," Poet said. "I won't need half to live out my days as a humble poet."

Marcus looked up to Ma. "I know, Ma, God provides for you, and I've seen this is true. But you can guide Boy and Aja to spend it wisely at the Abode of God in love and charity. On the children . . ."

"The children thank you. Each gold, coin will save an orphan's life, and each gem will save another hundred." Ma said and kissed him sweetly on the forehead.

"Dear friend." He returned to addressing Poet. "You've been the best, most loyal friend anyone could hope for. Rome is not my home. My home is with my family here with me now and the one above." Marcus looked at his comrades and then to the heavens. Marcus reached into his tunic and pulled out the letter with the emperor's broken seal to hand to Poet. "Post this letter to Senator Lucius Arruntus, smeared with my blood, a powerful man and dear friend to my father. It should redeem the House of Decia and prove the treachery of the emperor. The truth will be known." He handed the letter to Poet.

"I promise to have this letter posted and delivered, my loyal friend, and to tell the story of the hero that lies before me. A man who conquered evil, and defended innocence, to return home crowned in glory." Poet stood and bowed to his master. And then took Boy's place standing guard, unashamed of the tears that streaked his face.

"Boy, approach me, so I may gaze into your eyes once more. You now have my sword, but I pray you never have cause to use it. Keep it only as a memory of me. The man who slayed your father and then loved you as a father. Forgive me."

"Master, there is nothing to forgive, and I will keep the sword that slayed the giant and saved all our lives. My heart is full of love and gratitude for you and all that you have taught me, my spiritual father," Boy said with tears streaming down his cheeks.

"Now you have a spiritual mother." Marcus looked at Ma and then back to Boy. "You have served me well. I made a private oath to your father as he was ascending to Elysium to live a good life and die a good death that I might be worthy of his courageous death by my hand. I feel his approval to share that oath with you now." Poet was glad Marcus disclosed that long-standing secret to Boy. Marcus reached into his tunic pocket. "I've carried this proclamation of your freedom for years," he said. "Now, we only need Poet to fill in your given name. 'Boy' won't do. Do you remember it?"

Boy said, "They called me Ieyoub as a boy." Boy seemed proud to proclaim his real name after all these years.

"Ieyoub and Aja. I like the sound of that. Use that name when I am gone. And if you will, take mine as well—Ieyoub Decia." Marcus's voice trembled, and he handed Boy the official letter with his House of Decia seal. Poet will see it done. Now, when I am gone, they won't travel all the way to India to harm my Moroccan son."

"I will bear the noble name with honor," Boy said.

"Now, you are a free man. But I think you are learning with Ma an even more important liberty—of being at peace and aligned with God. Be faithful and giving and make Aja the most fortunate of women. She is a worthy mate for my boy. And—" Marcus raised his hand as if asking for a pause or Ma for more strength.

Ma looked to Poet with her eyes saying, *There's not much time.* She placed her healing hands upon Marcus's temples to dim the pain. Poet could almost feel her hands sending radiating warmth through Marcus's entire body to ease his suffering.

"I will," Boy said. "You will watch over me, and I could never dishonor you. I love you." Boy fumbled with his hands not sure whether to give the

Roman salute or a namaste bow. Marcus chose for him, tipping his head down to him. With their foreheads touching Marcus said, "Namaste."

"Namaste," Boy replied.

"Dear, sweet Ma," Marcus said. "Please hold me a little closer and so I may gaze into your sunny eyes once more." Ma gently raised his head slightly and twisted her body more fully around his so they were eye to eye. "My gratitude to you for a life fulfilled. Finding you—discovering the beauty and bliss of life with you—is more than this man of war could have asked for or ever deserved."

"Everyone is animated by divine love and bliss, and you have experienced it by aligning your heart and actions to God's will," Ma said. Poet could feel her love enveloping Salomon's Garden and giving Marcus peace.

After drawing one more painful deep breath, Marcus said, "Marching to Rome with God's son for revenge on a dying emperor was a mere childish fantasy. A story for another day. This reality is far better, thanks to you. You have been my guide to all that really matters in life and death: *Just love.* I wouldn't trade your presence here and now for a longer life or the entire empire. I am ready now."

"Yes, just love," Ma said. "And your story of discovery will return to Rome in the fullness of time, as Issa prophesied. You saved us all. And you go home now. No death—just life to life as our love rolls on. The same power that creates and destroys, creates again. That dance we perceive as time is but a passing play, and love alone abides. Jaya Bhagavan!"

Marcus, Poet, and Boy joined Ma in chanting, "Jaya Bhagavan!" As Marcus's voice faded away, they kept chanting to send him off, a blissful fare-thee-well as they all sat around the campfire once more, in joy and sorrow.

And so it came to pass a Roman poet, a freed slave boy named Ieyoub, a little-girl guru, a holy man called Issa, and his aging saintly mother buried Tribune Marcus Decia's body at sundown in the shade of Salomon's Garden.

I declare
That later on
Even in age, unlike our own,
Someone will remember who we were.
As the torch is passed,
From fire to fire,
Just love,
Knowing love alone will last.

—Sappho

July 1, 2029 — Day 90 at the Monastery

The mysterious author's ending with the Sappho poem reminded me of the invocation where he asks the gods to let the story's *end be never ending*. My last Sunday evening with Lama Chin was remarkable. I cut it close, but I finished before my deadline as I'm awaiting the arrival of my military escort to the airport. I was eager to hear his reaction to the ending and to discover the secret he had for me. I had already found a great secret of my own rolled up in the last scroll.

When I finished reading the Roman saga, we sat in silence for a long time, both waiting for the other to speak. I didn't want to render my judgment and influence him. Perhaps he was paying me the same respect. As the eight-bell warning approached, and still hoping he'd remember his promise to reveal his secret, a small epiphany came to me that I wanted to share with my friend. "Interesting," I said. "It just occurred to me—the two Roman rivals were like the two thieves crucified beside Jesus. Marcus, who came to Jesus, or Issa, and accepted his divinity, and Saltaurius, who witnessed his miracles yet mocked him and sought to kill him."

"Like Ma said," Lama Chin replied. "You gotta serve somebody. The eternal, defining choice of mankind."

"Amen," I said. "It also struck me. Perhaps the manuscript was Poet's work. Regardless, I believe I have performed my duty as Christ would have wanted." I was no longer worried about my archbishop and his punishing me for performing my duty. I might be reprimanded and given penance, but wouldn't be burned at the stake.

Lama Chin folded his hands together and put his index fingers to his chin as he considered my words before saying, "Perhaps Ma was the author. Poet had taught her to write in Latin, and she was a brilliant and prescient holy woman."

"Wow! I hadn't considered that. Or maybe it was a collaboration. We may never know."

"Does it matter? Isn't life better when we relish the unknown and dwell deep in the mysteries?" he asked with a devilish grin. "And now you want to know my sec—"

The first of the eight bells interrupted him. *Please, please don't say the secret must wait until morning when there might be no time before my military escorted departure,* I pleaded to myself. After the way the story ended, I was already dwelling deep in the mysterious. And now my curiosity was killing me about what secret he could hold for me.

"We will ignore those bells just this one night, and I ask that you follow me to see my secrets below." He handed me a warm vest of lamb's wool. "A gift. It's cold where we are going."

"Well, I'm glad it's not hell, though Dante's hell was a frozen lake in his Inferno," I joked.

Lama Chin's eyes were beaming with excitement like we might soon be headed up the stone stairs of the Temple of Solomon to meet Issa ourselves. My friend lit an oil lamp to lead the way. As we walked down long and twisted corridors behind his flickering light, I felt I was watching myself from above—such was my elevated state of spiritual anticipation.

After descending into a subterranean maze, in an area of the monastery I'd not explored before, we came to a set of great oak doors. Lama Chin removed ancient keys from around his neck to open the doors, releasing a blast of cold air and revealing a hidden cavern that seemed to go on forever. Standing at the threshold I stared into an endless black tunnel, causing me sideways vertigo.

As he proceeded reverently, the lamp revealed a room with twenty-foot-high arched ceilings and walls that stretched at least a hundred yards, though I couldn't see the far end. Stacks of manuscripts, books, and scrolls, many preserved in tubes, covered the walls. The haphazardly stacked collection rivaled that of the Vatican; my head spun at the magnitude of the collection. I exhaled slowly, trying to ground myself. I'd been welcomed into an Aladdin's cave of treasures designed for translators and lovers of the written word, and I felt like dropping to my knees, bowing respectfully, and singing hallelujah. Instead, I just said, "Wow!"

I wished I could read each text in the original Pali and Sanskrit. As we moved farther into the cavern, pausing to revel and marvel at the vast cliffs of ancient books, it was as if the infinite wisdom of the volumes was being imparted to me simply by being in their presence—a great gift granted to me by Lama Chin. I bowed to him in gratitude.

My friend played his fingers over the closest tubes. "Many scriptures, histories, and poems here date back even to before your grand story. When you leave, we will place your scrolls in tubes and secret them away here. Not knowing what they are looking for, the government could search for years and never find them. So do not worry, the treasure will not be lost."

I couldn't speak; my heart soared. My one hundred and eight friends would not be burned alive. I bowed again. "Dear friend, thank you, but won't that put you and the other monks at risk?"

"Not unless we leave the monastery grounds. They govern by harsh laws, but ones that prevent harming a monk inside the monastery walls. They could beat us outside the gates and burn the books in the public square but not here," Lama Chin said, smiling, as if this were not his first act of civil disobedience. "But come, there is more to show you, and it will get colder still."

I wrapped my lamb vest tighter around my chest. Lama Chin walked into the center of the vast, dimly lit dome-shaped catacomb, waving one hand for me to follow. At the far wall, an old wood panel mounted over stone concealed a hidden door. I only knew there was a door when he inserted a key into one notch of wood. The door creaked open, and we entered a tunnel inside a glacier that transported me back to an ancient time. I felt at once like a wary intruder and a welcome visitor blessed by the mystery.

At the end of the tunnel, an icy spiral staircase led upward. We made our way cautiously up the stairs. I followed closely to stay within the light of his lamp. When my head poked up behind my guide into a mysterious chamber, I saw a frozen floor and walls glistening with diamonds of ice. I gasped not at the beauty of the room but at a box—a coffin—positioned in the dead center of the chilly chamber. I suppressed the sudden hope that seized me, daring not to imagine . . .

The slippery floor was covered with gravel and stone pellets to give us traction. We approached the box—a coffin-like altar flanked by sturdy kneelers—without falling on our faces. Lama Chin lit three candles held by four-foot-high candlesticks, one in front of the altar and one on either side. Wind squeezed through cracks in the walls, making the candle and lamp lights flicker, casting shifting shapes upon the walls and floor, and resonating with the celestial sound humming through the natural ice and stone organ. The simple and reverential scene was magnificent. Exquisite. Humbling. Inwardly and outwardly, I felt like I had entered my own deep heart's core. Cold but warm. Dark but full of light.

My heart swelled with hope as I focused on the object before me: the bronze sarcophagus that had housed the scrolls for millennia. The brave lama, my dearest friend, with his monks, had saved it from the government. A heavy lock fastened the box—the sadly empty box—shut. That lock also shackled my soaring heart, as I wanted to inspect the inside too. I had an inexplicable desire to be as close as I could get to people who might have walked and talked with Jesus—as a fitting end to my exhausting work. My life-changing work.

I realized that no matter what the pope decided, my life—however long I had left—would not follow the same trajectory as before. I'd been reborn in Christ and knew for the first time what that phrase truly meant. My life would be dedicated to living as Jesus wanted me to live, under his tutelage and the guidance of the soft voice of the Holy Spirit.

The lamp lit up Lama Chin's round and lovely face, shining on his grin as he pulled yet another key from the chain around his neck and opened the lock. He motioned for me to open the bronze box. My heart pounded so loudly, I couldn't think or move. My eager blood coursed through my body, awakening every cell within me. Cold inhales weighed me down one moment, while warmer exhales lifted me up the next. Slowing my conspicuous breaths, I reverently opened the heavy lid—

Yes! The mummified body!

I fell to my knees onto the cushioned kneelers, and Lama Chin joined me—humble friar and monk gazing at the ancient figure resting peacefully before us. Though it was a relatively well-preserved body, laid to rest in a simple robe, I couldn't identify the sex. Did it matter? There would be time to think later. Now was a time for unbounded exaltation and gratitude. I closed my eyes, drinking in the whirling sensations. *Thank you, Lord*, I repeated in my head. "Thank you, Lama Chin," I whispered into the frosty air that hung between us, unintentionally using his abbreviated name. I wasn't sure he heard me, but I was sure he wouldn't care.

The body protecting the scrolls, the well-preserved body, hadn't vanished. I pressed forward, noticing an additional detail: a stone cross and prayer beads hung from the neck of the mummy. My entire being was overcome with love and gratitude as grace washed over me. In that moment of exaltation, in the mist and candlelight behind the mummy's casket, he appeared!

A towering vision of my Lord with arms outstretched to me. The light from his eyes filled me with his supreme consciousness. There were no words, only his loving presence and omnipotence.

That moment in eternity passed in an instant as the image of my Lord faded, becoming a shroud of mist that disappeared. But he would evermore be with me.

Lama Chin kindly leaned over to fasten my new wool vest shut clasp by clasp, unknowingly protecting the drum beating in my chest. Without his kind attention, I might not have been able to calm my heart. I didn't want to stop the warm tears streaking down my cheeks, even though they soon would turn to ice.

We knelt in prayer and contemplation for an hour. We might have frozen if not for our monk robes, lamb vests, and the warm spirits swirling within us. Eventually, my host and guide for the past three months rose and held out his hand to me.

"You will need to pack; we don't want your military escort to find you missing." He hadn't seen the Christ figure, or we were not to speak of the ineffable appearance. Even now, I only reduce it to words because I believe it is God's will.

"Thank you for everything. I am not the man I was upon arrival. I am twenty pounds lighter. My mind is clear and my spirit soars. I am forever grateful, Lama Chin-chin-anaga!" The joyful-sounding syllables of his full name brought tears to my eyes again.

As we retraced our steps, we didn't speak. A dream would have felt more real, but less fantastic. My friend—my dear, sweet friend—walked me to my small chamber door to say goodnight. We embraced and touched our foreheads together as we'd done before, this time to seal our shared secret. It would pain me to not tell Miles that the mummy wasn't lost, but I had made an unspoken promise.

"I love you, brother," I said without thinking and without looking for a response.

"And I you. *Just love*, as your good book says." We gently touched our foreheads one last time.

With that, he left as he had come, with a bright smile on his delightful face. I wasn't sure if I would ever see him again. I almost ran after him as I had one last great secret of my own, but the moment had passed, and I had to pack and seal my secret away.

It was past midnight when I opened my suitcase. Even before Lama Chin had shown me his great secrets, I experienced the elation of a great discovery of my own. Not because I accepted fully or rejected the story as whole cloth but because rolled up in the last scroll had been an image of Jesus— the picture our heroes had employed in their search—the words *Mortuus vel Vivus* written below his holy face.

I had rediscovered Jesus. The sacred picture was too great a treasure, or too great a temptation, to be left behind. I knew the lama would forgive me and prayed God would forgive me too, as I used a kitchen knife to carve a cavity inside my Bible to smuggle it out. A Bible that had been with me for decades— making a sacred sacrifice. My Kashmir military escort had searched the Bible upon my arrival to make sure it didn't hide a camera. There would be no reason, I hoped, to search my Bible on the way out. But I'd risk it for Miles and the Church. Surely the pope wouldn't suppress an image of our Lord. May Christ's beloved face and mesmerizing eyes guide him too.

They will take me to the airport at dawn, and the sun is about to crown the horizon. I have performed my mission of translating, editing, and presenting the story without rendering a personal judgment of truth or fiction upon it. My mission is complete, and my just-love ministry is just beginning.

In the end, I am not myself but am one with my Lord. And whether I was that artifact-saving abbot in a prior life, whether Issa was Jesus, whether the story was a true account or an incredible fiction, those unanswered questions have brought me to the truth—our union with Christ's divine love and his still living presence in our lives.

A beloved English professor's favorite saying was "All good fiction tells the truth with lies."

I will fly directly to Rome to present my truth to the pope. He will judge if the story should be told.

"Christ's body after
His Resurrection was of the same nature,
but differed in glory."

— Thomas Aquinas